BY LAURA ANDERSEN

THE BOLEYN KING TRILOGY

The Boleyn King

The Boleyn Deceit

The Boleyn Reckoning

THE TUDOR LEGACY TRILOGY

The Virgin's Daughter

The Virgin's Spy

The Virgin's War

The Darkling Bride

The

Darkling

Bride

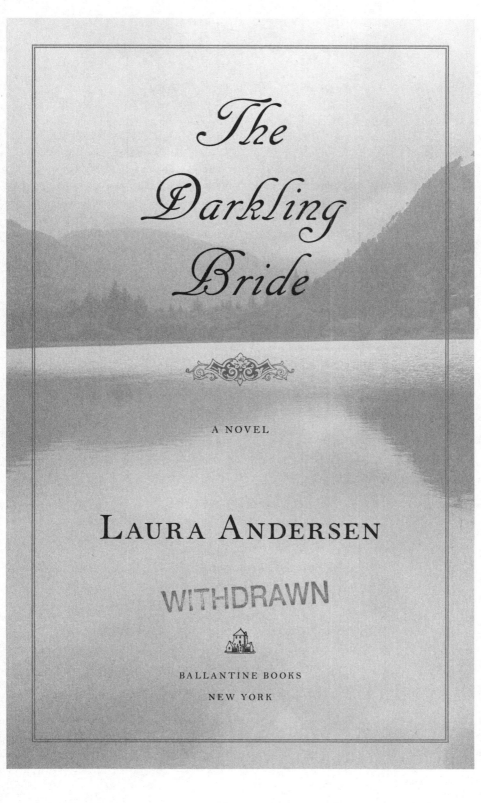

The Darkling Bride

A NOVEL

LAURA ANDERSEN

WITHDRAWN

BALLANTINE BOOKS

NEW YORK

Copyright © 2018 by Laura Andersen

All rights reserved.

Published in the United States by Ballantine Books, an imprint of Random House, a division of Penguin Random House LLC, New York.

BALLANTINE and the HOUSE colophon are registered trademarks of Penguin Random House LLC.

Hardback ISBN 978-0-425-28643-2
Ebook ISBN 978-0-425-28644-9

Printed in the United States of America on acid-free paper

randomhousebooks.com

2 4 6 8 9 7 5 3 1

First Edition

Book design by Caroline Cunningham

Title-page image: © freeimages.com/Dora Pete

For Mom and Dad
No parents could be more real than you

The Darkling Bride

CHAPTER ONE

DUBLIN WEEKLY NATION
May 1880

MARRIAGE: On Thursday the 20th ult., at St. Patrick's Cathedral, Dublin, Mr. Evan Chase of London to Lady Jenny Gallagher of County Wicklow, only child of Michael Gallagher, 13th Viscount Gallagher, and the late Lady Aiofe Gallagher. Mr. Chase will append his wife's surname, as she is the sole inheritor of the Gallagher estates.

DUBLIN WEEKLY NATION
May 1881

BORN: On Wednesday the 11th ult., James Michael Gallagher at Deeprath Castle, County Wicklow. He is the first child of Lady Jenny Gallagher and Mr. Evan Chase-Gallagher.

DUBLIN WEEKLY NATION
January 1882

DIED: On Sunday the 8th ult., Lady Jenny Gallagher, suddenly, at the age of twenty-two, leaving her widower and a young son. Due to the unexpected nature of her death, an inquest will be held in Rathdrum.

THE ILLUSTRATED LONDON NEWS
4 March 1882

We have it on good authority that Mr. Evan Chase-Gallagher, noted folklorist and author, has returned to England's shores following a sojourn of two and a half years in Ireland. Little could the author have expected such heights of joy and depths of despair as he has endured since he last crossed the Irish Sea. Love, marriage, fatherhood ... to be followed so shortly by the extremity of grief known only to those whose loved ones have perished in suspicious circumstances.

Lady Jenny Gallagher possessed, by the accounts of those few who knew her, a brilliant wit to match her dark Irish beauty, as well as the noted charm of her race. But such brilliance too often exacts a cost, and it is well known that the lady suffered an unquiet mind after the birth of her son. The strain on her husband, cut off from his London circle in mountainous isolation, we can only guess at. That he has published nothing since his marriage is, perhaps, telling.

We understand the inquest to have been generous in their verdict of accidental death, and hope that his wife's Christian burial will work its peace upon Mr. Chase. We look forward to once more reading his learned and captivating prose and sharing in the talent that has seen him compared to both Mr. Dickens and Mr. Trollope.

His son remains in Ireland, to be raised by his grandfather at Deeprath Castle.

Twenty miles south of Dublin, Deeprath Castle brooded in its shallow valley scooped out of the Wicklow Mountains. Thirteen hundred years ago, St. Kevin had come to these mountain heights for solitude. Eight hundred years ago, Tomas Ó Gallchobair had become Thomas Gallagher by marrying the daughter of a Norman lord—changing his name, if not his heart—and built a stone keep two miles from what was then the monastic city of Glendalough. And every hundred years or so since, a new descendant had made his mark on either land or castle until Deeprath was as idiosyncratic a mix of English and Irish as the family who lived there. "Rath" might mean "farmstead" in Old Norse, but those who lived in the Wicklow Mountains whispered that it should have been spelled "wrath."

Whether the Gallaghers were meant to be the instigators of that wrath, or its victims, varied according to the story and the mood of the storyteller.

Laughter, tears, joy, sorrow, love, hatred, birth, and death—every beat of every Gallagher heart resounded in the stone and wood and plaster of the castle, so that those sensitive to such things could feel the thrum of centuries through their bodies. Any animals brought into the house as pets must learn to live with the echoes or be driven out. The castle knew her own, and jealously kept their secrets.

Secrets in the Norman keep, its spiral stone steps worn by thousands of feet over the centuries. Secrets in the Tudor hall that housed spinet and lute and harp. Secrets in the Regency study, soaked in its aura of patriarchal privilege.

And, above all, secrets in the library, with its soaring walls and stained-glass windows, the Gothic fan vaulting poised loftily above the thousands of books in their bays. Books in glass cases, books on open shelves, books and manuscripts and journals and maps stored in great Renaissance coffers.

The library had secrets aplenty to reveal . . . to those who knew how to look.

CHAPTER TWO

2015

Carragh Ryan perched straight-backed on the reproduction nineteenth-century chair offered her by the interviewer and was devoutly glad she'd chosen her most sober gray-green tweed shift today. The woman seated before her was eighty at least, and dressed as though she were heading to a *Downton Abbey* funeral. *Do people still wear bombazine?* Carragh's mind rattled inwardly, as it did when she was nervous. *What even is bombazine? And do I really want this job if it's working for her?*

Perhaps the woman—who had declined to give her name when Carragh entered the anonymously expensive hotel suite—could read minds. Because she now asked, "Why do you want a job of which you know virtually nothing?"

Because those I do know about are all of them so deadly boring I want to claw my eyes out just applying for them . . . Carragh smiled, though it seemed unlikely this woman would be susceptible to flattery. "If a job has to do with books, I don't need to know much more."

"You understand the position is of limited duration. Three weeks at the most."

"I understand."

"It is also an . . . isolated situation. You would be resident with us, without reliable mobile phone service or Internet access."

Carragh couldn't help herself; literary allusions were second nature. "Sounds very Victoria Holt or Daphne du Maurier."

When the woman merely looked at her blankly, she babbled on. "Gothic writers. Mysterious manors, naïve governesses, brooding lords of the manor . . . never mind."

"Am I to take it you see me in the role of Mrs. Danvers?"

Carragh's eyebrows shot up at mention of the unpleasant housekeeper from du Maurier's *Rebecca*. It was the interviewer's turn to smile. "I am three times your age, my dear. It is just possible I have read as many books as you have."

The old woman had been reviewing Carragh's résumé, and now removed her glasses and let them hang from a chain. Without the lenses, her eyes were even sharper. "Your name indicates Irish heritage. But clearly you are not."

Carragh almost found this straightforward statement refreshing. "I am adopted."

"From China?"

"Boston."

They hovered there for a moment before the older woman moved on to the point of their meeting. "So, you are American-born, were raised in Boston, have a degree in English literature from Boston College and postgraduate work in Irish Studies at Trinity."

"Yes."

"And you have remained in Dublin since Trinity, doing freelance editorial work when you can get it. Secretarial work when you cannot."

"Yes." Were they ever, Carragh wondered, going to get to an actual question? Or the slightest hint about what this mysterious job would entail?

Once again the nameless woman proved remarkably adept at sensing Carragh's thoughts, for she began to question her closely and intently about everything from her familiarity with Irish ballads to her experience working in research libraries. When Carragh was ushered out twenty minutes later—a little dazed—she not only had no idea how well she'd answered, she still hadn't figured out what, precisely, the woman wanted her to do.

But she had a name, at least. Nessa Gallagher, the woman told her as she was dismissed. The surname struck a bell of familiarity, but she virtuously refused to jump to conclusions. No sense getting her hopes up unnecessarily. Within five minutes of going online, her virtue was rewarded: Lady Nessa Gallagher had been born and raised at Deeprath Castle in County Wicklow.

Carragh knew a moderate amount about Deeprath: originally a Norman castle, home of the Gallaghers for more than eight hundred years, and possessed of one of the finest Irish libraries still in private hands.

The castle where Evan Chase, Victorian novelist, had arrived in 1879 for research . . . and left three years later a broken widower who never published again.

Chase was the reason Carragh knew anything about Deeprath. In university she had studied Victorian novelists and had shelves full of Dickens and Trollope, Gaskell, the Brontës, Thackeray, Eliot, and Hardy. But she'd had a particular affinity for Evan Chase, whose books her grandmother had introduced her to before she was ten. It seemed—ironic? coincidental? miraculous?—that this opportunity would arise so soon after Eileen Ryan's death. At almost the very moment that Carragh had determined to drag herself out of the depression she'd fallen into after losing her grandmother. She didn't believe in signs. Or maybe she did. One thing Carragh had learned in the last three months was that she did not know herself as well as she'd thought. Not all of the learning process had been comfortable.

Still: *Evan Chase.*

Half Welsh, half English, the writer had been among the early fantasists, his gothic tales dripping with claustrophobia and tension and echoes of the supernatural twenty years before Bram Stoker. He had written five popular novels by the time he was thirty and seemed poised to take his place among the pantheon of English favorites.

Then he had come to Ireland to research a legend—a ghostly, vengeful woman known as the Darkling Bride—and had instead found love. In swift succession Chase married a Gallagher daughter, had a son, and lost his wife in a probable suicide. He left Ireland after that—along with his son, who eventually inherited the Gallagher lands and title—and died six years later without publishing another word. Of the book Evan Chase had come to Ireland to write, all that existed was a one-page draft outline sent to his publisher. If he'd left any further writing behind him at Deeprath, the Gallagher family had never revealed it.

Surely, if Nessa Gallagher was hiring someone to do something with books, it must involve the Deeprath Castle library. Experts estimated it contained between five and six thousand volumes, painstakingly assembled over generations. From simply wanting the job before, Carragh now felt she would walk through the Wicklow Mountains barefoot in winter to get to that library. But no matter how she recalled and fretted over every question and answer of that odd interview, she was no nearer knowing if she'd impressed Nessa Gallagher or not.

She complained about it later, while on the phone with the youngest of her three older brothers that night. "How can anyone give away so little? It was like a police operation—I don't know who I'm up against for the job, or how many, or even precisely what the job is! You'd think I was dealing with the government rather than one old woman who seemed mostly interested in staring me down."

Francis was always bracingly optimistic. "Who can resist you, Carragh?"

"Nessa Gallagher," she pronounced glumly, "could resist the Second Coming if the details weren't to her particular liking."

"Deeprath Castle," her brother mused. She could practically see his Irish-green eyes creased in thought. "Why do I know that name?"

"From Gran. She read us Evan Chase's books, do you remember?"

"Vaguely. Ghosts and witches and vampires—"

"Vampires was Bram Stoker. No, Chase wrote novels based on folklore and legends. Lorelei who was banished to a nunnery and threw herself off a rock in protest, Melusina the mermaid, the knights of the Broceliande Forest—Chase turned all of them into Victorian high romances."

"I'm afraid you're the only one who inherited Gran's love of old novels." A well-worn quip, one Carragh had always told herself she liked because it meant she was as loved as any child of blood. Family teasing meant family belonging.

"Anyway," she plowed on, "Evan Chase spent four years at Deeprath Castle. He even married the daughter of the family. That's why you've heard of the place. Gran talked about him a lot."

"Gran talked a lot about a lot of things."

Carragh laughed. "True. Anyway, say a prayer to St. Ceara for me. If I don't get this job, it's back to the temp agency. I've got contractor bills a foot high."

"Ah. How is the house?" he asked.

"Just like Gran left it."

"Dark, cold, and furniture from the sixties?"

"Less furniture now. But the floors are all in desperate need of refinishing, the wallpaper is giving me headaches, and I think the cupboards haven't been cleaned since the 1860s.

"Still," Carragh looked around the high-ceilinged reception room with its fine woodwork and graceful lines, "Gran left me a fully paid-off Merrion Square townhouse. What's to complain about?"

"Damn right. You'll sort it all in time, Carr."

But no one in her family knew quite how dire the situation was. Although Eileen Ryan had died a wealthy woman, as evidenced by the money left to Carragh's father and three brothers, she had not spent a penny on updates to her home or even repairs in at least thirty years. The Georgian moldings had woodworm, turning on the lights was a fire hazard, and she took her life in her hands every time she filled the bathtub.

The townhouse—one of the few in central Dublin not divided into flats—was worth a small fortune even in its present condition. Carragh knew the responsible thing would be to sell it and get what cash she could.

But she didn't want to be responsible.

"Maybe," she told her brother, "I only want the Deeprath Castle job to remind me that Norman keeps and Tudor halls must be even more impossible to heat in winter than Gran's house."

"That's not why you want the job. Face it, Carr, even a Georgian townhouse is modern when compared to an actual Norman castle. The older the better, as far as you're concerned. And if it comes with a mystery to solve? Even better."

Then Francis's tone of voice altered, becoming a shade too casual. "By the way"—a phrase always followed by something unpleasant— "Mom wants to talk to you."

"I know she does."

"Well, I happen to be at Mom and Dad's right now so I'll just pass the phone over—"

"I have to go, Francis. Someone else is ringing."

Carragh hung up on that lie with only a twinge of regret. She loved her mother. She respected and admired her. She even liked her, which was not always something that could be said between daughters and mothers. But she did not want to talk to her. Not just now. Not since her mother had given Carragh a letter her daughter did not want. A letter she felt had been stalking her ever since, laying whispery ink fingers on the back of her neck, pleading, "Read me, read me . . ."

To hell with that. Pacing idly in circles after she talked to Francis, Carragh went to the IKEA bookshelves where her grandmother's collection of novels rested and pulled out Evan Chase's first novel—*The Wandering Knight.* She didn't open it, but like a ten-year-old, she crossed her fingers and wished for the luck she wanted.

Who wouldn't want to know what happened at Deeprath Castle with Evan and his beautiful, insane wife? What book lover wouldn't jump at the chance to look for a lost novel?

Her inarticulate prayers must have worked, for the phone rang twenty minutes later and the voice was unmistakably that of the imperious Nessa Gallagher.

"Miss Ryan, you may have the position."

Clearly the woman was not one for unnecessary conversation. Carragh was glad Nessa couldn't see her mouth hanging open. She snapped it shut, then said simply, "Thank you." She did not think she sounded as matter-of-fact as she intended.

"I will send you a train ticket and necessary information for your time at Deeprath Castle. You understand that the castle has not been lived in for more than two decades. That, combined with its location, means you shouldn't expect reliable Internet service or mobile phone signals. I assume a woman interested in libraries is capable of entertaining herself without such conveniences."

"Of course." Carragh would give up almost anything for this chance. Though she wouldn't mind if the castle had a decent availability of hot water.

"You will technically be answerable to my great-nephew, Lord Gallagher, though it is possible Aidan will not even be at Deeprath Castle while you are. Nevertheless, I have given him your information should he care to contact you in advance. I think it unlikely. Aidan has always trusted my decisions."

Carragh made some noise that she hoped signaled agreement or interest or whatever the hell Nessa wanted to hear.

"And I trust," Nessa continued without a pause, "that you are not disturbed by ghosts."

Utter silence. "I beg your pardon?"

Surprisingly, there was a hint of humor—or at least mild amusement—in the old woman's answer. "Deeprath Castle is more than seven hundred years old. Where there is long history, there are ghosts. Ours are none of them particularly troublesome, so long as you do not provoke them."

Carragh somehow managed to assure the woman that she had no intention of provoking anyone—living or dead—during her time at Deeprath. When she rang off, Carragh stared at her phone for a long, blank moment before the sense of it all penetrated.

She had gotten the job. For three weeks, she would live at Deeprath Castle. She would spend her waking hours surveying a library that had taken centuries to build. The library where surely Evan Chase had read and researched and written during his brief tenure. Impulsively, she returned to the bookshelves and pulled out the rest of his novels.

"You're returning to Deeprath," she announced to them all, as though the books stood in place of the writer himself.

And maybe, she added silently, *I'll find out what happened to drive you away from writing forever.*

She dared not articulate, from instinctive superstition, her deeper hope . . . that somewhere deep in the castle's library might be found some fragment of the lost Darkling Bride tale.

There were only two things on earth that could have persuaded Aidan Gallagher to return to Ireland. As one of those would have involved people rising from the dead, he generally lived without an inordinate fear of having to go home.

He should have known better.

"No." Aidan had said that three times now, but it made little difference to his sister. Kyla just kept talking.

"The deeds must be signed before April thirtieth," she reiterated. "The Irish National Trust requires your signature. More probably twenty of your signatures, considering the amount of paperwork needed to donate a property like Deeprath."

"Send them to me. I'll sign and have it all notarized in London."

"I thought you were anxious to divest yourself of our heritage," Kyla said remorselessly. "You're not telling me you suddenly want to keep the place? That you've been stricken by a belated sense of family responsibility?"

"I have no issues with the donation."

"If you were having second thoughts, there's still time to consider creating a heritage trust and letting me turn the castle into a center for visitors."

He'd already turned his sister down four times. Aidan had no more interest in turning Deeprath into a guest house or historical studies retreat than he did in living there. Let the National Trust do what it would, but he had just enough family pride left to shudder at the thought of tourists tramping through the castle.

"Kyla, just send me the paperwork—"

"Nessa wants it done here."

"I don't answer to Nessa," Aidan said flatly. No matter how old he got, his great-aunt continued to treat him as a child who required direction. For eighty-eight years Nessa Gallagher had considered herself the steel spine of the Gallagher family, and the kindest word for her temperament was *tenacious*. A more accurate description was *bloody-minded*.

There was silence on the line, and Aidan hoped Kyla had finally accepted his refusal.

And then she spoke one of the two things guaranteed to gain his compliance. "The library will be opened once the trust takes possession. Nessa is hiring someone to do a cursory cataloging of its contents beforehand. Do you really want to leave that task entirely to a stranger?"

Damn, damn, and damn again. It wasn't as though he hadn't known the library would be opened. Its contents could hardly be donated without people entering the room and digging through its collection of books, documents, and family history. But like so many other unpleasant things in his life, he had kept that knowledge firmly out of mind.

"The notary is scheduled for April twenty-ninth, little brother. That gives us almost a month. I'll be going down next week. You should come as soon as you can."

With false brightness, she continued remorselessly. "I'll have Ellie and Kate with me part of the time. You could pretend you're a normal uncle who doesn't dislike every other Gallagher on the planet."

Because he was upset and tired and overwhelmed at the thought of going home, Aidan let himself be cruel. "But Ellie and Kate aren't truly Gallaghers. They are Grants, like their father."

His sister's reply was all sharp glass and brittle control. "Then you'd best be at Deeprath to ensure they don't sully the precious Gallagher heritage by pretending they belong. You can use your lord of the manor voice, Viscount Gallagher. I'll pretend it intimidates me."

If this were twenty or thirty years in the past, they both could have relieved their tempers by slamming down a phone. Aidan very nearly threw his across the room, but he didn't want the bother of buying a new one. Instead, he resigned himself to the paperwork on his desk and made a note to speak to the superintendent in the morning.

Under normal circumstances, a Scotland Yard detective inspector would find it difficult to take substantial time off with so little notice. But Aidan was about to be transferred from the downsizing Arts and Antiquities division to Sexual Crimes and Exploitation. As he was replacing a not-quite-retired officer, there was a lag time in which he knew he could manage to eke out at least two weeks in Ireland.

But that meant clearing his desk of last minute tasks a bit sooner than planned. Even as Aidan worked with outward diligence, he was conscious of a dim roaring that seemed to reverberate from the base of his skull through his eyes and ears. *Deeprath*, it beat a tattoo, *Deeprath, Deeprath.*

And beneath that, in echo: *death, death, death.*

➘ ➚

He was in the grimmest of moods when he got home that night and found Pen in the kitchen helping herself to leftover curry. Penelope Costa could eat an awful lot for a woman who had modeled seriously for five years before taking her degree as a psychologist. She still did something or other in the fashion world from time to time . . . Aidan wasn't quite clear what it was, besides attending a number of events that required her to look glamorous. An easy task for the half-Spanish, half-Jamaican Londoner who looked equally at home in bikinis or ball gowns and who spoke three languages fluently.

She took one look at his face and sighed. "So much for a pleasant evening at home."

Home was overdoing it, for Penelope did not share the London townhouse with Aidan. He had never lived with a woman and had no plans to start in the near future—but she was the first woman to whom he'd given a key, along with his tacit agreement that she could come and go as she pleased.

"I've got to go to Ireland," he said abruptly, removing his tie and helping himself to the white wine on the marble countertop.

"Ireland?" Penelope asked with extravagant surprise. "Your family will be turning in their graves."

As she realized what she'd said, she added, "Shit. Sorry."

Her apology was genuine, for all its brevity, allowing Aidan to skip over the matter if he chose.

Which he did. "Deeprath Castle is going to the Irish National Trust, but the library's contents are marked for the National Library. There are still plenty of personal papers and volumes that I don't intend to give into the hands of strangers. The professionals will do the real archival work, but I need to make a general catalog of things first."

Pen remained standing even as Aidan seated himself at the counter. Her face looked particularly striking when, as now, it was stripped of her usual irony.

"Then I guess it's time to return this." From her jacket pocket, she took the key to the townhouse and laid it on the countertop before him.

Aidan stared at it, then at her. "Why?"

"Because I knew from the first that Ireland would divide us. Now it's come, there's no use prolonging the inevitable."

"I don't understand . . . are you upset that I didn't invite you? It's not that kind of visit, Pen. And you'd hate my family anyway."

She smiled at him fondly. "I like you, Aidan. I'll always like you. But I knew better than to fall in love with you. You may live in London, but you don't belong here. Your heart is in Ireland."

The headache he'd been fighting all day now threatened tears of pain. Aidan gritted against it. "You could not be more wrong."

With an elegant shrug—Pen did everything elegantly—she came around the counter and rested a cool hand on his cheek. "You're a lovely man, Aidan Gallagher. Or you will be one day when you've dealt with your demons. Someday you will walk in your Irish mountains with a woman, and that woman will be the one you love. I think I like her already."

He turned his head and caught her hand to his lips. "Will you stay?" he asked. "One last night?"

She laughed. "Better not. Why make it harder for you to let me go?"

But she kissed him before she went, leaving Aidan with the bleak sense of having failed once again.

CHAPTER THREE

1992

IRISH TIMES

6 September 1992

Breaking News: Irish businessman Cillian Gallagher (16th Viscount Gallagher) and his wife, Lily, found dead in their Wicklow County home. Police say only that the deaths are not considered natural.

IRISH TIMES

7 September 1992

A statement released today by the Garda in Rathdrum confirms violence in the deaths of Cillian and Lily Gallagher. "Lord Gallagher died of head injuries in the family library where his body was found. Lady Gallagher died of injuries consistent with a fall. We are actively pursuing lines of inquiry."

A police source claims valuable items were in the library of Deeprath Castle at the time of the deaths—items that have vanished. Police are searching for any strangers seen in the vicinity of Laragh or Glendalough on the afternoon in question.

IRISH TIMES
14 September 1992

An inquest held today in Rathdrum into the deaths of Lord and Lady Gallagher returned an open verdict and was adjourned indefinitely. Lady Nessa Gallagher, aunt to the deceased viscount, issued a statement through the family solicitor:

"My nephew and his wife will be greatly missed. My sole concern moving forward is the care and protection of their children. I would appreciate your discretion in giving them space and time to heal."

The title passes to the only son, Aidan Gallagher, age ten. Lord and Lady Gallagher are also survived by a fifteen-year-old daughter, Kyla.

CHAPTER FOUR

September 1879

The Wicklow Mountains were a revelation of stone and sky. Considering the mist that kept shading into rain, it would have been wiser to hire a carriage, but Evan Chase had not become a popular gothic novelist without understanding the importance of presentation. How romantic to arrive at an ancient castle on horseback, greatcoat swinging. More romantic, of course, if one did not also have cold rainwater worming its way down one's back. But, though he may not always be sensible, he did possess the ability to laugh at himself.

Eighty years ago, determined to break the back of the Irish stronghold, English soldiers had forged a military road across the spine of the Wicklow Mountains. Today, Evan saw little more than the stark landscape, the high moorland and bog of Featherland Peak, until he reached the village of Glencree. Turning directly south there, he passed the old military barracks that now housed several hundred young male offenders and felt a pang of empathy. If not for his mother, he might have landed in such a place himself.

From Glencree, Evan rode through a vista of gentle slopes and sharp peaks. He'd never imagined that the color brown could be so

varied and so lovely; black-brown streams wending through the
dark chocolate peat, the light brown grass drooping heavily with
raindrops. After passing through Sally Gap, the road began to slope
down and the greens most commonly associated with Ireland gradually reasserted themselves. Six miles after the gap, he reached a
crest and below him lay Deeprath in the shallow, bowl-shaped valley
where, in 1196, Thomas Gallagher had erected a Norman keep.

Through the autumn light, Evan traced the angular lines of that
keep, rising distinctly at one end of the castle. For generations the
heart of the castle had been that rectangular structure: at once a
storehouse, living quarters, and the defensible retreat where an entire estate could take refuge in times of battle. There were Norman
keeps of this type dotted all over Ireland and the rest of the British
isles, though not many were still roofed and livable, as was the one
at Deeprath. The remainder of the castle was a jumble of stone and
brick and rooflines, wall walks and battlements, with two circular
towers framing the Tudor construction that comprised the front
façade of today's living quarters.

The road to the grounds entered through a crumbling gatehouse
whose central gate hung permanently open. The iron, wrought in
fanciful swirls that almost resolved themselves into woodland creatures before fading away when Evan tried to pin down the design,
had grass and wildflowers growing up and around it. Perhaps it was
the tremble of the growing things, silvered by rain, that gave off the
sense of a sentient welcome.

The drive wound through the remnants of an ancient forest.
Mixed with birches and poplars and pines were older trees, trunks
twisted with age. Might some of them, he wondered, have stood
long enough to have witnessed—if not the earliest Gallaghers—the
impetuous, violent woman who had passed into legend centuries
ago? Might the Darkling Bride have passed this way on her desperate flight? Having come here seeking her legend, Evan felt more
than ever the rightness of his choice.

After nearly a mile the path abruptly veered to the left. Without warning the trees ended and Deeprath Castle rose up before him, seeming to block the entire sky. He swallowed the last notes of the tune he'd been whistling and reined in his horse to stare.

Deeprath stared back with perfect indifference. Closer to, and despite the jumble of styles and materials, he saw an overall unity—as though centuries of habitation had imbued the castle with a personality of its own. Aloof, not easily impressed . . . watchful, perhaps?

All those impressions passed through him in the moment before a groom appeared to take his horse and the housekeeper materialized in a swirl of black. She chatted easily and volubly, so Evan had only to nod and smile with half his attention as he trailed after her, eyes roaming the castle interior.

"Lord Gallagher is with his manager in Rathdrum . . . back by dark . . . bedroom at the top of those stairs, second door on the right . . . see the library first."

The library cut cleanly through the architectural jumble of Evan's impressions, and he drew in a sharp breath of appreciation. Built as a private chapel, the space had been deconsecrated a hundred years ago, but its past lent an air of special grace even to a Protestant like him. Though the afternoon was late and the skies clouded, the wide windows marching down either side of the long room gave a sense of air and light. Actual light was provided by a single lantern set on the circular table ten feet in front of the door. For a moment he wondered at the wisdom of leaving a lamp burning in an empty library full of irreplaceable books. Then the shadows clinging to one of the bays broke and reconfigured into a woman's shape as she stepped away from the shelves.

Her face was a perfect oval, with a wide brow above deep-set eyes, framed by hair as black as the darkest night. In the uncertain light, without the identifying details of dress and grooming, she looked timeless and enduring. Evan had once described a character of his as "amaranthine": ceaseless, deathless, everlasting. Here, without the slightest warning, stood the word's living embodiment.

"I'm Jenny," she said. "Jenny Gallagher. And you are the writer who has come to capture the Darkling Bride."

He swallowed once. Hard. "Yes. And you are the one who will show me how."

DIARY OF JENNY GALLAGHER

12 September 1879

A man has come to Deeprath, a lovely man with brown hair as fine as silk floss and longer eyelashes than I have. Father told me a writer was coming to ask about the Darkling Bride—I did not dream he would be young. And kind.

I could tell he was kind from the first. I have not met many men these last few years, but the ones I have all look at me the same: as though I'm a cake they would like to devour. Though I know he finds me beautiful—I am not blind, nor stupid—Mr. Chase managed to look at me as though . . . as though I am a person. When I asked about his books, he gave me one to read. I am only twenty pages in, but already I can tell that he is a man who treats the world—and everyone in it—with care.

He said I would help him capture the Darkling Bride. I think he is well on his way to capturing more than a story.

CHAPTER FIVE

"Welcome to Deeprath Castle, Miss Ryan."

Nessa Gallagher made no move to shake her hand. Even if the old woman had seen fit to extend her own hand, Carragh reflected, it would no doubt only have been in expectation of some-one kissing her heavy silver ring. The ring was the only ornament Nessa wore. Dressed otherwise in neutral tweeds, she had a peri-winkle silk scarf around her neck that looked wonderfully chic against her white hair.

But Carragh repented her uncharitable thought when she saw the cane the woman leaned on with her left hand. No modern metal and plastic for Lady Nessa Gallagher: the gold top was heavily scrolled, and narrowed into a mother-of-pearl shaft that in turn led to a beautifully polished dark wood. In a concession to practicality it had been fitted with a rubber grip at the bottom, but it must be at least a hundred years old.

More to the point, Nessa looked frailer on her feet than she had seated with aplomb in the hotel suite. She might have all the pride in the world, but old age could not be entirely controlled by even the strongest will. Carragh vowed to not be so quick to judge.

She had a few moments to look around the Tudor hall while Nessa directed the driver with her suitcase. Like a royal great hall in miniature, it had dark wood floors and paneling to shoulder height, then white plaster rising to the lofty hammerbeam ceiling. The original beams achieved a feeling of airiness, thanks to the open spaces between them. Carved into the stone above the enormous Tudor hearth was the family crest and motto: three mountain peaks (for Wicklow), an Irish round tower (for Glendalough), and the central griffin, the mystical half eagle, half lion, standing rampant in deep crimson. The Latin motto? *Non Nobis Solum*. Not for Ourselves Alone.

Carragh had to shake her head to make sure she wasn't dreaming. Two hours ago she had boarded a train in busy Dublin, and even Rathdrum, where she disembarked, had been recognizably twenty-first century. But somewhere along the ten kilometer drive to Deeprath, she seemed to have passed into a different time and place and even climate. Dublin had been cool and damp, Rathdrum lit by occasional pale streaks of sun, but Deeprath sat beneath a steel-gray sky that felt . . . not malevolent, exactly. But definitely reserved. Taking its time while it weighed her in the balance.

"I thought you might care for a tour before going to your room," Nessa said courteously. "If you're not too tired."

Right, because at twenty-eight she would tell the eighty-eight-year-old woman in front of her that she required rest. "Thank you, that's very kind."

The woman who had answered the door stepped forward, but Nessa said, "I'll do it myself, Mrs. Bell."

"Are you sure? You shouldna overexert yourself, Lady Nessa."

Carragh liked the look of Mrs. Bell—her mother's age, perhaps, with the fading colors of the natural blonde and lines carved around mouth and eyes that hinted at a sense of humor. She spoke to Nessa Gallagher respectfully, but also with the familiarity of one who knew the house and family well.

That instinct was confirmed by Nessa. "Miss Ryan, if you do need anything at all, Mrs. Bell's study is next to the kitchen. She has been at Deeprath for forty-five years and knows it better than any-one but the family. She will gladly provide whatever you seek."

Carragh smiled at her. "I'll try not to be too much trouble, Mrs. Bell."

"No trouble. It's good to have people here once more. The castle has been too silent for too long."

And there, perhaps, was the reason for Nessa taking control of Carragh's introduction to Deeprath Castle: because twenty-three years ago, Cillian and Lily Gallagher had died here by violence. In the aftermath, Nessa had taken her nephew's two children and raised them in her own home in Kilkenny. Deeprath had stood empty ever since.

The moment Carragh had secured this job, she threw herself into research beyond merely Evan Chase and his Victorian tragedy. The murder of the sixteenth Viscount Gallagher and his wealthy American wife, Lily, in 1992, had clearly been a story on par with the death of Princess Diana or the disappearance of Lord Lucan in the seventies. The inquest had returned an open verdict. Reading be-tween the lines (and in the more salacious tabloids), Carragh found that many people had suspected Lily of having first killed her hus-band and then herself. Officially, the case remained unsolved.

Unofficially, Carragh had quelled a moment of panic. This house and family had been scarred by an intimate trauma. Her own de-mons were put to rest years ago. She had no intention of stirring them up again—which is exactly what she'd said to her mother about that stupid, intrusive, unread letter.

But then she had breathed deeply and reminded herself that she was going for the library and its past, not the contemporary family. Probably she wouldn't even meet most of them.

As Nessa led her out of the Tudor hall, she launched immediately into stories of the Gallaghers and their architectural and decorative legacies. She was a competent guide, if rather dry. Carragh would have preferred tales of the people and their lives, but got mostly a recitation of names and dates.

*The eleventh viscount's French wife imported the damask wallpaper . . .
Henry Gallagher painted his bedchamber black for mourning when the Act
of Union passed in 1801 . . . William Gallagher brought stonemasons from
Italy to restore the battlements in 1745 . . .*

From the Tudor hall with its enormous fireplace of dressed stone and lofty beamed ceiling, they passed into the Regency wing. Here the plasterwork and carved wood were still lovely, though signs of damp and age encroached. There was a breakfast room and parlor in the same wing that had been updated in the 1920s, and a heavily masculine study with its Victorian desk and bookshelves still in place.

"The work of Michael, the thirteenth Viscount Gallagher," Nessa said, and Carragh felt her interest prick. Michael Gallagher had been Evan Chase's father-in-law. No doubt the writer and the viscount had sat together in this room many times. Could this be the very spot where Evan Chase had the nerve to ask for the viscount's daughter as a bride?

The second wing they visited was the oldest. Here, remnants of the medieval structures had gradually been incorporated into newer architecture, meaning the Elizabethan and Stuart eras. Here, too, stood the chapel that had given way to a different sort of worship two centuries ago: the library.

To Carragh's intense disappointment, the library itself was locked. She could not repress a small sound of distress, enough to make Nessa stop.

"By orders of the viscount," the old woman said crisply, gesturing at the anachronistic Yale cylinder lock. "Since 1992. There are two keys. My great-nephew possesses one, and Mr. Bell, the estate steward, the other. We will have to wait for Aidan to open the library. He is due tomorrow."

"It was the family chapel once, right?"

"Correct. Built in 1512, as a replacement for the oratory."

When Carragh looked at her blankly, Nessa elaborated. "No doubt you noticed the old stables to the right of the castle. It's where

we keep the cars and gardening equipment these days. Just behind it
is the original oratory from the late thirteenth century. It's where
the family worshipped in those early centuries. There are still three
walls partially standing, and the remains of an altar, but not much
more."

Carragh's disappointment at the locked library vanished when
she realized the walls beyond it gave way to a roughly dressed stone,
which practically hummed with its centuries. Even without Nessa's
guidance, she would have known this for the original Norman keep.
Once exterior, this section of wall had been used to buttress a later
structure, and an arched opening carved through the ten feet of
stone so one could enter directly into the keep's ground floor.

"Various restoration measures have been carried out on the Bride
Tower over the generations," Nessa explained, as Carragh prowled
the empty, echoing space that would have stored grains and possibly
housed livestock in the winter.

"The Bride Tower? How long has it been called that?" Carragh
asked.

"Oh, for ages. At least three hundred years."

The steep, irregular stone stairs twisted out of sight, leading up
to the floors where the earliest Gallaghers would have lived and
worked, with the Great Hall at the top being the gathering place for
all. Though Nessa did not say so, Carragh knew that those steps
wound up to the chamber where Evan Chase's mad wife, Jenny, had
ended her days. She resolved to return as soon as she could to explore without Nessa's suffocating presence.

The wall to the right of the entrance possessed an alluringly narrow arched door that must lead directly into the library. Curious.
Perhaps it had been a convenient entrance to the chapel in those
days when prayers were observed with clockwork regularity. This
door had the same maddening Yale lock on it.

Backtracking through the Tudor hall, they arrived in the long
western wing ("early Georgian," Nessa said) and Carragh was led to
a comfortably shabby bedroom. Mullioned windows, the griffins of

the Gallagher coat of arms carved in dark wood above the fireplace, the bright primrose walls of the early eighteenth century faded to a pale lemon, the heavy four-poster bed with toile hangings . . . all very country-house proper.

Save for the single piece of artwork in the room. Carragh couldn't help but gasp. She might have expected a hunting scene or a romantic landscape or a formal family portrait. Instead, it was a painting of a woman, done in pre-Raphaelite fashion. With wavy black hair loose to her waist and wearing a vaguely medieval white dress, there was a fey quality to the woman's shy smile that was very Irish, Carragh thought. A powerfully evocative painting, with an undercurrent of unease to it.

At first Carragh could not understand why she felt uneasy. Then she noted a disturbing detail. The painted lady stood over a mirror-smooth pond, but the reflection showing in the water differed from the original. It was the same face, more or less, the same loose, dark hair and deep eyes and wide brow . . . but the mirrored figure wore black, not white, and her expression was one of deepest mourning.

Or, perhaps, terror?

"The painting . . ."

Nessa, on the point of leaving, slanted a look to Carragh over her shoulder. "The woman in white is Jenny Gallagher."

Carragh looked from poor mad Jenny to the sinister black-clad reflection at her painted feet. "And in the pond?"

Nessa raised a single eyebrow. "The Darkling Bride."

Aidan had not been any nearer to Deeprath Castle than Kilkenny since he was ten years old. He had two shots of whiskey in Dublin before boarding the train to Rathdrum, thinking it would calm the nerves that he refused to openly acknowledge. All it seemed to accomplish was to bring his nerves nearer the surface. He was abrupt with the driver who took him out to the castle—a stranger, fortunately—shutting down every attempt at conversation. It was as though all the skills of effortless deflection he had so long perfected were left behind in London.

Very little had changed. Why did that surprise him? Deeprath had been nestled in its shallow mountain bowl since the year 1196, its timeline running parallel to without ever quite intersecting that of nearby history. The iron gate of the entrance, leading to the badly eroded gravel drive, hung permanently open, frozen in position for so long that it now looked a deliberate part of the landscape. Aidan dismissed the driver and swung his leather duffel bag onto his shoulder. He did not want an audience for his homecoming.

He'd deliberately told Nessa he was arriving tomorrow so he wouldn't have his great-aunt causing a fuss over Viscount Gallagher Returning to His Ancestral Home. (Before signing away said ancestral home to the National Trust—Nessa had a gift for ignoring facts she found unpleasant.) So Aidan had the mile-long walk through the forest to himself, and when the castle appeared before him, he saw it as it should be seen—without a hint of human habitation.

And still with the power to reach into his chest and squeeze his heart into a fury of pride and pain. He had always been taught—had always believed—that Deeprath Castle did not belong to the Gallagher family. *Not For Ourselves Alone*, as their motto proclaimed. No, it was the Gallaghers who belonged to Deeprath. The castle knew its own and suffered its inhabitants so long as they were of the proper blood or family ties. The castle was not a property—the castle was a living heritage.

One that he was about to give into the hands of strangers.

Aidan took his time, scanning the windows and towers and echoes of battlements with deliberate care as though imprinting them on his memory. Last of all, he allowed himself to settle upon the unmistakable shape of the old chapel's roofline with its single spire still reaching heavenward, though its interior had known nothing but books for generations. The library, locked at the orders of a frightened child twenty years ago. No one had entered that space since, except the steward, Bell, who brought in an archivist once a year to check for damage.

He ignored the enormous doors into the Tudor hall and passed up the Palladian entrance to stop at last outside the library. From its past as a Catholic chapel under constant threat from the Protestant English, a door had been cunningly constructed in the narrow corner butted up against the thirteenth-century keep. Designed for unobtrusive escapes by outlawed priests, it provided as well the perfect entrance for someone who did not want to be met before he was prepared.

Aidan used his key—the only one, not even Bell could access the library through the priest's door—and winced at the screech of unoiled metal and then the louder scraping of wood on stone as he shoved it open with his shoulder. Dropping his bag at his feet, he passed behind what had once been the rood screen to emerge into the open space of the library proper.

He knew this room in his bones: the shelves groaning with books fitted beneath and between the arched windows; the stained glass skipping shards of color across wood and stone; the distinctive scent of old paper, glue, and leather. Aidan breathed in deeply and felt a dangerous crack in his walled-off memories.

At first he had wondered what his father was doing, sprawled across the flagstone floor. Then he'd seen the crater in the side of his head, the depression flecked with blood and bits of bone . . .

The memories were hazy from that point, swirled with panic and fear and the bewilderment of being told his mother was also dead. Twenty years on, and he had no more answers now than he'd had then. Just questions. And grief. And anger.

Aidan was wrenched from reverie by a sound to his right, where another locked door had been carved into the thick walls of the Norman keep. Visions of a woman in white, the ghost of his insane ancestress, rose unbidden to his mind. Jenny Gallagher, condemned by her own misery to haunt the place where she'd died, rumored to be seen when a Gallagher death was imminent . . .

But he was no longer ten years old. Aidan found his second key and wasted no time using it and swinging the door wide.

It wasn't a ghost, not unless ghosts these days wore jeans and jumpers and a sloppy ponytail above a face frozen in shock. The woman recoiled back a step, and Aidan had the impression that she'd been half expecting a spirit visitation herself.

"Who the hell are you?" Aidan didn't recognize his own voice, strangled with strain and temper. "And why were you trying to break into my library?"

"Ah. You must be Aidan. I thought you weren't coming until to-morrow . . ." She trailed off in a questioning manner.

"So that makes it all right to sneak around my castle?" He was shocked at how unbalanced he felt—and how possessive. *My library, my castle.* Nessa would be delighted. Modulating his voice to a calmer register, he asked, "How do you come to be at Deeprath?"

She was small and black-haired, with jewel-toned streaks of color painted beneath her ponytail. Her accent wasn't quite Irish. Asian blood, he thought, as he watched the color stain her high cheekbones. Chinese? Korean? He was embarrassed not to know.

"I was hired," she replied loftily, "to help catalog the library. I'm Carragh Ryan."

"Ryan? Nessa hired you, I remember. Sorry." He attempted a smile that wasn't as warm as he meant it to be. Beneath his culti-vated calm, his heart still beat with the tremors of fear. "I wasn't expecting to trip over you on the threshold of a locked door."

"I only wanted to look again at the keep." Unexpectedly, she broke into a cheeky grin. "And I wouldn't have minded finding a secret passage to the library."

"Any secret passages were locked up long ago. I was just going back out the way I came. Do you want to come through?"

She peered around him into the library, then said ruefully, "You shouldn't reward me for nosiness. I'll wait until tomorrow. It's nice to meet you, Mr. Gallagher. Or do you prefer . . . should I call you Lord Gallagher?"

"Please don't. It's Aidan."

"I'll see you later, Aidan," she said, and retreated back into the keep.

So this was the archivist Nessa had hired. Not quite what he'd been expecting.

What was wrong with her? Safely back in her room, Carragh closed the door and leaned against it. Why the hell hadn't she jumped at the chance to see the library she'd been dreaming about for weeks? And why, when Aidan Gallagher flung open that door in her face, had she been momentarily terrified of confronting something else?

Carragh did not believe in ghosts, not in the traditional sense. She was not afraid of the Woman in White or the Darkling Bride or any number of ancient monks who might drift down the slopes from Glendalough. She was not afraid of the dead, however uneasily they might lie, for her earliest memories encompassed death.

But in all her eager research into the Gallagher family, she had deliberately ignored a simple truth: tragedy casts a long shadow. Prying into the life and death of the Victorian Jenny was one thing. Meddling with a man whose mother was believed to have murdered his father and then jumped off the same tower as Jenny Gallagher? That was an entirely different matter.

Especially when the man in question was sexy as hell. Seriously, who looked like that? She'd seen a few pictures of the viscount as she'd scrolled the Internet looking for information on the Gallaghers, most of them of Aidan paired with various formidably fashionable women. But the combined effect of his height and dark hair and those bright blue eyes narrowed suspiciously at her . . .

Carragh shoved herself away from the door and glared at the painting of Jenny Gallagher. "I'm here for the library," she said aloud. "Not for men, and not for ghosts."

In the painted pond's reflection, the Darkling Bride stared back at her in warning.

CHAPTER SIX

"This is the catalog my grandfather had made just after World War Two."

Carragh flinched as Aidan dropped a leather-bound book that must be nearly a foot thick on the long library table. "Looks thorough."

"Typed, at least," he replied. "For any gaps in that report, you'll have to go further back, which puts you at the mercy of individual handwriting. First thing, check the general categories and locations and see which are still relevant. I don't think my father made many changes in layout, but those are a child's memories. He might have decided to shelve everything according to his favorite color, for all I know."

"Is there anyplace in particular you would like me to start?"

"Do you need direction?" he asked. "Look, whatever my great-aunt told you, I'm not interested in the library as such. My only concern is locating personal documents—diaries, travel journals, letters. I expect to find most of those on the smaller shelves against the road screen. For the rest, you are free to go on as you think best."

In contrast to yesterday's wariness, Aidan was perfectly polite.

And perfectly inaccessible, walling himself off behind impeccable manners. Was she quite sure she hadn't stumbled into the past? She imagined his Victorian and Edwardian ancestors had given off that same air of self-possession.

But as she kept insisting to herself, she was here to work. Nothing else. "I'll start with a look at your grandfather's catalog and see if I can locate at least general categories on the shelves."

Of course, the look was not all that quick. Though Carragh was itching to prowl through the library itself, she had been hired to work, not to satisfy her curiosity and book lust. Also, Aidan Gallagher's presence at the far end of the nave kept her professional. And the catalog was itself a fascinating artifact of the past. Typed on canary-colored onionskin, just turning the translucent pages required a degree of care that meant by the time she had marked the ten most general categories of organization, Mrs. Bell had delivered tea and biscuits.

"I didn't hear her come in," Carragh said.

Aidan arched an eyebrow, a trick she'd seen before and always viewed with suspicion. "I doubt you'd have heard anything short of an explosion."

She leaned back in the chair and stretched her arms above her head. When she had taken a sip of tea, Aidan asked, "How are you getting on?"

"Good. Ready to start checking whether your grandfather's main categories are more or less in the same places. If they are, then I can start sorting by content and age. How's your search?"

"More or less as I expected." Like turning on a light switch, he smiled disarmingly. "I'm sure you'll be happy to have the library to yourself this afternoon. I've a meeting in Rathdrum with the family solicitors."

"About the trust?"

"It's almost as difficult to divest oneself of a castle as it is to build one in the first place."

Which wasn't actually an answer. "Then why do it?"

"Do you have the faintest idea what it costs simply to keep the roof from falling in?" he asked. "It's a waste of money for a place that hasn't been lived in for twenty years."

She picked carefully through her reply, knowing it was none of her business but hopelessly curious all the same. Aidan was trying to get rid of a house, she was trying to hold onto one . . . "Does your family support the donation? You have a sister, don't you?"

"My sister has no more desire to live here than I do. She has a perfectly beautiful home in Kilkenny. And I don't see why any of us should be shackled to this castle simply because of our name. Would you like to live in a house merely because it had once belonged to your family?"

"I would. Actually, I do. I live in a Dublin townhouse owned by the Ryan family for two hundred years."

"Really?" In only two syllables he managed to convey a wealth of polite scorn.

"So it's not as impressive as a castle, but I love it because of family memories. My grandmother knew I appreciated our history, so she left it to me when she died."

"And were your parents murdered in that house?" She felt the blood leave her face, and instantly Aidan apologized. "That . . . I'm so sorry. That was a stupid thing to say. I'm afraid coming home has rattled me more than I expected. It's not fair to take it out on you."

"Is this the first time you've come back?"

"Yes." He looked around the library as though seeing it anew. "It feels like ages. And also, like it was just yesterday." A brief laugh. "I'm not acquitting myself very well. The Met would be disappointed with my people skills."

"The Met?"

"The Metropolitan Police. Scotland Yard, and all that."

"You're a police officer." It wasn't a question; Carragh had read about him online.

"I work Arts and Antiquities thefts. Or I did. Like all institutions, they're cutting budgets and personnel. When I return to London, I'll be working Sexual Crimes."

"Depressing."

"Someone has to do it." He uttered the platitude without conviction, then smiled at her once more. "I believe I was getting out of your way. If you need anything, you can let Mrs. Bell know."

Carragh stared at the door after Aidan left, until the catalog, precariously held open with paperweights, closed itself with a thump. Right, she thought. Back to work.

Aidan walked away from the library cursing himself. He'd been at Deeprath less than twenty-four hours and already every habit he'd developed over the last twenty years to cope with his past was crumbling. He was polite, he was reserved, and he was always controlled. So why had he nearly confessed: *I want rid of Deeprath because it turns me into a frightened ten-year-old who has no control over his world.* Not the sort of admission he could ever make, least of all to a stranger.

Instead he had managed to insult a perfectly nice woman in a handful of sentences—must be some sort of record, even for him. Not that he made a habit of insulting women. Deceptive charm and an ability to confine his relationships to the surface of his London life ensured that very few dared trespass on his inner world. Even Penelope, psychology degree and all, had picked her way warily along that path.

He'd known coming back here would test his control. He just hadn't guessed how quickly it would begin to unravel.

He had spent the morning skimming through the shelves and cabinets that held family documents. Birth, death, and marriage records. Property sales. Business investments. Georgian and Victorian travelogues written by Gallagher women with both money and time on their hands. Daily accounts of estate management. What one would expect to find in a family library of its age.

What he hadn't found were records of his immediate family. Aidan could still see in memory the distinctive peacock-blue binding of his mother's journals. He imagined most of them would be in her bedroom. But already Aidan suspected he wouldn't find the particular journal he was looking for. Not the one that had been left unfinished in 1992. He may have only been an Art and Antiquities officer, but he knew police procedures. Everything recent and personal that might have had a bearing on his parents' deaths would have been taken into evidence long ago. If he wanted it back, he would have to go to the police.

And that was his purpose for going to Rathdrum today. He had allowed Carragh Ryan to think it was about the trust. Instead, when ushered into the family solicitor's office he asked as soon as could be decently managed, "Who should I speak to about having my parents' papers returned to us from the police?"

Gerald Winthrop—of Murphy, O'Byrne, and Winthrop— answered with the customary caution of solicitors everywhere. "I would advise any such request to go through me, and not come directly from the family."

"Why?"

"Because for over twenty years I have been the family liaison with the police. You understand, it is an unsolved crime. It is wiser to have a buffer between what you say and what the police hear."

Aidan scoffed. "Because I might be a suspect? I was ten!"

Winthrop avoided answering—also in the tradition of solicitors everywhere. "Besides, the evidence has long since left the county. As it remains an unsolved case, it is in the hands of the Siochana Garda. I can speak to them, if you like."

"Fine, you speak to the Garda." But Aidan felt a faint stirring of unease. Dealing with the local police was one thing. Even those who didn't know him personally had known or knew of the Gallaghers and Deeprath. They would understand. They would be . . . accommodating. But strangers in Dublin? That could be trickier.

"Lord Gallagher." Trust the man who had known him since birth to use his title now. A reminder that Aidan was more than an individual—he was the embodiment of a long history. "If it is information you are seeking, there are some papers in my possession you might find useful. I have copies, for instance, of the initial police report. And the transcripts from the inquest."

"That would be helpful, thank you."

"I'll have my clerk make copies. And I will let you know my progress with the Garda." As Aidan shook the man's hand, Winthrop added, "It is good to have the family at Deeprath again."

Don't get used to it, Aidan nearly said. But he retained enough of his manners to simply smile noncommittally.

Sibéal McKenna was lost. To be fair, Phoenix Park was an enormous place to navigate. But if one were not inclined to be fair, one might wonder about an inspector who could not even manage to find her own office.

Inspector McKenna. She still couldn't say or even think the title without grinning inwardly. There'd been a time when a woman could not have hoped to reach that level in the Garda, and certainly not at the age of thirty-five. But Sibéal was tenacious. And smart. And, galling though it may be, she knew how to manipulate men's expectations to her advantage. If she had to play games, she'd make sure that she won.

Which was why she gritted her teeth, pasted on a smile, and asked a passing constable to show her to Serious Crimes Review, making light of her directional difficulties. Before she knew it, she was in the first office she'd ever had all to herself. That it was little bigger than a broom closet and had apparently been furnished with pieces left over from various historical eras didn't matter. She enjoyed the space for all of five minutes before being summoned by Superintendent O'Neill

"Settled in, McKenna?"

"Yes, sir."

"Good. On to your first assignment. An unsolved double murder from 1992 in County Wicklow. The family is about to donate their home—which was the crime scene—to the National Trust. I want you to review the case as thoroughly as possible before that happens. This is the first time the family has been in residence since the murder. That might shake some things loose."

And with just those few words, Sibéal was launched on her first independent investigation.

She returned to the new office where she met her new partner, Garda Sergeant Derek Cullen. He appeared to be a year or two younger than she was, and had been in Serious Crimes Review for three years. If he had reservations about reporting to someone new—and a woman, at that—he kept them concealed for now. But she could feel him weighing her up even as he sketched the outline of their case.

"Family called Gallagher. The late Viscount Gallagher was found dead in the library in September 1992. Cause of death, blunt instrument to the head. When the police arrived, they also discovered the body of Lady Gallagher at the foot of an ancient tower. She died from the fall, however it occurred. By all accounts theirs was a happy enough marriage—at least, no one offered a plausible motive for a murder-suicide."

"With the wife imagined in the role of killer and then suicide?" Sibéal asked.

"Seeing as her husband could hardly have hit himself in the back of the head, yes. But there was another significant fact. Being not only an amazingly old family but also an amazingly wealthy one, the Gallaghers had accumulated a number of historically significant Irish artifacts. They were usually kept securely off-site or on loan to museums. At the time of the deaths, the artifacts were purportedly at Deeprath Castle. Except they weren't. When the police arrived they had vanished from the library."

Sibéal leafed through the reports until she found the itemized list of stolen valuables:

Three gold neck rings (late Bronze Age)
Celtic mirror (1st century BC)
Two Viking seax (10th century AD)
Book cover of carved whalebone (12th century AD)
Two silver and jeweled reliquaries (14th century AD)

She whistled when she saw the estimated value of the stolen items. "What's a seax?" she asked Cullen.

That he could answer promptly boded well for their partnership. "Viking dagger."

"So, robbery gone wrong? Except it must have been an extremely specialized crime. Deeprath Castle is not an easily accessible location. And a common thief looking to make ready cash would hardly take such antiquities. I don't suppose any of these items have ever resurfaced?"

"They have not. In the absence of other evidence, the inquest returned an open verdict of murder by persons unknown. And that's where it's stayed for twenty-three years."

"The family has never complained at the lack of resolution?"

DS Cullen shook his head. "Not formally. Read the file for yourself. I'd say the local police stuck to the surface of the case. They were glad to leave it unsolved rather than risk tarnishing the family name. They didn't even call in help from Dublin. But you will find in the case notes that at least one officer was dissatisfied with the casual nature of the investigation. A lowly constable in his first year, so no one paid him any mind. His name was Jack O'Neill."

Sibéal's head shot up from the case file opened before her. "Superintendent O'Neill?"

"One and the same."

Interesting. Why hadn't the super told her that himself?

"Well, O'Neill told me the castle is about to be donated to the National Trust, so we have a deadline if we want to get into the place without having to make official requests in triplicate and waiting months. Let the local force know we're coming. Ask them to keep it quiet. I don't want any solicitors getting word and prepping the family in advance."

Cullen nodded and they each set about their tasks. Sibéal was deep in the depressing story of Cillian and Lily Gallagher when her sergeant returned. He looked bemused.

"What?"

"You know how you didn't want any warning going to solicitors? Well, there's one on the line, name of Winthrop. He called us, completely out of the blue, asking to speak to whomever could tell him about the Gallagher evidence still in hold."

"Put him through," she said.

Sibéal closed her eyes, did two rounds of yogic breathing, then opened her eyes and with the sort of brisk expression she would have used with someone sitting across from her, picked up the phone. "Mr. Winthrop. I'm DI McKenna in Serious Crimes Review. What can I do for you?"

"I represent the Gallagher family. My client would like to know the status of the physical evidence taken from Deeprath Castle in 1992. There were personal papers, letters and journals, that must be of only limited interest to anyone outside the family. And if they have not been of evidentiary use in the last twenty-three years, what realistic reason can you have to hold onto them?"

As a daughter, sister, niece, Sibéal was sympathetic—when missing the dead, of course one wanted as many of their words as possible. But as Inspector McKenna, her suspicion piqued. It seemed too coincidental that within an hour of being handed the case, a lawyer came calling wanting a portion of the evidence returned.

"As it happens, Mr. Winthrop, this case is currently under active investigation. I've been assigned to review it. As such, I require to hold onto the evidence for now. I should like nothing better than to finally close this case. Surely your client would agree."

There was a wary, calculating silence. "I see. Do I take it we will soon have the pleasure of your company in Wicklow?"

Damn. No surprise arrivals. Sibéal made the most of what she had. "I'm coming down tomorrow to speak to the local police. I should like to speak to the family members as well."

"I can arrange for a meeting in my chambers."

"That won't be necessary. I prefer to see them at Deeprath Castle, which also allows me to view the crime scene at the same time. Surely it's best not to drag this out longer than necessary?"

"Do you have a warrant?" the solicitor countered, all business.

"Do I need one?" she shot back. Then she deliberately softened her tone. "I understand that you represent the Gallagher family, and have done for decades. Surely you are as eager as they are to finally know the truth of what happened in 1992. No need for you to tell them I'm coming. I'll place a call directly when we are finished and arrange matters with the family myself."

"Then I imagine you and I will be meeting before too long, Inspector."

"I look forward to it, Mr. Winthrop."

And that was the biggest lie Sibéal had told in at least a week. She was not at all interested in the Gallagher family solicitor. All her interest was reserved for the Gallaghers themselves.

CHAPTER SEVEN

October 1879

Evan walked beside Jenny Gallagher in the clear autumn air and told himself to focus on what he'd come for. Which was not, however tempting, Jenny herself.

"You promised to tell me your version of the Darkling Bride legend," he noted. "So why are we going to Glendalough?"

It was two miles to the ruins of the monastic city that had once thrived in these mountains. When Jenny had proposed a visit, Evan looked doubtfully at her fashionable dress in white and purple stripes and asked, "Are you sure you want to walk?"

"Afraid you won't be able to keep up?" she'd answered, eyes widened in innocence.

Now he dragged his attention away from her profile, the sharp, neat line of her nose and the curve of cheek and mouth, and asked again, "Why Glendalough?"

"Because that is where the story begins. There can be no bride without a man. And where, this far in the mountains, was she most likely to meet a man?"

"You're telling me your bride ran off with a monk?"

"You haven't heard that version?"

"It sounds unique." He smiled. "Rather like you."

A London woman would have accepted the compliment as her due. Jenny eyed him sideways and said, "Flattery will not get you the story before I'm ready to tell it. Fortunately for you, this," Jenny said, sweeping her right hand to encompass the scene before them, "is where the story begins."

The Gateway of Glendalough had been the entry to the monastic city, though all that remained now were bits of four walls enclosing a small, square space with arches front and back. When the gateway had been intact, these would have allowed entrance through the gatehouse.

"Here?" Evan asked.

"More properly, just here." Jenny led him through the second arch and directed his attention to a large stone on the side of the path.

Evan squatted down and tilted his head until he had a better angle to see what she was pointing out—not the stone, but the carving on it. Faint, but unmistakable—the plain outline of a cross, with an unusually wide flared base.

"What was its purpose?" he asked. "And what does it have to do with the Bride?"

"This is a Sanctuary Cross," Jenny told him. "It marked the space where one who was being pursued could cross into holy sanctuary, where they could not be touched by civil or military authorities. This is where the Darkling Bride was first seen in these mountains . . . on a stormy night, when the monks found her clutching fast to the stone as though begging its protection."

Evan had heard a lot of versions of a lot of folktales over the course of his life. Never had he heard anything like Jenny Gallagher's version of the Darkling Bride. Part of it, he knew, was the setting. Anyone who could stand in the Valley of the Two Lakes—surrounded by the stern peaks and ancient bogland to which St. Kevin had retreated twelve hundred years ago—and *not* feel the eerie slipstream of time and place had no sensitivity at all.

But he was honest enough to recognize that most of the allure came from the storyteller. Jenny could be reciting the periodic table of the elements and he would still be enthralled. Not just because she was lovely, not just because she was charming, but because he could envision her as the Darkling Bride. Even in the light of day she retained that timeless quality he'd first noticed in the library.

The bones of the Gallagher version of the Darkling Bride retained recognizable similarities to others Evan had read: the mysterious woman who appears from nowhere; her inability to communicate; her enchantment of a respectable man who abandons all responsibilities for her sake; the revelation of her identity by either saintly or demonic means; the resulting curse, either from goodness defiled or evil unmasked.

But as with all folktales, it was the differences that were most illuminating. The Darkling Bride of the Wicklow Mountains had "skin of palest moonlight and hair of darkest night," and she further possessed "eyes of an unholy blue." Evan noted that phrase, for it was most commonly found in the legend of St. Kevin and Kathleen, the woman who would not stop troubling him. An interesting fusion there.

The name the monks gave their mysterious woman was Aine, the traditional Queen of the Fairies. In this version, her inability to communicate was not because she was mute or traumatized or even, as in one bloodthirsty version, had had her tongue removed. More simply, she spoke a language not recognized even in this learned community.

As she was so clearly distressed—and wore a gown and mantle of fine soft wool, marking her as a woman of wealth—the monks installed her in their guesthouse and awaited whatever or whoever pursued her.

The longer Jenny Gallagher spoke, the more Evan fell under the spell of the soft Irish voice, until he began to feel the edges of reality fold inward. When he blinked, he could almost see Glendalough as it had been—prosperous and vibrant, the Round Tower and St. Kevin's Church made new amongst the outlines of other buildings. They rose from their ruins like ghosts of stone and wood, and Evan let himself follow the illusion until he could have sworn he had fallen into the story itself.

"Is there naught I can do for you, lady?" Niall asked. He was eighteen, romantic, and as a younger son of the Gallagher family, chivalry had been bred into his bones. And though he had lived and been educated at Glendalough since he was a child, he had taken no vows as yet.

She did not answer—Aine rarely spoke, and then in words none here could decipher—but she appeared happy to see him. Each day, they would sit in this sheltered spot near St. Kevin's Kitchen and Niall would talk enough for both of them.

Stories of his family and childhood, Irish tales of heroes and tricksters, Bible lessons (when the prior came close enough to overhear) . . . Niall would talk and Aine would listen.

Every day, he ended by asking her a few gentle questions.

"Can you not tell us your name? Where you come from? We will protect you, lady, you need not fear what any man can do while you are protected by Our Lord's grace in sanctuary."

And every day, she would simply regard him gravely with those eyes of unearthly blue and remain mute.

Until the fifteenth day. As Niall rose and dipped his head to her in farewell, Aine said, in clear and perfect Irish, "Thank you."

It was then that Niall Gallagher took his vow—that he would never become a monk.

It took a moment for Evan to realize that, first, he was not Niall Gallagher and, second, that Jenny had stopped speaking.

"That's it?" he asked. "What about the rest of the story?"

"I thought you were the storyteller, Mr. Chase. Why should I do your work for you?"

"It's not as though I'm going to write a faithful account of any single Darkling Bride legend. I'm just looking for as many variations as possible, to provide . . . inspiration."

"And have I not provided sufficient inspiration?"

Evan had never met any woman who could make his brain stop working with just a mischievous smile. He spent a precious few moments gathering himself, which allowed Jenny to drift away from the sanctuary stone.

"Wait!" he called. "Just tell me this—does your Aine have a happy ending?"

"If you want to know more, Mr. Chase, you'll have to do your research." She turned on her heel then and said over her shoulder as she moved away, "I suggest you start in the library."

DIARY OF JENNY GALLAGHER

5 October 1879

I felt my father's eyes on us long after we'd passed from view of the castle. I was frankly surprised that he didn't object to my walking to Glendalough with Mr. Chase, or insist on coming along. I am so accustomed to him watching—night and day, body and soul—and mostly I bear the weight of it without thinking. It is only since Mr. Chase arrived that I have found my father's brooding concern at times unbearable.

Mr. Chase is an antidote to that watchful fear. He is a cheerful, self-assured man who knows who he is, where he comes from, and does not intend to change himself for anyone else's convenience. For all that—or maybe because of it—he has a deep and genuine interest in other people. Probably that is why he is such a good writer.

He even manages to pay me the most banal of compliments while sounding genuinely sincere. Can any man truly be that transparent? I want to believe in his native goodness, but I have never learned to trust my own instincts. How could I, when my father is always watching—and warning.

You are fragile. Vulnerable. Likely to be swayed by those of stronger minds. You must be watchful, never too violent in your likes and dislikes. *I am too like my mother, they say.* Weak.

Evan does not make me feel weak.

CHAPTER EIGHT

In the early afternoon, Carragh allotted herself half an hour to abandon her measured work and indulge her curiosity. While reading and noting and cross-checking pages in the fifteenth viscount's catalog, she had felt the pull of thousands of books calling to her, waiting to seduce her with language and imagery and story—always and above all else, a story.

She took a few minutes to walk the length of the library, taking her time to admire the lofty fan-vaulted ceiling that, more than any other feature, branded this space as a former chapel. There was a Catherine window high on the wall opposite the main entrance, and she shivered at the crimson and azure and plum glass set in the wide circle. It was—rarely for its time period—original, Deeprath Castle having been just far enough removed from Anglo-Irish society to protect some of its Catholic beauties. Along with this chapel, the castle grounds contained the walls and much of the stone floor that had been the original oratory for the Gallagher family, constructed in the early thirteenth century.

Apart from its archetypal architecture, the remaking into a library had been done with sensitivity and a desire to match, rather than overwhelm, the chapel's original design. No Restoration opulence or Regency flamboyance here, just dark wood beautifully finished into twelve-foot-high bookshelves that marched the length of the room on either side of a wide aisle, dividing into a number of bays with Gothic windows lighting the western side. The table set in the middle of the aisle looked as though it had been made for that spot—quite possibly it had—at six feet wide and almost twenty feet long. It would have fit a monastery, for a flock of literate monks copying and illuminating manuscripts. The only discordant notes were her laptop and the commercial-size fire extinguisher next to the main door. Aidan had ensured she knew where it was first thing.

When she had paced off the length of the room, she stopped and studied the fitted cases with glass doors that covered the end wall in front of the rood screen. They might once have been curiosity cabinets, she thought, and there were still a few displays of a natural history sort. But mostly the cabinets were now filled with ledgers and diaries, boxes of papers and newspaper clippings that documented much of the Gallagher family history. It was where Aidan had spent his morning, though from what she could tell, he had not been very thorough. It seemed he was looking for something in particular, and not finding it, had quickly set aside whatever else came to hand.

Prying into personal affairs was not part of her job description. Indeed, it might well get her fired. But it was so bloody tempting to see if there remained any trace of Evan Chase in those cabinets. Letters, articles, outlines . . . she knew it wasn't likely. Surely the Gallaghers knew all about the promised Darkling Bride book that had never been published. If an unpublished manuscript by Evan Chase were somewhere in these papers, someone would have made it public by now.

Despite all those good, sensible reasons to walk away, Carragh opened the first door of the first cabinet and breathed in the concentrated scent of the past.

"How are you getting on?"

If she'd had anything in her hand, she probably would have dropped it from guilty surprise. Carragh took a moment to compose herself before turning to face Nessa.

"Off to a good beginning," she replied. Nessa wore another simple and expensive outfit today, a charcoal wool skirt with a navy silk blouse and another of her lovely scarves, this one in shades of ivory and teal.

"Good."

Carragh braced herself for more questions, but Nessa seemed distracted. She approached the table and the catalog put together by—Carragh quickly sorted family ties—her older brother? That was right, surely, for the fifteenth viscount had been Aidan's grandfather, and if Nessa was his great-aunt, it meant she'd been his grandfather's sister. One thing Irish families taught you was an ability to calculate relationships to a ridiculously convoluted degree.

"Do you know where Aidan has gone?" It was asked with apparent casualness, but Carragh sensed the woman disliked having to ask an outsider anything concerning her family. And it put her in an awkward position, for if Aidan had not told anyone about the solicitor, she didn't think she should.

"He went into Rathdrum, I believe. Told me to carry on." All of which was strictly true.

Close to, Nessa's skin had nearly the same fine texture as the onionskin of the catalog. "I had thought that returning to the library would be . . . unpleasant. As though it had been permanently tainted by what happened here. But now?" She looked around the space she must have known intimately since childhood and smiled faintly. "There isn't a room in the castle that hasn't seen death or grief. This one feels no different. I'm glad." With a brisker tone, Nessa added, "If you don't mind, Miss Ryan, I've arranged for you to have dinner in your room again tonight. Mrs. Bell will bring you anything you need."

"Of course. Thank you."

Just as well, Carragh decided as the woman left with the same abruptness with which she'd arrived. *I don't know if I can take any more Gallaghers today.* Repressed and abnormally controlled, the lot of them, as well as arrogant. She'd take her three rowdy Ryan brothers any day. At least you knew where you stood with her family.

But beneath her I-don't-care attitude, Carragh knew she was indulging in one of her least likable traits: preemptively dismissing people before they could decide they didn't like her. "Defensiveness," her mother told her, "means you're judging in advance of the facts. Which is exactly what you are accusing others of doing to you."

Appropriately chastened, by the interruption and her own conscience, Carragh stayed away from the family cabinets and worked flat out, with only sandwiches and tea sent in by Mrs. Bell, until six o'clock. After a long hot bath—the Deeprath pipes might groan, but they were made of sterner stuff than the ones in her grandmother's townhouse—she put in her earbuds and listened to vintage U2 while reviewing her notes from the day's work. Mrs. Bell, as promised, had brought her lamb stew and fresh bread on a tray, and she was in a perfectly relaxed mood and looking forward to her well-earned bed.

When she finally heard the knocking, it sounded like it had been going on for a bit. "Sorry," she called, scrambling out of the window seat where she'd been reading. "I had headphones in."

She opened the door to Aidan, dressed, as earlier, in black jeans and dark gray Henley. It looked very good on him, accenting his height and build. And what was she wearing? Sweats and a Red Sox hoodie, wet hair twisted into a knot atop her head.

"Aren't you coming down for dinner?" he asked.

"You eat at nine o'clock at night?" she blurted out.

"My sister's just arrived with her girls. Nessa held dinner back for them. Won't you come?"

"I wasn't invited," she said, hearing that defensive note creeping into her voice. "And I'm hardly dressed to meet anyone."

"So you're just going to lurk up here like a discontented servant?"

"I'm not discontented. And I'm no one's servant."

"I agree. So come downstairs and prove it."

She had never been able to refuse a dare. Aidan wouldn't even let her change, as though fearing once she closed the door she would never open it again. He underestimated her. Facing down Nessa Gallagher in sweats wasn't even close to the most uncomfortable thing she'd ever done.

She heard the newcomers halfway down the main stairs—the shouts of overexcited children in a new place. She imagined that horrified Nessa, and the thought made her grin as she entered the music room.

There were only two children making the noise of four or five. They were running literal circles around a harassed woman who looked far too young to be their mother.

"Ellie, Kate, that is enough." Nessa knew how to command. It quieted the girls, if not completely silencing them, so that she was able to say in a more moderate voice, "Kyla, it's time to send them to bed."

"Yes, yes, go along with Louise, darlings. I'll see you in the morning." Kyla Gallagher was tall and long-legged, with the elegant bone structure of Nessa and thick russet hair. The caustic edge to her voice was so like Aidan it was eerie.

The girls whirled around their nanny—or au pair, possibly governess?—like miniature tornadoes before the older one came to an abrupt halt. The younger fell against her sister, and stopped with the same sudden air of concentration. They were fixed on Aidan.

"You're him, aren't you?" The older girl stared at him with bright blue eyes just like his. "Our uncle."

"You can call me Aidan." It was the softest Carragh had heard him sound. "And you are Ellie."

"I'm nine, and Kate is six."

"I know. I send you birthday gifts."

"But you never come and see us. Mama says we met you in London years ago. I don't remember you."

Carragh realized her fingernails were digging into her palms as she tried to cope with the terrible tension that had sprung up. What kind of family went years without seeing each other?

"I'm seeing you now," Aidan told the child. "I hope you like the castle."

"If we do, does that mean you won't give it away?"

Ellie should have been cross-examining in courtrooms, Carragh thought. It was one thing you could always trust children to do: speak the truth.

Aidan's cheek twitched, but his voice was even. "If you go up to bed now, you'll find Mrs. Bell has put scones and jam in the old nursery."

Ellie pondered that, then nodded decisively. "We're going."

The little one, Kate, hadn't said a word. But the look she gave her uncle as the girls left with Louise was thoughtful beyond her years.

"I do apologize for my terrors," Kyla said, addressing Carragh. "I hope they haven't frightened you off all children."

"I have five nephews and nieces under the age of twelve," Carragh replied quickly. "They don't frighten me."

"My sister, Kyla Gallagher," Aidan interposed. "And this is Carragh Ryan. Whom Aunt Nessa seems to think is some sort of servant to be hidden away in her room."

"Aidan—"

Ignoring her great-aunt's protest, Kyla looked Carragh up and down. "So you're the archivist who's cataloging the library. You don't look like an Irish expert."

"Because I'm half Chinese?" There were times when Carragh truly tired of making other people comfortable with the dichotomy between her name and her appearance.

Kyla had the same polite, distancing smile as her brother. "Because you are young and pretty. But then, as my husband would say, I'm likely just jealous."

"Dinner's ready," Nessa intervened decisively.

There was only so far Carragh was willing to go to prove she wasn't a servant, and sitting down with this barb-tongued, wary group of three was too far for tonight. "I've already eaten, and I have work to do. It was nice to meet you." She didn't know what to call Aidan's sister. He'd introduced her as Gallagher, and she had no idea of the woman's married surname.

"One moment." Aidan stopped her. "It's only right you should hear this news, since there will be strangers coming in and out of the house for several days. It seems the Siochana Garda has decided to review the . . . incident of 1992."

That seemed a wild understatement. In what world did "incident" mean your parents' murders?

"I took a call from an Inspector McKenna from Serious Crimes Review a few hours ago," Aidan continued. "She and her sergeant are coming tomorrow to speak to all of us who were here at the time."

"And you have agreed to allow this?" Kyla asked icily.

"It's not a matter of allowing. The case remains open. Until it is closed, it will always be subject to review. It would be as well to be helpful to the police."

"Are you advising me as my brother or as a police officer?"

His eyes darkened. "Both."

"And you really want to rake it all up again, to talk about it and think about it and dream about it . . ."

Carragh was already edging her way to the door, for she had no wish to be caught in the middle of this.

"Kyla." Aidan spoke in the same tone of command that Nessa had used to quiet the children. "Are you afraid of dreams? Or of answers?"

"I am not afraid," she replied firmly. "I am annoyed at what the press might make of it. And so would you be, if you hadn't abandoned Ireland long ago."

Aidan shrugged. "I won't apologize for my choices."

"I would die of shock if you did."

That was the last Carragh heard before she managed to slip through the door and escape to her room. She knew all about sibling rivalries. Her brothers had settled their differences with shouting and the more-than-occasional wrestling bout. But never had she felt such vicious tension as evinced by Aidan and Kyla in just a handful of sentences.

Better stick to the library and Evan Chase. At least those griefs were too old to cause damage.

Aidan had a punishing headache by the time dinner was over and he could go to bed without incurring his great-aunt's displeasure. But it was the same bedroom he'd had since birth, which just now seemed unbearable. He didn't want to sit there surrounded by Lego sets and comic books and the ghosts of nights spent reading in bed with only his torch to hand. One learned early at Deeprath Castle not to mind the dark.

Tonight it was too much. He snagged a bottle of scotch from the butler's pantry and went back to the music room. It was an elegant, refined space, but its greatest virtue just now was that he had very few memories of being in here. Just the times he and Kyla had come investigating in the dead of night, waiting to hear the phantom music of the unhappy French girl who'd married a Gallagher and wasted away in the wild Irish mountains.

Aidan had never heard so much as a note.

He sat in the pool of amber light cast by the chinoiserie lamp on the table next to his chair and opened the folder of documents copied for him by Winthrop's assistant. It was thinner than he'd expected—hoped—but no doubt the Garda had not released every-thing to the solicitor.

As a detective in the Arts and Antiquities squad of the Metro-politan Police, most of Aidan's cases had involved an abundance of data analysis, research, and interviews. He knew not only how to read a police report and witness statements, but how to assess them. And he was not overly impressed by the quality of the Rathdrum Garda station's work.

It must, he conceded, have been overwhelming. Violent crime was fairly rare in Ireland, certainly outside of Dublin and the drug networks and/or political affairs. As an officer, he could sympathize with the police constable who had answered the urgent call from Deeprath Castle and arrived to find a viscount lying dead in his own library. But those who came after appeared to have done no better. Yes, they had secured the crime scene in the library. Yes, Aidan read now, they had instituted an immediate search of the house and grounds—which resulted in the discovery of his mother's body at the base of the Bride Tower. They had continued the search in hopes of finding evidence, but only halfheartedly, it seemed. It wasn't their fault that the castle was almost fifteen thousand square feet and had more than a hundred rooms. And the grounds were no less extensive, giving way rapidly from decorative and kitchen gardens to the ever-encroaching mountain landscape. Aidan could forgive them for those things outside their control.

But the witness statements were almost laughable in their brevity. He flicked through those of the adults who had been in the castle at any point on that September day: Robert and Maire Bell, estate manager and housekeeper by description, friends and trusted companions in reality; Mrs. O'Toole, who had cooked at Deeprath for forty years; the gardener and his assistant; the cleaners who came twice a week and had the bad luck to have been there that day; Nessa, who was spending the week with them; the solicitor, Winthrop, who had stayed the previous night while doing business; and Philip Grant. He'd come back to Philip Grant later. For now, he shuffled and recounted and examined every piece of paper front and back to make sure he hadn't overlooked something.

He hadn't. Which meant there were two critical witness statements missing from these reports: Kyla's and his own. Surely the police had talked to them both. Aidan could just recall the mustache of one of the policemen who'd asked him . . . what? They must have asked him something. He was the one who had found his father's body, after all. Of course they'd interviewed him. So why couldn't he remember it? And why wasn't that statement, or his sister's, accounted for here?

Aidan dropped his head and ground his hands against his closed eyes. Only now did he acknowledge that he'd been almost as eager to read Kyla's statement as his own. He had gone long years without consciously thinking about that day, but there were a handful of impressions he'd carried with him, which arose now and then to disturb the surface. One was the sight of his father's body on the library floor. Another was the memory of Kyla, looking over her shoulder as though ensuring she wasn't being watched. Aidan knew he had seen her somewhere that day. No, not just "that day"—somewhere and some time perilously close to his discovery of their father.

He had never been able to remember more. He'd never wanted to remember more.

Until now.

CHAPTER NINE

June 1972

"Susa!"

Lily Morgan threw her arms around her cousin, suffocating her in an enormous hug, until Susa laughingly protested. "I can't breathe, dearest."

Lily loosened her grip enough to look at her while still keeping Susa trapped in her arms. "You have no idea how relieved I am to have you here! Cillian's family is lovely, of course, but I am rather drowning in Gallaghers at the moment."

"That's what happens when you decide to get married at your fiancé's home in back-of-beyond Ireland instead of in New York like a rational woman. Or London, even. But who's going to come all the way out here?" Susa pulled a hand free to wave at the surrounding landscape. Despite the lightness of her tone, Lily knew her cousin was truly baffled. But that was all right. She'd understand soon enough.

"Thank you, Rob," she said to the steward, who was directing the gardener's assistant in taking Susa's luggage. "To the Jade Room in the Jacobean wing, please."

She stepped away from her cousin to give her an uninterrupted view. "Welcome to Deeprath Castle, Susa."

Lily knew that Susa would be impressed—as who wouldn't be? The cousins had grown up in New York City, with summers in Newport or the Berkshires, traveling to London and Paris and other chic European cities. Ireland was not chic. Nor was Deeprath Castle. But how could anyone fail to be impressed by the sheer weight of age and history embodied here? Yes, the cousins had toured many Renaissance palaces. But this was not a showplace. This was a home.

For all that, Lily also knew that Susa's first comments would be critical. No one could pick out flaws like she could. *It's isolated. It's crumbling. It's ridiculously outsized. It's positively medieval. The lights/plumbing/heating are going to kill you all* . . .

But Susa surprised her. "I can feel why you love it, Lil. You have always had one ear tuned to the past."

Yes! Lily wanted to say. *That is right. And this place speaks to me. Not the ghosts, not the history—the castle itself.* The first time Cillian had brought her here, her immediate impression had been of an enormous, imposing specimen composed of hundreds of years of architectural styles, but nothing that made it substantially different from dozens of other castles dotted across Ireland.

And then, she had touched a wall. Like a jolt of electricity, the castle had come crashing into her, flooding every inch of her body with the power and passion of seven hundred years, until she couldn't breathe. Just as suddenly, it pulled back . . . and took her heart with it. She'd known in that moment that she belonged to Deeprath, though Cillian would not propose to her for another six months.

"Come along." She squeezed Susa's arm. "We'll say hello to Cillian."

He was in the drawing room with his mother and aunt. Tall, broad-shouldered, and with a quiet intelligence and sensibility that kept Lily grounded, Cillian went straight to Susa and kissed her on the cheek. "Welcome to Ireland," he said.

"I don't think I really am in Ireland," she retorted. "It isn't raining."

He laughed and made the proper introductions. "Mother, this is
Susan Morgan, Lily's cousin. This is my mother, Lady Gallagher,
and my aunt, Lady Nessa."

"Call me Fiona, please," his mother said. "We're so delighted to
meet you. Lily sings your praises day and night."

"Lily sings everyone's praises," Susan retorted drily. "She's inca-
pable of seeing faults in anyone."

Aunt Nessa—though Lily was pretty sure the woman would
have asked to be called Lady Nessa, if only Aidan's mother weren't
so determinedly informal—greeted Susa with a cool nod. "A charming trait in Lily, I'm sure. If not always a practical one."

"That's why I'm here, Aunt Nessa." Cillian drew Lily to his side.
"I'll be practical, and she'll be everything else. This castle could use
some fresh and enthusiastic blood."

Nessa's expression softened. Perhaps the only thing she appreciated about Lily was her love for Deeprath. "I'm sure all of the Gallaghers are very pleased to have such an enthusiastic advocate."

Lily met Susa's eyes, her cousin conveying whole phrases in her
expression: *Does she really talk like that all the time?*

Lily answered in the same silent manner. *You haven't heard anything yet.*

CHAPTER TEN

In the twenty-six hours between being assigned the Gallagher case and arriving in Wicklow, Sibéal spent all but five immersed in study. She had no memory of the case—she'd been eleven at the time, and though it certainly made the news, her family had little interest in nonpolitical crimes. The domestic murders of a rich lord and his eccentric American wife paled beside IRA ops and hunger strikes.

By the time the train pulled into Rathdrum, Sibéal had pulled together not only the information she needed to be getting on with, but also the persona demanded of an inspector about to trample all over a family's most painful memories. Sergeant Cullen had been admirably silent while she studied and when they exited the station he asked, "Deeprath Castle first?"

It had not been their plan. She'd told the solicitor, Winthrop, that they would call on him first, and courtesy dictated she also make their presence known to the local force. If Cullen continued reading her mind like this, they'd do very well together.

"Right," she confirmed. "Find us a cab."

It wasn't a cab, per se, but the car was adequate and the driver willing. Sibéal had never been to County Wicklow before. Growing up in Donegal, so far removed politically and geographically from the rest of the Irish Republic, she was not easily impressed by landscape. What could be more dramatic than the sea lochs or the Slieve League sea cliffs?

Still, the Wicklow Mountains in April had an eerie feel, she decided as they drove into the hills, though she knew that impression was likely influenced by her recent reading. Ireland was a country alive with ghosts. She was just particularly sensitive at the moment to those of Cillian and Lily Gallagher.

Her first sight of Deeprath Castle left her breathless. At her side, Cullen whistled softly. "I'm surprised there haven't been dozens of murders out here," he said. "Looks exactly the kind of house people are dragged to on purpose to be murdered."

"It's just old," she said sharply, reproving her own response, not his. "And damp, no doubt."

Sibéal, who preferred her architecture modern, clean, and minimal, felt a reluctant appreciation as Cullen paid the driver and extracted a promise for him to return at four o'clock if they hadn't called before. She studied the various frontages of the castle before her, neck craned to an uncomfortable degree. What would it be like to be responsible for such a place? she wondered. And could that responsibility have had anything to do with the Gallagher murders?

Considering the size of the castle, it didn't take an inordinate amount of time for the elaborately traceried door to open. Disconcertingly, two little girls stared up at them.

Fortunately, Sibéal was not cowed by little girls, being the mother of one. "Hello. Is your mother here?"

The woman who followed the children was too old to be their mother. She addressed the girls first. "Back to your au pair now, and no more dashing about on your own." Only then did she acknowledge Sibéal and Cullen.

"I'm Maire Bell. I assume you are the Dublin police?" She would have looked more enthusiastically at a rat catcher. If there were such things still. A place like this could no doubt use one.

Sibéal showed her warrant card. "I'm Inspector McKenna, this is Sergeant Cullen. I believe we're expected."

When Sibéal offered nothing more, Mrs. Bell narrowed her eyes and allowed them in. Sibéal knew that the woman had been the housekeeper at the castle when the murders occurred; it appeared she'd never left. They were kept waiting in the echoing space of the hall, complete with original wood paneling, beamed ceiling, and a fireplace that could have roasted a whole cow. Add in the family crest carved into stone—she'd seen a drawing of it in the case notes, with its winged lion/eagle creature dead center—and Sibéal didn't know if she wanted to burn the aristocracy to the ground or find a wall to put at her back. Beneath his breath, Cullen said, "Colder in here than outside."

The woman who returned was elderly, of the type that age had distilled into the essential qualities of bone and personality. She was well-dressed, with a decorative cane used, Sibéal guessed, for balance.

"I'm Lady Nessa Gallagher. It has been a long time since we've had police at Deeprath Castle." The introduction was unnecessary. She could not have been anyone else.

"I'm Inspector McKenna, Ms. Gallagher. I am sorry about this, but my business is with unsolved crimes. I'm sure you can appreciate that this one looms rather large in our conscience."

"A cold case, isn't that what they call it? I can't imagine what you think can be learned now."

"New eyes, new information . . . one never knows. As this is the first time since 1992 that family has been gathered at the castle, it seemed convenient to do this now. We'll need to speak to each of you in turn, if you don't mind."

"If I do mind?"

The woman might be privileged and elderly, but Sibéal was

cowed by no one. "Then my job will be harder, and you will lose the opportunity to tell your story first."

She held her breath. Nessa Gallagher looked the sort to cause trouble if she felt others were being less than respectful. But she also looked intelligent, and Sibéal's reasoning won out. "Is there a particular order in which you'd like to speak to us, Inspector?"

"Might as well begin with you." Better to do it at once than allow this self-possessed woman to armor herself even more thoroughly.

As if she knew Sibéal's reasoning, Nessa Gallagher gave a slight, scornful smile and escorted them to a less enormous but no less imposing room. A music room, for there was a harp, what Sibéal thought was a spinet, and a grand piano of more recent vintage. She sat directly facing Nessa in a matching set of black painted chairs with faded embroidery seats. Cullen sat to her side and a little withdrawn, to be less obtrusive in his note taking.

Sibéal opened her own notebook, with the relevant facts and a few loose lines of questioning already written. "Tell me about your nephew's wife, Lily Gallagher."

If Nessa thought that an unexpected beginning, she didn't show it. "As lovely and charming as a butterfly, and approximately as responsible."

"You didn't like her."

"Does my liking enter into it? If so, then please note that I liked Lily quite a lot." Nessa sat perfectly still, hands in her lap, the overly decorative cane resting against the chair. "It was impossible not to like Lily. That did not change the fact that she was not entirely suitable for the marriage she had made. Her flightiness caused some damage."

"What sort of damage?"

"Beyond getting herself and her husband killed?"

Ten points to Gryffindor, Sibéal thought. Or, more likely, Slytherin. (She'd been reading Harry Potter with her daughter for several months.)

"You think Lily was responsible for the murders? How, exactly?"

"It was Lily who wanted to see the antiquities the Gallaghers have collected over generations. It was for her sake that Cillian arranged to have them brought to the castle that week. Winthrop, the solicitor, was not happy about it—nor were the insurance adjustors; there's a reason we've never filed for compensation—but Lily nearly always got what she wanted."

"So you think, as the police apparently did, that it was a crime of opportunity that went badly wrong. What do you believe happened to those antiquities afterward? They haven't surfaced in twenty-three years."

"Truth be told, Inspector, I spent as little time thinking about it as possible. I had two children on my hands in the aftermath, both traumatized and angry, and all my efforts went to raising them to be a credit to their family. It may seem heartless to you, but what was done, was done. Cillian and Lily were gone. The why seemed . . . less relevant than the mere fact of it."

"If it was not a robbery gone wrong, then it would be irresponsible of me not to consider every possibility. Double-murder, murder-suicide, murder-accident . . . but such domestic crimes do not erupt from nothing. And yet, there was no hint of any serious discord in the marriage itself. Unless there was information you did not choose to share at the time?"

Grudgingly, Nessa conceded, "No. Cillian adored Lily. Even when exasperated with her, he never gave her cause to doubt his loyalty and affection. And for certain he never hurt or threatened her, if that is what you mean."

"Did Lily ever give him cause to doubt her loyalty? You told the police at the time that she was . . ." Sibéal pretended to look at her notes for the phrase she had actually memorized. "'. . . a natural flirt who didn't always know where to draw the line.' But you declined to provide the name of any man with whom Lily might have been seriously involved. Has anyone specific come to mind in the last twenty years?"

Sibéal was enjoying this; maybe too much, she reflected. It wasn't always a good idea to antagonize a witness. Though Nessa didn't seem antagonized so much as wary. Interesting.

"I assure you, Inspector, if I had thought of anything that would have led to resolution for my great-niece and -nephew, I should have contacted the police at once. It is a cruel thing to lose both parents at one stroke."

Sibéal nodded noncommittally. Deciding to stop here for the moment—let Nessa think she'd controlled the interview—she added, "Thank you for your time. I'd like to see your great-niece next. And I'd prefer you not speculate with anyone about our discussion."

"I wouldn't dream of it."

She slanted a look at Cullen as the woman exited and said, "A bit too much protesting on her part. So Nessa Gallagher doesn't believe that the crimes were robbery gone wrong. Sarcastic and defensive. Is that pertinent, or simply a feature of her personality?"

"Of her upbringing, more like. She comes from the days when class mattered."

"It doesn't matter now?"

"You know what I mean," Cullen answered. "Nessa Gallagher was born in the Old World. She grew up in this castle with probably a dozen servants and a father who never had to work a day in his life. She can hardly help being arrogant."

"I almost think you like her."

The sergeant snorted. "She might have been born to her arrogance, but that's no excuse for rudeness."

"Let's see if Kyla Gallagher tempers her arrogance with better manners."

Kyla Gallagher did have manners of a more engaging sort than her great-aunt. But Sibéal quickly realized that the woman was very nearly as guarded. She simply hid it with a flow of words and a rueful air of wanting to help and sorry that she couldn't. Tall and even better-dressed than her great-aunt, Kyla's copper-brown hair was pinned up in a deceptively casual French twist. Sibéal knew that if she tried to adopt the same style, it would be all messy ends and loose strands.

"I was so young," Kyla told them, as though confiding a great secret. "Well, at the time I thought I was very grown-up and knew everything. Fifteen-year-olds do, you know. In my case, I'm afraid it meant I'd been fighting with my mother for some months. Normal adolescent things—she didn't like my clothes, I thought she was controlling, all the things mothers and daughters fight over. We would have got over it with time. Sadly, we didn't have more time."

"Did you notice anything in your mother's behavior in the month or so before the deaths that was . . . different? Out of character?"

"My mother always had changeable moods and interests. She would take up knitting with religious fervor, only to abandon it three months later for gardening. She always had a passion, but nothing held her interest for long."

"What was her passion that summer?"

"Gallagher history," Kyla answered promptly. "Drove me mad chattering about the castle and our various ancestors. She seemed determined to authenticate as many of the stories as possible, so they wouldn't be forgotten or changed too much in future. I also remember her going on about the Darkling Bride and the many variations in that legend. She wanted to find the truth of it if she could."

"The Darkling Bride?" Cullen queried.

Kyla turned her practiced smile on the sergeant. "It's a mainly Celtic legend; you'll find versions of it throughout Ireland and Scotland. Wales, parts of Cornwall and Brittany. The Wicklow version had some unique details that my mother hoped could be substantiated, used to show that our local legend derived from an actual history."

"How did your father feel about that project?" Cullen asked. "Was it something over which your parents disagreed? Perhaps he did not care for her digging in his family's past."

For the first time, Sibéal saw a flicker of real feeling in the eyes of the woman before her. So Kyla wasn't entirely immune to her loss. "In my memory, my parents never disagreed. It was a happy marriage, insofar as a child could tell. If you're thinking that my father was so enraged by my mother's foray into his family history that she was driven to kill him and then herself . . . no. Never over something so trivial."

So Kyla knew about the gossip that claimed the deaths were a murder-suicide. Taking back the reins of the interview, Sibéal asked, "What about something less trivial?"

"Like money, or cheating, or drugs? You'd have to ask someone else. I never saw it. And children, for all their self-absorption, are aware of emotional undercurrents. Just ask my girls about the state of my marriage, if you don't believe me," she said bitterly. "If my parents were half as unhappy as I have been, I would have known it."

Now that was information to take note of, seeing as Kyla's husband had also been at Deeprath Castle in 1992. Philip Grant had been a twenty-one-year-old intern to her father, and according to the records, was a troublesome presence as far as the fifteen-year-old girl was concerned. Sibéal had a great deal of interest in Philip, and if his marriage to Kyla was faltering, that might give her a wedge she could use in the future.

"What do you think happened to your parents?"

After a moment, Kyla said, "Someone murdered them both, Inspector. I don't know who, and I don't know why. But my mother was no coward. She might have hit my father with something—in a moment of madness, even—but she would have admitted it. Not jumped off the tower and left us to cope all alone."

Mrs. Bell delivered the news of the police's arrival to Aidan sotto voce in the library. He was surprised by his instant surge of adrenaline, considering that he'd known they were coming, and he stared sightlessly at the tray of tea and scones the housekeeper had left behind for long minutes. He had forgotten he had company. When he finally looked up, he saw that Carragh was regarding him steadily.

"Are you all right?" she asked.

"Of course. It's just a few questions, after all."

"I'm sure all they want is to go over your testimony from before. You were just a boy, they don't expect much from children." Spoken as though she knew.

"That's just it," he said almost without thinking. "I realized last night that I don't remember giving a statement back then."

"I thought . . . Didn't you find your father?"

"Yes, I did, and yes, I should have been questioned. Surely I was, a little. I remember sitting with Nessa and a policeman from Rathdrum. I don't remember anything else."

"Well, maybe these people will help you remember. They'll have all the evidence and stuff. Whatever." She shrugged.

He smiled at that. "Yes. Whatever."

But a growing sense of unease followed him to the music room when he was finally summoned.

There were two detectives waiting: a man about his own age, with fairish hair and a ready smile, and a woman with serious brown eyes who offered her hand.

"Inspector McKenna," she said. "We spoke on the phone yesterday. And Sergeant Cullen. Thank you for your time."

"Am I to assume this is a result of my asking for evidentiary materials in my parents' case? You didn't say when you rang." He knew he sounded pompous and overbearing.

She was undaunted. "Coincidence, believe it or not. I was assigned your case shortly before hearing from your solicitor."

"So you're not going to return the things I asked for? May I at least ask if you have them?"

"We have letters written to both of them, as well as your father's account book."

"But you won't return my mother's diary?"

"We don't have it. The police never did, there's no mention of a diary or journal. Are you sure it hasn't simply been misplaced?"

"I've looked."

"Everywhere? That could take weeks." He saw a flicker of sardonic humor as her eyes took in the space of the music room.

Only if it was hidden, Aidan thought. And why would it have been? "Why has the case been reopened now?" he asked.

"I'm sure you can figure it out, Detective Inspector Gallagher."

He didn't flinch. "Because it's technically unsolved, whatever fuss the police made of the stolen antiquities and possible assassinthieves. Because the deaths occurred within and without this castle, and the castle will soon be handed over to bureaucrats at the National Trust. And probably because you are new and so they gave you a case that's not a high priority."

"That's not very flattering."

"For me, either. It means no one really cares about what happened here. Except us."

"I care."

When she said it, he believed her. For whatever reason—probably more than one, including advancing her career—Sibéal McKenna was committed to solving this case.

"Then ask your questions," he said. "Inspector."

CHAPTER ELEVEN

Carragh would never have expected anything could distract her from the glory that was the Deeprath library. Turned out a police investigation was sufficient.

After Aidan left, she wasted an hour before she realized that she hadn't taken a single legible note about the current shelf she was studying. Guiltily deciding that there was no use working when she couldn't concentrate, she left her notes on the long table and allowed herself to simply browse.

She'd located the Victorian novels section yesterday and now indulged to her heart's content. The chief find was a complete set of first edition Anthony Trollope novels—forty-seven altogether—including all of the Palliser series and the Chronicles of Barsetshire. Sitting cross-legged on the floor, she immersed herself in the domestic worries of *Framley Parsonage*, of which Trollope himself had said, "There is much church, but more lovemaking." She only stopped reading when the light grew too dim to make out the type on the 150-year-old pages, reminding her that she was supposed to be working.

Floor and table lamps had been brought into the library, and

Carragh turned them all on. She hoped the electrical circuits could take the strain. If there was a power cut, as Nessa had suggested often happened, she'd have to wander around the place with a flashlight. She managed to work her way to completion of the first two bays, which fortunately retained their order from the days of the fifteenth viscount (Greek translations, French philosophers, and, intriguingly, the American Revolution). She admired an English translation of *The Iliad* by John Dryden, three early printings of *Candide* in Voltaire's original French, and a copy of *The Federalist Papers* that appeared to have been signed by John Jay, James Madison, and Alexander Hamilton. She set that last one aside for Aidan to decide whether to keep in the family or donate.

Blinking to loosen the muscles around her eyes, she turned off the multitude of lamps and weighed asking Aidan if she could take *Framley Parsonage* to her room, then decided just to do it. He had not reappeared—nor had she seen anyone—since he'd left to talk with the police. That was hours ago. She was pretty sure the Gallagher family had other things to worry about than her borrowing one Victorian novel.

She had her own worries for tonight: her presence had been requested at dinner, perhaps due to Aidan overriding his great-aunt's protocol. What did one wear to attend dinner in a castle with a viscount and two ladies, especially when one's presence might not be wholly welcome?

Carragh would have called or texted Francis or her sister-in-law Abbie for advice, except that Lady Nessa had not exaggerated the lack of mobile signals at Deeprath. Aidan had told her that one could usually be picked up where the drive met the road, but that was almost a mile long and she didn't need advice that badly. It's not as though she had a wardrobe full of choices.

She finally chose tights, ankle boots, and a tunic dress edged with silver-threaded embroidery. After leaving her room, she came down the main staircase—the Hollander staircase, she remembered from her tour; she couldn't remember why—and came to a perplexed stop in the Great Hall. Where, exactly, did she go? The dining room, she seemed to recall from her tour, was somewhere to her left. But then she heard voices from her right and went cautiously in their direction. For all she knew she would end up in the kitchen.

But no, it was Gallagher voices she'd heard coming from the open doorway of what could only be termed a drawing room. She blinked, dazzled by the blaze of double chandeliers on the gold leaf that seemed to be everywhere. The room was even larger than the library, with a wall of French windows at the far end. Critics might have thought it too-sparsely furnished, until they looked closer. Then they would have realized that each piece was original and gorgeous and chosen specifically to complement each other and the overall design.

For a brief moment Carragh wished she were eating on her bed in pajamas. It was like entering an Edwardian dinner party before the Great War; what would she do if Nessa was wearing a corset and trailing skirts?

"Blinded?" It was Aidan, who blessedly wore the same casual dress pants and button-down shirt he'd been wearing earlier today.

"By all the Gallagher brilliance," she quipped. "Pity we don't have those chandeliers in the library. Would save our eyes considerably."

She saw Kyla, with a glass in her hand, wearing a pair of perfectly tailored black trousers and a crisp white shirt that looked simple but probably cost more than the contents of her entire suitcase. Nessa was dressier than the rest of them, but not outrageously so. Carragh relaxed slightly, before remembering the tension last night among the three of them together. She vowed not to drink more than a sip or two of anything alcoholic and slip away as soon as she decently could.

They ate, as she had predicted, in the cavernous dining room at a table that would have seated twenty with ease. Two adults on each side, facing one another across the exact middle of the mahogany expanse, with china so fine it could almost be seen through and silver so heavy it could do serious damage if dropped. Or thrown. Ky-la's daughters—Ellie and Kate—were escorted in by their au pair and allowed to sit with her farther down. Their china and cutlery was not so grand.

Carragh was next to Nessa—less, she thought, because the older woman preferred her company, and more because she wanted to keep a piercing attention on her younger relatives. There were barbs delivered over and between the food as it was served by Mrs. Bell, but they were all Gallagher aimed and directed, until she began to wonder if they even remembered she was sitting here.

"Kyla, have you given further thought to accepting the position on the Children's Cancer Research board? After the strings I pulled, it would be a pity to turn it down."

"I didn't ask you to pull strings. I am capable of choosing my own activities."

"Your work with Kilkenny Marketing is quite good, but we must all be willing to offer our talents in service as well as in business."

"The Kilkenny Civic Trust takes a considerable amount of my time," Kyla said, sounding defensive.

"Yes," Aidan interposed smoothly, "it must take loads of work to turn heritage properties into hotels."

"What would you know about it?" Kyla snapped. "Your only in-terest in business is how much your investments bring in. At least I know where our money comes from."

"It comes from the dead," Aidan answered.

It was like being caught in the crossfire of a particularly mean-spirited Victorian novel: the cool matriarchal figure, the ambivalent heir, the disappointed and sarcastic sister. Carragh would have writ-ten them all off as unlikable—were it not for the undercurrents of loss and fear that ran just beneath the surface. She knew something about being unlikable in order to keep people away.

Nessa diplomatically turned her attention to Carragh. "How are you finding Deeprath, Miss Ryan?"

"Everything at Deeprath is most interesting," she answered diplomatically. In truth, she found the empty corridors and rooms a little grim. Beyond the showpiece areas of the castle—and despite evidence of physical care and cleaning—there was a melancholy air to the place. Deprived of the family it had sheltered for centuries, it was as though Deeprath had turned brooding, twisting ever more inward . . .

Which was exactly like something out of a novel. "That's what imagination does to you," her mother had often warned. "Don't let your imagination make you see what you want to see."

"No sign of our ghosts?" Lady Nessa asked, perfectly serious.

"I don't think so. What sort of sign should I be looking for?"

"It depends on the ghost. Thomas Gallagher, who built the original keep, can be seen by moonlight walking the battlements. Marthe lingers around the music room. She was French, very delicate, and spent most of her time singing to herself. You might catch a few notes from her if you're quiet. She's sensitive to interruption."

"Don't forget the Darkling Bride," Kyla intervened. "She's rarely seen, but it's said she can frighten Gallagher men into flight."

That gave Carragh a perfect opening. "There was an author who came here in the 1880s to write about the Darkling Bride. Evan Chase. He married Jenny Gallagher. She had such a tragic life and death . . . are there any ghost stories about her?"

Lady Nessa said sharply, "If she walks, she does so only in the tower. And we do not disturb her."

"Maybe that was mother's mistake," Aidan said. "Maybe she disturbed Jenny Gallagher and ended up at the bottom of the Bride Tower as punishment."

Carragh was as shocked by his bitterness as by the words themselves.

Kyla blanched, and in a whisper meant to keep the end of the table from hearing, she said, "Aidan, please. Whatever grudge you bear my girls, there's no need to be brutal in front of them."

"That wasn't—" Aidan stopped himself, almost as pale as his sister. "I'm sorry. I didn't mean it."

That effectively ended conversation, while Mrs. Bell brought in the second course of poached salmon. Carragh was aching to leave. It's not as though she came from a conflict-free family. Even without alcohol, the Ryans knew how to argue. Loudly. They could be even louder when agreeing with each other. But loud, she decided now, was far and away better than painstaking chilliness.

Kyla continued to drink, Ellie and Kate began to squirm, and Nessa conveyed distaste for both those activities with no more than a tightened cheekbone and a hard flick of her consonants.

And Aidan? After his enigmatic statement, he resumed his distant and distracted air. It seemed he could change personalities at the drop of a hat. When he'd yanked open the library door and confronted her that first day, he'd been hostile—and then switched to an obviously well-practiced charm. Carragh imagined there were many who wallowed in that charm.

After yesterday's unthinking rudeness about her family, Aidan had appeared genuinely apologetic, and when discussing the library with her, he was focused and straightforward. How was she supposed to know how to behave when he kept switching on her with dizzying speeds?

Just be professional, she told herself sternly. *All I have to do is not openly antagonize him and get thrown out of Deeprath before I'm finished in the library. I can do that.*

With the third course (spring lamb and carrots), Lady Nessa turned her attention back to her. Probably because she was the only one at the table who would feel compelled to be polite.

"Tell us about your family, Miss Ryan. Do I recall correctly that you have siblings?"

"Three brothers."

"Older or younger?"

"They are fourteen, twelve, and six years older than I am."

"I assume your mother wanted a girl and couldn't have one, until she took you in."

As though Carragh was a puppy dog that had strayed too far from home. "You would have to ask my mother that."

And wouldn't that be a conversation, she thought in amusement. Lady Nessa Gallagher might have name and title and position on her side, but Judge Anne Ryan bowed and scraped to no one. If her mother were sitting at this table tonight, no one would have been left in doubt of her opinions on . . . well, everything.

Nessa tried another tack. "You said last night that you have nieces and nephews."

If the old woman wanted a family tree, Carragh would oblige her in spades. "Sean and his wife have two boys and two girls and live in New York. He's a professor of economics, like my father, and Abbie is a pediatrician. Patrick and his husband"—*let the lady linger on that one*—"live in Boston and have a three-year-old daughter. They're both finance professionals. And Francis, who is nearest me in age, is still trying to find himself. So far that has involved a stint in the Peace Corps, teaching English in Vietnam, and starting—and dropping out of—graduate study three times."

Kyla laughed, and raised her third—or fourth?—glass of wine in toast to Carragh. "To your family. I hope you see more of your brothers than I see of mine."

Nessa stopped trying to interrogate her after that. They shared a few stilted comments about Dublin traffic and the weather before the old woman turned her attention back to her great-niece. For fifteen minutes Kyla and Nessa bickered over the children's behavior and lack of table manners. ("Those are habits which can only have been learned at home, Kyla dear, for their breeding is impeccable," to which Kyla replied, "They are children, not horses.") Eventually, the problem sorted itself when Nessa insisted the au pair put the girls to bed. Kyla protested halfheartedly, then bid her daughters goodnight with open affection.

When Kate whispered in her mother's ear, Kyla laughed without any of her previous cultivated bitterness. "Miss Ryan, the girls would like to know if they could play with your nieces and nephews."

She smiled at the sisters. "I wish you could. They all live in the United States. Perhaps next time they visit Ireland?" As though she would have any connection with any Gallagher after she'd finished this job.

Carragh attempted to excuse herself as the children left with the silent au pair, Louise, but Aidan said to her, "I rather think you're the only reason we're still speaking to one another. If you go, the rest of us will soon retreat to our separate corners." He raised that irritating eyebrow. "On second thought, perhaps that's preferable."

"Really, Aidan!" Nessa's voice held both reproof and weary affection. Though maybe it was simple weariness. "What will Miss Ryan think of us?"

"If Miss Ryan has a brain in her head—which she certainly seems to—she must already think us either mad or wicked."

"Not a chance," Carragh retorted. "If you want family drama, you should be in the Ryan household when Boston College plays Notre Dame in football. The odds then aren't on bloodshed, but on whether an ambulance will be needed to clean up afterward."

Aidan raised the glass of white wine he'd scarcely touched through dinner. "To families. Long may they haunt us."

From the doorway behind Carragh, a voice drawled, "What a bloody depressing welcome! No wonder you're still single, Aidan, if that's your attitude to domestic bliss."

The speaker moved into the dining room and into Carragh's line of sight. A handsome man of early middle age with the kind of silver-streaked hair called distinguished and a London suit to go with his London accent. Arrogant, she'd called him, the night they'd met, and nothing about him had changed.

"I let myself in," he added unnecessarily. "Hello, darling."

For a long, appalling moment, Carragh thought he was speaking to her. She had wondered what it meant when someone said they were frozen in shock. Now she knew.

Sensation returned with a rush as he sauntered to the other side of the table and leaned down to kiss Kyla's cheek. Carragh knew that she herself had paled and then flushed, and took a hasty drink to hide her face.

"Nessa," the man purred. "Looking perfectly elegant as always."

"Your lateness is not excused by flattery. And especially not when we have a guest."

He looked at Carragh then, and she thought she saw the glimmer of her own shock reflected in his eyes. But he recovered smoothly as Nessa introduced her. "This is Carragh Ryan. She is helping Aidan catalog the library."

"Are you? You don't look the type."

"Forgive my husband," Kyla interposed, with syrupy sweetness. "There are only two types of women in Philip's world: those he'd like to sleep with, and those he wouldn't. The former group is rather larger than the latter."

"Don't exaggerate, darling. Nice to meet you, Miss Ryan. I'm Kyla's long-suffering husband, Philip Grant."

It was the second time Philip had introduced himself to her. And God help her if any of the Gallaghers ever found that out.

CHAPTER TWELVE

October 1879

Evan took to the Deeprath library like an ocean fish that had been deprived of seawater for far too long. From the very first day he'd been struck by the aura of time past mixed with time present in the former chapel, thanks in part to Jenny's dramatic appearance from the stacks. Whatever the reason, the library retained its mystical air.

As Jenny had suggested, he turned an investigative eye to the Gallagher family history. It took him many hours of tracing names and dates, deciphering spidery handwriting until his eyes crossed and his head ached, before he finally located a Gallagher son by the name of Niall. It was an eighteenth-century copy of a history compiled by a family cleric in the late 1400s, stretching back to the first Gallagher—Tomas Ó Gallchobair, who anglicized his name and married the daughter of an Anglo-Norman settler in 1214.

Evan knew better than to take everything the cleric wrote as gospel truth, especially as he repeated several of Gerald of Wales's more startling assertions about Ireland as though they were proven fact—such as kingfishers never decaying after death, or migratory birds spending the winter in some mystical state between life and death. But the man seemed reasonably well-informed of dates and, after all, one did not expect to find hard facts when tracing the origin of legends. The most one could hope for was a distinct beginning point—a story's inspiration, as it were. And in this fading and crumbling history, Evan found the basis of the Wicklow version of the Darkling Bride.

Niall Gallagher was born in 1273, a great-grandson of the founding lord Thomas. As the third son to live to maturity, he was designated from birth for the Church, and where better to learn and be called to service than at Glendalough? The anonymous cleric recorded that *guileless as Nathan and ever obedient to his fathers, earthly and spiritual, Niall would have made a great saint.*

And then . . . disaster. In the shape—as so often in men's recounting of history—of a woman.

In 1291, Acre, the last remaining Christian stronghold in the Holy Land, fell to Muslim armies. Among those few who escaped was a distant relation of the Gallaghers, who came to Deeprath to recuperate from the trauma of it all. With him came his wife and her servant, Maryam—*though many tongues,* wrote the cleric two hundred years later, *whispered that she was no servant but the Crusader's concubine.*

Whatever the truth of that relationship, all fell to pieces when Niall encountered Maryam upon a visit home. *And with her hair dark as sin and eyes of unearthly blue, the sorceress wove her spell and enslaved the boy so that he forgot all he owed to his family and God.* Niall left the monastic life to marry her, a crime for which his family would never forgive the woman. In one of those twisted medieval intrigues, Niall and his wife were invited to visit Deeprath Castle, where Niall was killed by his own brother and Maryam locked securely in the keep. The keep now fittingly known as the Bride Tower. There the story ended, the chronicler concluding with a smugly pious lesson: *Surely man must be always vigilant against the snares Satan lays in his path, for never is evil more dangerous than when cloaked in beauty.*

Interesting. No mention of the Sanctuary Cross or Maryam having spent time at Glendalough, though he supposed her speaking in an unknown tongue referenced Arabic. Evan was not surprised that the more paranormal aspects of the story Jenny had told him did not make an appearance in this earliest version, nor even the Darkling Bride name. (Though he did rather like "hair dark as sin" and knew that phrase would make its way into his book.) He was well-acquainted with how legends twisted and turned through the generations and different storytellers, so that the same essential story could have myriad differences within just a fifty-mile radius. As much as he enjoyed spending time with Jenny, he needed to interview more widely in the area.

But that was for later. He had his beginning, handed to him as though tailor-made for a gothic novel: crusaders, monks, a castle, a beautiful woman, and family treachery. What more could one ask?

DIARY OF JENNY GALLAGHER

16 October 1879

Just because Dora helped deliver me at birth, she takes it upon herself to give me advice while helping me dress or brushing my hair. Yesterday she called Mr. Chase "A fine young man. For a writer."

I know exactly what that means. It means that however handsome, however presentable, however well-spoken and successful he is, Evan Chase is not the sort of man society would judge suitable for the only daughter of a viscount. Barring another attempt by my father to marry and have a son, I will inherit Glendalough and his fortune. No novelist, however popular, need apply.

I have my own opinions about that. On paper, I am considered an excellent match. But marriages do not exist on paper. Where is there a man who will want, not only my money, but my person?

Evan is the only man I've ever met who I think I could trust with all of me.

CHAPTER THIRTEEN

For the first time since her arrival, Carragh fiercely missed having a connection to the wider world. Even a chance to ignore her mother's emails would have been a pleasure after that dinner. She had escaped to her room but could think of nothing that she wanted to do. Watch downloaded episodes of *Project Runway*? *What were the chances Philip would stay far away from her while at Deeprath?* Play solitaire for the thousandth time on her phone? *What other secrets were this house and family going to throw at her?* It was all just distraction, and tonight none of that distraction was sufficient. If she were smart, she'd return to the library and work.

But when she considered the library, another thought snagged at her mind and quickened her pulse: the Bride Tower. She hadn't been inside it yet, hadn't even asked Aidan about it, but she knew where the key was kept—right there in the library with the same set Aidan had brought from London with him. As he no longer locked the library itself, he had put them on the top shelf of one of the family history cabinets.

Right—she would investigate the tower. The unelectrified tower. At night. There was no need to add more gothic trappings, like candles or flowing nightgowns. She wore her flannel pajama pants, tank top, and oversized Boston College sweatshirt, and carried the enormous flashlight her father had given her when she moved to Ireland. It was as much a weapon as a light, for it must weigh five pounds with its solid steel casing. With it, Carragh felt suitably prepared for whatever lay ahead.

She couldn't decide if Nessa Gallagher had put her alone in a wing of the castle to emphasize her position as a hired employee, but at least it made covert exploring convenient. Carragh had never been anyplace so dark. And quiet . . . She would never know if all the inhabitants of the castle just suddenly decided to leave. Sound seemed to have no ability to penetrate here. She couldn't even hear herself breathe, which set off a momentary panic that made her try to inhale and speak at the same time, and that led to a ridiculous fit of choked coughing.

If asked—or accused—she would have instantly denied being superstitious. Certainly she did not believe in conventional ghosts. But she did believe in the energy of strong emotions. And the Deeprath walls fairly vibrated with tension—and not all of it, she thought, from its current occupants.

Knowing the route to the library, she arrived there without hearing anything more than the noises very old houses made. Creaks, groans, the settling of centuries old wood and stone, the whistle of wind against ancient windows and the abrupt hushes of tapestried galleries. She was not afraid, she told herself. But she had the same feeling as on the day she'd arrived at Deeprath—that the castle knew its own and recognized her as an outsider. Not an enemy, perhaps, but definitely not family.

The library was as she'd left it, with no sign that Aidan had returned after speaking to the police, and Carragh found the keys where she'd expected. She let herself through the short rounded door that led out of the library to the tower's ground floor and switched on her light before pulling the door (mostly) closed behind her.

The space was much more imposing at night, with only the flashlight to throw uneven light across the stones of floor and wall. The ceiling seemed miles above her and yet claustrophobic at the same time. What might be lurking in those ancient beams, ready to fall on her?

No point panicking before she'd even properly begun. She crossed to the farthest corner, where two walls jutted into the room to enclose a space maybe eight feet square. There was a door here, made of planked wood with heavy iron fittings and a ring to pull it open. Her heart dropped when she saw it also bore a lock. It was older by far than the Yale locks used to seal the library—though certainly not medieval—and Carragh shivered, suddenly certain it had been installed during Jenny Gallagher's life. To keep her out of the dangerous tower—or to keep her in? Had Jenny leaped from the tower's height because she'd had no other way out?

She was concerned that her exploration would end then and there, but when she turned the engraved handle, she discovered the door wasn't locked. It opened smoothly. As though someone were welcoming her . . .

I am not Catherine Morland, she reminded herself crossly, *to be played with by Jane Austen as an example of foolish, easily persuadable girls. I don't believe in ghosts and I don't believe in sentient houses.*

But she did believe in history, and centuries of it almost choked her as she stepped inside and turned her flashlight upward. As expected, the enclosed space contained stone steps spiraling tightly out of sight.

Focusing the beam on the first of the steps, Carragh began to climb. There was an iron rail—no doubt added much later to replace an earlier rope—fixed to one wall. The spiral was not the usual clockwise direction (received wisdom claimed it was for the ease of defenders swinging swords in their right hands against invaders from below) but counterclockwise. She couldn't imagine anyone swinging a sword in this narrow space unless from directly overhead. Clinging to the rail with one hand, she kept bumping the flashlight into the other wall as she went up.

The first floor was as bare as the ground room, save that it had six narrow windows, three each on the north and south sides. The second and third floors were nearly identical, differing only in the height of the ceiling. Each floor had the same ancient openings off the stairwell, no doubt once covered by tapestries. Carragh knew she was approaching what had been the livable areas. Where Thomas Gallagher and his household would have kept court.

When she emerged onto the fourth floor, she was so startled that the beam veered wildly. She had expected another bare space. But this was furnished. No, more than furnished—lived in. At least, lived in once. Which gave weight to the theory that Jenny had been kept here at some point. It must have been her . . . what? Sitting room? What need had a madwoman of such a civilized space?

Through the dust and webs and mold, Carragh crept noiselessly, as though she might disturb the absent occupant. There was a writing desk and a sofa that must once have been comfortable before mice (she hoped nothing more than mice) had made use of its stuffing. There was a bookshelf that now held only a handful of books with water damage and foxed pages, and an embroidery stand with the rotting remains of whatever had last been worked on.

There was no bed. Had Jenny slept on the sofa? But then the beam picked out the stairs, continuing its spiral up, and with a sense of increasing dread, she followed it up to the last level.

Here was Jenny's bed. The frame was Victorian, she guessed, a rather institutional-looking plain iron bedstead. Bare of mattress or linens, it did not look in imminent danger of destruction. She could probably sit there if she liked.

She did not like.

Other than the bed, there was only a wooden chair and a table designed to fit against the curved outer wall. Carragh swung the flashlight around to the extremely narrow door that gave onto the battlements. But the door did not hold her attention, for it was then that she realized the stone walls were not blank. At first she thought it was a bizarrely patterned wallpaper composed of intricate lines

and sweeps in gray. She moved closer and touched her hand to the
wall. Her palm felt cold stone. And now, only inches away, she could
see that the pattern was not decorative.

The walls were covered in writing.

In the pressing blackness, with only the flashlight for illumination, she strained to make out individual words. *Love's terrible fierce-
ness . . . racked with the torment of one fallen from grace . . . iron-bound
and thrice betrayed . . .*

Though the phrases themselves were well worn with melodrama, Carragh's whole body shuddered. There was power in these
words: an intelligence and passion and a singular voice that was
greater than the sum. Someone— Oh, who was she kidding? She
knew who it was. Jenny Gallagher had written on the walls of her
cage, these walls, pierced only by two narrow arrow-slits and an
ancient door to the outside that was, indeed, iron-bound.

Carragh ached for more illumination so she might read the whole
of it, though she knew it would not be as simple as that. It had been
written with who knows what ink on medieval stone in a room that
was unheated and damp. She would be lucky to get even a hint of a
coherent narrative.

She would return tomorrow, if she could steal an hour in daylight. Aidan Gallagher need not know. Carragh told herself he was
burdened enough just now, that she was being positively altruistic in
keeping quiet about it. But she knew the truth of the matter: she was
afraid Aidan would forbid it. And nothing would keep her from trying to piece together Jenny's last days, in hopes of discovering what
had happened later to her husband and his missing book.

Aidan couldn't sleep, tossing restlessly, his mind in more turmoil
than his body. This was exactly why he'd never come back to Ireland. He'd known he would find Deeprath disturbing. What he
hadn't anticipated was the police. What an idiot! He knew how these
things worked. He knew his parents' case was still technically open

and unsolved. Of course the police would want to look into it with all the family gathered together and before the castle became contaminated, as it were, by outsiders.

But he wasn't a police officer where this case was concerned. He was a son who wanted answers.

He gave up after midnight and flung back his covers. In London he had weights and a treadmill for when he couldn't sleep; here he would have to settle for walking around the castle. That should be good for several miles.

Thankfully for the strain on his memories, he hadn't spent much time in his childhood wandering Deeprath at night. Not alone, at least. Kyla had always been there, the two of them spying on the dinners and parties their parents held with clockwork regularity. Despite the five years' difference in their ages, his sister hadn't minded her little brother tagging along. Not that they'd had a huge number of playmates to choose from, Deeprath being so far off the beaten track. Even when Kyla went to boarding school at age twelve, she'd been willing to hang out with Aidan when she was home.

Until that last summer. Turning fifteen had changed her into a moody, irritable stereotypical teen girl—at least in his ten-year-old eyes. The only time she'd smiled that whole summer had been when Philip was around. Aidan had disliked Philip even then, and twenty-three years' acquaintance had not improved his opinion of his brother-in-law.

After a jog around all three floors of the Regency wing, Aidan headed for the library. Knowing that the police did not have the missing account book and journal he'd been looking for, he would have to begin looking somewhere, and there were enough shelves in the library to hide a dozen books. He'd turned on one of the table lamps and debated flipping through his grandfather's catalog for inspiration when he heard a thud, like something heavy falling. He turned, searching for the source, and realized that the door to the tower was open. And a beam of light, swinging crazily, was coming through it.

He reached the door just as Carragh came from the other side. Startled, she dropped the flashlight on the flagstone floor, making the same sound he'd heard before. Her underlit face was all shadows and hollows, her eyes like dark stars flung down from heaven . . .

Only when her shoulders sagged in relief did Aidan realize he must have scared the hell out of her. He picked up the flashlight—it was ridiculously heavy—as she said, "You have got to stop looming out at me from doorways."

"*You've* got to stop wandering around where you don't belong."

He didn't mean that. He didn't even know why he'd said it, but her expression closed off as she took the flashlight back. "Couldn't sleep," she said briefly. "And curiosity is my original sin. Here's the key."

"You're welcome to explore the empty rooms as much as you like," he said apologetically. "As long as you promise to be careful—the last thing I need is someone falling through a floor and suing me."

"Because the tabloids would have a field day? Or because the police would be suspicious? Or maybe because Nessa would decide I'd offended one of the castle ghosts?"

He was almost sure she was teasing him. "Just promise to be careful and not go wandering alone at night with only that torch."

"That I promise you," she said with real feeling.

"How did you like the Bride Tower?"

She hesitated. "Have you been up there?"

"Not since I returned," he said briefly. And he'd prefer to keep it that way.

"I'd better get to bed," she said, and only much later would Aidan realize she hadn't answered his question about the tower. "Lots of library to get through tomorrow."

"Ah, as to that, I forgot to tell you earlier. The police have asked for access to the castle tomorrow, and the library especially. I've given them leave to examine whatever they like, save Nessa and Kyla's personal items. They'll leave you alone, of course, but it would be easier for them if we were not in the library in the morning."

"Of course. I could take the catalog to my room and do some work there."

It was his turn to hesitate. Then, in an impulse he didn't understand, he said, "I'm going to walk up to Glendalough in the morning. Would you like to come?"

"The monastic city? I'd love to. What time?"

"Eight o'clock? Wear comfortable shoes—it's two miles there and back on foot."

"I'll see you then."

As she walked away, Aidan imagined he could hear Penelope's light, amused voice in his ear: *Walking in your mountains with a woman? Be careful, Aidan. You never know where that might lead.*

It had taken a surprisingly short time for Carragh's borrowed bedroom to become a sanctuary. At least there she wouldn't be disturbed by imperious old women or bitter older sisters or disconcerting Irish lords with the kind of stunning blue eyes and black lashes that her grandmother had described as being smudged in with a sooty finger.

Although, after what she'd found in the tower, she wasn't all that wild about having that spooky double portrait staring down at her while she was in bed.

It wasn't staring at her. It wasn't there at all.

Carragh stopped in her tracks when she saw the blank expanse of wall unbroken by any painting. Had someone removed it for some reason? In the middle of the night?

No, it was still there, just leaning against the wall at floor-level. She wanted to believe it had fallen, but oil paintings did not fall and manage to turn themselves front to back in midair. Because all she could see of it now was the thick brown paper glued around the back of the frame. Very odd.

She hesitated before picking it up and returning it to its rightful place. She was tempted to leave it where it was, if only not to spend the night with those doubled eyes looking at her, but she didn't want Mrs. Bell or, Heaven forbid, Nessa to think she had tampered with it. Better to endure the imaginary disdain of painted faces than the actual disdain of the formidable Nessa.

I'm sorry, she said silently to the white-clad Jenny after she'd re-hung the painting. All she could think of were those two disturbing rooms behind a locked door, and the young wife and mother who had ended her life there.

CHAPTER FOURTEEN

It was a perfect day for walking—the morning misty and cool, with pale sunlight filtering through the trees. Aidan felt himself unbending as he followed the path he'd taken so often as a boy and thought wryly of Penelope's pronouncement: *You belong there.*

Carragh, by his side, was a good companion, neither a chatterbox nor a silent burden waiting to be entertained. She asked a few questions about the landscape, but otherwise seemed content to drink it all in. And when the Round Tower of the ancient settlement came into view on the horizon, she caught her breath with a delight that pleased Aidan as though he were personally responsible for it.

"Welcome to Glendalough," he told her. "Pilgrims for hundreds of years would have greeted the sight of the Round Tower with relief and gratitude. Ireland wasn't easy to travel in those days, especially not the mountains."

"The mountains are still not easy to travel, especially on foot," she pointed out. "And it wasn't so many generations ago that the British tried to split the mountains in two with their road. I believe it only worked to a limited extent."

"You're right. Even with the British road and military outposts, hundreds and hundreds of starving Irish made it past them to take refuge in our mountains during the Famine. The Gallaghers were among the landed of Wicklow who helped keep them alive."

"And the English didn't like that?" she teased.

"I don't think the English have ever liked anything about Ireland. We have always been a grim duty, not a prize."

The lines and peaks of other roofs and walls continued to sharpen against the misty morning as they came nearer. "How much do you know about Glendalough?" he asked Carragh.

"Historically?" She shook her head. "Only the basics. St. Kevin, hermitage, monastery."

"Then I have some stories to tell you."

His mother had been an avid and zealous student of Wicklow history and, instead of chapter books at night, she had told him tales of saints and kings and banshees and changelings. The white cow who appeared morning and evening to provide milk to the infant saint. Kevin's retreat into hermitage in the Valley of the Two Lakes, and his rebuke of the larks for singing too early, so that now its song is never heard in the valley. The banishing of the monster from the Upper to the Lower Lake. The blackbird who built a nest on Kevin's upraised arm while he was praying, and the otter who brought him salmon to eat in his final years. Aidan shared all those legends and more. Some of them Carragh knew, from her Irish Studies at Trinity, and she provided a few interesting comparisons to other Irish tales.

He had packed bread and cheese, dried apples, and Mrs. Bell's homemade sausages. They ate by the river that ran out of the Lower Lake, just off the path maintained by the National Park Service. By the time they finished, other voices and footsteps had begun to echo through the air. The guests at the Glendalough Hotel were up early, to enjoy the site before the rush of outside visitors. It was located within sight of the gatehouse and its unusual Sanctuary Cross, and Carragh asked idly, "What do you think the monks would have made of a hotel in their holy city?"

"They entertained hundreds upon hundreds in their day."

"They didn't make money off them."

"Of course they did. Not from a room rate, maybe, but they could not have afforded such hospitality without generous recompense from the wealthier pilgrims and novices."

"Cynical," she noted. Her face was as open as the sky, not watchful, as she always seemed to be in the castle.

"Practical," Aidan retorted. "Hermitage can never be more than a solitary experience. The monastic city, on the other hand, educated thousands and sent most of them out into the world to spread their knowledge. I find it . . . admirable. Perhaps because I recognize in myself the instincts of a hermit. I used to roam around here as a child, wishing I could be one of those who never had to leave Glendalough." He smiled at her wryly. "I had yet to grasp the full concept of what being a monk entailed."

"You came here when you were little?"

"Mmm. Sometimes I'd walk, sometimes I'd catch a ride with someone leaving the castle and spend hours exploring."

"By yourself?"

"Mostly—at least that last year. Hermit, remember?"

Not a hermit, though, so much as a spy. As a child Aidan had liked setting his imagination loose, and nothing fueled it like people. Not those familiar faces he saw day in and day out, but strangers whose lives he could only glimpse in fragments, snatching at their conversations without context, weaving epics from the threads of tone and glance.

He'd thought himself so clever, hiding in plain sight. Looking back, he supposed he'd mostly appeared lonely. If he were to see a little boy today, following couples and families with wary intensity, he would guess at an unhappy home life. A child substituting an imaginary world for a colorless reality.

But he had not been unhappy. There were the normal tensions of families with disparate personalities—especially Kyla, moody and erratic as any teenage girl. She'd had screaming matches with their mother that last year. Or would have, if Lily Gallagher hadn't been so unprovokable. Not serene, no—no one would have called his mother that; but her enthusiasms were just that. Enthusiasms that might swing from highs to lows, but never to anger. Of that, Aidan was certain. Lily Gallagher could never have murdered her husband in a fit of fury.

What did that leave? Thieves after the antiquities? Aidan had spent his professional life working exactly those kinds of cases. Thieves like that rarely made mistakes and were never that messy. A demented stranger, then, stumbling across the castle, killing his parents and vanishing without a trace? A hired assassin sent by one of his father's business rivals? Highly unlikely on either count. That left the people who'd been in the castle: the Bells, the gardener and his two boys, the cook and maids-of-all-work from the town, Winthrop visiting for business matters, Philip interning for his father . . . and the family.

He startled when Carragh touched his arm. "Are you all right?"

Just trying to solve the twenty-three-year-old murders that unraveled my life. Thinking about it had leached the pleasure from the day. "We'd better go back. I have work I can do outside the library until the police are finished."

Carragh had remarkably dark eyes that seemed to reflect back everything he was feeling but without losing herself in the process. There was a clarity to her gaze that was almost as refreshing as the Wicklow air.

Her words, however, were not as soothing as her expression. "Do you really think you'll stumble across fewer memories in the castle than out here?"

"I moved away more than twenty years ago, but I never really left Wicklow. I thought I had grown beyond the pain. I was wrong. And I appear to be taking it all out on the only wholly innocent person at Deeprath. I apologize."

"You do not consider your nieces innocent?"

"Are you always this direct?" He looked at her compassionate eyes and opinionated mouth and bright streaks of blue and green and purple in her black hair. She'd worn it conservatively down at dinner last night, hiding the colors, but he preferred it pulled up and back like this.

"Only when it's other people," she conceded. "I can delay and avoid and lie to myself with the best of them." She gestured to the monastic ruins all around them. "It's a pity to go back without finishing the tour. I'd love to hear more about these mercenary monks who profited from an early form of spiritual tourism."

Aidan shook his head, but conceded. As long as he kept the conversation firmly set in the Middle Ages, he should be all right. "I can spare another hour. What do you want to know about Glendalough?"

Once Carragh distracted Aidan from brooding, he continued to be an engaging tour guide. Unlike Nessa, he didn't recite a list of facts, but wrapped information in stories. Before she knew it, their conversation had ranged from the missionary efforts of the Glendalough monks to the Book of Kells to the holy islands of Lindisfarne and Iona. They argued about the relative influence of Irish and Scottish ballads on American country music, and Aidan told her some of the strangest places he'd recovered stolen art (including buried beneath the dirt floor of an eighteenth-century Welsh barn).

Upon their return to Deeprath Castle, Aidan thanked her courteously and vanished, leaving Carragh to decide what to do next. She didn't feel like staying in her bedroom, so she went up just long enough to grab the Trollope novel and make sure Jenny's portrait was still on the wall. It hung where she'd replaced it, two pairs of unrevealing eyes watching her.

Did you enjoy yourself?

Carragh was not in the habit of speaking to paintings. But without thinking, she answered aloud. "At Glendalough? Yes."

And with Aidan?

Now that was her imagination taking things one step too far. She was not going to stand in her bedroom and engage in a one-sided conversation with herself about Aidan Gallagher.

After careful scouting to ensure she was alone, Carragh settled down in the music room with *Framley Parsonage*. She was busy giving passionate advice to Lucy Robarts when the sudden strumming sound of music jolted her to her feet. But because she'd been sitting curled up in a chair, her legs had locked and she tripped, dropping the Trollope. "Damn it!"

For a moment she thought of the ghostly Marthe. But the Frenchwoman's music was supposed to be delicate and faint, and this had been anything but. A rush of giggles confirmed it. Carragh got herself balanced and confronted the two Gallagher-Grant girls.

"How did you get away from Louise?" she asked mock-sternly.

Ellie wasn't fooled. With a defiant tilt to her chin, which had disconcerting echoes of Aidan, she said, "We're playing hide-and-seek. It's not our fault if Louise isn't very good at it. What are you doing?"

"Reading."

"We saw you go out with Uncle Aidan."

If she was to be interrogated by these little spies, why not turn them to her own use? "Do you know where he is now?"

Kate piped up. "Play with us and maybe we'll find him."

Carragh could only laugh at the steely little negotiator in yellow tunic and leggings. "As long as we don't play hide-and-seek."

As she'd told Nessa, she was used to children. She understood the combination of overexcitement and boredom she saw in the girls, but she wasn't accustomed to the edge of anger beneath their interactions. Children were meant to express all their emotions at full volume. This kind of hidden, denied anger was likely because of their parents' strained marriage, Carragh thought, and then felt a wave of guilt at the realization. What a mess people could make of other people's lives without ever meaning to.

The girls' idea of play seemed designed mostly to explore the family castle that they'd never before seen. Carragh went into so many rooms trooping after them that she lost count; most of them were bare or contained only a few dust-shrouded pieces. She supposed all of it would go to the National Trust—or maybe Kyla was here to choose any pieces she wanted to keep.

They ended in the vast kitchens that stretched through three rooms. Carragh tried to name each as they might have been used in Jenny's time: pantry, scullery, kitchen proper. Though the Victorian bones were still there, they had been turned into a warm and welcoming combination of cooking and sitting space. This was clearly the domain of the Bells.

Mrs. Bell was warm and welcoming, not self-effacing, as she seemed around the older Gallaghers. "Call me Maire," she told Carragh, then proceeded to make a great fuss of Ellie and Kate.

"Do you have children?" Carragh asked.

"Two girls, and three grandchildren."

"Were your daughters raised here?"

The housekeeper laughed. "No, the days of live-in servants had passed by the time Rob and I married. We have a house in Laragh. Sometimes, in the last twenty years, we'd spend a week at a time here when repairs were under way or there was a great push on to get something done to the house or grounds. But this house has seen little enough of people of late. I think it's happy to have family here again."

Maire Bell had settled the girls at the long table with its marble top, shortbread and milk at their elbows, and she looked down at them fondly. Ellie had Kyla's russet coloring, but Kate had the same black hair and bright blue eyes as her uncle Aidan.

"You go on, love," Maire said comfortably to Carragh. "I'll keep them busy with me. They can learn how to wash dishes."

With shortbread in hand, Carragh made her way back to the music room to retrieve the book she'd left behind. She bent over the chair to pick it up and a voice said, "Hello. Who are you?"

Carragh faced the woman, whom she'd missed standing near the harpsichord, and said with annoyance, "Who are *you*?"

"Inspector Sibéal McKenna. Siochana Garda, Serious Crimes Review."

Carragh felt immediately foolish. "Of course. Sorry. Everything around here is out of sorts today. I suppose you're used to dealing with that."

The DI smiled briefly without replying. She was mid-thirties, maybe, with the creamy skin of the natural redhead, but Carragh could not decide whether the woman was attractive or not. Compelling was perhaps the best word, for despite her no-nonsense bob and inoffensive trouser suit, she was hard to look away from. And it wasn't just that she was a police officer. DI McKenna had a presence beyond her warrant card.

"I'm Carragh Ryan. I was hired to help catalog the library before its contents are donated. I arrived three days ago."

"Were you previously acquainted with the family?"

"No. I'm American—well, my father's from Dublin but has lived in the States for forty years. I only came to Ireland to live three years ago."

"So you knew nothing about the Gallaghers?"

How had she ended up on the defensive so quickly? "I knew about the library and the castle. And of course I looked into them before coming. But all I know of the family is what I learned from the Internet."

DI McKenna paced thoughtfully between the harp and the grand piano. "What, exactly, are you looking for in the library?"

"I'm not looking for evidence of murder, if that's what you're implying."

That actually made the officer laugh, which in turn made her look younger and far more approachable. "Miss Ryan, I promise I'm not trying to trap you into anything. You would have been . . . what? Four or five years old when Lord Gallagher was murdered? Even if you had been in Ireland, I'd hardly suspect you of involvement."

"Then what is it you do want?" Carragh asked impulsively. Maybe it was because she'd spent so much time alone the last few months, but this place seemed to be turning her into her mother. A woman who always asked the things she wanted to know.

"I've heard that Lady Gallagher was interested in family history before she died. I wondered if you've come across anything that would add to that picture. There must be family records in there."

"Those are not part of my job description. I'm working on items of general, not personal, interest." But Carragh's curiosity was piqued. So Lily Gallagher had been looking into the family's past. Trying to keep the interest out of her voice, she asked, "What do you think you can learn from history?"

"I won't know unless or until I find it . . . and then, like as not, only in retrospect. This job is a matter of sifting information. The more of it I have, the more likely I am to find what I need." She studied Carragh thoughtfully. "So what do you think of the Gallaghers?"

"What do you mean?"

"Do they get along? Do they seem happy to be gathered all together in their castle once more?"

Choosing her words with care, Carragh replied, "I've hardly met Kyla, and Nessa has not interested herself in me since I was hired."

"And the viscount, Lord Gallagher?"

Lord Gallagher. The reminder of his title threw her for a moment, until she remembered that he was just a man. Carragh thought of the things Aidan had said and the more things he'd left unsaid, of the twist of his mouth when he'd spoken of finding his father's body and the way his smile managed to be both mocking and sweet. "I think Aidan Gallagher does not know if he wants to be here or not. He is doing his duty. We speak of the library and its contents and that is all." *Or mostly all,* she amended to herself.

"Right." DI McKenna had the same trick Carragh's mother did—to speak neutrally and yet imply volumes of disbelief. "Well, I'm sure I'll see you again before this is all finished. If you think of anything else, let me know."

"Right," Carragh parroted back.

That made DI McKenna grin widely. "I do so love Americans." She sounded wholly sincere.

It was dark and rainy when the train returned to Dublin, and Sibéal went straight home after planning to meet Sergeant Cullen at eight in the morning at Phoenix Park. After two days of traveling back and forth to Wicklow, she needed a quiet, safe space in which to think. Her promotion was too new and her office too bare to provide that yet.

Sibéal lived in the same one-bedroom flat she'd had since she was twenty-four. West of Christ Church and north of St. Patrick's, the neighborhood went from privileged to struggling in a matter of blocks. She and Josh had bought it in their first year of marriage. When Josh left, she'd struggled for a while to make the rent, but she loved her oddly shaped corner flat with its view of St. Audoen's Church. She could lie in bed and touch the window that framed the medieval spire across the street and it always made her feel safe.

But her daughter, May, was nearly eight, and it wasn't fair to keep her sleeping on a fold-out couch behind a screened section of the lounge. May was with her father this week, and Sibéal had promised they would look for a new place when she returned Josh had more than two thousand square feet in his detached Ranelagh villa, so May could have her own room, even with two little half brothers.

She spoke to her daughter on the phone ("Daddy says I can go with them to France this summer."), and then, wanting to soak up however much time she had left in this flat, Sibéal sat at the dining table and spread out the files and notes she'd made from the last two days, St. Audoen's lit up outside the bay window.

The Gallaghers and their ilk were a species of Irish she hadn't come across much. The McKenna family was decidedly downmarket and owed their connections to clannishness rather than birthright. She'd tried to go into Deeprath with an open mind, but it was hard not to be affected by wealth—especially the old blood, old money wealth that made a virtue of threadbare furniture and a casual elegance that meant their jeans and jumpers cost more than Sibéal had spent on her wedding dress.

But once she'd stopped looking at the high coved ceilings and antique furniture of the castle and focused on the family themselves, she'd found her footing. Sibéal knew people. She had a knack for discerning the motives and emotions that most people kept locked away—often even from themselves. Her first partner had disliked a lot about her, but he'd admitted without grudge that Sibéal was the best officer he'd ever met at going to the heart of a story.

And that's what crimes were: stories. Of lust and love and anger and hate, of boredom and alcohol and principle.

Well, here was a story unlike any she'd ever encountered in life. Lily Morgan, an orphaned American heiress, meets Irishman Cillian Gallagher in New York, and following a whirlwind romance, becomes Viscountess Gallagher. After twenty years of marriage and two children—including the all-important male heir—Lily Morgan Gallagher is a lovely, bubbly, generous woman who is equally at home entertaining her husband's business partners in London or Paris as she is doing her marketing in the local village. The most critical thing said about her—from both twenty years ago and in the last two days—was that she flitted from project to project, not out of boredom, Sibéal judged, as much as an excess of curiosity and a desire to do everything.

No obvious problems in the marriage (though she knew how difficult it could be for outsiders to crack a carefully constructed and agreed upon façade), and the family's finances had been in excellent order. A fifteen-year-old daughter who'd been squabbling with her mother, but Sibéal was more inclined to be suspicious of daughters who didn't. And a ten-year-old son who had realized only yesterday that some questions that should have been asked of him at the time had not been.

The most difficult of all the Gallaghers to gauge was Nessa. Lady

Nessa, as she could properly be called, had been married once—Cullen had tracked down the information—to a landowner and MP in Kilkenny when she was thirty-six. He was thirty years older, they didn't have children, and he'd died just three years after the wedding, leaving her to add his fortune to the family name she refused to relinquish.

The only significant witness Sibéal had still to meet was Philip Grant, Kyla's English husband. When reached by phone, he'd promised to meet her in Dublin tomorrow, then left a silky voiced apology on her voicemail while she was on the train, saying he'd actually gone down to Deeprath "to be with my wife in this difficult time." If Grant thought she wouldn't bother to run him down, he was sadly mistaken.

Tomorrow, she'd assign DS Cullen to track down Cillian Gallagher's former business interests and see if there might be anything of interest after all this time. But in her gut, Sibéal knew this was not a crime about money. Everything about Deeprath Castle shouted to her that the two deaths were a crime of great and terrible passion. The question was: what kind of passion?

There was something else pressing on Sibéal, a tiny detail—the fact that the Deeprath Castle library had been locked up since the murders. Had opening it again released an atmosphere from the past, something to stir the echoes of time and place and lead her to a killer?

Because that was what she was looking for. Just as she doubted this was a story of a robbery gone wrong, she didn't believe it was a simple story of murder and suicide. Maybe she could not wholly discount the possibility that Lily Gallagher had killed her husband and then herself, but if so, then it had been done for a deep purpose. Or else it was double murder, plain and clear. Either way, she was going to solve it.

CHAPTER FIFTEEN

December 1879

Proposing to Jenny was easy. Facing down her father was an altogether different matter. Evan had always proudly proclaimed himself unaffected by issues of class and background—but when sitting across from a man in the house his family had built over the course of seven hundred years, a man of title and wealth and enormous family expectations, it took all Evan's control not to let either his hands or his voice shake.

"Lord Gallagher," he began, and was immediately stopped.

"I think we can dispense with the formality, son. If you're going to marry my daughter, then you should at least feel free to address me without the honorific."

"Yes, sir." He said it a little dizzily, not quite grasping that he had been handily anticipated.

The viscount didn't look overjoyed at the thought of Evan as a son-in-law, but neither did he look outraged. The quality of his silence began to press on Evan, mingling with the aura of the castle itself, until it began to seem that all the Gallaghers of the past had gathered to weigh him in the balance. Would he be found wanting?

When the viscount finally spoke, it was as the businessman

rather than the lord. "Let us be straightforward, Chase. You are in love with my daughter. I would think you an utter fool if you were not. Far more important to me, Jenny is in love with you. But there are impediments. Perhaps serious ones."

"I know I am not of high birth—"

"That is of little import. No, Chase, I have no quarrel with your family or past. I respect men who work hard for their success, and you have done that. You have earned your place in the world."

"Then what impediments do you mean?"

Gallagher's brow furrowed and he seemed to be searching for the best words. "Despite three marriages, I have no male heir. Although the title is entailed, the estate itself is not. Upon my death, Jenny will inherit all my wealth and properties. When she has a son, the title will go to him. I want all of this to remain in the Gallagher name."

"I will gladly take the Gallagher name if it pleases you. One of the benefits of being without position—I do not have that sort of pride."

The viscount inclined his head. "That is one impediment settled. But I must speak plainly—if I had a living son, I would not allow this marriage to occur whatever concessions you might make. But I am willing to risk much for a chance of the Gallagher line continuing through my grandson."

"I do not entirely follow."

Gallagher seemed to be wrestling with some serious qualms. "My daughter is not well. No, it is more than that. My daughter, Mr. Chase, is not . . . stable. Her temperament is at times erratic and impetuous. There have been periods of melancholy. It was a condition that also afflicted her mother."

Bewildered, Evan asked, "Are you trying to tell me Jenny is mad? Because, sir, I have met many of the mad in the course of my research. And Jenny is nothing like any of them."

"This castle is her refuge. Here she is more likely to remain well. No doubt if she were confined in a madhouse, she would soon be as markedly mad as anyone else there. I have no faith in asylums." He grimaced, as though the words stuck in his throat. "I will understand if this changes your intentions."

I will understand, his tone added silently, *but I will be greatly displeased.*

How little he must think of me, Evan realized. But he didn't think it wise to insult the father of his future wife. He was a writer, and it helped him now find the right words for how he felt. "If Jenny were an orphan in a poorhouse with nothing more to her than the soul I have come to love, I would marry her just as gladly. I am not afraid of illness. Not even illness of the mind."

He had never seen Lord Gallagher smile. Seeing it now told Evan that whatever else Jenny might have inherited from her mother, she was a Gallagher in both looks and charm.

"You are a good man," the viscount said. "I would not risk Jenny with any but a good man. I give my consent to this marriage with one condition—other than adding Gallagher to your name."

"And that is?"

"That you never remove Jenny from Deeprath. This castle is her home. If she left it, I feel certain she would soon die."

DIARY OF JENNY GALLAGHER

18 December 1879

Evan and I are engaged! He asked me to marry him at Glendalough, kneeling next to the Sanctuary Cross. Any other girl might find that odd. But he is my Niall—my light in a life of murky shadows. I haven't had a single headache since he came, and there has been no need for the tower. I haven't come nearer it than the library for months—and I only visit the library to visit Evan.

He is hard at work on his book. He will not read it to me as he goes. He says he must write a story, not talk about it, or else there is no story left. But he has promised that I will be the first one allowed to read it.

I told the Bride of my happiness. Sometimes I forget which is me and which is her . . . but surely I am the happy one tonight. Even she cannot begrudge me my love, for she had her own happiness. Brief as it was.

CHAPTER SIXTEEN

After staying up until two in the morning and meeting with DS Cullen at eight, Sibéal devoted several hours to paperwork and drinking Diet Coke. She knew she would pay for it later with a massive headache, but she needed caffeine, had never liked the taste of coffee, and as far as she was concerned, tea was little more than stewed grass. While she worked, she kept an eye out for Superintendent O'Neill. Though it was Sunday, she knew he usually came in for a few hours in the morning. He needed updating on the Deeprath case—and Sibéal needed answers about O'Neill's involvement there twenty-three years ago.

He appeared as expected, and five minutes later Sibéal stood in front of his desk and rattled off her list of interviews with and plans for the Gallagher family. He listened in silence and with an inscrutable expression. O'Neill looked more like a quiet accountant than a police officer—not much more than five and a half feet tall, with wire-rimmed spectacles that obscured the acuteness of his eyes—but no one who knew him would mistake his mildness for incompetence.

Her recital completed, she launched straightaway into the critical question. "Why didn't you tell me you were previously involved with the case when you handed it over?"

"Do I take it you have questions for me?" he parried.

"No questions . . . yet. First, you can tell me everything you didn't before." Sibéal sat down as calmly as though she'd been invited.

He fixed her with an unamused expression, then launched directly into recitation. "It was my first year in the Garda, 1992. And Deeprath Castle was my first crime scene. But even without experience, I knew something was not right. The castle was . . . wary. Unwelcoming. And no, I don't believe in sentient buildings. But I do believe in the atmosphere of families. There was something badly wrong with the Gallaghers. I just didn't know if that wrongness lay with the living or with the dead."

"Why weren't Aidan and Kyla Gallagher interviewed?"

He sighed. "They were. At the castle, within two hours of the murders. It was decided there was no need for further questioning."

"Or formal statements, apparently."

"You have the boy's brief statement of finding his father's body."

"But nothing of his earlier movements that day, where he was just before the library, his impressions of his family . . . and nothing at all from Kyla Gallagher."

"It was not my call. However, I was the constable taking notes at the scene. During both of their interviews. I may have retained them."

She blinked. "Yet you didn't think to include them in the case file."

"I could say I didn't want to prejudice you beforehand, and that is true. But it's not the whole truth. This case is not simply about the Gallaghers, Inspector McKenna. It's about what kind of investigator you are. Do you settle for the surface answers, or do you look deeper? Are you creative? Are you easily distracted or intimidated?"

"You thought withholding information was a good way to test my skills?"

"I thought it a good way to test your character. Some officers

believe that the end justifies the means. I am not one of them. I want
success, but not at any price. And I never want the kind of hollow
success that comes from grasping the most convenient solution or
from looking the other way. I will not work with such officers. Now
I know that you are not one of them. Congratulations."

Sibéal didn't quite know how to respond. *Thank you for making
things difficult?* She settled on standing up and asking, "When can I
have the notes you made in 1992?"

O'Neill pulled open one of his desk drawers and handed over a
file folder. "This one has bothered me for a long time, Inspector. I
want it resolved."

Her spine straightening automatically, she snapped back, "Yes,
sir."

On Sunday, Carragh returned to the library with a vengeance. She'd
brought protein bars with her from Dublin and chose to eat one of
them before she went to work, rather than take the time to eat a
proper breakfast.

She worked furiously, keeping her mind fixed on the printed titles on shelves, her fingertips quickly growing black from the spines
and title pages of the volume after volume she perused. She cataloged encyclopedias of natural history, two shelves of English translations of Latin and Greek classics, and now, sitting at a table, studied
four slim and startling volumes of Japanese erotica. Were some of
those positions even possible for humans?

"Who'd have thought," a smooth male voice said from behind her,
"that Deeprath Castle could offer up such a pleasurable surprise?"

Carragh shut her eyes and swore inwardly. How did people keep
sneaking up on her in this place? You'd think an ancient structure
would creak and groan with warnings, but Deeprath somehow managed to strangle all sound until the last person in the world you
wanted to meet was speaking right over your shoulder.

Over her shoulder, Philip Grant plucked the Japanese book from her hands and, with raised eyebrows, studied it. "Looking for inspiration? I admire the sentiment, but you're not a woman who needs tricks."

"What are you doing here?" It was hard to be authoritative and dismissive when your face was flaming red.

"In my wife's home? I came to offer support. And look how the universe has decided to reward me for that virtue."

"Virtue?" Carragh snorted. "Go away."

"I remember when you didn't want me to go anywhere."

"And I remember that the last time I saw you I told you to go to hell. Go on, then."

His eyes flickered briefly with dislike. "You're not a Gallagher. You can't order me out of the castle."

"I can order you out of this library. I'm here to work, and unless you know a great deal more about books than I think, you'll be of no earthly use to me."

He smiled, a deadly smile promising all manner of dark desires. "You found me to be of very good use before."

Philip moved close enough to touch, and Carragh jumped up from the table to get away. In the process she banged against the chair and knocked it over. She and Philip moved to right it at the same moment and he took the opportunity to put his arm around her.

"Get out of here and leave me alone," she spat.

"Harassing my staff, Philip?"

It was Aidan, with an upper-class drawl that simultaneously humiliated and infuriated Carragh. Philip straightened up with lazy good humor as she snapped at his brother-in-law, "I don't need your help."

Aidan's face was a mask of indifference as he remained focused on Philip. "Kyla's looking for you. And I don't have time for you to interfere with estate matters."

"Really, Aidan, estate matters? Is that what you call it?" Philip stooped and picked up the book Carragh had dropped. He laid it on the table, open to one of the more flagrant erotic illustrations, before sauntering to the library door.

Before he pulled it shut, he shot an eloquent glance at both of them and winked. "Lock it behind me before working on those . . . 'estate matters.'"

"Bastard."

Carragh thought she'd spoken quietly enough not to be heard, but Aidan said drily, "Quite."

As casually as possible, she closed the book and turned it facedown. Aidan gave no sign of having seen it. Not that she'd be able to tell from his controlled expression. However easily he'd spoken to her yesterday at Glendalough, today the barricades were back up and the gates firmly shut.

"Progress?" he asked neutrally.

She walked him through the morning's work, but he seemed distracted. When she finished speaking, he said abruptly, "I'll leave you to it, then. I'm going up to Dublin for the day. I may or may not return tonight. If I were you, I'd have Mrs. Bell bring supper on a tray and stay in your room. Kyla drinks more than normal when she's unhappy, and Philip seems to always make her unhappy these days. I doubt dinner will be any more pleasant than last night."

"Can I ask why you're going to Dublin?"

He raised an eyebrow and said coolly, "Maybe I'm looking to be entertained."

She almost laughed aloud. Entertainment did not seem to be high on Aidan's priority list. Even in the tabloids, he'd always appeared as a partner to someone else and all the photos gave the same impression—that of a man forbearing for the sake of the woman next to him.

Then she saw the slightest crack in his detachment. "Carragh— keep away from Philip. He's always been nasty where women are concerned. Don't be fooled by the charm."

She met his eyes with all the steadiness she could summon. "I'm not swayed by charm. Or married men."

Only when I'm miserable, she amended to herself as Aidan walked out. *And drunk. And clearly God is punishing me for those errors in judgment.*

It took a while to get back into the flow of work. Mrs. Bell, alerted by Aidan, brought her soup and bread for lunch. When she'd finished, Carragh decided to indulge herself by taking a closer look at the Evan Chase novels in the library.

They had several copies of each of the five, including all the first editions, and each of them signed by the author. But only one of them was autographed directly to his wife.

> *To Jenny*
>
> *Who led me from darkness to light. May your darkling shadows be friendly ones.*
>
> *Evan*

Christmas Eve 1879, he'd added below—five months before their marriage and three months after they'd met. Had they already been engaged? For the first time, Carragh pondered the significance of such a hurried marriage. But their son was not born until eleven months later. She supposed it was just possible that Jenny had been pregnant with an earlier child that she'd miscarried after the wedding . . . and got pregnant again within weeks? Hardly likely. Besides, she didn't want to believe that Jenny had only married Evan Chase because he'd seduced her. Though he was undoubtedly a romantic. *Your darkling shadows* . . . It was a phrase telling of both romance and mystery.

Of all the copies of Chase's books, this was the most well-worn, and Carragh was certain that Jenny herself had turned these pages often. She did the same now, catching phrases from the story as she idly skimmed. *The Mourning Bell* was his second book, the plot a little uneven and the writing a bit uncontrolled compared to his later work, but it contained Carragh's favorite character: Mercy Harris, a clear-headed, plain-spoken Quaker girl who is hired as companion to the aging mother of the quintessential tall, dark, and damaged hero. There were elements of Jane Eyre—the character—in Mercy, but despite the occasional clichés, she still read today as an original, flawed, and engaging character.

What caught her eye first was so small that she'd flipped past it before her brain registered the fact that someone had written in the book by hand. Carefully, she returned to the page and laid the book on the table, moving the swing-arm lamp to see better.

Whoever had written, it hadn't been Jenny herself. The ink wasn't nearly faded enough. The lettering was fine and precise, but sufficiently small to make deciphering it difficult. Carragh picked up the magnifying glass that was a requirement in an old library and read.

Could this be the catalyst of Jenny's final—fatal—breakdown?

Carragh knew this part of the story well: when Mercy discovers that her own mother is not, as she has long been told, dead—but rather, an inmate in an asylum for the insane.

She studied the handwritten query, coaxing it to tell her more. Someone in this house had been curious about Jenny Gallagher in the past. It could have been anyone in the last hundred years. But Carragh had a feeling she already knew who it was. Hadn't Inspector McKenna mentioned that Aidan's mother was interested in Gallagher family history the last year of her life? Where better for Lily to begin than the tragic tale of love and madness that had unfolded at Deeprath in the 1880s?

Carragh examined the rest of the book, turning each page carefully to ensure she missed nothing. There were a few other notes—not immediately revelatory, the sort of half phrases a person writes to spur their own memory—that she copied into her notebook. Tucked between two pages near the end, she found a loose piece of stationery, folded once and embossed with the initials LMG. Lily Morgan Gallagher.

The page contained a numbered list.

1. *Dublin Weekly* and Wicklow People archives
2. Baptismal records
3. Father Hennessy
4. Bride painting
5. Chase's literary agent
6. Eileen Ryan

Beneath that last name was an address: 41 Merrior Square East, Dublin.

Carragh's own address. The house that for sixty years had belonged to her grandmother, Eileen Ryan.

Sibéal didn't have time to go through O'Neill's notes right away. At 11:00 A.M. she was in the Financial District north of the Liffey, meeting with Philip Grant's business partner, who had agreed to see her despite the fact it was Sunday. Happily for her, the man had known Grant since secondary school and thus had known the Gallaghers from the moment Philip met them. If the man himself did not want to talk to Sibéal, she had no problem interviewing everyone in his circle. Eventually, he would get the message.

"Kyla," Thomas Ealey ("Call me Tom") said. "Yes, Philip met her the summer of 1992. Not that he was especially interested in her at the time—she was only just fifteen. But his default is always charm, and he couldn't keep from flirting with a pretty girl if his life depended on it. Being young as she was, probably Kyla took it more seriously than he did."

"Why exactly was Mr. Grant in Wicklow that summer?" Sibéal had the bare-bones statement given by Philip to the local police at the time—two paragraphs that provided almost no useful information—and she wanted to see if the story he'd told matched what he'd told his friends at the time.

"He was there for a summer job," Tom Ealey replied. "Mind, he took it more for the connections than the money. Lord Gallagher—the previous Lord Gallagher—was something of an investment genius and had all sorts of ties to all sorts of wealth around the world. Philip craved that kind of personal scene. He didn't just want to make money, he wanted to make money with the right kinds of people."

"So he was working for Lord Gallagher?"

Ealey stretched back in his seat, hands resting on his comfortably prosperous stomach. "Mostly, yes. Though I believe he also did some work for Lady Gallagher. I met her once when she came to Dublin to arrange matters for the summer. Her usual secretary was off having a baby that summer, and she asked Philip if he'd mind lending a hand from time to time—and of course Philip seized the chance. He might even have done so without her husband's position. She was a . . . very warm person."

Sibéal's ears pricked up. "Too warm?"

He shook his head. "She wasn't hitting on him, or hiring him to provide . . . other services. No matter what gossips might have said about her afterward. No, it was simply who she was. So overflowing with joy in her own world that she couldn't help pulling others along with her. Lady Gallagher could look at you, as the cliché goes, and make you feel you were the only person in the world who mattered."

Coming from someone whom had met her only once, it was a compelling description. "So Mr. Grant liked Lady Gallagher."

"It was impossible not to. And yes, before you ask, I'm sure Philip had something of a schoolboy crush—whatever his age—but personally I thought it was good for him to have the tables turned for once. Let him pine after a woman who wouldn't have him. Anyway, that's why he went to Deeprath that summer. He was working for them."

"Doing what, precisely?"

Tom shrugged. "You'd have to ask him."

The police had asked, at the time, but in only the most cursory fashion. "Executive assistant," Philip had replied. And no one had bothered to press for details. He'd been twenty-two that summer— plenty old enough to commit murder.

Sibéal thanked Thomas Ealey for his time and exited the office, only to stop short at the sight of Aidan Gallagher in the reception area.

"What are you doing here?" they asked in unison.

Aidan recovered first. "Never mind, I know what you're doing here, Inspector. The same thing you were doing at Deeprath— trying to catch a killer."

"And you?"

He didn't blink for an alarmingly long time. "The same."

It was as if he was daring her to warn him off, to caution him against interference. No need for that . . . yet.

"I shall probably come down to Deeprath again tomorrow to speak to your brother-in-law." She did not ask permission.

"Lucky Philip." With that, Aidan stalked past her to take the chair she had just vacated and, no doubt, to repeat many of the same questions.

Though he had her at this disadvantage: no matter how young he'd been, Aidan Gallagher had lived through that summer. No doubt he knew things she didn't. Perhaps it would be worth making an ally of him. He was a fellow police officer, after all. It couldn't hurt to try.

An optimistic point of view that had kept Sibéal in an unhappy marriage for far too long. She'd tried patience, she'd tried under-standing, she'd tried ignoring . . . until one day she woke up and knew that was the day she was going to leave.

Whatever his faults, Josh had been cooperative about it all. Let-ting her have the flat, promptly paying child support, and no one could accuse him of being a neglectful father. He was such a good father, in fact, that his second child was born to his current par-amour just four months after the day Sibéal asked for a divorce.

Never more than a nominal Catholic, he'd blithely married again in a registrar's office. To his credit, he'd managed to stay married to this wife, though Sibéal's mother and grandmother considered both the divorce and remarriage religiously invalid. If ever she decided to marry again, Sibéal would have a battle on her hands.

As though on cue, her mobile rang with the doom-laden tune assigned to her mother's number. Sibéal had long ago learned that avoiding calls only meant greater trouble later on, so she sighed deeply, forced a false note of patience into her voice, and said, "Hi, Mam. What's up?"

There was never much of import, just a long litany of gossip about the neighbors and the village and the sorry state of the country and when was Sibéal going to move home so that her family could help take care of May like a proper family should.

She knew it so well she only had to listen with half her attention, inserting the appropriate phrases and encouraging sounds along the way.

"Your grandfather's looking forward to seeing you both for his birthday."

Which was next week. "Mam, I told you that with my promotion, I might not be able to manage it. I've got a case."

"A dead case," her mother answered with no sense of irony. "It's not like anyone's in a rush, are they? It's just solving a puzzle, not stopping danger. And I can't see that a puzzle matters more than your family."

"Mam, I have to go. I'll ring you later." She hung up abruptly, the only way she could escape from those kinds of conversations.

What stung was that her mother wasn't entirely wrong. She'd only been promoted because then they could stick her away in Serious Crimes Review where the work was mostly tedious and unappreciated. Whoever killed Cillian and Lily Gallagher had been quiet for more than two decades. It was the very definition of a cold case, with no one in imminent danger should she fail to solve it.

But she thought of Aidan Gallagher's eyes—the only part of his expression he could not control—and the anguish in them of a child who deserved answers. A family had been destroyed all those years ago. And what was left of that family deserved to know who had done it, and why.

CHAPTER SEVENTEEN

After pondering those mysterious notes found in Chase's book, Carragh helped herself to the tower keys and made her way up the stairs to the very top. With at least some sunlight coming in through the arrow slits and the small door she wrested open, now was as good a time as any to photograph the wall of words. It was a pity all she had was her phone, but who carried a real camera these days unless they were a serious photographer? She tried to go about it systematically, dividing the walls into grids in her head, but no doubt she overlapped too often and probably missed some sections. By the time she was finished, she'd taken almost five hundred pictures. She would load them onto her laptop later and see if she could make sense of it all.

She spent another two hours working hard on the library catalogs and felt pleased with what she'd accomplished—six bays completed—until she looked at the fourteen bays remaining. Then she took the least-traveled route to her bedroom and successfully avoided contact with anyone. Mrs. Bell had left a cold meal for her on the desk and Carragh decided on a bath before anything else.

There was something decadent about these enormous old tubs,

as though one should be surrounded by maids pouring fresh pails of steaming water—which would be an improvement on the temperature. The plumbing wasn't as bad as at her grandmother's house, but the size of the tub and open space of the bathroom meant it cooled quickly.

Afterward, Carragh ate cheese and bread and apples and ham while she uploaded the photos and studied them on her laptop. Try as she might, however, it was impossible to decipher more than a few words at a time. Zoom in too close, and everything went blurry. Zoom back out, and it was too small. She sat back, rubbing the bridge of her nose where strain had settled in a knot, listening to the wind that had picked up enough in the last hour to sound as though it were battering at the stone walls. Carragh knew she needed help with the photos. She had a friend who did graphic design in Dublin— perhaps if she emailed him the photos he could manipulate them into clarity, blow them up, then print them out? It would be easier to figure out if there was a narrative line if she could lay them all out at once.

There was a knock, and Nessa Gallagher entered without waiting for a reply.

Carragh scrambled to her feet, closing her laptop as she did so. It was like having one's headmistress or tutor show up unexpectedly, and she began thinking how to justify the work she had done thus far.

But Nessa had not come to call her to account. "Have you spoken to Aidan at all tonight?"

She shook her head. "Not since he left for Dublin earlier."

"I thought he might have been in touch with instructions."

"No."

Nessa was dressed more informally than Carragh had yet seen her, though *informal* was a relative term. She wore a dressing gown of cream-figured silk with dark red cherry blossoms trailing across the fabric. "Aidan used to be such an obedient child. Not like Kyla, she had an opinion on everything from the time she could walk. But

Aidan has always understood and accepted his position and responsibilities. Now, I feel as though I do not know him at all."

It was the first time Nessa had ever sounded old to Carragh, and it made her sympathetic. "I'm sure he does not mean to worry you."

She realized that Nessa had moved her walking stick so she could lean on it with both hands. "Would you like to sit down?" Carragh moved forward to provide support or help her to a chair . . .

But Nessa seemed not to hear her. She gazed around the room, from toile drapes to heavy bed hangings to limestone fireplace surround. "This was my bedroom when I was a young woman. I'd stayed in the nursery wing, of course, until I went to school in France."

"Where did you study?"

"A convent school outside Paris. I had to leave when the war came. I was thirteen when I came back, and insisted I was too old to return to the nursery. Papa let me choose whatever room I wanted. I'd always loved this one. And Fiona didn't mind me having it."

"Who was Fiona?" Carragh's mind had too many Gallaghers in it to place them all.

"My brother's wife. Eamon was from Papa's first marriage—he was twenty-four when I was born. I was glad when my brother married Fiona. She would ride and hunt with me. Fiona was always quite kind, and the castle could be lonely."

Considering that Deeprath could—and had—comfortably housed dozens upon dozens of servants, not to mention the much larger families of the past, Carragh was not surprised Nessa had been lonely. She was only surprised that she admitted it.

Cautiously, she probed. "You must also have been glad when Lily came to the castle. It seems she loved it here, as much as any Gallagher."

"Lily." The softer, mellower tone was gone. Nessa clearly had mixed feelings about Lily Gallagher.

Before Carragh could press the issue, the room was plunged into darkness without warning.

She gasped despite herself, then bit her lip and cautiously felt for the desk to her right and her industrial flashlight. She switched it on, to find that Nessa had unerringly made her way—in the dark and with her cane—to the fireplace mantel and the candles there. Without comment she lit them from matches set beside them.

"Well," Nessa said, all her authority returned. "Your first Deeprath blackout. I hope you don't find it too tiresome. It's not stormy, just windy, so Bell should be able to find the trouble and get it sorted before too many hours. We don't bother with the utilities company unless necessary."

Then she visibly startled. "My goodness, what on earth have you done with that painting? Why would you take it down?"

Carragh moved the flashlight beam to where Nessa was staring: the painting of Jenny Gallagher propped against the pillows of her bed. She could not have missed that earlier in the evening. The thing was four feet tall! If that enormous picture had been there when she'd come in, she would most definitely have noticed it.

Nessa said frostily, "I appreciate your interest in our home, Miss Ryan, but unless you have an art history degree of which I am not aware, I would prefer that you admire our paintings from a distance. Do you need assistance to rehang it?"

"No," she said slowly, too shivery with curiosity to be much embarrassed. "I can do it."

"See that you do."

Carragh offered to light Nessa to her room, and returned almost reluctantly. Would the painting have moved again? No. It continued to look at her from the bed. Whatever her promise to Nessa, she didn't rehang it immediately. How could she? This was the second time it had been taken down, and that could not be accidental—never mind the fact that she'd just found it noted on the list Lily Gallagher had made years ago: 4: *Bride painting*. It seemed someone wanted her to look at it. She tried to ignore questions about whether that someone was alive or dead, propped her flashlight at an angle, and sat cross-legged on the bed staring at Jenny Gallagher and the Darkling Bride.

The portrait had been painted in 1880, Jenny's wedding gift to her husband. Its outstanding feature, of course, was the subject and her reflected double. It tended to block out all else. But tonight Carragh deliberately avoided the painted women. Instead, she studied all that surrounded them.

The background appeared to be little more than generic woodland, though she'd seen enough of the Wicklow Mountains now to recognize the distinct shadings of brown and ochre earth beneath the pines. The longer she looked, the more details began to appear— like invisible ink turning brown beneath lemon juice.

Reflected in the pond behind the Bride's shoulder was the outline of a Norman keep just like the one at Deeprath. At the base of the trees surrounding Jenny were woodland creatures—hares and foxes and sika deer. There were faces, as well, like gargoyles lurking in the trees, mischievous and cruel.

Carragh sighed in satisfaction when she found the most recognizable symbol—the wide, squat Sanctuary Cross from Glendalough. Not the entire rock on which it was carved, but just the outline of the cross itself, etched beneath the hem of Jenny's dress. As though she were standing on it. She played the light at different angles until she got the best one, and leaned in so close her nose wasn't more than six inches from the canvas. There was something else etched inside that cross. Two letters: *EC*.

A shudder went through her, like a rush of air beneath wings. Jenny Gallagher had chosen to make a deliberate statement with this painting: her sanctuary was Evan Chase.

So how had it all gone so disastrously wrong?

After a long day in Dublin and an uncomfortable train journey, Aidan's ill temper was not helped by having to navigate the castle in darkness, illuminated only by a penlight. But he managed to find his bedroom without falling over anything . . . and then wished he hadn't, since his great-aunt was sitting in the chair before his empty fireplace. The paired candelabra on the mantel gave off a light that licked her face eerily.

"I heard you return," she informed him. "Has Bell found the issue with the power?"

He shook his head of excess rainwater and took off his wet coat. For once, Nessa did not complain about his manners. "It's started to rain. I told him to leave it until first light. Were the girls frightened?"

"Kyla told them they could have a campout. They piled all their blankets and quilts on the floor and fell asleep in two minutes."

He expected her to inquire about his trip to Dublin, but instead she asked, "Are you quite sure Miss Ryan can be trusted?"

"What do you mean? You're the one who hired her."

"I didn't know you would be leaving her so much to her own devices. She's spending quite a lot of time alone in the library. Is that wise?"

"You think she's going to pocket some of the books? More power to her. There're more than anyone needs down there, even the National Library. Miss Ryan can take what she likes as far as I'm concerned."

"And are you at all concerned about your family's reputation?"

Aidan sighed. He pulled out the heavy oak desk chair so he could sit across from her. In the candlelight, Nessa's face seemed to flicker between past and present, from the stern but fair guardian of his youth to the hollows and angles of old age. For the first time, he really grasped the fact that she was nearly ninety.

It led him to speak more gently. "How much more damage could be done? If there was anything incriminating in the library, the police would have taken it long ago. They didn't—I have looked at the evidence lists. There is one missing journal of my mother's. The police don't have it, and unless it has been pulled to pieces and scattered page by page, it's not in the library. If Carragh wants to look at dress pattern books from Great-grandmother Isabella or family letters from the 1700s, I have no objections to whatever she might learn."

Nessa dipped her chin, her carefully shaped bob a flash of white in the shadows. "Things cannot go on like this, Aidan."

"What things?"

"I know I have not been the maternal figure you would have liked over the years. I raised you the best I knew how, and made allowances for trauma. But you are thirty-two years old, and the last Gallagher male. However old-fashioned you find it, the name matters. You must marry and have a son."

"And I suppose you would like to play matchmaker?"

Sarcasm never deterred Nessa. "Certainly, if you will permit me. Enough of our ancestors married for money that it need not be the deciding factor. And there are any number of blue-blooded girls anxious to increase their titles. Just because the English queen's grandson married a commoner doesn't mean you need follow suit."

He would have laughed if he weren't so tired. Just like Nessa to dismiss the Duchess of Cambridge as nothing but an ambitious commoner. And he thought he would gladly marry a woman like Kate Middleton, if it meant marrying a woman who looked at him the way she looked at William.

"Your father was in his fifties when you were born," he pointed out. "And my father was forty. I wouldn't worry so much. No doubt there will be just as many willing girls in ten years as there are now."

"I will not let you evade me with flippancy, Aidan." Just that easily his great-aunt could slip into the stern watchdog of his youth, the guardian who reserved her greatest warmth for the dead and had only patient responsibility to offer the living. Even the traumatized living, as he and Kyla had been. No wonder his sister married Philip almost the minute she turned twenty-one. If their parents had lived, would his sister have naturally grown out of that unsuitable passion?

"Let us do one thing at a time," he countered now. "Finish the catalog, deal with the National Trust, finalize the paperwork, and see this new investigation through to the end."

"Don't forget the reception Friday night," Nessa said.

Aidan just managed not to roll his eyes. "How could I forget that you've invited the whole of Wicklow to tramp through the castle one last time? Do you really think it's a good idea? None of us are feeling especially social."

"It's not for us," she answered sharply. "But hopefully the police will be finished long before then. Do you really think that young policewoman will find any answers?" Her tone was not as dismissive as her words. Nessa was an excellent judge of character; she would have recognized Inspector McKenna's determination.

Aidan shrugged. "It's all guesses now, isn't it? There's nothing new turned up recently—so no, I don't think we'll find definite answers. I've learned to live without them."

That was a lie. He'd only learned to survive, not to live. And that, he mused later, before he finally fell asleep, would simply have to be good enough.

Except, it turned out he had been wrong. There *was* something new to discover. Something revealed by a combination of the heavy winds and the night's drenching rainfall and two lost hikers in the mountains. Something whose discovery spun a new angle on the tragedy of twenty-three years ago.

The Irish antiquities stolen from Deeprath Castle on the day of his parents' murders.

CHAPTER EIGHTEEN

June 1982

If Lily had known what pomp and circumstance the baptism of a Gallagher heir would involve, she might have wished to have another daughter. Kyla's birth and baptism had been a private joy allotted to her and Cillian, with family and ceremony secondary to the new parents and baby.

But the newborn Aidan Cillian Gallagher was not just a baby—he was "the living embodiment of generations of Gallagher viscounts past and present." To Lily's surprise it was not her father-in-law, the current viscount, who made such a pronouncement, but his half sister. With no children of her own, and only a brief marriage in her past, Nessa considered herself the repository of all family traditions. One would think, if not for her age, that *she* was Aidan's mother.

Before Lily had even left the hospital—and that was something Nessa didn't like, in her view all Gallaghers should be born at Deeprath—Father Hennessy had already been informed of the baptismal date and the names of the godparents. Lily gave in on the date, but no way in hell was she going to let someone else choose her son's godparents. Nessa wanted Viscount Gormaston, whose peerage was the only one in Ireland older than that of the Gallaghers, and Eleanor Butler, widow of the last Earl of Wicklow. Lily knew neither of them beyond making small talk at various receptions.

After a vicious battle between the two women (both Cillian and his father were of the school that preferred to stay out of emotional conflict), Lily conceded on the issue of Lord Gormaston in order to obtain the godmother of her choice: Maire Bell.

"The housekeeper!" Nessa had been horrified.

"My friend," countered Lily. "Who has been my everyday companion for ten years, who loves my daughter as fiercely as any sister of mine could, and who will put the good of my son above all else."

Aidan's baptism, like Kyla's and his father's and grandfather's and great-grandfather's, was conducted at St. Kevin's Church in Laragh within sight of Glendalough. The chapel had been constructed during the Famine years in the Celtic style, small and severe in design, calling worshippers' attention to the mysteries of God and the sacraments rather than earthly embellishments.

Afterward, the Gallaghers welcomed their guests at Deeprath Castle while the guest of honor slept in the nursery and five-year-old Kyla darted through the gathering like a hummingbird. Lily made a point of thanking Father Hennessy for his patience in the face of changing orders for the baptism.

He waved it off. "Not to worry. It comes with the territory. I think your choice of Maire Bell is very wise."

"Thank you."

"You know both she and her husband come from families that took refuge in the mountains during the Famine. It was the Gallaghers who helped feed and resettle them, once the worst of it was done."

"So you are enjoying being assigned to St. Kevin's parish, I take it?"

The young priest—no more than twenty-five—grinned widely. "I like the countryside. And the past. Glendalough and the mountains are a good fit for me. Legends and myths and history as far as the eye can see."

"You must let me know if you'd like to use our library. And no doubt Nessa would be more than happy to speak with you about local history. Though I must warn you, Father, it will be biased."

"I am well warned."

Cillian came over to add his thanks to the priest, and then husband and wife had a brief moment alone. "Tired?" he murmured.

"A bit."

"Happy?"

"I'm the mother of a future Viscount Gallagher. According to your aunt, I should spend the rest of my days giving thanks that I've been allowed such an honor."

He kissed her. "It's Aidan and Kyla who are honored, to have you as a mother. It was a good day for the Gallaghers when I went to that awful New York party and met you."

She allowed herself thirty seconds more of pretending it was just the two of them, before sighing. "Kyla appears to be trying to make Lord Gormaston eat a daisy. I'd better intervene before disaster occurs."

CHAPTER NINETEEN

Sibéal hardly said a word to Sergeant Cullen between Phoenix Park and the mountains. She'd chosen to drive down herself, and parked at the Glendalough visitors center, where they met the local officer and the rescue team that had made the discovery this morning.

The lost hikers, three fraternity boys from America who deserved whatever punishment they'd taken overnight in the storm, had been questioned and taken to Rathdrum to make formal statements. They didn't know much—it was a member of the rescue team who recognized anomalies in the hillside where one of the boys had slid down. Also something of an amateur archaeologist, he quickly realized that what appeared to be random stones beneath the earth slide were in fact meaningful.

"Very old," he told Sibéal as she followed him, legs aching from the unaccustomed surface, DS Cullen swearing softly now and then behind. "Not St. Kevin old, mind you, but medieval. Old enough to have been here when the monastery was a thriving city. Maybe eleventh or twelfth century."

"How far are we from Glendalough?"

"Bit more than a mile. Close enough for communal worship, iso-lated enough for private prayers. I'm guessing the stones are from some kind of holy well. We've got a call in to the National Museum. They'll want to send a team."

"They're not to come any nearer than the Glendalough car park until the police are finished and I've given clearance," Sibéal told him.

"Of course." He didn't point out the obvious—that any evidence had likely disappeared long ago. But Sibéal was not taking any chances. She'd been handed this case to ease her into SCR, expected to do little more than cover the same ground and, no doubt, reach the same conclusion. Unsolved.

But now, if what this man said were true, she had something the police twenty years ago didn't—the stolen treasures whose disap-pearance had allowed them to point responsibility for the murders away from the castle. Unless the inhabitants of these mountains made a habit of hiding valuable artifacts in out-of-the way places, this was a significant find.

The well must have been quite wide originally, Sibéal realized after going down and crouching beside the dislodged box—a coffret, the rescue worker had called it—without disturbing it or its con-tents. However deep it had once been, it had filled up over the cen-turies so that now she stood only four feet below ground level.

She leaned closer, her flashlight beam flaring briefly against the coffret. Two feet long and at least a foot wide, carved and inlaid with mother of pearl—she had studied a photograph of this box recently enough to be certain of its identity. It was the Victorian coffret last seen in the library of Deeprath Castle the day of the Gallagher deaths.

With time and the fall of earth and stone, thanks to the hikers, the lid was half open with one hinge twisted back. She could see in-side enough to identify several of the items listed as stolen in 1992: a Celtic mirror, a Viking-age dagger, the dull gleam of silver.

"I'm coming up," she called, and once out of the well, used the crime scene lights that had been delivered to illuminate the box below. "I want that up straightaway. Did you get photos in situ?" she snapped over her shoulder at the police photographer, who had arrived ahead of her and taken pictures of the well's interior.

"Yes, Inspector."

The amateur archaeologist protested about removing the coffret, but Sibéal shook her head when he claimed that history came first. "Not this time," she told him. "If it eases your conscience, I promise you that this box hasn't been down there long enough to interest an archaeologist."

Once carefully lifted to ground level with the help of Cullen and the techs, the police photographer took more photos, while Sibéal bounced impatiently. When every crime scene protocol had been fulfilled, she borrowed a camera cloth from the photographer and gently rubbed the tarnished oval plate set in the lid's center. Silver cleaner would have been useful, but it shone up enough to convince her she was looking at the Gallagher crest: the mountain peaks, round tower, and distinctive griffin with its wicked claws.

With care, she had Cullen hold the lid up enough for her to take a quick inventory. Everything was there. Every single missing item that had persuaded the local police the murders were committed by outsiders bent on profit.

And one item that did not belong—not with these antiquities, at any rate.

A marble Celtic cross, about a foot high, plainly carved and heavy-looking. And on one side of the distinctive ringed arms, an irregular stain. Sibéal caught her breath. "Light," she called out.

Someone thrust a flashlight at Cullen, who shone it on top of the cross.

"Blood?" Cullen said softly, crouching next to her.

"We'll find out."

Leaving Cullen at the site to await the scene-of-crime officers— and ensure the local police did not intrude on her investigation— Sibéal went directly from Glendalough to Deeprath Castle. It was only ten minutes by car, even with the windy roads. The overgrown gate looked less menacing today and more . . . sad. As though the castle knew why she had come.

Get a bloody grip, she commanded herself. Nessa Gallagher would eat her alive if she exhibited the slightest weakness. Such as kindness or sympathy.

Directed to the music room where she'd done the interviews, Sibéal found the family gathered together: Aidan, Nessa, Kyla and her erstwhile husband, Philip Grant. She had not forgotten Mr. Grant, but his interview would have to wait a bit.

"I know you have heard from Mr. Winthrop, your solicitor," she told them. "I've just come from the site where the discovery was made. In what appears to be the remains of a medieval well, we found a coffret containing various items detailed as stolen in 1992. The coffret itself matches the description given to the police at the time as the one last seen in your library, including the silver plate with your coat of arms engraved on it."

"What does this mean?" It was, perhaps surprisingly, the non-Gallagher who asked.

She studied Philip, but it was Aidan who answered him. "It means the odds of this being an outside crime are now astronomical. Professional thieves do not dump their take immediately and never come back. It means whoever stole those artifacts took them solely to divert suspicion from those of us in the castle at the time."

"But they're just . . . things." Kyla looked younger than before, and close to tears. "And my parents are still dead. What does any of this matter?"

Aidan moved, as though to put his arm around his sister's shoulder, then didn't. Sibéal caught his eye, and he supplied the answer that any police officer would give. "Everything matters in a murder investigation."

"Especially a murder weapon," Sibéal said, trying to watch all of them at once.

"What do you mean?" Aidan asked.

"The coffret also contained an object that may have been used to strike Lord Gallagher. We will let you know more when it's been tested. I'm sure you'll understand if I decline to be more specific."

"Waiting for one of us to know more than we should?" Aidan noted. "Am I to take it this discovery has narrowed your suspect list?"

"Until we know for certain if it is the weapon that killed Lord Gallagher—and where it came from—I'm keeping an open mind."

She would leave her remarks at that. For the moment.

After the emotional upsets of the previous night—not to mention the fact that the lights had come back on at four in the morning, startling her awake just when she'd managed to fall asleep—Carragh dragged herself out of bed feeling awfully like she was back in university. Once again she avoided the family, but snuck into the kitchen to see if she could find coffee. Maire Bell handed her a cup and a fresh scone but seemed preoccupied and unwilling to talk.

Carragh entered the library and looked around the lofty space with something like despair. Four days she'd been here—and she still hadn't even touched three-quarters of the shelves. She decided to forgo the fifteenth viscount's catalog today and simply make her own general notes, marked on a roughly drawn map. She would use her camera phone to take pictures of each shelf so she could re-create sections as necessary.

She began by taking the volume farthest left on each shelf, beginning at the top, to give her the roughest overview of subject (which, so far, had been the primary organizing principle). After recording the subject of each far left volume on the eleven shelves, she went back and randomly examined them to see if they conformed to the subject she'd marked down. When she pulled a book that seemed especially fine or old, she photographed the spine, the cover, and the frontispiece, and made a note of its precise location—fourth bay to the left, third shelf from the top, ten books in, for example. She was distressingly aware the whole time of how underqualified she was for this work. Why on earth had Nessa Gallagher chosen her?

Carragh was on the wooden rolling ladder, examining the third shelf down from the top, when she heard someone enter. She looked down on Aidan, who was unaware of her presence, and saw a painful vulnerability to his face, which plucked at her sympathy and made her look away.

He looked up. "Still hard at work. I'm trying to remember the point of it all."

From her perch on the ladder, she said, "The point is, I'm being paid. Unless you want rid of me?"

"Why would I?"

Because I'm criminally underqualified, I'm having a hard time focusing, and I care more about a lost Victorian manuscript than any other book just now.

To buy herself time to think of an answer she could say aloud, she descended the ladder, putting her at the disadvantage of being ten inches shorter than Aidan. But she had three much older, much bigger, brothers, so she'd learned early not to be intimidated by size. And all her instinctive sympathy came to the fore when she found herself close enough to see the misery in his eyes.

"Aidan, what is wrong?" She touched his arm without thinking and felt the fine tremor of tensely held muscles beneath the skin.

"They've found the items stolen from the library the day of my parents' murders." He must have seen her incomprehension, for he added, "A collection of especially fine Irish antiquities gathered by generations of Gallaghers. They were occasionally loaned to museums for special exhibits, but they were brought to the castle that last week because my mother wanted to examine them more closely."

Did she? Carragh thought. Did those antiquities have something to do with Jenny?

"Where were they found?"

"At the bottom of a medieval well in the mountains. Not two miles from here."

She thought aloud. "That means it wasn't thieves, right? Not outsiders?"

"Not outsiders," he agreed grimly.

"You must have considered that," she said. "Most murders are domestic."

"So they are. Did you pick up that knowledge in your folklore classes?" His smile was so full of bitter mockery she almost recoiled. "Surely the question isn't whether I want rid of you, but whether *you* want to stay. Being confined with possible murderers cannot have been part of the job description."

Leave, when she had that tantalizing list hidden by Lily Gallagher? When she didn't yet know what the writing on the tower walls said? She met his eyes steadily and told the exact truth. "Murder doesn't scare me." *Not since I was four years old.*

"Really." Aidan stared at her. "Someday, I'd like you to tell me why."

"Someday I will. Not today." Carragh hesitated, feeling odd about asking a favor after declining to explain herself. But she felt a pressing need to get to Dublin and follow whatever clue linked Lily Gallagher to her grandmother. "Aidan, would you mind if I took the evening train to Dublin? There are a few things I need to see to, but I'll be back here by dinnertime tomorrow."

He didn't answer for such a long time that she almost apologized and retracted her request. Finally, he said. "No, that's fine. Things are so unsettled just now, I'm having a hard time focusing on the library. I've even thought about calling the National Trust and putting off the acquisition date."

"I'll work up until the last minute today," she rushed to assure him. "Is there anything specific you'd like done before I go? Or anything at all I can do for you?"

Had it been Philip, she expected she would have gotten a leer and been the recipient of various suggestive comments. Aidan merely said, "Just keep on as you're going. You seem to know what you're doing."

Which only proved how little qualified he was to hire an archivist. She was about to tell him so when he unexpectedly added, "Just promise you'll come back."

It sounded remarkably like a personal appeal. If he was less gorgeous, less sexy, less titled, and less often in the tabloids, Carragh would have thought he wanted her company for something other than the library. But men like Aidan, the seventeenth Viscount Gallagher, did not look twice at half-Chinese adopted daughters of middle-class Irish American families. It was only shock and grief speaking.

Nonetheless . . . "I promise," Carragh said firmly.

CHAPTER TWENTY

Carragh fell asleep on the train before it finished pulling out of Rathdrum. Waking an hour later in Dublin, she thought groggily, was a little like a time traveler returning home or a cloistered nun leaving a convent. She hadn't realized the all-encompassing weight of Deeprath Castle and its history until she stood blinking on the pavement outside Heuston Station, ears assaulted by engines and horns and locust-like crowds, every other person in loud conversation on a mobile. She had planned to take the bus home, but instead grabbed the first cab she saw.

Merrion Square had the virtue of belonging half to the Georgian past, so it was less jarring than the city center. But if the outside was all red brick and white stone and glossy front doors, stepping into her grandmother's house was a suffocating embrace from the sixties. The first thing she did was run upstairs to check on the bathroom. She groaned at the state of it, unchanged despite the contractor's promises, and wished she'd managed a bath before she'd left the castle.

She threw the backpack on her bed and rummaged through drawers for a clean pair of leggings and a sweatshirt from her years at Boston College. Just how many sweatshirts did she own? She'd always thought that the best part of living alone—no one to dress up for. But maybe when she returned to the castle she'd pack something other than jeans and T-shirts.

It was a luxury to use her laptop for more than note-taking. She felt days of tension drain from her shoulders as the Internet welcomed her in as though she'd never been away. The first thing she did was send the tower room photos by email to her friend Duncan, along with a careful mix of flattery and begging. She'd seen him do magical things with computer programs she didn't understand, and crossed her fingers for good results as she pressed Send.

Sadly, there were plenty of unpleasant things waiting for her in this real world that also demanded attention. Bank statements, contractor bills, emails from the temp agency with some office administrative jobs on offer, and belated Easter cards from her nephews in New York containing bunny confetti and personalized crayon art.

For all that she'd missed having a mobile signal, she only turned on her mobile now with great reluctance. Sure enough, in five days she had missed nineteen calls from her parents' house. Only her father had left a voicemail, and it consisted of just three sentences: "Francis told us about the castle library. I imagine you're in Heaven. Call your mother."

She would have ignored it if she hadn't just come from a man who was so clearly suffering the loss of his parents. She had already lost one mother in her lifetime—she shouldn't allow resentment to alienate her from the one who'd loved her since she was four.

But as usually happens, she steeled herself to call and reached only a message. Probably her mother was at work. She could at least send her a text before she changed her mind.

Hi, Mom! Hope the criminals are giving you a break this week.
Having an amazing time in the Deeprath Castle library. You know
me—where there are books and old buildings, I'll always be happy.
I can't get a mobile signal there, so don't worry if you don't hear
from me for another week or two. Love you!

With that, she switched her phone off again, determined not to think any more tonight about her mother and their last argument, and that wretched, dangerous letter hid away in this house. To distract herself, she did the sensible thing: she pulled out the list Lily Gallagher had made decades ago.

1. *Dublin Weekly* and Wicklow People archives
2. Baptismal records
3. Father Hennessy
4. Bride painting
5. Chase's literary agent
6. Eileen Ryan

What connection had Lily made with Eileen Ryan?

The obvious answer was that—somehow—Lily had discovered that Eileen, with her magpie-like tendencies to gather up bangles and baubles on subjects that intrigued her, had collected some Evan Chase memorabilia. Carragh had only been allowed to see a couple of items over the years—usually her grandmother claimed she couldn't dig them out from wherever they were—and what she recalled wasn't terribly personal. Mostly copies of letters from Chase's publisher, some of them referencing Chase only in passing. But for Lily Gallagher, had her grandmother been able to dig out something more critical?

There was only one logical place to look: the attic. Carragh climbed all the way up to the space she had ignored since her grandmother's death three months ago. This was why she wore things like sweats and trainers—because she could hardly wear designer clothes to root around in dirty, spider-infested attics.

Her grandmother had an enormous trunk in which she'd kept her most "precious" items: an ancient, battered thing that had sat in the maids' attic bedroom for as long as Carragh could remember. It was latched but not locked, and she wrestled a moth-eaten brocaded wingback chair next to it since she wouldn't be able to reach inside if she sat on the floor.

She held her breath as she opened the creaky top . . . and let it out in a sigh of exasperation. Why had she expected her grandmother to have stored anything in order? Hoping there wasn't anything alive in the accumulated detritus within, she resigned herself to being filthy and began to pull out items one at a time.

Newspapers, magazines, dress patterns, a stack of gorgeous brocade fabric samples that had faded almost into neutrality, a tarnished silver box that held photos from as far back as the 1920s. Someday, when she had time, she resolved to spend a few satisfying hours trawling through all of it.

Beneath a stack of genealogical charts she found a wooden box carved on all four sides with the chevron and shamrocks of Eileen's Lynch heritage. Reverently, she lifted it out. As long as she could remember, this box had stood on her grandmother's desk, a piece of polished symmetry amongst the normal chaos. She had never been allowed to open it, but spent hours of her childhood staring at the fluid grain of black walnut and the intricate shapes of the young Irish clovers.

Gladly leaving the attic, Carragh took it with her to the dining table where she'd set up her laptop and turned on a Tiffany lamp with a cracked shade for better light.

The lid was a single piece that she had to cautiously wiggle off, swollen as it was by months, maybe years, of damp. The box was filled with envelopes tied together with string and a single, folded sheet atop them with *CARRAGH* dashed across the front in her grandmother's sloping handwriting.

Maybe it was the days spent in Deeprath's evocative atmosphere that made her fingertips tingle and the back of her neck crawl. It was almost as if her grandmother stood behind her, speaking the words of the message she'd left her one and only granddaughter.

Darling girl, how long have I been dead? If I were a betting woman, I'd lay odds you either came up here before even my funeral . . . or have put it off until months and months later. I

rather hope it's the latter, as that would mean you've managed to hang onto this house against all good sense.

Either way, I thought you might need a little project. You
know I was a collector of Evan Chase memorabilia. Years and
years ago—when you were just a tiny lass—a member of the
Gallagher family contacted me, trying to track down information about Evan, his wife Jenny, and the missing story of
the Darkling Bride.

Lily Gallagher and I corresponded for some time, and met
once in person. Tragically, just weeks after that meeting, both
Lily and her husband were killed. I held onto her letters out
of—well, who knows? I hold onto a lot of things for a lot of
reasons. But when you got older and I introduced you to
Mary Stewart and Victoria Holt and Daphne du Maurier
and Evan Chase—and you became a dedicated fantasist
yourself—I thought one day I would give you her letters so
that you might know what a member of the Gallagher family
knew or guessed about the tragedy in 1882. Consider this my
last gift to the girl whom God sent to us by such crooked
paths to bless our family.

With all my love,
GRANDMOTHER

Just as she finished reading, the lamp sparked and went out.
Though Carragh knew it was simply the bulb dying, she shuddered.
It felt like a hand had reached out from the past and extinguished
the light in order to prove its presence. Whether that presence was
her grandmother or Lily Gallagher or the long-ago Jenny . . . Maybe
it was all three. Maybe Heaven was a place where anyone could meet
anyone else and the three of them were playing games with her, giving her information little by little, seducing her with Deeprath's library, teasing her with Chase's missing manuscript, taunting her
with both a man she wished she'd never met and a man she was beginning to devoutly wish to know better.

"Just stop it!" she commanded, and didn't know if she was addressing interfering ghosts or her own runaway imagination.

By this time she had an irritable headache and knew she would have to sleep before attempting to make sense of Lily's letters. But she allowed herself to untie them at least, and pulled out the letter from the last envelope, dated ten days before the murders.

It was brief, agreeing to a time and place to meet in Dublin on the following Saturday.

My husband will be in Italy for business, so I need not make excuses. What a surprise I hope to present him with on his return! I cannot wait to show you the letter I found from Chase to his publisher. I am quite sure that, with your help, it will lead me to what I seek. Without your help, I would never have found it.

After that long, draining, and event-filled day, the last thing Carragh thought of as she slid into sleep wasn't her grandmother's unusual prescience or the possibility of actually locating Chase's missing book . . .

It was the vulnerability in Aidan's eyes when he'd said, "Just promise you'll come back."

Sibéal did not return to Dublin that night. Instead, she took a room at the Glendalough Hotel and grimly set herself to defending her case from those who might try to poach it. It wasn't a scenario she'd anticipated when accepting promotion to Serious Crimes Review— the very definition of cold cases was that no one wanted to touch them. But the Gallaghers were as much a part of Wicklow as the mountains, and the local force felt proprietary.

She'd had a discussion with a Rathdrum officer that swiftly moved from cautious probing to political threats to—from her—insults.

Though more than two decades since the murders, Inspector Burke was still a sub-district garda, just as he'd been when handed the Gallagher case.

"Why would anyone let your men near this case again?" she shouted, temper snapping. "I've found nothing in your records but sloppy police work and social pandering. There is only the briefest possible statement from the witness who discovered the viscount's body, and you seem to have written off the entire household as suspects solely because, and I quote: 'Such violence is doubtless the mark of an outsider.'"

For a minute she thought the man would have a heart attack, considering his purple face and popping eyes. "I don't need you to tell me how to conduct a proper investigation," Burke finally replied. "I've been solving crimes in Wicklow since you were guzzling at your mother's breast, and I don't like girls with no name and no proper history messing about with my district and my families."

Sibéal had left before she might be tempted to hit him, deciding instantly not to return to Dublin until forced to. So she called Josh, talked to May, and bought the necessary toiletries for a night in a hotel. She also picked up leggings and a hoodie that said EIRE across the chest in block letters and—after checking into the Glendalough Hotel, showering and changing—sat at the small desk and began to study Superintendent O'Neill's notes from 1992.

There were two types—those taken during the interviews, and those he'd written a little later, a mix of commentary on what had passed and questions to consider in the future. Sadly, no one had paid the new Garda officer enough attention, or it might have been a different case. At least, a lot more questions would have been asked.

Even through the medium of pen and paper, ten-year-old Aidan Gallagher's distress remained evident all these years later. His distress, as well as his attempts to control it and be helpful. An intelligent child, clearly, and one used to pleasing adults.

Sibéal was accustomed to the difference between notes taken

during an interview and the cleaned-up formal statements that followed. Mostly what she noted in this particular case was the lack of follow-up by the investigating officer.

I came home for tea. I was at Glendalough. I asked Mrs. Bell where my father was.

How long were you at Glendalough? Why did you go there? Did you talk to other people there? Did you see anyone on the way home? Did you go straight to the library? O'Neill had tried to prompt one or two of those questions but was slapped down by either his boss or Nessa, who sat in on the interview. No need to distress the boy more than necessary his great-aunt had insisted.

With Kyla, Nessa had apparently been just as watchful if not quite as sympathetic. O'Neill's asides on the lady, scribbled in one or two word phrases during the interview, were things like *Wary* and *Protective—of the children? or reputation?*

The other interviews—the Bells, Winthrop, Philip Grant—had been more straightforward, if not as probing as Sibéal would have liked. Which would have been fine if there had been follow-up interviews later on. But there hadn't, except for a few cursory conversations with the solicitor about Lord Gallagher's business that seemed more leading than probing. Definitely pushing for outside involvement from the first. Which, granted, with the theft of the antiquities, might have seemed reasonable. But follow-ups with those who had known of their temporary storage at the castle yielded nothing useful, at which point the Rathdrum police had more or less thrown up their hands and allowed a verdict of murder by person or persons unknown.

When she had finished, Sibéal found two items of note, details that were not offered in the original case file.

First, the day after the funerals, Kyla Gallagher had asked Constable O'Neill how she could get her mother's journal back. The same missing journal that Aidan had gone to his solicitor about just days ago? The one the police didn't possess—and never had? Definitely worth following up.

Second, even more curious for its oddity, Maire Bell had described Aidan's return from Glendalough thus: "He asked where his parents were and dashed off in that direction when I said the library. All dirty and rumply like lads get when they're outdoors, and gripping some of the late roses he'd brought back with him in his fist."

Roses. That detail had not appeared in the formal statement. It probably meant nothing—but it was odd, and the odd should always be followed up. She made a note to ask Aidan Gallagher what he'd been doing with wild roses the day of his parents' murders.

With that fizzing sense of interesting work ahead, Sibéal fell asleep, with the hotel window open to whatever night sounds might drift from the Glendalough ruins.

Carragh had planned to spend the morning working at home. But when she woke up to a bedroom that was more chilly and damp than even the Bride Tower at Deeprath, she threw on jeans and a red jumper and went to the nearest café with Wi-Fi and hot tea. She'd put the letters from Lily into a legal envelope, since she couldn't fit the entire wooden box in her bag, and after fortifying herself with caffeine and oatmeal, took out her notebook and began to read the letters of a dead woman.

Lily Gallagher had a distinctive voice, with the kind of personality and energy that leaped off the page and made her words a portrait as much as a written record. Though they focused mainly on the subject of Evan Chase and Jenny Gallagher, there were some scattered references to her family: *I really think fifteen-year-old girls should be locked up until they're stable. A temporary convent would stand Kyla in good stead just now.* Of her husband, she wrote in terms of great affection, which made it hard for even a stranger to believe that she would have had cause or inclination to murder him. And there at last was the name Carragh had been half consciously searching for: *Aidan is such a solemn child, but with the sweetest temper, which makes Kyla's tantrums bearable. Please tell me he won't be so different at fifteen as he is at ten! I should hate to say goodbye to my dearest boy.*

Lily never had a chance to say goodbye to that ten-year-old, or mend things with her difficult teen daughter. Blinking back tears, Carragh told herself firmly that this would never do. She needed an appropriate detachment if she wanted to find answers.

So she began again with a professional research eye, taking notes and marking questions to follow up on as she went. From the first letter, she learned that Lily had been told of Eileen Ryan's collection of Chase esoterica by the local priest, Father Hennessy. By way of introduction, Lily wrote that she had recently begun researching the Gallagher family history in order to compile the most interesting people and stories into a book to give her husband on his upcoming fiftieth birthday.

There are, of course, any number of "official" histories, Lily wrote, *but they focus rather too much on the ideal for my taste. I have always preferred the skeletons in the closet—or in the case of the Gallaghers, the skeletons in the tower. And the least talked about, most glossed-over skeleton is that of Jenny Gallagher's suicide in 1882. Considering that she went from pampered and secluded only child to wife to mother to death in the three years that followed Evan Chase's arrival at Deeprath Castle, he certainly presents as the obvious point of entry into those events.*

The local priest, who seemed to have been some sort of antiquarian or collector of Victoriana—it wasn't quite clear from Lily's letters—had also directed Lily to a London bookseller who actually had in his possession a handful of correspondence between Evan Chase and his publisher, Charles Maxwell, during Evan's first two years at Deeprath. That made Carragh practically salivate—even more so when she found that the Londoner had allowed Lily to make copies of the letters for her personal records. Sadly, those copies were not included in the letters she'd written to Carragh's grandmother, but Carragh's pulse quickened. They might even now be in the castle, if not the actual library itself.

Was the local priest who helped Lily still serving in Laragh? She'd have to find out. But while reading the letters, she'd had several sharp texts from Duncan about her plea for blown-up photos of the mysterious tower writing. After questioning her sanity, accusing her of having lost all sense of how time worked while in the Wicklow Mountains, and proclaiming dramatically that he was not a miracle worker, Duncan told her to meet him at a café across from St. Stephen's Green at three o'clock and he'd give her what he could.

Perfect. That would allow her to take the four-fifteen train to Rathdrum and be back at Deeprath by dinner as she'd promised. And she had four hours until meeting Duncan, in which to harass the plumber in person about the lack of progress on her bathrooms and to locate someone to check the heating.

Dealing with contractors was always guaranteed to put her in an exasperated mood, and when Duncan raised his eyebrows at the state of her clothes—she'd had to get on the floor to point some things out and there hadn't been time to change—he said, "I thought you were at Deeprath Castle to catalog the library, not serve as a kitchen maid."

Carragh glared at him as she dropped into a seat, and Duncan rolled his eyes. "In one of those moods, are you? It almost makes me regret doing you a favor."

"Give over," she commanded, one hand extended across the table. "And don't talk to me about favors. You'd never have graduated if not for me."

"True enough. And frankly, what I've been able to look at so far is fascinating. My only request is that you fill me in someday on what all this means."

"I have to figure it out myself, first."

Carragh took the file folder Duncan slid across the tabletop and opened it. There were ten of her photographs, enhanced by whatever digital wizardry he commanded and blown up to eight-by-ten size.

"I tried to keep to the order you'd taken the pictures in, so if whatever this is has any sort of narrative, you can start to piece it together."

Just like last night with her grandmother's box, Carragh's nerve endings felt exposed, as though equally craving the photos and afraid of them. Abruptly, she shut the file folder and put it into her messenger bag. "Thank you, Duncan. I will pay the costs, if you can finish the rest quickly."

"Sure." His curiosity was plain. "Want to at least tell me where you took these photos? I'm assuming at Deeprath Castle."

She hesitated. "Yes. But that's all I'm going to say just now. The family received some . . . difficult news yesterday. And until I can talk to one of them about whatever this is, I don't think it's fair to speculate with anyone else."

"Right. Well, just know I'll be anxiously awaiting news about how a story or poem or whatever about fairies and changelings and evil curses came to be scribbled on a wall in an old castle."

"When I know, I'll be sure to share."

CHAPTER TWENTY-ONE

May 1880

Evan and Jenny were married on a spring day of surpassing beauty at St. Patrick's Cathedral in Dublin. He had watched his new father-in-law struggle with indecision, caught between two impulses: to keep Jenny as near to Deeprath as possible with a ceremony in the parish church at Laragh, or to fulfill societal obligations by having his only daughter properly married in a Dublin society wedding. It was Jenny herself who decided him, for she insisted on being married at St. Patrick's as her parents and grandparents and great-grandparents had been.

Being a popular and fairly well-paid author, Evan knew how to move in society, but he was not accustomed to the level of scrutiny he received now that he was impudently "marrying up." Let them talk. His mother had died three years earlier and he had no other close relatives to invite to the wedding, so who else could they insult?

In the end, his only personal guest was his publisher from London—and Charles probably came as much to check on the progress of the book as for the wedding. When Evan introduced Charles to Jenny, he could see the instant spinning of his publisher's mind at the marketing possibilities. A novel called *The Darkling Bride*, with the author newly married to a woman who could be the title character? Doubtless Charles was already figuring out how to introduce Jenny to the reading public.

Their wedding night was spent at the Shelbourne Hotel. Evan's intimate experience with women had been limited and mostly awkward—if not downright professional—and he had worried a great deal about frightening or hurting Jenny. But she was as trusting as she was lovely, and responded to him with an ardor that assured him their marriage was well begun.

The viscount expected the two of them to return immediately to Deeprath while he traveled on to London for business. But once her father had departed, Jenny begged Evan to stay on in Dublin for a few days. "I have seen so little of it in recent years. I have seen so little of anything," she said plaintively.

Of course Evan agreed. They remained at the Shelbourne and spent the days walking on St. Stephen's Green across the street and visiting the National Museum and its hoards of ancient treasure. They also browsed through the National Gallery, and it was on that evening that Jenny presented to him her wedding gift.

He'd known she was being painted, but he hadn't expected this half portrait, half fantasy. Jenny had been depicted as Evan first remembered her, that amaranthine timelessness caught on canvas as she smiled at her reflection in the water. Except . . . it was not a reflection. Or not a completely accurate one. Though portrait-Jenny smiled, her watery echo was grave. And even the soft blurring of the reflected image could not hide the haunted expression in the eyes.

"It's the Darkling Bride," Jenny told him proudly. "I have always felt connected to her. And why not? God must have known it was the Bride who would bring you to me."

When she twined her arms around his neck and kissed him, Evan allowed himself to forget the concern caused by the doubled portrait with its disquieting expressions.

But from the next day, Jenny's moods began to shift. So quick and subtle at first, like American fireflies at dusk, that it was easily dismissed. A snap of temper that vanished the next moment into smiles, an absence of attention that she apologized for so charmingly it was forgotten. Even so, after two days of this Evan suggested they return to Deeprath. Her father was expected back from London in a week, after all, and Lord Gallagher would not like to find them still in Dublin.

But the logic served only to strengthen Jenny's stubbornness. Frowning, she insisted that the two of them deserved "a proper wedding trip." Beneath her stubbornness, Evan could glimpse in snatches a franticness that frightened him enough to speak soothingly and agree to whatever she wanted—if only to erase that look from her eyes. The same trapped look that the Bride gave him from the portrait.

Ten days after the wedding his world came completely unmoored. Jenny'd had difficulty sleeping for several nights, awake and sometimes pacing until dawn, so when she remained deeply asleep at noon, Evan let her be and was grateful for it. Perhaps she was simply exhausted. She woke just before sunset and insisted on going out. She chattered and laughed and teased as the hotel maid dressed her hair, but it was a false brightness like nothing he'd seen in her before. As though she were only pretending to be Jenny.

Against his better judgment, she had persuaded him to take her to the Gaiety Theatre. But she lasted only a quarter hour inside before coming to pieces. She could not stop talking, her speech increasingly fast and disjointed, and she flinched away from him when he tried to soothe her. At last, he told her firmly they were returning to the hotel and practically marched her outside. When a carriage pulled up, she would not get in and began to shriek that he was hurting her, forcing her, calling upon passersby for aid . . . but Evan looked the part of the Victorian gentleman in charge of his hysterical wife and managed to keep calm and get her inside the carriage and back to the Shelbourne without being questioned.

He summoned a physician—who gave her laudanum to keep her

calm—and then wired Jenny's father in London. Lord Gallagher arrived sooner than Evan dared hope, and whatever anger he felt at the flouting of his expectations he kept well in check while speaking in a kind but no-nonsense tone to his drowsy daughter. The three of them left Dublin in the still, dark hours before dawn. When they reached Deeprath, Lord Gallagher gathered Jenny into his arms and carried her inside.

Evan followed, expecting the viscount to take the main stairs to the rooms that had been prepared for the new couple, but his father-in-law went directly to the oldest part of the castle. The door at the base of the Bride Tower was unlocked and open, with gaslights illuminating the ancient steps. With increasing foreboding, Evan tagged his father-in-law's steps all the way to the top.

Jenny's childhood nurse, Dora Bell, stood waiting for them in the tower's top floor, which contained only a bed, a desk, and a chair. Drowsy still from being drugged for the trip, Jenny murmured a little when laid on the bed but made no other sound or protest.

Lord Gallagher looked at Dora. "Let me know when she's awake."

He brushed past Evan as though he wasn't there, leaving him to scramble after with a growing anger. At the foot of the stairs, he grabbed his father-in-law's arm. "What the hell are you doing?"

Lord Gallagher shook him off and opened the door to the library. "I told you to bloody well bring her straight home after the wedding. How could you have been so stupid?"

"You never told me what would happen if I didn't! How was I supposed to know?" Evan sat abruptly in a chair and dropped his face in his hands, fighting against anger and despair. And fear.

At last, he raised his head and met his father-in-law's eyes. Lord Gallagher looked years older than his age, and no longer angry. Just very, very weary.

"What's wrong with her?" Evan asked softly.

"Alternating fits of hysteria and melancholia, exacerbated by too much excitement and best treated with solitude and rest." Delivered in the flat monotone Evan had heard at other times and other places—the clinical words used in asylums to disguise the true horror of madness.

Even now, he couldn't believe she was really mad. Not his Jenny. "Why didn't you tell me all of it?"

"Because you wouldn't have married her if you'd known . . . and Jenny wanted you."

"And you wanted an heir," Evan shot back. "Right? You couldn't risk marrying her to someone of name and rank who might well walk out on a marriage based on a lie. You must have been over the moon when I showed up—too starry-eyed to ask questions and not important enough to make demands. You knew I'd simply count myself lucky when you agreed to the marriage and never look closer for the reason why."

"Are you going to leave her?"

Evan shook his head in disgust. "You don't know me at all, do you? I love her. And the saddest part of all is that, if you'd told me before, it would not have changed my mind. I'd still have married her. All you accomplished by your lies of omission was to ensure that I put my wife in danger because of my ignorance. I find it hard to forgive you for that. No more. I want to see the doctors you've consulted and I want a full history of Jenny's illness and treatments."

Lord Gallagher still looked weary, but some color had returned to his face. "Very well."

"And no more lies about anything to do with Jenny. Ever. Is that clear?"

"Perfectly clear."

CHAPTER TWENTY-TWO

After a refreshingly restful night in the mountains, Sibéal woke at dawn and went for a long, long walk. She did not attempt to return to the old well that had offered up its unexpected contents yesterday. Instead, after a brief study of the literature provided by the hotel, she explored Glendalough itself.

As a schoolgirl she'd visited the ruins of Red Hugh O'Donnell's Franciscan friary in Donegal. About the only thing she remembered was that it had been destroyed in an explosion during a siege in 1600 or thereabouts. County Donegal was known mostly for its natural attractions—the peninsulas and cliffs and golden beaches that made it one of Ireland's top tourist destinations. Other than being a significant Gaeltacht (Gaelic was the primary or only language), her home county's connections to Irish history had mostly eluded Sibéal.

The Round Tower, medieval cathedral, St. Kevin's Kitchen (so-called because its own miniature round tower integrated into the roof made it look like a chimney), St. Kevin's Cross . . . she was astonished by how moving she found it all. Perhaps there was more to history than she'd ever learned. Probably a good lesson for someone working cold cases.

It was a surprise to her that the cemetery contained recent graves. She would have supposed its days of use long past, but it seemed the local parish church continued to bury their dead in the monks' graveyard. Alert and curious, Sibéal began to examine the newer stones.

She found the Gallagher family in its own section, set off from the rest by a rusting iron fence. Like the gate at the castle, this one hung open as it clearly had for years. Within lay a jumble of stone and grass, wildflowers peeking through at odd angles from those memorials that had broken or sunk slantwise into the ground over the passage of centuries.

The oldest marker that she could decipher was for a Henrietta Gallagher, who had died in 1704. Sibéal had her notebook out and drew a simple plan of the plot, marking the readable gravestones as she went. There were no mausoleums as in fancier graveyards, but there was evidence of carving and design on many of the headstones: winged death's heads and Celtic crosses and even the Gallagher griffins. The littlest markers, those of infants and children, wormed their way into her heart like poison, and she knew they would haunt her in her dreams. Many of the children's gravestones bore stone daisies or depictions of broken flower buds.

Despite her professional curiosity, she took her time approaching what looked to be the newest markers. There she found the most recent of them all: CILLIAN GALLAGHER, 16TH VISCOUNT GALLAGHER, 1942–1992; LILY MORGAN GALLAGHER, 1945–1992. *Too Soon.*

Just that. One stone shared, no protestations of having been greatly loved or dearly missed. Following that line of thought, who had chosen the stone and the engraving in the first place? Not his children, surely. No child or even adolescent would propose such restrained phrasing. Most likely it had been Nessa, Sibéal mused as she left the graveyard, as it had been Nessa who had taken care of everything else, from business to guardianship.

After showering and changing, she returned to Deeprath warily, wondering if the local police had wormed their way back in with the

family and were looking for a fight. But the grounds were as quiet
and remote as ever, with the brooding feel of a coming storm. Sibéal
locked her car door—her little VW had protested the uneven and
neglected gravel drive—and decided to prowl around the grounds
before announcing herself. The police photos taken at the time allowed her to now fill in a great deal of color and structure where
there was the bare minimum of upkeep. In 1992 the castle frontage
had been offset by the neatly raked gravel drive drawing a large
circle before the house. In the center of that had been inner rings of
manicured turf, beds of Irish wildflowers, and a stone fountain.
Today, the fountain was the only recognizable element remaining,
though it had long ago stopped running and the only water it held
was that caught from rain. Both flowers and grass had succumbed to
a free-for-all of waving fronds almost waist-high in places, and the
circular drive was full of potholes.

It was not for lack of money. Sibéal had seen the pages Sergeant
Cullen had compiled about the family's finances over the last thirty
years. Aidan Gallagher could have chosen to keep the castle maintained even if he preferred not to live here. Instead, he'd locked up
the library and more or less the castle itself, with only the Bells and
the occasional hired hand to see to the most necessary repairs. He
had a townhouse in London and various rental properties throughout Dublin. Kyla Gallagher's Kilkenny manor house represented
less than fifteen percent of her personal worth. The amount of zeros
in their finances tempted Sibéal to make the murders a matter of
money—except children, when they killed, did not do so for even-
tual gain. They acted on immediate needs or fears. Aidan Gallagher
had not murdered his parents just so he could get his inheritance
early.

She walked the perimeter of the castle, appreciating the unique-
ness of its various wings and angles and rooflines and trying to
match the interior plans with the exterior. It was almost hopeless,
especially for someone who barely knew the difference between
stone and brick, let alone the various architectural periods.

The library was by far the easiest to identify, with its former identity as a private chapel. Sibéal paused by the hidden outside door—for fugitive priests, Cullen had told her; her sergeant knew all kinds of odd trivia—and pondered it with interest. The police at the time had hastily concluded that the killer had entered and exited the castle by this unobtrusive priest's door. It wasn't a bad theory—if it didn't have the air of being grasped at as the one most convenient for the family. Personally, she didn't see how a random outsider could have even known about the door. Or for that matter, been able to open it. It possessed a sturdy enough lock today.

"Trespassing, Inspector?"

She didn't flinch, didn't even blink, simply assured herself that the door was, indeed, thoroughly locked, before turning to face Philip Grant. When she'd spoken to the family yesterday, he'd been dressed in a bespoke suit that made him look sleek and satisfied. Today he wore khakis, boots, and a tweed jacket that made him look like a countryman. Only his cynical, practiced expression remained the same.

She didn't respond to his jibe, but seized upon the moment. "Would this be a convenient time to speak, Mr. Grant?"

"About what?"

"About what happened here in 1992, and how you came to be mixed up in all of it."

"Mixed up?" he repeated, amused. "Only in the most peripheral sense. Do you want to conduct an interview lurking outside the walls?"

She wanted to conduct the interview without risk of being interrupted. She nodded to a wooden bench, silvered by age and exposure, at the edge of what had once been trimmed turf. "We can sit."

Philip agreed, and when they were seated launched into the story he'd no doubt been preparing since he heard the case was reopened. "I was an intern, more or less, hired for that summer by Lord Gallagher thanks to my father's connections. I had business aspirations that have proved to not be entirely foolhardy."

"Helped, no doubt, by Gallagher money."

A man may smile and smile and still be a villain definitely applied to this man, with his custom-made clothing and easy air of belonging and fair-haired good looks . . . and yet, there was something reptilian at his core. This was a man devoted entirely to his own ends.

"Not so much the money, as the name. You're quite right, Inspector, marrying Kyla did me no harm. Nor her. And isn't that the ideal marriage—where both partners benefit?" His eyes flicked to her bare left hand. "You'll just have to take my word for it."

Sibéal wouldn't have taken his word if he swore that the earth was round. She wondered if Kyla felt she'd benefited as much from the marriage as her husband.

"Mr. Grant, what was the nature of your relationship with Lady Gallagher during your internship? I believe you were resident in the castle."

"I was. In one of the more remote wings. There are more than a hundred rooms in Deeprath Castle. I could go days without seeing anyone but his lordship and the steward."

"Mr. Bell, the estate manager? You reported to him as well?"

"I wouldn't say reported."

Of course not, she added mentally, *you wouldn't want me thinking you were ever subordinate to a mere steward.*

"Whatever Lord Gallagher asked, I did. I studied estate records and past investments, I learned about the running costs of property as balanced against income, and I studied stock reports and practiced picking winners."

"And your relationship with Lady Gallagher?" she asked again.

The reptile flickered behind his eyes. "Her secretary was off having a baby or some such that summer. When she needed it, I helped with her correspondence."

"Did Lady Gallagher have a large circle of correspondents?"

He shrugged one elegant shoulder. "American, mostly. They're all so . . . friendly. Don't you find? Like Miss Ryan."

Sibéal was taken aback by the hostility of the apparent non sequitur. "The library archivist? Is she American?" For some reason, she didn't want Philip to know she'd already spoken to Carragh.

"I'm not entirely sure what she is. She had a grandmother in Dublin, but Carragh was raised in Boston. I suppose that makes her American, whatever mongrel bloodline brought her into being. She's adopted, you know?"

He'd called her Carragh. Now why did Philip Grant feel the need for such a personal attack on someone wholly unconnected to Deeprath Castle before now, someone who could have nothing at all to do with the murders? Yes, obviously, Sibéal thought, he is trying to distract me. But why Carragh in particular? An interesting puzzle.

One that could wait. "Mr. Grant, I would appreciate a list of all the correspondents you recall Lady Gallagher being engaged with that summer. My colleagues were not especially searching in their questions at the time."

"Understandably. All the signs pointed at robbery gone wrong. No need to disturb a devastated family more than necessary."

"But it wasn't robbery, was it? No, Mr. Grant, I'm afraid it will not hold. Someone killed them both, someone who knew enough about Deeprath and Glendalough to hide those antiquities in an unmapped holy well, along with the gun. Someone who has gotten away with it for twenty-three years. That someone? Should be very, very worried."

However unwise it might have been, Sibéal felt vicious satisfaction at knocking the smug expression off Philip Grant's face.

Aidan spent much of that Tuesday in Rathdrum dealing with Winthrop on estate matters. It was straightforward—as much as it could be—for the solicitor had done an excellent job over the years keeping track of the many spinning plates that constituted a heritage like Deeprath and a fortune like the Gallaghers'.

But when Aidan complimented him on his work, Winthrop said, "You owe as much thanks to your sister as you do to me."

"Kyla?"

Coolly, Winthrop replied, "You did appoint her to oversee the books."

So he had, fifteen years ago before he'd started university and Kyla had just earned her business degree. Aidan had given it little thought since then, assuming she saw it as he'd intended: a figure-head position, meant mostly to ensure he wouldn't be bothered too much by Ireland.

No wonder she thought him arrogant and detached. Fumbling to ask without sounding more condescending, Aidan ventured, "I'm glad she has had something to keep her occupied. We don't discuss it much."

"I know." Could it be disapproval shading the solicitor's tone? "I thought it a pity you weren't more receptive to her thoughts on the castle's future—alternatives to donating it to the National Trust."

"Hotel, conference center, historical archives . . . Wicklow is not Dublin. If we ever managed to turn a profit, no doubt it would be eaten up at once by expenses."

"No one thinks it would be easy, but this was no idle dream, Lord Gallagher. Kyla worked hard for months putting together a viable business plan, complete with possible grants and sponsors for the project. Did you not read it?"

"I assume you know I didn't."

Winthrop removed a hefty file from one of his desk drawers. He must have come prepared for this meeting, in more ways than one. Passing it to Aidan, he said, "You should read it. If you have questions—ones that you cannot bring yourself to ask your sister—talk to Robert Bell. He also thought this an excellent proposal."

"Is there not one person in Ireland who thinks the trust donation is a good idea?"

"Of course there are—those persons who work for the trust."

Uttered with a dry humor that pierced Aidan's pride, so that he answered more humbly, "I will read it. Carefully."

That promise given, Aidan borrowed a conference room and Internet connection in Winthrop's offices, attending to what business he had in London. There wasn't a lot professionally, seeing as he was on leave and between assignments. He almost wished he had friends, just so he could communicate with someone outside Wicklow, someone who could remind him that nothing lasted forever. Not even grief.

He thought he'd learned that lesson as a boy—but had begun to realize that grief denied and ignored will come back to bite you in the ass. Look at Kyla's drinking. Look at Nessa's iron avoidance of emotion. Look at his own tendency to shy away from anyone or anything that came too near his boundaries.

Impulsively (or as near to impulse as he was capable of), Aidan texted Penelope.

> What are you doing?
>> Not waiting around for you. How is Ireland?
> Not as horrible as I feared. The castle, at least. But the family? Let's just say the Gallaghers are not fated for personal happiness.
>> Fate?
> I'm Irish. We believe in Fate.
>> I'm rolling my eyes at you so hard a passerby just stared at me in concern. How's the woman?
> What woman?
>> There's always a woman where you're concerned, Aidan. Usually more than one. And don't tell me you don't notice them . . . you're a sodding police officer. Didn't your aunt hire someone for the library?
> How do you know it's a woman?
>> Ha! If you're stalling, it's because I'm right. What's her name?
> . . .
>> Aidan?!
> Carragh Ryan. She's adequate to the job.
>> The job of the library . . . or the job of walking with you in your mountains?

You're an unnatural creature, you know that? You were sleeping
with me three weeks ago.
    And I broke up with you two weeks ago. So Carragh Ryan likes
    your library and likes your mountains . . . what else does she
    like?

He almost ended the conversation there. But apparently impulse,
once indulged, could run riot.

Pen, if I asked you to come to Ireland for the weekend—would
you?
    What on earth for? If it's to protect you from this archivist, for-
    get it. And I won't sleep with you. What other use could I be?
Am I really that selfish a bastard? I suppose I am, because I do
want something.

Aidan paused. Did he really want to do this? Taking a deep
breath, he started typing again.

You told me before that you use hypnosis in your psychology practice.
    To relax people, yes.

Even through text, he could feel her caution.

And when people are relaxed, they can sometimes remember
things they didn't want to before?

She took so long to respond he thought she'd given up in disgust.

    What is it you want to remember?
I don't know. There are definite gaps in my memories of that day. I
thought the police statements would help me fill them in. But it
turns out the police barely spoke to me at all.

That was accurate, as far as it went. But Aidan knew what he wanted to remember, something that had been tugging at his mind and conscience since his return. He had seen Kyla just before the murders. He knew he had. But he couldn't remember anything of the context. Had she seen him? Had they spoken? He didn't even know if this had happened inside or outside the castle.

This, he knew now, had always been lurking beneath his detachment, the cold fear that had seeped into his relationship with his sister, which he had buried long before he went to London to work. He could not keep it buried any longer.

> So you want me to come all the way to Ireland to maybe or maybe not hypnotize you. What an enticing proposition.
> There's a party on Friday night. Half of County Wicklow is coming to the castle to kiss my hand before I throw away my heritage.
> I'll think about it.

With that, he had to be satisfied. As he drove back to Deeprath in the battered Land Rover that had been part of his childhood, he thought about what it was he wanted—needed—to know.

First: *Who murdered my parents?*

Second: *Why?*

And a very distant third: *What do I do with those answers once I have them?* For years he'd lived his life based on the trauma of one day. If ever that day was explained and understood . . . who would he be?

The unusual introspection meant he had not anticipated Inspector McKenna in his house. He'd hardly even noticed the strange car outside, assuming it was the cleaners. But the detective was in the Great Hall, having just finished an interview with Mrs. Bell. The housekeeper looked flustered, and Aidan felt a flash of empathy. After his parents' deaths, the only thing close to open affection he'd received had come from his godmother. Maire Bell had been a faithful correspondent, writing him weekly through all his years of boarding school and university. Nessa had never approved. She'd considered the friendship between Maire and Lily Gallagher improper. "The American in Lily," she used to say. "Never knowing where to draw the proper lines."

Which was precisely why people had loved his mother. For the first time since his return, Aidan realized that if he wanted a more complete picture of his parents from an adult point of view, Maire Bell was the one to ask.

Noting that for later, he said, "Any news, Inspector?" He had asked various Dublin contacts about Sibéal McKenna, knew the basics of her family and upbringing and history in the Garda. She looked serious, but then, he suspected she always did. Something about the steadiness of her gaze and the set of her chin.

"Only that the antiquities have been definitely identified by your solicitor. Which seems to upend the conclusions reached by the police at the time. As you noted, few thieves would commit murder for such items only to bury them away for decades."

"Does that upend *your* conclusions?" Aidan asked. "I had the impression from the first that you didn't believe in an opportunistic robbery gone wrong."

"No, I didn't, no more than you did. Which makes me wonder, Lord Gallagher, what exactly you have concluded about what happened."

"I was ten at the time. Too young for theories."

"And since then, you have grown up and joined the police force. As an Arts and Antiquities officer, interestingly. Did you join that division in order to keep an eye out for your family's missing antiquities?"

His temper flared at the implication he couldn't make rational decisions. "Are you a cold case officer because you have an unsolved crime in your past?"

Her smile was ripe with understanding. "For whatever reason, you are a police officer. So don't tell me you don't have theories now."

"I don't." He stared her down.

"Already, I am being encouraged by the local police to admit that the most likely remaining scenario is a business rival who wanted your father out of the way and perhaps didn't anticipate your mother getting in the middle of it. Hired assassins seems to be the desired conclusion, who took the antiquities as a distraction."

"Hired assassins who relied on finding a convenient weapon at hand? And how the hell would a hired killer know about any holy well near Glendalough? It's not in any tourist literature. I didn't even know about it!"

"Quite." She nodded once, as though approving an apt pupil. "We both know it was not a stranger, Lord Gallagher. It was someone who knew your family, someone who knew this castle, someone who knew the landscape of these mountains. And if that is true, then it is almost certainly someone you know."

"I have nothing to add to that very logical piece of deduction."

Her brief smile of acknowledgment was without warmth. "You are no longer ten years old. And you are not simply the seventeenth Viscount Gallagher. You are a detective inspector in the Metropolitan Police, and what I want to know is . . . who are you protecting?"

"I have no answer to that." He met her stare without blinking.

"I didn't expect an answer. And I don't really need one. I may not be wealthy and titled, but I'm an inspector, the same as you. I think I can work it out on my own."

CHAPTER TWENTY-THREE

Carragh used the return train ride to transcribe the first of the enlarged photos. She disciplined herself to treat it as an academic project, to not look through them all at once and anticipate what she would find. But it didn't take long to see the strangeness Duncan had hinted at.

. . . and envy is not to be borne. Why should the girl be happy, why should she live with joy in the world, while disdaining those spirits who walked with her through darkening days and endless nights? Ingratitude is the first sin of the fae, disloyalty punished by exile and death.

The Bride had forgotten them. She had fled her bright world for the darkling shadows of the mortal one and counted her people well lost for her pride. But sin casts a long shadow. Where one child is lost, another may be found. If the girl would not return of herself, then let her pay the price.

So . . . a narrative. Of sorts. And a suggestive narrative at that, what with the reference to the Bride and the use of "darkling" as a description. Written, Carragh guessed, by the beleaguered Jenny Gallagher during her periods of confinement to the tower. Whatever illness or madness had caused her confinement, she wrote lucidly enough, though it would take many more transcriptions to tease out a storyline from it all. Was that what had drawn Evan Chase to Jenny—that she had literary talent as well as beauty and birth?

She was glad to see the electric lights shining at Deeprath Castle when the cab dropped her off. There was a blue Volkswagen parked near the stables, and Inspector McKenna approached it from around the house as Carragh drew near.

"Been away?" the inspector asked.

"Only overnight."

"I believe Lord Gallagher just went in to dinner. You're in time to join them."

More like she would be unable to avoid them, what with the dining room opening off the Great Hall. Carragh's heart sank. She was itching to continue transcribing the enlarged photos and reread Lily Gallagher's letters to her grandmother. She was also itching to keep as far away from Philip as possible.

Uncannily, Inspector McKenna asked, "Why does Philip Grant dislike you?"

"Did he say so?"

"He didn't have to. He tried every trick he knows to get me to take a closer look at your role in all of this. Which is beyond absurd. That can only mean he has a vindictive wish for you to be put to questioning. So again—why does Grant dislike you so much?"

"You said yourself I can't possibly have anything to do with the Gallagher murders."

"That's not what I asked, Miss Ryan."

While Carragh fumbled for a response, the inspector smiled knowingly. "However, that doesn't mean I don't have other questions for you. I'm interested in the family and their current state of mind. I'm curious about what you think of it all—being an outsider, as you are. Can we speak again tomorrow?"

"I'll be working flat out after taking today off."

"I'll come to you, in the library. Nine o'clock?"

One could hardly say no to the police. She would just have to think up some good stories from the Gallagher history to keep the inspector from asking about Philip again.

As expected, she was not ten steps inside the castle before her presence was noted and Nessa directed her to join them at the long table. Carragh tried to sit at the end next to Kyla's little girls, so Ellie and Kate would be between her and Philip, but Nessa insisted she come to the other side to help balance things. At least that didn't put her next to Aidan.

The conversation at the table, already tense, required little from her. They were discussing the etiquette of going ahead with the reception planned for Friday night. "In light," as Nessa said delicately, "of the unforeseen situation in the mountains."

"You mean everyone will be wondering about the stolen antiquities that weren't actually stolen?" Aidan asked. "What a pity we couldn't wait to mark ourselves as the chief suspects until after the party." She'd never heard him talk this way before, and suddenly realized he'd been drinking even before dinner.

"There's no need for sarcasm," Nessa replied calmly. "I feel it would be wrong to cancel things at this late date. It's not as though we will have another chance to bid goodbye to the district before you sign away their castle to strangers."

"Their castle? It's *my* castle, aunt. For as long as I care to keep it. And no one can have anything to say about when and how I choose to give it up."

"Your father would never have indulged in such selfishness."

"My father is dead."

Like magnets, the two non-Gallaghers at the table locked eyes, Philip for once appearing as uncomfortable as Carragh felt. But only for a second, before his expression slid into its usual provocative look. Kyla did not notice. Pale and furious, she said to her brother, "I agree with Aunt Nessa. You may not care about our responsibilities here, but I do."

"Is it responsibility you care for, sister? Or the opportunity to complain to a larger audience that I am robbing you of your precious business plan?"

"Aidan." In just two stinging syllables, Lady Nessa Gallagher infused eighty-eight years of privilege and position into a reprimand sufficient to make Aidan's mouth snap shut and the spines of everyone else at the table straighten automatically.

"No one," Nessa continued, "disputes your legal rights so far as the property is concerned. It is not entailed—you may dispose of any asset as you so wish. But this castle is not merely an asset, Aidan. It is your home and the home of nearly eight hundred years of your ancestors. Gallaghers who have fed and protected and served the people of these mountains for all of those centuries. Do you really wish to sneak out of here like a thief in the night?"

Carragh wished she dared look at Aidan without fear of being caught. But she thought if she did look, she would have seen that queer vulnerability edging his eyes when he answered, for his tone had softened considerably. "We will keep to the date and the arrangements for the party. But you know as well as I do we won't be able to keep yesterday's discovery quiet until then. By the time people gather here on Saturday, the rumors will be flying."

"Then all the better to meet them head-on and set the record straight."

How? Carragh wondered. Did they even *have* a straight record yet? But she reluctantly admired Nessa's nerve. She imagined it came from a heritage of upper-class disdain for other people's opinions.

As though they were all children, Nessa dismissed them from the table. Though Ellie and Kate had remained commendably quiet through dinner, only fidgeting a little, they now claimed Carragh with insistent voices.

"Play with us, please," pleaded Ellie. "You're ever so much more fun than Louise."

The maligned Louise kept a blank expression, and Carragh began to wonder if the au pair spoke any English.

Kate, who seemed the naturally more suspicious one, unbent enough to add graciously, "We don't have to play hide-and-seek. You can choose the game if you like."

Philip seized the opportunity. "I've no doubt Miss Ryan is very fond of games." He smiled at Carragh. "Will you be at the party Friday? After working you so hard, the least my brother-in-law can do is let you out for a little fun."

Aidan abruptly said, from so close behind Carragh that she could swear she could feel his breath, "Of course she'll be there. Miss Ryan is not my servant. But while she is in this castle, she is my responsibility."

"Is that a warning, my lord?" Philip asked with deadly civility.

"Do you need one?"

Kyla swung her gaze between her brother and her husband, while Carragh devoutly wished she were elsewhere. Beneath the humiliation of it, she felt a spark of anger at being used in a power play between the two men.

She spoke up firmly. "No one needs warnings. And if you're going to fight, do it over someone who cares."

At that dramatic moment, thunder crashed and the lights flickered and went out. Carragh flinched, wondering if ghosts could control the weather.

"For goodness sake," Nessa said irritably. "Mrs. Bell!"

Carragh didn't dare sneak away in the dark, for it was difficult enough finding her way around with light. But she grabbed the first candle she could when the housekeeper appeared and—with a moment's pity for the little girls she was so ruthlessly abandoning—left the Gallaghers behind, icily ignoring one another.

Her plan was to bathe by candlelight and then go to sleep as soon as she could. She couldn't transcribe the photos with any accuracy, even with her strong flashlight, and the tension of the day, heightened by the almost nonsensical squabbles at dinner, had worn on her. Best to sleep and wake up to a new day's work. The way things were going, she wouldn't be surprised to be bundled out of Deeprath at any moment, so she wouldn't waste her daylight hours with anything but work.

But someone at Deeprath—breathing or not—had different plans for her. Once in her room, she used the candle she carried to light those on the mantel and the table and gratefully stretched her arms and neck. And froze.

Jenny Gallagher stared at her from the pillows, the portrait placed on the bed exactly as it had been the last time the power went out. Why the hell couldn't the damn thing stay in one place? And who, exactly, was sneaking in and out of her room for such a bizarre reason? She had half a mind to put it out in the corridor, but didn't want to be scolded by Lady Nessa. Or worse—turn around to find it back on her bed once more. Her brothers had once made her watch a horror movie in which the man being haunted threw a ball into the river just to keep it from moving about . . . and came back home to find the ball—the *wet* ball—rolling down the stairs at him.

Gingerly, she approached the bed and put her hands on either side of the gilt frame. She meant to simply lean it against the wall as she had before but could not look away from the combined weight of the two women staring out at her. Jenny and the Bride—one real, one not—one lost, one found—both beautiful, both loved, both tortured—

We are the same.

Part of Carragh wanted to drop the portrait, but the other part refused. There was a singing in her blood, whispers along the beat of her heart, the sense of a hand in the small of her back pushing her forward, leading her on to . . . what?

"What do you want me to see?" she murmured, only half aware that she spoke aloud.

She sat on the bed, angling the portrait to get as much light as possible from the candles. But she searched by touch as well, hands running all along the frame as her nerves pulsed and twitched. Nothing. She hesitated, imagining Lady Nessa's horrified exclamation if she could see her, then let her fingertips touch the surface of the painting. The curve of Jenny's cheek, the gloss of the Bride's hair, the falling leaves and deep water of the pool . . . She didn't know what she expected, but there was nothing there except paint.

Carragh sighed and gave up. She grasped the painting by the frame, and in her frustration one side slipped out of her hand. She made a desperate grab for it, fingers splayed wide against the back, making the glued paper backing crinkle. And a bolt of inner energy surged through her.

"You've got to be joking!" she exclaimed, even as she turned the portrait over and laid it facedown on the bed. This was ridiculous. She'd already been warned about moving or touching the paintings. What on earth would they do to her if she started tearing one apart on a hunch?

It's okay, she imagined assuring Aidan. The thought of explaining to Nessa was beyond even her imagination. *I took the framing apart because the ghost of Jenny Gallagher told me to. Or possibly, you know, the mythical Darkling Bride.*

She should wait until morning, sleep on the idea before acting. Wait until she had sufficient light. Wait until she could move with care and precision.

She didn't wait. Thank goodness for the old-fashioned nature of the castle—her desk held crested notepaper and a wickedly sharp letter opener in the shape of a long sword. Offering a silent prayer to whichever saint was the patron of absolutely insane ideas, Carragh began to work on the top right section, since it appeared to be the least firmly attached.

Carefully, centimeter by centimeter, she inserted the sharp point between the backing paper and the frame. As she worked, she realized the backing could not possibly be as old as the portrait itself. Victorian paper would surely be more brittle, easily split if not shattered by too-vigorous movement. This paper was thicker than she would have expected, more pliable and resilient. It seemed that at some point in the last, say, thirty years, the portrait had been repapered.

She labored away at the backing, eyes straining against the flickering candlelight, until she had made an opening across the right corner, three inches down and three inches across the top. Dropping the letter opener, she began pulling the paper backing away with one hand while cautiously reaching in with two fingers of her other hand.

She almost snatched them back again at once for there was something inside, something more than just the back of an oil painting. Even though that was why she'd done all this work, the confirmation was shocking . . .

Then the lights came blazing back on. She was pretty sure she hadn't left them on when she'd gone to Dublin . . . She swore, beginning to feel that the castle was playing with her. As if, now that she knew something was inside the painting, Deeprath had decided to give her the necessary illumination to accomplish the task.

"Fine!" she said aloud. And jumped at the echo of her own voice.

With anger fueling her curiosity, Carragh proceeded to remove the rest of the paper backing—with a little less care than before. Now that she knew it was not original, she didn't feel so bad about damaging it.

But having been trained to handle archival documents—part of her graduate studies—her native respect for the past combined with her training to ensure that she didn't just rip the backing off, despite the temptation. When the last of the glue finally came free, she screwed her eyes shut to release the tension she felt and shook her head to loosen her neck muscles. Then she opened her eyes and removed the backing entirely.

Inside, she found a sealed A4-size envelope. On it was written, in the hand Carragh now recognized as Lily Gallagher's: CLUE #1.

She knew she should take it straight to Aidan. Instead, she used the miniature long sword to rip open the top of the envelope. It contained four sheets of paper, the first page handwritten, the remaining ones photocopies of what looked, on first glance, to be newspaper articles. Carragh read the handwritten page.

Happy birthday, Cillian! What to get the viscount who has everything for his 50th birthday? How about a Gallagher mystery solved?

You know how fascinated I've become with the portrait of Jenny Gallagher/the Darkling Bride. Jenny's story had such a tragic end . . . but was it really the end? Jenny left her son, after all. And a writer-husband who seemed to decide if he could no longer be a husband, then he could no longer write, either.

Do you know that the literary world is still interested in Evan Chase's time at Deeprath? Do you know there are those who hope that some version of his final book will be found after all this time? And where else could such a search begin than here, my darling?

I will not tell you what I have found. But I have found . . . something. Of greatest interest to all the Gallaghers. And for your birthday, you will follow the trail I have laid for you. With sighs and rolling eyes and mock boredom, no doubt, but I know you too well to believe in them. You love my mysteries.

And here is the first—on the following pages, you will find the necessary hints to lead you to the next step and the next clue. Good luck, dearest!

Love always,
Your Lily

Her throat tight with emotion, Carragh lay the page down gently on the bed without looking at the photocopies. She knew about sadness, she knew about untimely death, she knew about unfinished business . . . but this was a voice speaking from the grave. She didn't know how close to his fiftieth birthday Cillian Gallagher had died, but clearly he had never made it to the first clue of his wife's whimsical fantasy of a gift. Carragh was interested in Victorian violence and its aftermath. But there was more recent violence here, the kind that still wreaked its way amongst the living, leaving behind children damaged by early grief and fear. If she had known that searching for Evan Chase's lost manuscript would entwine her in the lives of those Gallaghers still living—

Who was she kidding?

Her native honesty brought that sentimental train of thought to an abrupt end. Even if she had known, she would still have gone looking. For her, there was something talismanic about the lost Darkling Bride story. And for certain the castle seemed interested in her search. The castle—or someone in it. With the lights back on, Carragh knew her sensitivity to the possibility of spirits had as much to do with her dislike of darkness as any actual direction from the beyond.

If the beyond were going to speak to her, then why would it be in the voices of strangers and not that of the woman whose death was so intimately tangled with her own early life? Was that why she was so stubbornly involved in this house and this search? Because if she was going to hear the voices of the dead, better those of strangers than her own?

CHAPTER TWENTY-FOUR

June 1880

DIARY OF JENNY GALLAGHER

15 June 1880

Several years ago my father gave me a volume of Tennyson, including "The Lady of Shallot." "I am half sick of shadows," says Tennyson's lady. For five years shadows have been the essence of my life. Until I stepped into the lamplight of the library and saw Evan looking at me as though I were . . . real. Solid. Flesh and blood, not fear and sorrow. And because of him, I stayed solid for months and months until I had dared to think myself well.

That I am not—that I will never be—wholly well is the bitterest pill I have faced since my mother's death, and if it had not been for Evan, I might well have stayed in the tower for months out of sheer lassitude. As I have so often before. But my husband—my husband, my mind sings in an echo of remembered joy—would not let them keep him from me.

Evan will pull me from the shadows.

At first Evan did little but sit by the bed and hold Jenny's hand. For the first few days, she was only hazily aware of his presence, wrapped as she was in laudanum and the fog that apparently followed her episodic outbursts of mania. But then he began to talk, trying to reach through the fog and wrap her in a storied web of his own design. And when he stopped talking, her eyelids fluttered open and she said, "Tell me more."

He blinked back tears, and obligingly continued his stories. He had legends from all over the world to tell her—from as far as the China Sea and the African deserts and the American plains. Evan's success and popularity lay in the fact that he was a master storyteller.

Eight days after their return from Dublin she got up from her bed voluntarily so that, when Evan came, she was waiting for him in the chair in which he usually sat.

He kissed her, gently, and hesitated when she pressed herself against him. "I do not want to hurt you, love," he murmured.

"You won't. Take me downstairs, Evan. Please."

He wavered, but paternal and medical warnings avail little against both love and instinct. So he took her to bed for the first time in the room with the coffered ceiling and blue-and-white linens that Jenny had so carefully decorated for this purpose weeks before.

Afterward, lying twined together, she answered the questions he had not asked her. "I have had these spells since I was thirteen. My mother was also . . . unstable. She died when I was ten. My father has had two wives since then, you know, both of whom died in childbirth along with their girl children. Finally he decided he was cursed. He put all his efforts into ensuring I would remain healthy enough to marry and breed."

"That sounds rather cold."

"He loves me, I know. But he loves the Gallagher in me more than the Jenny. When I bear you a son, Evan—when I bear him a grandson—he will leave us be."

"And what then? When you can have what you want, my love, what will it be?"

She sat up and took his face in her hands, her black hair spilling over bare shoulders. "I want you. I want children. I love Deeprath and the mountains, I do. But I want a chance to love it on my own terms! Without my father and everyone waiting and watching me all the time. Maybe I will have to start small. Maybe I cannot go far, or for long. But I want to try, dearest. I don't want you to lock me up in your head the way everyone else has. Let me be Jenny. And if Deeprath is truly the only place I can be well, then when we have a son, I will ask my father to go away and leave the castle to us." She paused, then added in a rush, "Oh, Evan, I'm truly sorry that you are getting more than you bargained for. I know you must have wanted a London wife, a woman more fit for society . . ."

For all his storytelling glibness, Evan was never careless with his words to her. "I swear to you, Jenny, that my first care for the rest of my life will be your happiness and well-being. I will strive to never act against your will. And if Deeprath is to be our home forever, you must not mourn that on my account."

He kissed her and whispered, "Wherever you are, my bride, is home."

CHAPTER TWENTY-FIVE

Carragh woke still undecided about when and how to approach Aidan with his mother's unsolved treasure hunt. She decided to wait and see what sort of mood he was in this morning. Probably not a great one, if dinner last night was anything to go by. As had become her habit, she went straight to the library to avoid the family.

When she opened the library door, she heard voices.

"It's the story of Seamus and Eileen and a magical donkey who takes them on adventures."

"Like Harry Potter?"

"By no means. This is Ireland, child, we have stories enough of our own. Does Harry Potter have Finn and the Salmon of Knowledge?"

For a disconcerting minute, Carragh thought her ghosts had manifested themselves in a discussion of children's fantasy literature. But before she cleared the concealing shelves, she had identified the speakers: Nessa and the skeptical Ellie.

At the long library table, Nessa sat with Ellie on one side and Kate on the other, a book held with obvious care in the old woman's hands. She looked up at Carragh's arrival and, surprisingly, smiled. "Perhaps you can convince Ellie of the story's merit, Miss Ryan. Do you know *The Turf-Cutter's Donkey*?"

"By Patricia Lynch," Carragh answered readily. "Yes, my grandmother read it to me often. I still have the copy."

"And you enjoyed it?" Nessa slanted her eyes in Ellie's direction, a hint of the answer she wanted.

"Very much. My favorite was always the talking teapot."

"See, girls?" Nessa asked. "Just because a story isn't new or popular doesn't mean you won't like it. I used to read this to your mother when she was little. Perhaps she will do the same for you."

Kate, who seemed to speak only when she was prepared to render judgment, said, "Will you read it to us?"

It was impossible to miss the surprise and grief and affection that briefly painted Nessa's face. But her voice never faltered. "Perhaps. But now it's time for you to report to your au pair. You must never keep others waiting, particularly those whose livelihoods depend on you."

Surely that speech went right over the heads of the two little girls, but it gave Carragh a glimpse into Nessa's sense of responsibility. It was easy to look at her and deride the upper-class arrogance, the privileges of wealth and family that she clung to so stubbornly. But there were virtues to the old aristocracy: virtues of duty and public service and an obligation to use one's position for good. Those virtues might be well hidden—and did not erase centuries of a problematic class system—but Carragh considered for the first time that Aidan must have gotten his sense of responsibility from somewhere. And no matter how wonderful his parents had been, Aidan spent almost half his childhood with Nessa as his guardian and guide.

When Nessa did not follow the girls out of the library, Carragh said awkwardly, "I was going to work, but I can come back later if you like."

"Not at all. I was simply going through the shelves of children's books to see what might be worth keeping. For the girls. Someday Ellie and Kate may wish to own a piece of Deeprath." Nessa stroked the cover of the Lynch book, with its depiction of two innocent children and one slightly alarming donkey. Her hand was shaky. "I wish Aidan understood that I am not trying to force him to hold onto the castle for pride's sake. I fear he will regret it someday. A day when he will wish he could walk in the steps of his parents, could touch the walls that hold all his own earliest happiness, a day when Aidan will realize that people and places can be inextricably bound."

Nessa laid down the book and fixed Carragh with her usual cool expression. "But I suppose the young rarely understand such things."

"I understand it," Carragh retorted. "I know you think I cannot have any real family feeling since I do not share their genetics, but I loved my grandmother and her Dublin house as much as anyone could."

A moment's silence, then Nessa said, "I did not realize I had insulted you quite so much. I apologize."

Carragh pulled out Ellie's discarded chair and sat. "I'm actually having the opposite problem with my family. My grandmother died in January, and she left me the house that has been in her family for two hundred years. My parents want me to sell it. They think there's too much work that needs doing, that I'm in over my head, that I shouldn't be saddled with a relic of the past."

"And what do you think, Miss Ryan?"

"I love it," Carragh said simply. "I love everything about it. Well, maybe not the plumbing or the rotting roof, but every time I open the door, I'm surrounded by love. Not just my grandmother's, but family I never even met. Those who died generations ago. It doesn't feel right to walk away and let strangers invade their home."

Nessa regarded her thoughtfully, as though seeing her for the first time. "I underestimated you. I thought I was bringing you to Deeprath to catalog books. But if you could speak to Aidan as you just spoke to me . . . It's no secret young men pay rather more attention to attractive young women than they do to ancient relatives. Perhaps he would listen to you."

Carragh didn't know which part of that was most surprising— that Nessa would contemplate using her to change Aidan's mind or that she considered her attractive enough to do it. Picking her way cautiously, she said, "I doubt Aidan could be persuaded to do anything he doesn't want to do."

"And that is why, for centuries, women have learned how to make men think that a particular course of action was their own idea."

She tried—and failed—to imagine manipulating Aidan Gallagher into keeping his family castle. She couldn't even convince her own family that keeping the Dublin house was a good idea.

Nessa rose with the aid of the cane that had been leaning against the table. She picked up *The Turf-Cutter's Donkey* and handed it to Carragh.

"Would you like me to reshelve it for you?" Carragh asked.

"No, my dear. It's a gift. I think you will appreciate it more than the girls."

"I can't take this—"

"It's a first edition, and signed by the author. Valuable, I suppose, but you seem a girl to treasure a book for something other than its price. It pleases me to think of it in your grandmother's home."

Carragh fumbled her way through a thank-you that Nessa waved off. The old woman paused at the door, and looked slowly around the library with the expression of someone seeing more than was actually there. As though the past had unwrapped itself and spread its layers over bookshelves and cabinets and leather and paper. Did she ever see Jenny Gallagher? Carragh wondered. Or did Nessa have other ghosts?

Aidan woke with an unaccustomed hangover, as much a result of last night's tension-filled dinner as the wine he'd drunk. Wine, and half a bottle of scotch. No wonder he felt like shit. And it wasn't as though drinking had erased any of the unpleasantness. He remembered clearly the sarcasm and malice he'd directed at his sister, and wondered just how far he'd have gone if not interrupted by the blackout. Was he really prepared to accuse Kyla of—

His mind snapped shut on the unspoken word and propelled him out of his bedroom looking for distraction. He found himself in the kitchen, as though he were a ten-year-old once again taking refuge from Kyla's tantrums with the equable Mrs. Bell.

It seemed all children had the same impulse, because he found his nieces elbow deep in bread dough and chattering like magpies. Until they noticed him. It was insulting how fast they shut their mouths and stared at him as though he were a strange dog who might bite.

Mrs. Bell spoke as if everyone was behaving normally. "Make room, girls. Your Uncle Aidan has shaped a few hot cross buns in his time. Let's see if he remembers."

He stood frozen for a moment, but his godmother fixed him with a fierce stare until he joined them. Kate continued to watch him sideways, but Ellie was as naturally friendly and outgoing as her mother had been and her reserve didn't last long.

"Is it true you lock up people in London?" she asked. "Like murderers?"

"I investigate art crimes. Thieves who steal paintings and things like that."

Ellie was unimpressed. "That doesn't sound very dangerous."

Leaving aside the threats of mobsters and terrorists who financed their work through stolen art, but he wasn't going to explain that to a nine-year-old. "It's not. Mostly talking to people and writing things down."

"Like the police who came here about Gran and Granddad," she said matter-of-factly.

"Right," he agreed cautiously. What had Kyla told her children about their grandparents? Enough, it seemed.

It was Kate, finally speaking, who surprised him thoroughly. "I heard Mama say you want the police to take Papa away."

"I don't—where did you hear that?"

Maire Bell shushed Aidan quietly, reminding him to gentle his tone. But the six-year-old answered straightaway. "I'm very small. There's lots of places here to hide and listen."

Like the minstrel's gallery above the Great Hall and various alcoves that might once have been meant for prayer or private study or even—because the past was not always so different—for spying. Aidan had made use of them in his own childhood. It was how he'd learned so much about Philip and Kyla and his parents' dislike of the relationship during that last summer.

One memory in particular came to his mind now, an afternoon spent wandering around the lesser-used parts of the castle. It had been raining for three days and he was bored. There was a little-used staircase in the Tudor wing that served only to join the portrait-filled long gallery with the private chapel above. Commissioned by a long-ago viscount for the delicate French Catholic wife who was now rumored to haunt the music room, the angular stairs were nearly hidden by the wooden fretwork that rose from ceiling to floor. Aidan had spent a listless half hour counting the different animals carved into the fretting when he was startled by voices below.

"They just want to keep the perfect family image intact." It was Philip Grant, whom Aidan did not like, no matter how often the young man turned a forced joviality in his direction.

He peered between the fretwork, knowing that as long as he remained still—and they didn't decide to use the stairs—he would be unseen by those below. Kyla was with Philip, of course. She clung to their father's intern whenever she could manage, with an eager air of wanting to please that made Aidan squirm.

"They don't need me for their image," Kyla said now. "Maybe two or three hundred years ago when daughters were needed to make necessary alliances. But today, all they need is the heir. I'm nothing but an inconvenience—and I can be extremely inconvenient when I want to."

Philip's low laugh was swallowed up when they kissed. Aidan squeezed his eyes shut. *Go away*, he implored them silently. Kyla would never forgive him if she knew he'd been watching.

They did, finally, go away. But not before he heard Philip say something else about their parents. "Why run away when you can get everything you want with just a little patience?"

"Uncle Aidan?" His full awareness snapped back into the kitchen, with two pairs of bright, suspicious eyes watching him. Ellie had taken over again as the sisters' voice. "If you arrest Papa, does that mean we'll never see him again?"

Dark, bitter grief flooded him. He hadn't asked for any of this. If they'd all just left him alone in London, none of this need be said aloud. "I can't arrest anyone in Ireland," he told his nieces bluntly. "It's nothing to do with me."

With that half-lie, Aidan escaped, leaving behind a disapproving godmother and two little girls who would probably never dare speak to him again. How had he become this man who snapped at children and whose only remaining family members either disliked him or didn't even know him? This wasn't him. And it wasn't who he wanted to be.

Leaving aside the question of who he did want to be, Aidan headed for the drawing room. But discovered he was not the first one to have that idea. Kyla sat on the Louis XIV settee, in black trousers and cashmere jumper, her wavy hair around her shoulders and a glass in her hand. Within reach stood a bottle of cabernet.

She looked at him without surprise. "Hiding?"

"Drinking?" he shot back, and instantly regretted it.

"Only because the men in my life are unmitigated bastards."

"So send Philip away."

"Will you go with him?" she asked sweetly.

"I'm nothing like Philip."

"Aloof, arrogant, dismissive—"

"Don't be ridiculous."

"More interested in talking to a pretty outsider than your own family. Ready to sell your birthright to the highest bidder. How can you be so eager to get rid of Deeprath?"

"How can you not be? This place is full of nothing but memories."

"Exactly! Every single happy memory of my life—save two—happened here. Why wouldn't I want to remember the years before my world ended?" She banged down the heavy crystal glass, so unsuitable for wine, and he saw tears in her eyes.

He regarded her silently, then ventured, "Ellie and Kate?"

"What?"

"Your two non-Deeprath happy memories."

"Yes. But even their births were bittersweet at best, for I had no one to be happy with me. Philip despises hospitals and mess, Nessa cared only that they were not boys. And all I got from my brother were flowers no doubt ordered by an assistant."

Aidan would have liked to deny it, but couldn't. He knew he was a rotten brother, and a worse uncle. But he didn't know how to go about explaining. Until he'd come back to Ireland, he hadn't realized just quite what a bastard he'd chosen to be in cutting off all that was left of his family. He had thought he was merely being practical.

"No witty comeback, brother? No protestation of unstained innocence? You must be feeling rather smug about the fact that you are the only one here not under suspicion of murder."

There, at last, was the word hanging between them. *Murder.* "I don't think it will come to that. There's no way to prove Mother didn't fall instead of jump, and as persistent as DI McKenna is, I imagine the Gallagher name will win out in the end. If they can't blame it on outsiders, then better to blame everything on the American wife and consign it all to history."

With more soberness than her drinking indicated, Kyla said, "Mother did not commit suicide." His sister looked away, as though seeing something in the farthest reaches of the drawing room.

When she looked at him again, Aidan felt a thread of that sibling bond that had frayed so long ago. Both Kyla's face and voice were bare of irony, sarcasm, bitterness . . . only the flatness of truth. And loss. "She would never have left us."

For a handful of breaths the two of them were joined in perfect understanding, and Aidan knew that whatever he asked now, Kyla would answer.

Did Philip kill them? Did you help? Why can't I remember when and where I saw you that day?

He couldn't form the words. And with a slight twitch of her lips, his sister retreated from the moment's intimacy and the chance was lost.

After a second night at the Glendalough Hotel, Sibéal pulled up to Deeprath five minutes before her nine o'clock appointment. She'd managed to dash into Wicklow town the night before and pick up clean underwear, a black T-shirt, and a knit skirt, figuring that cheap was better than wearing the same clothes three days in a row.

Was it her imagination, or did the castle manage to look more hostile every day? Logically she knew it was simply pressure and the weather getting to her, the muggy air during the day giving way to thunderstorms at night. She certainly hadn't imagined the downed tree lying parallel to the gravel drive she'd bumped down today—it seemed the wind was battering the castle.

Logic also told her that the scene-setting didn't matter, that her techniques and her questions and every other aspect of this case would proceed the same whether she was interviewing people in a suburban villa or behind castle walls. But logic was wrong. People were people, yes. But people also grew up in families and in communities, and for the Gallaghers, Deeprath Castle lay at the heart of both. Crime—plural—could be quantified. Crimes—individual— could not. Whatever had happened here all those years ago had happened because of the place as much as the people.

How that applied to Carragh Ryan, she wasn't sure. The woman was perplexing, and Sibéal took the unusual step of admitting it to her once she'd been shown to the library. The librarian—archivist? temp worker?—certainly looked as though she'd been working for several hours already. Her hair was pulled back messily, showing the layers of jewel-toned colors beneath the surface black, and her eyes were red-rimmed. Too much reading? Too little sleep? Tears? Perhaps all three.

"I must confess that I don't know what to make of you and your presence here, Miss Ryan."

"I'm just doing a job."

"What is it you normally do? Unless bouncing from castle to castle looking at old books is a career path I'm unaware of."

"I wish," Carragh said with feeling. "My degrees are in English Literature and Irish Studies. I've cobbled together work since leaving Trinity three years ago. Internships at a few specialist libraries, some temp secretarial positions, but mostly freelance editing. Helping writers get their manuscripts into readable shape is becoming more of a thing with the rise of independent publishing."

"But you prefer castles."

She shrugged. "This one, at least."

"Because of the Gallaghers?"

"Sort of."

Sibéal cocked her head invitingly. She was not taking notes, considering this was little more than a conversation to assuage her curiosity. It seemed to put Carragh at ease, because the American went on to elaborate. "Have you heard of the Darkling Bride?"

"Someone mentioned it. Kyla, I think. A legend from the mountains?"

"Yes. But more relevantly, that legend brought a Victorian writer here in 1879. He came to write a book, and ended up marrying the daughter and heiress of the house."

"So he wrote a book on the Darkling Bride?"

Carragh's smile was full of mischief. "That is the question, Inspector. If you're interested in cold cases, they don't come much colder. Evan Chase wrote an outline that he sent to his publisher in

London, but nothing more than that was ever seen. His wife had a breakdown after the birth of their only child and eventually committed suicide. Evan returned to England afterward but never produced the promised book, or anything else, before his death ten years later."

It was no accident that Sibéal was a good detective—she could read people. There was no mistaking true enthusiasm. "So that's what brought you here. You're hoping to find the missing book."

The mischief died. "A faint hope. A child's hope. I'm just here to make lists."

I don't believe that for a minute, Sibéal wanted to say. "And is there anything in these lists you're making that can give me insight into the Gallagher family?"

"They're rich, they're old-blooded, and they're territorial," Carragh answered flippantly. "But I'm sure you've worked all that out for yourself."

"Any information about the previous viscount and his wife?"

"No."

Carragh Ryan was a very bad liar. "So no sign of the missing journal Aidan Gallagher has been looking for? The one police never found?"

"No."

Sibéal studied her, trying to decide what pressure points would work. "You know, Miss Ryan, a crime like murder is not a discrete event. Its roots reach into the past, and its effects ripple far into the future. Just because you don't know anything about the murders directly doesn't mean you don't know something useful."

"I don't," she retorted firmly. "And you do not have to tell me about the effects of murder. I have lived them every day since I was four years old."

Sibéal's eyebrows shot up. "May I ask—"

"No. It has nothing to do with Glendalough or Gallaghers or even Ireland, which makes it none of your business. If you've gotten all the gossip off me you wanted, then I have work to do." She stood up, notebook in hand, to tackle another shelf.

Amused and intrigued, Sibéal left her to the library, realizing only long afterward that she had failed to press Carragh Ryan on the subject of Philip Grant.

When the library door closed, Carragh stopped pretending to look at whatever shelf she was standing by and slid to the floor. With her back resting against the volumes (she only hoped they weren't irreplaceably valuable), she dropped her notebook and rested her head on her knees, arms wrapped around her legs. And though she knew she should feel guilty about not telling DI McKenna about the notes and letters she'd discovered in the last forty-eight hours, it was her own past that was swamping her just now. The past so casually summoned by McKenna's description of murder: "Its roots reach into the past, and its effects ripple far into the future."

Twenty-four years, she thought bleakly. I haven't been that little girl for twenty-four years and I never will be—never can be—again. So why is everyone determined to make me go back there? Even those who are supposed to protect me?

It was her mother who'd started it. Anne Ryan believed in plain speaking, a judicial trait not always comfortable for her children. Especially her only daughter. One week—just one week!—after the death of Eileen Ryan, Carragh's mother had sat her down and said bluntly, "I have a letter for you from your grandmother." At Carragh's instant look of shock and hope, Anne had corrected herself. "I'm sorry, I mean your Chinese grandmother."

Carragh's reply was instant. "The one who never even tried to stop your adoption of me? I'm not interested."

Which was exactly the way Carragh liked it. She had a family, what did she need with people who'd never even met her? And when her mother had once lamented in an argument during college that, "Maybe if I'd given birth to you I'd understand you better," Carragh burst into genuine laughter and hugged her. "The fact that you can drive me crazy faster than anyone else on this planet absolutely guarantees that you're my mom," she'd assured Anne.

So Carragh had looked her mother in the eyes earlier this year and said a firm "No, thank you" to the proffered letter from a stranger. She didn't want to read it. When her mother tried to talk to her about it, she didn't want to hear what was in the letter or why it had been written now. And since her family's return to Boston after Eileen Ryan's funeral, Carragh had steadfastly avoided the conversation.

She was aware, however, that her mother had slipped the letter inside one of her favorite books when she left. She had looked at it more than once—at the expensive handmade paper and the precision of the fountain pen strokes spelling out in English her original name: *Mei-Lien*. Her parents had retained it as her middle name, but Carragh never thought of herself that way.

Her mother told her it was a mistake. The therapist they'd made her go to in high school told her it was a mistake. *The only way out is through, pain is fear leaving the body* . . . All the platitudes written by people who had no idea what it was like. Finally, when she'd had enough, she raged at her parents one night at the dinner table, "If you don't like who I am, then why the hell did you bother to bring me home? I like being me. Just let me do that!"

She knew, because she was not stupid, that wasn't really the point. She could even concede, at her most reasonable, that her mother was not wrong. You probably couldn't hide away an entire person inside you forever. But so far, so good.

Until that damn letter had arrived from Hong Kong. She had coped badly after her grandmother's funeral and her family's departure from Ireland—hence the clubbing and drinking—so Deeprath Castle appeared a shining refuge. A chance to immerse herself in someone else's painful past. To find the answers to someone else's questions.

Except that someone else had turned out to be Aidan Gallagher.

And Kyla. Two children who suffered their violent loss later than she did, but who had not had a large and warm family ready to sweep them in afterward. Only Nessa.

"What are you doing down there?"

Would Aidan ever stop being able to sneak up on her? And would she ever stop jumping when he did, managing to look both surprised and astonishingly clumsy at the same time?

A woman laughed in her ear. Carragh's head whipped around as she was halfway to standing up, and the next thing she knew, Aidan had to put his hand out to keep her from falling at his feet.

"Are you all right?"

Did you hear that disembodied laughter? was not a question she wanted answered just now. So she said crossly, "I was fine until you loomed over me. I was working."

"On the floor," he noted without inflection.

"Every single bookshelf has floor-level books." She glared at him, daring him to contradict her.

He didn't. "Look, Carragh, what I wanted to say is that this assignment with the library . . . everything's become more complicated, obviously. I've put off the National Trust for a few weeks. They didn't like it, but there's really nothing they can do about it. That means there's no longer an imminent deadline and—"

"And you're firing me."

Startled, he opened those irritatingly blue eyes wider and said, "No. But I thought it only right to give you the chance to back out. I mean . . ." He waved his hand, indicating the thousands of volumes around them. "This was never going to be an easily defined job. Mostly, Nessa wanted to make sure nothing extremely valuable was overlooked."

"And you? What did you want, besides answers?"

"To ensure that any answers discovered did not further destroy my family's reputation. But unless someone's going to take issue with the admittedly racist and imperialistic views of my traveling ancestors and their accounts of other cultures, there's nothing in this library I need fear. Whatever I was looking for, it's not here."

He shook his head once, then—unexpectedly—smiled at her. "However, you were hired for a specific term and I certainly intend to pay you for the whole of it. So if you were of the mind to continue doing what you could in here, I would be very grateful."

Her hesitation had nothing to do with the request, for she would have stayed even if he didn't want to pay her. Nothing drove her like curiosity. But how much should she tell him?

In for a penny, in for a pound. "Aidan, what if I told you that I found something that may be pertinent to your search? Something about—something written by—your mother?"

He would never be a man to lightly lose control. His cheekbones tightened, but he said calmly enough, "I would say it depends on what exactly she wrote."

He was afraid that his mother had done something wrong, wasn't he? "It's not like that," she rushed to assure him. "And it's not her missing journal. It's probably nothing at all to do with their deaths, just a project she was putting together. A gift for your father. All about Jenny Gallagher and Evan Chase and the Darkling Bride."

"In that case, Carragh Ryan, I say lead on."

Aidan stared at the painting laid flat on Carragh's bed, the doubled woman making his head spin as she/they always had. "I'm pretty sure I need you to say that again," he pronounced carefully.

She flushed, but did not retreat from her unusual statement. "I think the castle wanted me to find this."

"Because the castle . . . ?"

"Took the painting off the wall. Three times. If I hadn't been yelled at by Nessa for it, I probably would have explored the why sooner. But she had me fearing I'd be locked up by the National Art Police."

"Not really the type of thing we do," he answered automatically.

"All right. I agree, it sounds wild. Maybe it's not the castle. Maybe it's intuition or . . . I don't know. Whatever. The point is, we've got an envelope labeled clue number one and an outline of the quest she was setting your father. I know this was on her mind not long before . . . everything . . . because she also wrote to my grandmother for help."

Aidan shook his head as though clearing it of bees or wasps. Or something equally odd and stinging. "What the hell does your grandmother have to do with this?"

With a postgrad degree from Trinity, she knew how to put together information logically and persuasively. But that skill had apparently deserted her tonight, as words and explanation and tangents tumbled out one over another, each almost more unbelievable than the last.

"So," he finally interrupted. "Let me get this straight. My mother came to your grandmother trying to track down information on my ancestors in the 1880s."

"Well, really, she was looking for stuff about Evan Chase—"

"Who was married to Jenny Gallagher. Yes, I got that part, thank you. May I see those letters?"

Aidan thought he sounded perfectly normal as he asked, but she shot him a glance of concern as she pulled a file folder out of the top desk drawer. Before she could hand it over, however, her face changed. She let the cover fall open so that the inside could be seen . . .

Nothing. An empty file folder. Carragh turned back to the desk, searching first the drawer she'd pulled it out of, then all the others. Next was her bag, which she ended up dumping on the bed. More nothing. Whatever letters she had found, they were no longer there.

"Aidan, I swear to you, I'm not making this up."

"Why would you? I can think of much easier ways to either bribe or torture a man. I believe you."

"Then where are they?"

"You said the castle wanted you to find the—" He flicked his fingers at the portrait. "—treasure hunt. Maybe the castle didn't want you examining too closely the letters to your grandmother." The castle, the policeman in him thought, or someone in it.

"I took notes on the letters. I can give you the basics. And the dates—I noted the dates they were written."

She gave Aidan her notebook and he scanned the list of dates. The last one was 26 August 1992, and the breath caught in his throat. He had to clear it before he could speak.

"This was written ten days before the murders."

"I know."

"Did you also know that my father was murdered the day before his fiftieth birthday? Just one day before, it seems, my mother intended to lead him to some sort of Gallagher family secret. That seems more than coincidental to me." His head was spinning, but the thought of doing something—anything—made him feel a tiny bit better. Especially when the path in question had been laid by his mother. "What do you say, Carragh? Would you like to go on a treasure hunt?"

CHAPTER TWENTY-SIX

"I've always hated riddles." Carragh moved to shove her chair back from the library table—except the chair weighed maybe forty pounds and so barely rocked on its legs before settling back. Great, now the castle was mocking her melodramatic gestures. *You're not so impressive*, the library seemed to say. *No hiding behind theatrical emotions here.* In her imagination, the library had the voice of a Catholic school nun, just as her primrose bedroom sounded like the kind of friend who was always coaxing you into dangerous situations.

She was pretty sure Aidan's cough was an attempt to cover his laughter. He sat next to her, the four pages of the first clue spread before them on the table, with notes and highlights scribbled by both of them that so far had done little to advance their understanding.

"My mother loved them," Aidan explained. "Riddles, puzzles, games. Every Christmas, she hid at least one of our gifts somewhere in the house and we had to follow the clues to find it. Just like this."

"Then, please, solve it for me." Take that, Deeprath, she thought spitefully. Just try to take my sarcasm away.

For no apparent reason, a book fell off the far end of the table, with a distinctly insulting thud. Seriously? Carragh thought crossly at . . . whatever. Whoever. *You're being childish,* she told herself.

Aidan looked briefly in the direction of the fallen book, then returned to the papers. "Here," he said, putting his finger on the first photocopied newspaper article.

DUBLIN WEEKLY NATION
May 1880

Marriage: On Thursday the 20th ult., at St. patrick's Cathedral, Dublin, Mr. Evan Chase of LOndon to Lady Jenny GallaghEr of County Wicklow, only child of michael, Viscount Gallagher, and the late Aiofe Gallagher. Mr. Chase will append his wife's surname, as she is the sole inheritor of the Gallagher estates.

Carragh looked dutifully once more at the two lines she had already committed to memory. "If you're telling me that your mother intended your father to take this hunt to St. Patrick's in Dublin—"

"No," he cut in impatiently. "That's not the rules. The games always took place inside the castle. Look at each letter, Carragh. One at a time."

"Are you this annoying at work?" she grumbled. As though he were trying to teach a four-year-old to read, Aidan's finger moved from letter to letter, pausing at *St. Patrick's.* When she said nothing, his finger tapped beneath the name. "Look, Carragh."

"The p is blurry," she said.

"No. It's been altered. Turned into a lowercase p."

She studied it doubtfully. "Really? How can you tell?"

"Find the next one."

She rolled her eyes, but the second letter was easier to identify. "The first o in London. It's been capitalized."

"Yes."

"So you can say something positive." The retort was instinctive;

already her eyes skimmed ahead and caught the next two. "Capital E in Gallagher and lowercase m in Michael." Her tongue was quicker than her brain and she said the word before she consciously knew it. "Poem."

Triumphantly, she grinned at Aidan, and he smiled back. *Please stop doing that,* she almost said. He must have been perfectly aware that his smile could make the susceptible drop in their tracks.

"So, *poem,*" she repeated hastily. "There's more, I take it?"

The second article capitalized an entire word—OF—and the third article capitalized THE. On to the fourth and final article, the opinion piece from London that had followed the tragic death of Jenny Gallagher and Evan's departure from Ireland.

THE ILLUSTRATED LONDON NEWS
15 September 1883

We have it on good authority that Mr. Evan Chase-Gallagher, noted folklorist and author, has returned to England's shores following his sojourn of four years in Ireland. Little could the author have expected such heights of joy and depths of pain as he has endured since he last crossed the Irish Sea. Marriage, fatherhood . . . to **B**e followed so shortly by the extremity of g**R**ief known only to those whose loved ones have perished in suspicious circumstances.

Lady Jenny Gallagher possessed, by the accounts of all who knew her, a brilliant wit to match her dark Irish beauty, as well as the noted charm of her people. But such brilliance too often exacts a cost, and it is well known that the lady suffered an unquiet mind after the b**I**rth of her son. The strain on her husban**D**, cut off from his London home in mountainous isolation, we can only guess at. That he has published nothing since his marriage is, perhaps, telling.

We understand the inquest to have been generous in their verdict of accidental death, and hope that his wife's Christian burial will work its peace upon Mr. Chase. WE look forward to once more reading his learned and captivating prose and sharing in the talent that has seen him compared to both Mr. Dickens and Mr. Trollope.

His son remains in Ireland, to be raised by his grandfather at Deeprath Castle.

Carragh raised her head, met Aidan's gaze. "Bride. The Poem of the Bride."

"Exactly."

"Well," she said drily, trying to damp down the excitement that made her want to believe they were sharing something beyond an intellectual puzzle, "I hope you know what that means, because I haven't the faintest idea."

"I do, in fact, know what it means. Or I'm pretty sure." He stood up and looked thoughtfully at the rows of shelves. "Tell me you've cataloged the section on local legends."

Carragh reached for her notebook and flipped to the version of a table of contents she'd made for herself. "I think so," she mused. "I remember looking at quite a few volumes about St. Kevin and the founding of Glendalough. Would that be what you're looking for?"

"That section, yes."

"Second bay on the left. Shelves three, four, and half of five. I numbered from the top down."

"Come help me," he said.

Once on the ladder, she asked, "What am I looking for exactly? Unless you want me to pull down every volume?"

"We're looking for an old book—"

"You don't say."

"You needn't be rude. I remember my mother reading me the poem at bedtime . . ." Aidan closed his eyes, and Carragh took the chance to study his face. From her angle sideways and above, his closed lashes were annoyingly—seductively—long and thick, and his mouth looked like it had been made for the precise purpose of kissing.

A laugh in her ear, a laugh that was now becoming familiar. But who was laughing at her? She could only hope it wasn't Lily Gallagher, considering the improper thoughts Carragh was beginning to have about her son.

"Red cloth binding," he murmured. "Gold-embossed griffin and round tower on the front. Vanity published by an ancestor, I think. At least someone connected to the family. Tradition says the poem was written by Evan Chase after his wife's death."

What? Carragh nearly shrieked aloud, managing to swallow it at the last second. *You've had something written by Chase in this library that no one's ever seen? And you didn't bother to tell me?* Except why would he, since Aidan didn't know that was more than half the reason she'd accepted this job in the first place.

With increased motivation, Carragh took out every book on the third shelf that looked remotely as though it might have been red at some point in its life. But it was Aidan who finally found it on the fifth shelf, tucked between a monograph on Wicklow mountain goats and a history of the rebel Michael Dwyer.

"This is it," he said, fingertips caressing the imprint of the family griffin.

Carragh nearly jumped off the ladder in her eagerness, expecting to follow Aidan to the table. But he simply opened the book where they stood in the bay and carefully turned pages until he reached the endpapers.

"Interesting," he mused.

She could nearly have ripped the book out of his hands. Rising to her tiptoes, she put her hand on his left arm to pull it down. He obliged, tilting the book until she could see what he was looking at.

"It's handwritten?" she asked.

"I never knew that. Look, here at the bottom, it says: 'Copied 1892 by James Gallagher.'"

Hope surged, for surely a poem copied out by Evan's son was likely to have been composed by his father. Aidan began to read aloud. And as he did, every aspect of Deeprath Castle that had teased and taunted the edges of Carragh's awareness since she'd been here rushed in and twined around them as though they were standing in a storm of time and memory.

> *When mist grows thick and demons ride*
> *And all small things begin to hide*
> *Then cross your heart, eyes open wide*
> *To keep you from the Darkling Bride*
> *Her curse will let no secrets lie*
> *Between her and her vengeful pride*
> *Against the place where she did die:*
> *The Dark Bride of Deeprath.*

When Aidan finished all six stanzas, Carragh shivered. "This is what your mother considered appropriate bedtime reading for a child?"

"We lived in an eight-hundred-year-old castle. In Ireland. Ghosts and curses and tragedy are what our blood is made of."

At her skeptical and probably horrified expression, Aidan gave that particular half laugh of his. "More to the point, this is definitely the Poem of the Bride. And we were right—it's the second clue."

He held up the folded notepaper he had palmed while she was coming down the ladder. Inside was written: *Clue #2. Well done, darling.*

She wondered if he could hear his mother's voice as he read the words, and knew she would never dare ask. And then, for a moment, her mind slipped and she wondered if that was why she was afraid to open the letter from Hong Kong: because, when she read it, might she hear an echo of the voice that had been silenced so long before?

"Carragh?"

"Yes, sorry. Time to decipher the next riddle?"

"I think we should eat first. You're looking a bit drawn around the eyes."

"Because we've been deciphering twenty-year-old photocopies and examining hundred-year-old books for the last three hours."

He closed the red and gold book and held out his hand. "Food. And away from here, I think. There's a place I used to like in Laragh."

What could she say? He was, technically, her employer, and set the terms of her work. If he wanted to have lunch, they'd have lunch.

It was definitely not, in any shape or form, a date.

Upon Sibéal's return to Dublin Tuesday night, she'd fallen into bed and, unusually for her, slept without stirring until her alarm sounded at six. She rose with the sun, did a three-mile run along the Liffey, had a tense chat with Josh and a more amiable one with May before her daughter went to school, and was in her Phoenix Park office by eight-thirty. Where she was almost immediately summoned to Superintendent O'Neill's office.

"The Gallagher case," he said.

Feeling like a primary schooler giving her first oral report, Sibéal presented the pertinent information of the last five days.

"Good. By the by," O'Neill said when she had finished. "I've had a call from Theodore Grant, MP for Galway . . . Philip Grant's father."

Of course you have, she thought mordantly. She could guess what was coming.

"He is raising questions about your . . . technique. Seems to think you've been harassing his son."

"Sir—"

"And I told him to fuck off."

Her eyebrows shot up and O'Neill grimaced. "Not out loud. I'd never have been made superintendent if I couldn't play politics. But you're my officer, McKenna, not his, and if he'd known me at all he'd have known his call was practically the one thing guaranteed to make me keep this case running."

"Thank you, sir."

"Don't go thinking you can get away with the same attitude, mind. I've got both years and gender on you and I don't want a fine officer ruined because men don't like a woman asking questions and forming opinions. You can have until Monday, and then I'll need you to have reached some conclusions. Understood?"

It was Wednesday. Three days, plus the weekend. But no way was she going to complain. She'd come in this morning expecting to have it shut down at once. "Yes, sir."

He—almost—smiled at her before waving her off with a curt, "Get to work."

She grabbed Cullen and pulled him into her office. Before she could launch into a list of tasks, the sergeant said, "I've been on the phone with Forensics. Officially, they're still running tests. Unofficially, they think it likely that the marble cross found with the antiquities was indeed the weapon that killed Lord Gallagher."

"Great."

"And," Cullen continued with a cheeky grin, "I found something interesting in Philip Grant's past. Not financial—well, obviously we now know he hadn't stolen and sold the Gallagher antiquities—but intriguingly relevant. We know that he was at Deeprath interning for Lord Gallagher in 1992. But in 1991, Grant had been forced to leave Oxford because of a scandal with a dean's daughter. He was twenty, the girl was fourteen when he got her pregnant. 'Course they all hushed it up between them, but that's what brought him back to Ireland for university. And I don't imagine it was something he put on his résumé for Lord Gallagher."

"No," Sibéal said thoughtfully, mind spinning with possibilities. "No, I don't suppose Gallagher would have allowed him anywhere near his home—and his daughter—if he'd known all that. Kyla was fifteen . . . what if the Gallaghers found out about the Oxford scandal? Or worse—what if there was a repeat scandal in the making at Deeprath Castle? I could imagine tempers getting very heated over the seduction of one's daughter. Heated enough—"

"For murder? I agree. So what next, boss? Back to the castle?"

"Let's see if we can get Grant away from the Gallaghers. Phone him, will you? See if he'll be in town for business today or tomorrow . . . And Cullen?" She remembered the veiled hostility in Philip Grant's eyes when he'd brought up Carragh Ryan. "If he's reluctant, tell him we want to talk to him about the archivist working at Deeprath. Imply . . . well, whatever you think will work. I trust your instincts."

"Because I'm a man?"

"Because you're a damned good officer. Stop trolling for compliments and do it."

"Yes, ma'am."

She could get used to being in charge.

They walked to Laragh, just past the intersection of three roads, where they could see the Round Tower of Glendalough rising to the sky as it had for centuries. Aidan directed her into a white-fronted low building with a sign proclaiming it THE WICKLOW HEATHER.

"The first restaurant I ever came to. I was six and my mother brought me here for lunch. It was practice, to ensure I had good enough manners to dine in company with guests. Or Aunt Nessa, who was much scarier."

"How did it go?"

"Fine. Until she gave me a bite of wild game and chicken liver pâté. I promptly spit it back out. Fortunately, my mother always had a sense of humor. I didn't get to dine in company for another year, but once or twice a month she and I would come here together."

"Note to self: don't order the pâté."

Everything they ate was delicious: from garlic mushrooms to the grilled goat cheese on ciabatta that Carragh ate almost embarrassingly fast. Except, unlike some men, Aidan didn't make her self-conscious about her appetite. He was a very good conversationalist—

which shouldn't surprise her, what with the women he dated and the society events he attended—and told her a string of funny stories about fraudulent art appraisers and the perils of underground antiquities dealings. By tacit agreement, they didn't talk about Deeprath or the library or the book he'd slipped inside his coat pocket. She knew he'd brought it because he had not forgotten the missing letters from her bedroom. However they had vanished, he wouldn't risk losing more precious fragments of his mother's voice from the dead.

"Dessert?" Aidan asked, without the inflection she so often heard in men's voices, the implication that she either wouldn't, or shouldn't, indulge.

"You're paying?" she teased.

"Depends on what you order."

Just for that, she ordered the most expensive item—crème brûlée. Aidan chuckled and followed with Banoffee pie. "Nostalgia?" she asked.

"Mmmm. Not quite as good as our old cook used to make."

"Cook, housekeeper, boarding school . . . So what's it like growing up rich?"

"I don't know. Children never think to question their positions. It was just my life. A very country-house life, I now recognize. Lots of horses and hunting. Not that I was old enough to hunt when I left, but Nessa tried to get me interested in shooting waterfowl. But after the murder of my parents, I wasn't all that interested in killing anything." Aidan raised that eyebrow. "Your turn. What's it like growing up with three older brothers?"

"Loud." She considered. "Protective."

"I suppose that's natural."

"Is it an age thing or a gender thing? Did you protect Kyla because she's a girl, or did she protect you because you were younger?"

That darkened his face, and she knew she'd tread on a sensitive point. But he answered readily enough. "You wouldn't believe it by the behavior you've seen, but Kyla and I became very, very close after our parents died. We were at different schools, so it wasn't really a question of protection. But we understood one another in a way none of my friends ever could."

"I get that." *In ways you can't fathom. Because I never talk about any of it.*

"And then she married Philip, the minute she turned twenty-one and got control of her trust fund. And every year since it's gotten harder. How do I protect her from the life she's chosen, the life she wants?"

That was coming perilously close to discussing the many sins of Philip Grant, a conversation Carragh would give anything to avoid. So she dragged their pleasant lunch conversation back to the matter at hand. "I don't suppose there are any conveniently altered letters in the Bride poem this time?"

"That would be cheating," Aidan explained. "My mother never repeated clues in a single hunt."

"Then I hope you remember some of those hunts and know where to point us next."

"I would imagine she made my father's a little more difficult than she made a child's. I think we should make a copy of the poem for you to study. I've moved my father's personal safe into my room— I'll keep the book in there when we aren't using it."

"So you do think someone is going through my belongings?"

"Best to be safe. And Carragh—lock your door at night."

But that was only protection from the living. And whether or not a living hand had stolen her grandmother's letters, Carragh felt in her bones that the constant moving of the portrait in her room was intimately connected with forces that had been in the castle for much, much longer.

CHAPTER TWENTY-SEVEN

September 1991

Lily had never been much for New Year's resolutions. She was perfectly happy to dance and drink and kiss at midnight, but January always felt like a letdown month. Who had the energy for ambition in the middle of winter? She'd always felt that autumn, and the start of a new school year, was much more appropriate for taking stock of one's life.

Kyla was back at school, and Lily hoped she would have a good term. Her daughter had shot up five inches in the last year, and at five-foot-nine towered over most fourteen-year-old boys. Not that Kyla had wanted sympathy. "What would you know?" she'd cried to Lily. "You're the perfect size. You're the perfect *everything*."

As logic was clearly not going to be of any use in the matter, Lily kept her advice to herself and did her complaining to her husband in private. Cillian was unconcerned. "All girls go through hormonal hell at this age. All boys, for that matter. She'll come out the other side in a few years and we'll find her perfectly delightful."

Anyway, with Kyla boarding and Aidan working diligently at a Catholic primary school and with private tutors, Lily needed a new project. Her last one—lace-making—had ended with several dozen imperfect doilies and an abundance of handkerchiefs even Nessa wouldn't use. She knew she could go back to one of her previous interests, but that felt like failure. Surely there was something new, something useful, she could do . . .

The answer came as she was checking the conditions of the drapes and linens in various unused rooms. A very traditional task that she could never do without a faint sense of the ridiculous. She would have made a very bad Lady Gallagher in any age before this one, for she simply could not take herself seriously. Not like Nessa.

Lily was in the primrose bedroom of the Jacobean wing, running her hands the length of the drapes to feel for weak spots or loose stitching, when she caught herself staring at the portrait hanging by the door. She knew it well—the portrait commissioned by Jenny Gallagher for her marriage, with her own image reflected back in the pond as the Darkling Bride. Now there was a family story she would like to know more about. She'd heard a few references about the Gallagher connection to the old legend, mostly from Father Hennessy, but that was only gossip. What if she could find out more? What if, in that labyrinth of a library, there were answers?

And not just about the Bride. The Gallaghers had a long and varied history. Nessa made sure she knew all the best stories by heart. By Nessa's lights, that meant those that were the most flattering to the family. Lily didn't want historical gilding—she wanted the odd, the funny, the tragic. All the communal, messy memories that go into making up a family.

She knew just where to start. Leaving the rest of the curtains unexamined, Lily went straight to the Bride Tower.

It was a place the family mostly avoided. From the moment Kyla was born, Cillian had ensured that the two entrances were securely locked night and day. There had been no children in the castle since World War II, and no one wanted to take risks with centuries old wood and stone. Not to mention that the tower was creepy as hell.

That last phrase was Cillian's. Lily didn't find the remnants of Jenny Gallagher's life creepy so much as sad. Now those remnants were the perfect starting place for her new project: surely Jenny'd had some affinity for the Darkling Bride, or else why that doubled portrait?

Lily prowled the sitting room level, mind whirring with what she knew of the story. Jenny's isolated girlhood in the mountains, her father's only heir, the arrival of Evan Chase, followed by marriage, motherhood, and madness. Her fingers itched to start making notes . . . and that was before she'd even reached the top floor and its walls of words.

This was it. This was her project. And it would be a surprise for Cillian.

CHAPTER TWENTY-EIGHT

Sibéal and Cullen met Philip Grant in his Financial District office at eight o'clock Thursday morning. She wouldn't have pegged him as the work-all-hours type of man, but whatever Sergeant Cullen had said to him had sufficed. He was there and ready to talk. About Carragh Ryan.

With Cullen taking notes, it gave Sibéal pleasure to disabuse Philip of his notions of why they were there. "I don't care about what's happening at Deeprath today, Mr. Grant. Except insofar as it sheds light on what happened there in 1992. Miss Ryan was four years old at the time and living in the United States. She is not relevant to this case."

As she'd noted at Deeprath, he was handsome, in that sulky, well-groomed way of public school graduates who move through life without any awareness of their own privilege, believing they have earned their good fortune. Definitely not Sibéal's type. She might not be brilliant in her personal life, but at least she had the sense to avoid a man who would never truly think of anyone but himself.

And yet, she could see the appeal for some women. But if Philip Grant's resentment masked a personal interest in Carragh Ryan,

Sibéal would wager he didn't have a chance with her. Not with Aidan Gallagher around. There was a man too good-looking for his own good, but (mostly) without the arrogant edge of entitlement. Probably the traumas of his childhood had knocked the edges off some of those tendencies, though it seemed a harsh way to learn to think of others.

"You spoke to the police in 1992," Sibéal noted.

"I remember. I remember that I had nothing useful to contribute. And I remember quite clearly that you and I have already discussed this."

"You lied to them." She had gone over his statement word by word, and planned this attack with meticulous care.

And, as she almost could have bet, he neither denied nor confirmed. He simply said, "You think so?" He had a carefully schooled expression of cool disinterest, but his eyes flicked restlessly between Sibéal and Cullen.

"When asked about your internship with Gallagher, you told the police at the time that it had been arranged while you were at Oxford. But you had not actually been at Oxford for almost a year."

"I told them that, too."

"You told them, and I quote: 'I left Oxford for personal reasons.'"

"There is no lie in that." The self-assurance slipped a little more, his shoulders beneath the tailored suit tightening.

"Perhaps I should have said that you lied by omission. You left Oxford because you had to, because it was part of the deal your father struck to keep you from being prosecuted for illicit sex with a minor."

The first rule of the arrogant: place blame when confronted. "The girl lied to me about her age—"

"Ah yes, don't they always?" she murmured.

"And it has nothing to do with Deeprath or what happened there. So why on earth would I have mentioned it to the local plods?"

"Because, Mr. Grant, you were living with a family that had a fifteen-year-old daughter. With your history, it is not a far stretch to imagine you might have overstepped your bounds with Kyla Galla-gher. If I had been investigating the murder of her parents, I would have been very interested to know about your history. Because I can easily imagine outrage, an argument, violence that may not have been intentional—"

"Bloody hell," he breathed. "You think I killed them? Over *Kyla?*" He infused his wife's name with contempt.

"Someone killed them over something."

"It damned well wasn't me! And I never touched Kyla that sum-mer. Not much. I'd learned that lesson. But it was bloody difficult keeping her off me. Any compromising positions that ensued were wholly her idea."

"And yet you married her several years later."

"I didn't say she wasn't attractive."

"I'd imagine her trust fund was especially attractive."

Grant had regained some of his confidence. He leaned forward, hands clasped on his desk, and said smoothly, "Look, my marriage had nothing to do with that whole affair, except that I felt sorry for the girl and so I kept in touch longer than I otherwise would have." Directing a smile at Sergeant Cullen, he said man-to-man, "And she grew up very nicely."

"And you didn't mind pissing off Nessa Gallagher," Sibéal coun-tered. It was a shot in the dark, but as it turned out, a very effective one.

"Too bloody right," he retorted indignantly. "Damned woman had it in for me from the beginning. Tried to tell the police I'd made advances on Lady Gallagher."

Now that was something else that hadn't made it into the written reports. "And had you?"

"Nessa Gallagher has been a cold-blooded bitch since the day she was born. Yes, I talked to Lady Gallagher, but talking isn't 'making advances.' And I couldn't help it if Lily flirted as naturally as she breathed."

Was this how Philip Grant ran his entire life—convinced that every woman he met was mad for him and he was helpless in the face of it? It made her want to gag. "Are you saying that Lady Gallagher took a personal interest in you? And if so, was it the sort of interest her husband might have disliked?"

"Who are you trying to pin this murder on, anyway? Look, I don't know why they died. But it was nothing to do with me. I wasn't important enough for that." The flash of bitter insight vanished as quickly as it came, and his mocking smile returned. "Not then, at least."

"If you're implying that you're important enough now not to be investigated, you're wrong."

She proceeded to prove it to him by putting him through an hour's interrogation, taking apart his original statement sentence by sentence.

What did you do that morning? *Compiled a summary of stock reports from the last ten years for Lord Gallagher.*

Where were you working? *His study.*

Alone? *Gallagher was in and out. Taking phone calls. Writing letters. Arranging a trip to New York for the following month.*

Did you see anyone else? *Lady Gallagher came in once and took her husband off for some reason. No, I don't know why. Mrs. Bell brought tea late morning. After lunch, Mr. Bell reported on estate matters while I took notes.*

When did you last see Lord Gallagher? *I was dismissed at two in the afternoon. I left Lord Gallagher with Winthrop and Bell, with orders to retrieve some old ledgers from the library and go through them on my own. Which is where I last saw Lady Gallagher, in the library with Aidan.*

Where were you between the library at 2:00 P.M. and 4:30 P.M.? *Working in my room.*

Can you prove it? *Can you disprove it?*

Sibéal finally allowed the questions to lapse, the only sound that of Cullen's pen. She studied Philip Grant as though he were a natural history museum specimen. *Here is an excellent example of twenty-first-century man, notable qualities being self-interest and utter disregard of the common good.*

She asked one final question. "Where was Kyla during the relevant afternoon hours?"

"Ah, the question no one bothered to ask me all those years ago. Very good, Inspector. As a reward, I'll answer you: Kyla and I were together."

"Doing what? I thought you said you were working."

"I was. And so was she. Some summer essay for school. She just liked to be where she could see me."

"So you claim you have an alibi from the impressionable adolescent girl who you later married. It's not terribly strong. For either of you."

"It doesn't have to be. Not unless, after twenty-three years, you have produced evidence from thin air. You are grasping at straws, Inspector. If you want to know what happened at Deeprath, then you should return to Deeprath. That castle . . . I'm not an especially sensitive person, but nothing happens there that the castle doesn't know about."

Although she made a skeptical noise, Sibéal felt a shiver down her spine. "What a pity I haven't learned the art of questioning inanimate objects."

Grant regarded her speculatively. "A great pity."

Carragh found a note in the library when she showed up to work: *There's a stack of family genealogies in the last cabinet on the left against the rood screen. Take a look through. My mother must have been referencing those when she noted baptismal records on the list you found. I'll be back later. A.*

There were indeed genealogies in the specified cabinet, as well as supporting documents such as birth, death, and marriage certificates. Baptismal records, confirmation dates, and newspaper notices.

It was like Christmas day for a lover of the past. Carragh had to resist the urge to throw them all into the air and see what came down to her first.

It took a while to sort through them, for they were in no easily discernible order. She separated handwritten from typed, then roughly by decades. She indulged herself for a few minutes with Aidan's and Kyla's birth certificates (Aidan Cillian Gallagher; 10:20 A.M., 5 March 1982, and Kyla Serene Gallagher; 16:31 P.M., 17 May 1977) and noted sadly the absence of records after those dates. Would Aidan choose to add his parents' death certificates to this collection? At the least, Kyla's daughters should be included here, even if one would prefer to forget her marriage.

Going backward, Carragh pulled out documentation for Aidan's grandparents and his grandfather's half sister, Nessa, born of the fourteenth viscount's second marriage nineteen years after her half brother. The fifteenth viscount, James Michael Gallagher, who was himself the only child of Jenny Gallagher and Evan Chase-Gallagher.

But Carragh only knew that because of her own research into the novelist. If she'd been relying on family records to tell her anything, she'd have been sorely disappointed. From the birth certificates of Nessa in 1931 and her half brother in 1912, there stretched backward a long, empty gap. She took her time, two hours all told, reading every single sheet filed in the genealogies section, and was finally forced to admit she hadn't missed anything. There was a record of Jenny Gallagher's birth in 1860, and then . . . nothing. No marriage certificate, no death certificate, no record of burial, no acknowledgment at all of Evan Chase or their son—not a single record for fifty-two years.

Someone had blown a hole through the Gallagher genealogies. Who? And why? The most likely suspect, she supposed, was Lily. She was the one interested in family history, had reminded herself in a note to look at baptismal records, and told her husband she'd found out something "of greatest interest to all the Gallaghers." Very possibly she had gathered the pertinent records in order to support those findings. But where the hell could she have left them?

Aidan, when he returned, had no more idea than Carragh did. "All we can do is continue to follow her clues," he said. "I'll ask Winthrop if she entrusted anything to his care. Though I doubt he would have forgotten to tell the police something like that."

So they returned to solving riddles. They compared their separate notes on the Bride poem, Aidan's much messier than Carragh would have expected. He saw her puzzling over the lines and circles and arrows going every which way and said, "It helps me see connections I would otherwise miss. Investigations need inspiration as well as logic. This allows the subconscious to make leaps I haven't knowingly thought of yet."

"All right. So what do . . ." She squinted at two circled phrases joined by a line. ". . . 'the Lady Church' and 'Aiofe Gallagher' have to do with each other? Who even is Aiofe Gallagher?" She gave it the soft Irish pronunciation corresponding to the English name Eva.

"Aiofe was Jenny Gallagher's mother. She died before Evan Chase came to Deeprath, and I seem to recall she was considered delicate in her lifetime. I've got a family history somewhere in here that talks about her—a second cousin, I think, who liked to gossip about the wealthier members of the family and call it history."

"And the leap between that and the Lady Church? Which is where?"

"Glendalough. You saw the ruined walls the other day, though we didn't go near it. The little church north of the Round Tower. It was built outside the walls of the city, but was still part of the monastic community. It was a church for women, maybe a convent church for nuns associated with the community. Or maybe more general. We should go look at it. It has another unusual cross—engraved beneath the lintel on the main door."

She could feel the pull of curiosity, that instinct of all true scholars to follow a meandering path of inquiry merely because it was

intriguing. But right now, she reminded herself, they had more specific concerns in mind. "And Aiofe Gallagher?"

"Hmmm, yes. I must dig out that history, but I do remember that
she had several stillborn children who were buried near that chapel.
There's a little graveyard there, meant for children who died without baptism. Although no longer much used, Aiofe wanted them
buried there."

Pity was even worse than curiosity—Carragh had a nearly overwhelming urge to go straight to that little graveyard. She had always searched out the graves of children in old cemeteries, maybe
because she knew she had been lucky not to have joined them at the
age of four. She couldn't imagine the bleakness of a spot where
mothers laid their children while believing them to be beyond salvation's reach. Just because she was Catholic didn't mean she sub-
scribed to all the traditions that had accumulated over centuries and
through sheer weight of time had become fixed.

"Carragh?"

"Sorry. It's just very sad."

"There is grief enough and to spare in this world." He sounded
as though he were quoting someone. "But pertinent to our search
are the references in the Bride poem to lost children. Did you note
them?"

"Not particularly." She skimmed through her copy now, wanting
to find them before he had to point them out. "Here," she said. "Third
stanza: 'A son of joy, a lullaby/Till jealous eyes did peek and pry/
And vow her heart to mortify./They made her baby seem to die,/
The Dark Bride of Deeprath.'"

Aidan pointed further down. "And in stanza five: 'My child, my
heart, my baby lost,/I will find though balked and crossed.'"

"I see it." She read over them both several times. "Are you telling
me that the next clue is somewhere at this church or graveyard? It
seems a little thin. I thought you said your mother laid her puzzles
strictly within the castle itself."

"For me, yes. But I was a child. Maybe for my father . . . ?"

Carragh sighed. "What you're saying is that we're going back to Glendalough. I suppose you've considered that even if your mother made this church the third clue, whatever she left will be well gone after all these years."

He shrugged. "Can't hurt to try. Tomorrow?"

"Tomorrow is Friday."

"So?"

"Do you really need reminding of your grand Gallagher Farewell Ball or whatever Lady Nessa is calling it? I doubt she'll let you go anywhere tomorrow."

"We could sneak out." It was hard to tell if he was teasing.

"Are you twelve?" she asked. "You may not be scared of your great-aunt, but I am. Look, this chapel has been there for hundreds of years. An extra day won't make any difference."

He gave her a look full of long-suffering concession. "Saturday it is. But don't come crying to me when Nessa runs you off your feet tomorrow like a nineteenth-century housemaid. When it comes to impressing outsiders, she knows no limits."

CHAPTER TWENTY-NINE

Aidan hadn't been exaggerating his great-aunt's zeal for forced
labor. The moment Carragh poked her head out of her bedroom Friday morning, Nessa pressed her into service. Aidan's own
service seemed to be more of an advisory role (listening to his great-
aunt move militantly through her list), but Carragh was detailed to
carry in flower arrangements and move tables and generally do
whatever other unskilled work needed doing.

She was concentrating so hard on ensuring that the table linens
were laid without any wrinkles that Aidan had to speak to her three
times before she heard him. "What did you say?"

"I said, there's a phone call for you. You can take it in the study."

How did he manage to still look cool and crisp and freshly pressed
when she knew she must look as grimy and tired as any historical
housemaid after hours of physical labor?

He must have mistaken her frustration for curiosity, for he added,
"I don't know who it is, sorry."

The telephone in the aggressively masculine Victorian study fit
its surroundings as much as any newer invention could, cast in
bronze and finished with filigree flourishes on the rotary dial and

the antique handset. A little dubiously, Carragh picked it up and said, "Hello?"

She'd left this number with only one person—the contractor for her grandmother's house. *Please*, she prayed silently, *don't let it have flooded or burned down or collapsed . . .*

It was much, much worse. "Hello, love," said her mother.

"How did you find me?" Not, perhaps, the smartest thing to say.

"So you admit you have been hiding from me? I found out from your Dublin neighbors who has been working on the house, and then I tracked him down and he was only too happy to give me this number."

"I'm rather in the middle of something just now—"

"Of course you are. Look, Carragh, I'm not calling to harass you about that letter. What you do with it is your business. But your father and I are concerned that you are shutting us out entirely. You're twenty-eight, I know. But you've been saddled with a house in poor condition in a city where you're alone, you've been incommunicative since your grandmother's death, added to which your birth grandmother is trying to make contact and we're worried about you. That is all. And we want to help. With the house, if nothing else."

"Yes, I'm sure you're all eager for me to put the house up for sale and take the cash so I can split it amongst my brothers."

There was a long silence, and even through the static Carragh could tell that what she'd said had stung. "Why would you think that?"

"It's what everyone is thinking! How is it that the Chinese girl ended up with a two million dollar house, when the son and grandsons of Eileen Ryan's blood got only half that between the four of them? Of course I'm expected to sell the place and share the money."

"Carragh—"

"I have to go. I'll talk to you when I'm back in Dublin."

Accustomed as she was to mobiles, Carragh now discovered the visceral satisfaction of getting to slam down a telephone. Then she sat at the desk and buried her head in her hands, a few hot, angry tears slipping through her fingers. She knew her family loved her. But no matter how hard she tried, she would always be instantly recognizable as not one of them. Different. Other. The daughter who had to prove her gratitude every day by being better and kinder and smarter than any child by blood would have to. The girl who had to be always good and always useful, or she might once more find herself locked in a closet and left behind.

"Is everything all right?" Nessa stood in the open doorway, one hand resting lightly on her cane.

How could it be so hard to find privacy in a ten thousand square foot castle? "Of course. Sorry, I'll go right back to work."

Nessa waved her free hand negligently and crossed the vast expanse of hand-loomed rug to a seat before the desk. Despite the fact that Carragh sat in the ostensible seat of power, she felt much like she had in her first interview with the woman.

So it was disconcerting when Nessa said, with real sympathy, "I have some experience with distressed children. Not to say you're a child, naturally, though at my age anyone younger than fifty seems impossibly young. The point is, I know the look of someone frustrated with a near relative. Can I take it you were speaking to your family?"

It seemed easiest to answer. "My mother."

"That explains it. Mothers and daughters . . . an eternal conflict."

Carragh's surprise must have read as skepticism, because Nessa added, "I had a mother once, hard as that may be to believe. My father's second wife. She was younger even than my brother Eamon. From the vantage point of adulthood, I can recognize that her position must have been very difficult. But I'm afraid that, as an adolescent, I found her meek and spineless. And as she died when I was sixteen, I never had the chance to alter my opinion."

"I'm sorry." Was that the right thing to say about a loss seventy years in the past? What else could she say—that there appeared to be a multitude of dead mothers crowding into her life these days?

"I appreciate the sentiment, but there is no need. If my mother and I were never close, I had the compensation of my father's love. To be part of a family means that the loss of one need never mean the loss of the whole. Whatever Aidan and Kyla may think, I provided them all the love I knew how. And if their choices are different than those I would make, at least I am certain that family matters to both of them. If it did not, they would hardly be so combative about it."

"I see." Carragh couldn't think of anything else to say. "I should get back to work." She slipped out of the study with a grim determination not to think about anything but simply do as she was told. At least she would be left alone tonight, she thought. Nothing more had been said about her attending this party, and she couldn't wait to escape to her room.

But Aidan cornered her two hours before the reception, in the kitchen with the catering staff. "I'm taking her off now, Mrs. Bell," he said with authority.

"I've told you to call me Maire," she grumbled affectionately. "Go on, then."

As they walked out, Carragh said, "Thanks. Though I'd be more grateful if you could grab me some food before I hide away in my room."

"Hide away? Don't be ridiculous. You're coming to the party."

Her first objection was about as silly as they come. "I don't have anything to wear."

"Kyla will have plenty to choose from."

Had he really not noticed that his sister was at least six inches taller than she? "Aidan, I'm tired and sweaty and my brain hurts from puzzle-solving and all I want is to take a bath and curl up in bed with a book. Preferably one not written in verse. Why would I give that up for a party full of people I've never met?"

"Because I'm asking you to."

And this, she thought crossly, is how Aidan Gallagher gets anyone to do anything—by turning the full power of those blue eyes and cheekbones and sheer concentrated personality on whoever he's manipulating. He probably didn't even know he was doing it.

With a martyred sigh, she said, "You'll have to ask your sister to lend me something. I don't have the nerve."

After a quick bath, Carragh found four outfits to choose from delivered to her room. She laid them on her bed, each one exquisite and expensive and perfectly tailored to the five-foot-ten-inch Kyla. She knew that no matter how she tried to adjust any of them, she would look like a little girl drowning in fashion she couldn't handle.

Having brought a black cashmere sweater with her, Carragh looked despairingly between the only two options she had to pair it with: a pink-and-orange-plaid pencil skirt or black cropped trousers. Which impression did she wish to give—ebullient schoolgirl or goth-in-training?

A knock on her door proved to be, of all people, Lady Nessa, and Carragh had a momentary—hope? fear?—that the woman would disinvite her downstairs. Her customary elegance had been accented tonight by a silver-beaded dress straight out of Central Casting from the thirties, her chignon highlighted with two ruby-set combs.

Carragh only realized she was carrying something when Lady Nessa held out her arms. Automatically, she took what was being offered and discovered she was holding a weight of heavy fabric.

"Aidan is a thoughtful man, but not a very practical one," Nessa told her. "Surprisingly unobservant for a police officer. Kyla's clothing would never fit you, in size or style. I thought you might prefer other options. They're old-fashioned, but some things are timeless."

As Carragh gaped at the luxurious items—was that velvet?—Nessa said as she left, "Half an hour. The family is meeting in the music room."

If Kyla's items were gorgeous, Lady Nessa's were something beyond that. Vintage fashion houses, beading and pearls and velvet and silk and tulle . . . was there any way she could wear them all?

It came down to two: a black silk dress with blue beads of various shades draping down the skirt in folds, and a vintage Dior skirt and top. She settled on the latter, swapping out the matching top for her own black cashmere. The skirt was steel-gray silk organdy with hand-embroidered flowers in pinks and purples scattered from the wide-banded waist to the calf-length hem. She dried her hair, twisting back pieces from her face and pinning them up to show hints of the peacock coloring beneath, and slipped on her black satin ballet flats. Thanks to Nessa's unexpected generosity, she wouldn't embarrass herself in appearance. She could only hope she managed to say the same about her behavior by the end of the night. Best to avoid alcohol. Aidan Gallagher made her nervous enough when she was sober.

Aidan could make it through fancy parties without having to think twice. But those parties and receptions and cocktail hours took place in London, where people knew him mostly as a silent escort to various women. Models, actresses, socialites . . . the one thing they all had in common was that they were beautiful and they were far more outgoing than he was. That suited him perfectly.

But he couldn't get away with that tonight. Tonight he was Aidan Gallagher, the seventeenth Viscount Gallagher, trustee of Deeprath Castle and the living representative of generations of Wicklow history. And with Nessa at his back, there was no chance he could get away with not talking. Was that why he'd insisted that Carragh come? Because he wanted someone there he could speak to without second-guessing every word?

But when she walked into the music room, he realized he might have misjudged. He had been thinking of the companion from the library, the mind and personality that could match him thought for thought, and when he was rude, wasn't afraid to be rude back. He had not imagined this woman in a fitted black top and elegant skirt flaring out from her waist like a highly decorative storm cloud, the whole of it highlighting curves he'd never really noticed before.

Next to him, Philip managed to whistle near-silently. "Who

knew the bookworm was so sexy? Oh right—I did." With a wink at his brother-in-law, he wandered back to his wife, who was watching him closely.

Could he get away with hitting Philip? Probably not till the evening was over. Nessa would never forgive him. She entered just behind Carragh, as though she'd been watching and planning the perfect entrance. While Carragh hovered awkwardly as the outsider, Nessa surveyed them all silently, one by one, like a general surveying her troops.

"This night is important. If we must leave Wicklow, let us do it with our heads held high as worthy successors to all who have come before us."

Aidan did not miss her stress on the word "must." He had known Nessa would never forgive him for handing over Deeprath. No doubt she would still be complaining about it on her deathbed.

"I expect each of you"—her gaze lingered on Philip—"to be on your best behavior. Drink no more than necessary to be hospitable. And no huddling in corners or isolating yourself with one or two people. Mingle. Be gracious."

"Is that an order?" Kyla asked with thick irony.

"You may consider it whatever you like so long as you obey."

It was like being young again, Aidan reflected, with Nessa and Kyla at odds and he left to be the peacemaker. Recognizing it didn't make his response less instinctual. "We will do our best. Won't we, Kyla?"

Her eye roll held all the long memories of siblings, the first time since he'd returned to Ireland that he could see beneath his sister's brittle poise and cynicism. It made him smile in return. A good beginning to the evening.

Aidan had almost hoped that no one would come, but as usual, Nessa had judged the community wisely. Curiosity ensured a crowd, even if memory and affection didn't. Deeprath Castle had not seen a party since the summer of 1992, and no one would miss the chance to see inside the place where a double murder had happened.

Of course the Gallaghers were overdressed, what with Aidan and Philip in dinner jackets and the women in high fashion. But it was what people expected, so no guest looked twice between their own High Street clothing and the bespoke dress of their hosts.

Aidan had never attended a party like this at Deeprath; he'd been always too young. But he remembered them, remembered many of them, for his mother had loved parties and people and laughter. He'd spent many hours pressed up against the banisters of the gallery overlooking the Tudor hall, Kyla beside him spinning stories about the guests. She'd always had a wicked sense of humor.

He found he was quite capable of behaving appropriately by putting on a slightly different mask than his London one. The mask of the viscount was a little stiff, a little formal, but the people here had not seen him since he was ten years old. They were in no position to judge the authenticity of his public persona.

Some of them he remembered, but many were strangers. If this had been England, the night would have passed without a single awkward reference to the past and what had happened here. But the Irish knew all about tragedy and had no problem talking about it. They called it "the calamity" and referred to it as casually as the weather, moving in and out of their conversations without any awkward pauses.

Nessa, dressed in timeless black, was in her element, and so—in a manner he had never seen before—was his sister. Kyla also wore black, an off-the-shoulder lace dress with a long, sheer overlay that highlighted her legs. She might have physically resembled their great-aunt, but as he watched her in animated conversation with a gentleman who looked ninety if he was a day, all he could see was their mother. Lily Gallagher'd had the same expressive hands and face, and the generosity of self that made every listener feel they were the most important person in the world. How had he missed that in his sister all these years?

Probably because their interactions had been mostly confined to texts and phone calls since her marriage. And that was as much his fault as hers—though Philip took a large share of the blame as well.

Speaking of whom . . . no one could accuse Philip Grant of not being sociable. As Aidan watched, half listening to the church organist pouring out two decades' worth of parish gossip in his ear, Philip moved easily from Father Hennessy, nodding at the solicitor, Winthrop, before inserting himself into a group composed of local teachers and Carragh. Aidan's blood pressure rose correspondingly the nearer his brother-in-law got to her.

When Philip managed to cut Carragh neatly away from the group, Aidan abruptly said to the organist, "Do excuse me, Mrs. Donovan. I've got to see to the music."

A total lie, for Nessa had the quartet in perfect order, and even as he moved across the hall they began to play dance music. Big band, swing . . . he supposed he should be grateful they weren't playing waltzes. At one point Nessa had wanted this to be a masquerade ball.

Carragh's face was set in an expression that he guessed meant Philip was being offensive. He sailed straight in. "Time to find your wife, Philip. Nessa will expect us to lead out the dancing."

"With you partnering your great-aunt? More luck to you."

"Nessa made clear that she would not be dancing tonight." Aidan extended his hand. "I'm going to dance with Carragh."

He was feeling quite pleased with himself, leading her to the center of the hall, when she asked, "Do you always snap your fingers at a woman and expect her to follow?"

"That wasn't . . . I didn't mean to. I only wanted to help."

"Next time, you might try asking if I need help. Or if I want to dance."

He tried not to smile, chastened though he was. "Would you like to dance, Carragh?"

"I don't know that I'd *like* to, but I will. If you promise me that you know what you're doing and won't let me trip over myself in front of everyone."

"No tripping," he promised.

The skirt she wore was perfect for dancing, swishing against him as he led her through the simplest of box steps. Perhaps there was something to be said for a dress made with ten yards of fabric as opposed to slinky gowns falling straight to the floor. He almost wished Nessa would request a waltz.

Carragh broke his moment of sentimentality with an abrupt question. "Do you think Philip might have stolen the letters from my room?"

"The ones my mother wrote to your grandmother? Why would he?"

"Why would anyone? Because he thought there might be something in them he didn't want me to read."

He didn't answer for several beats, then lowered his voice for good measure. "Carragh, if you think those letters were taken to protect someone, then you're implying that whoever took them is the person who killed my parents."

"I know."

By now he was speaking so quietly he was more or less whispering in her ear. "Do you think Philip capable of that?"

"You tell me."

He thought Philip careless and reckless with other people's lives, he thought him of questionable business honesty, and he knew him for a marital cheat and liar. But a murderer?

"It has to be someone, Aidan," Carragh insisted as the music swelled to its close. "Someone you know. You're going to have to deal with that fact if you want the truth."

With that, she slipped away, and Aidan's affability went with her. He retreated into the aloofness and meaningless politeness that had long been his shield. In that mood, the only way to make the rest of the evening tolerable was alcohol. He never drank more than he could handle, for he desperately hated being out of control, but tonight it failed even to deliver the customary effect of knocking off the too-bright edges of everything.

Instead, he found himself recalling long-ago moments with as-
tonishing clarity. It was as though memories overlaid everything he
saw, giving an odd impression of time flickering in and out of per-
spective.

Philip, busy being charming to a sixty-year-old retired judge,
altered between one breath and the next in Aidan's eyes from the
slightly dissolute mid-forties businessman to the sharp-featured
university student whose fair hair flopped over his eyes and whose
laugh rang through Deeprath with unnerving regularity.

As a ten-year-old, he'd distrusted anyone who laughed so easily.
Especially anyone who had the habit of ruffling his hair, as Philip
did.

*"I can't decide if you're lucky or not to grow up with beautiful females
in your family,"* Philip said, *leaning his arms on the gallery railing and
musing aloud to Aidan as his mother and Kyla passed through the Great
Hall. "It might come as a shock to you when you move into the world and
realize most women are nothing like her."*

Her, singular. Philip had definitely been talking about his mother.
And Aidan could recall, distinctly, the expression in Philip's eyes. He
hadn't been able to name it as a child, but now knew it for what it
was—a mix of lust and resentment. Men had been known to kill for
such emotions.

As he moved around the edges of the hall, ignoring those who
looked like they didn't quite have the nerve to approach him, he
caught sight of Nessa, and his eyes pulled that doubling trick so that
her white hair darkened into the faded chestnut of her sixties and
the lines on her face softened and drew back. Her stance, her expression, her upright figure remained the same.

"Stand up straight, Aidan . . . Elbows off the table, Aidan . . . Make
your grandfather proud, Aidan." Virtually everything his great-aunt
said to him was a command or a reminder of who he was and what he
was expected to be. His father only laughed and told him to ignore
her. His mother had been more indignant on his behalf—and her
own, perhaps? An adult Aidan realized Lily might not have liked

someone else correcting her child—and she did not hesitate to quarrel with Nessa when she overstepped her bounds.

That had been a source of tension, Aidan remembered suddenly. Nessa had resented his mother's tenancy of Deeprath Castle, had hated that a strange woman from America could come in and do whatever she liked to a house that had stood for hundreds of years. He could even recall a specific argument between them . . .

"If you will not keep your daughter from ruining her reputation, then I will."

"Keep away from Kyla. It is none of your business."

"Kyla is a Gallagher. She is far more my business than yours."

Of course, Nessa hadn't lived with them at Deeprath. Even through what he could remember of his childhood, Aidan knew she had lived mostly in the dower house in Kilkenny that her brief marriage had brought her. But being a Gallagher, Nessa considered the castle to be as much hers as her nephew's. Certainly, Aidan himself had been exposed to that point of view as he'd come into his inheritance.

And Kyla? Aidan knew, somewhere inside him in a place he did not want to acknowledge, that he was reluctant to look at his sister. What would he see when he did? The unhappy, sometimes difficult woman she'd become? The angry and temperamental teenager? Or the girl who'd often been generous to her little brother, letting him follow her around the castle, even just letting him draw quietly in her room while she did whatever mysterious things a twelve- or thirteen-year-old girl did.

He had to search for Kyla tonight, and finally he found her dancing with Winthrop. But stare as he might, the double-vision trick did not work with his sister. His vision of her stayed stubbornly in the present. He still could not remember where he'd seen her the day of the murders, or when.

Did he remember her in the immediate aftermath? He recalled Nessa more clearly than anyone else, and Maire Bell, who had been the first to appear when he screamed. He remembered the usually serene housekeeper visibly shaking as she knelt by his father and then took Aidan by the shoulders and gently pulled him out of the library. Nessa had come somewhere in there. Aidan could not remember the moment when he'd understood what had happened—could only recall himself shouting.

Make it not true! Make it not true!

His hand jerked, sloshing scotch onto his cuff, as his voice echoed in his head. He had forgotten that completely, forgotten screaming with his hands over his ears until Nessa had to slap him to bring him out of it.

And then . . . yes . . . Kyla had been there by then, for the two of them sat in silent misery in the music room while footsteps came and went and lots of conversations occurred just out of their hearing.

Someone touched his arm then, and Aidan sloshed his drink again. Swearing under his breath, he put on his mask of remote politeness to keep whomever it was from wanting to linger.

"Penelope!"

"Hello, Aidan darling." As always, Penelope had matched her attire perfectly to her environment. Her vibrant red dress was conservatively cut by London standards and she wore no jewelry save a single silver chain. Even so, most of the men in the room were eyeing her.

He kissed her on the cheek. "Why didn't you tell me you'd decided to come?"

"Because I wanted to be free to change my mind at the last moment without guilt."

"Where are you staying? You must come here, of course."

"Don't be ridiculous. The Glendalough Hotel is perfectly charming. Where else could I have a view of ruined churches outside my window? Though I must say," she let her eyes drift around the hall, taking in the enormous fireplace and the tapestry-covered walls and Tudor beams, "when you told me you grew up in a castle, I didn't really think Castle with a capital C."

"So have you come to see me or Deeprath?"

"Deeprath, of course. Maybe that's why I broke up with you, when I realized you weren't going to marry me and let me live like an Irish princess."

There were so few people in his adult life who'd dared tease him. Kyla (always bitterly these days), Penelope . . . and Carragh.

Penelope touched his arm. "Seriously, how are you?"

"It's been . . ." He considered, surprised to find that he could honestly say, "It's been not so bad. I mean, families are always families. But there have been some developments about—" He broke off, unsure how to describe the hunt he and Carragh were embarked on without a good deal of explanation. "Tonight's not the best time to go into it all. I would like to talk to you. Does your being here mean you're willing to hypnotize me?"

"Tonight's not the best time for that discussion, either. Tomorrow? In the meantime, tell me about the young woman in the rather gorgeous gray skirt that you danced with earlier. Is she your archivist?"

"Carragh's helping me go through the library, but she's not really a professional. She's an editor, I think, who studied Irish folklore."

"Interesting."

"She can read Irish as well as English and she knows how to take notes," Aidan said defensively. "For my purposes, that's all we needed. And before you get any ideas, may I remind you that it was Nessa who hired her."

"It wasn't Nessa who danced with her," Penelope murmured.

"Pen." It was a warning, in response to her eloquent expression. "What?"

"Nothing, I'm sure. You just go on being aloof and gorgeous. It's a lethal combination. Who can fight it?"

"*You* had no problem walking away."

"Because I have a well-developed sense of self-preservation, darling. Not everyone does. You should take care."

He was uncomfortable with her assessment. Did she mean he should take care of Carragh's feelings, or his own? He offered Penelope his hand. "Since you've come all this way, will you dance? I wouldn't want you to miss out on a princess moment."

"You," she said softly, placing her hand in his, "are a dangerous man, Aidan Gallagher. It's a good thing I only like you."

CHAPTER THIRTY

Autumn 1880

When Evan wrote to Charles that the first months of his marriage were not what he'd expected, his publisher returned a wry reply: *I don't think there's a man alive who has the faintest idea what to expect. If we did, we'd never risk it. Work on the book and you'll get over it.*

Evan wrote to others infrequently and cautiously, for he would not risk the slightest stain on Jenny's reputation. Her health was no one's concern but their own. He watched her closely the first weeks after she left the tower, and blessedly she returned to the Jenny he'd met and fallen in love with.

And he learned it was possible to love her even more. He loved her stubbornness in the face of fragility, and the way he could actually see her battling at moments. The terrible kind of internal fight that is so much more difficult than those fought with fists. He began to recognize how closely she was watched—and how much that watching affected her. From the housekeeper to the chambermaid, eyes followed his wife everywhere she went, and he was quite certain all their reports ended up on Lord Gallagher's desk.

Evan nearly brought up the subject with Jenny a dozen times, but every time he began, she steered the conversation artfully away from her health. He told himself he would respect her wishes. Or maybe that was just cowardice talking. In the event, he held his peace throughout the summer and early autumn and poured his frustrations and observations into his novel.

He used much of the skeleton of the Gallagher family history as the origin story for his own Darkling Bride: the embittered Crusader, the young woman taken far from her home, the idealistic monk-in-training. He also used—how could he not?—the details of their first meeting as told to him by Jenny: the Sanctuary Cross, the stay at Glendalough, the one-sided silence as the woman (he altered Maryam to Miriam) listened to the eager and impressionable Niall Gallagher.

But that was only the backdrop to the main story. For however many versions of the Darkling Bride legend he had found, in none of them was she a heroine the reading public would accept. Too strange, too vengeful, too *other* (in some versions she was faerie). Readers wanted their lovers to be accessible, honorable, and, on the woman's part, pure. So he created Anna, an intelligent, self-willed, but kindhearted orphan who finds in Ireland a forbidding castle, a secretive family, and a stern master. Evan knew how to write a bestseller—give them beauty, give them brooding atmosphere, give them a taciturn man who can only be redeemed by the right woman and the kind of mystery that can be tied up neatly with a bow at the end, leaving them to live happily ever after . . . with just enough darkness in the story to highlight the good.

Evan was not blind to the similarities to his own life this last year, although he didn't especially fancy himself as the innocent orphan. He poured into the book all that he had felt since his arrival, his attraction to both people and places, the sense of rightness by day that couldn't erase the distant air of foreboding in the dark. As though every person at Deeprath was waiting for something to happen.

Although Charles asked—often—Evan refused to write a synopsis. Nor did he send early pages, as he usually did, for critique. This story was his and he would not risk its too-early entry into the world. When pressed—pushed—harassed—he reluctantly wrote a one-page outline in the barest possible terms and told Charles that was all he was getting. He also ignored every question about when he would return to London.

So the days passed at Deeprath Castle quietly, becoming more and more like a space set aside from the normal world. Everything in Evan's life had narrowed to Ireland, to Wicklow, to this particular structure and landscape known to the Gallaghers for centuries. He still felt himself something of an outsider, but one being inexorably absorbed into the larger whole.

A feeling that intensified on a wildly stormy day in November, when Jenny told him she was pregnant.

DIARY OF JENNY GALLAGHER

26 November 1880

All shall be well and all shall be well and all manner of things shall be well . . . never have the words of St. Julian so resonated. This baby will be my salvation. I can feel it.

CHAPTER THIRTY-ONE

To her own surprise, Carragh quite enjoyed the evening's festivities. Except for university and those few disastrous weeks of clubbing and drinking after her grandmother's death, she mostly preferred going out in small groups to quiet places. But tonight, buoyed by her borrowed fashion and one carefully sipped glass of champagne, she moved through the crowd with ease. She danced twice more, once with the teenage son of a Rathdrum family and once with the local doctor. It helped that no one really wanted to talk about her, but were only probing for inside information on the Gallaghers. She confined herself to physical descriptions of the library, her pleasure and interest in the mountains and Glendalough in particular, and her degree in Irish folklore.

That last brought an unexpected response from the Laragh priest, who turned out to be the very same Father Hennessy referenced by Lily Gallagher years ago. After learning of Carragh's interest in the Darkling Bride, he immediately invited her to visit him. "I've got some privately printed material not easily found."

They settled on the next afternoon and parted with well wishes, Carragh already wondering how to question him about Lily Gallagher and that fatal autumn. And then she learned all over again how swiftly one's emotional state can change, as Philip slid to her side and in a malicious tone said, "Well well. Who is that smashing woman with Aidan?"

He might be malicious, but his description was accurate. The brunette was tall and striking, willowy in a red sheath dress that made Carragh feel simultaneously overdressed and as though she'd rummaged through a child's dress-up trunk. And no one could accuse Aidan of simply being polite, for he was not only speaking to her while they danced, but his expression was open and engaged. So the woman was not only gorgeous, but someone he liked. Carragh thought maybe she'd seen her before, in one of the tabloid photos of Aidan.

"Don't look like that, sweetheart." Philip didn't touch her, but he might as well have. His voice was as intrusive as his hands would have been—or almost. "I could make you forget all about Aidan Gallagher. Everyone will be busy for the next hour and this place is enormous. I'm sure we could find a quiet corner."

He did touch her then, his hand coming to rest lightly in the small of her back just above the waistline of her skirt.

"Go away, Philip." She said it as firmly as she could without raising her voice. The last thing she needed was to draw attention.

So of course that was the moment Nessa chose to check on her. The old woman's steel-trap eyes lingered for a moment on Philip's hand, which he kept where it was, then regarded Carragh. "Enjoying yourself, my dear?" It was hard to tell if she was saying more in subtext, since the woman's normal voice always sounded like she was implying two or three things at the same time.

"Yes, thank you."

"Lovely. The supper buffet will be served in a few minutes. Make sure you don't miss it." Which could mean *Eat something* or could equally mean *Don't even think about going somewhere I can't see you.*

Another gothic novel moment, the intruder who doesn't belong being reminded of her position by the superior family matriarch. Or maybe simply Victorian, when being a woman—whatever her position—meant being constantly put in your place. Was that what it had been like to be Jenny Gallagher?

Yes.

Carragh could swear she felt a ghost of laughter against her flushed cheek and startled, leaving Philip's hand dangling in the air for several surprised seconds. *Really?* she yelled internally. *You want to talk here? Or am I just too close to drunk and imagining things?*

"I'm just going to powder my nose before supper," she said distractedly. Now she was even talking like a character from the past. She needed to get out of this skirt and out of this party and out of this damned castle before she forgot who she was and what year she was living in. She was no one's governess, she was no servant who needed to be reminded of her manners, and was most definitely not the lower class girl falling inappropriately in love with the master of the house.

So there.

She didn't have the means to powder anything even if she'd meant to, and the nearest cloakroom had several people waiting, so she slipped around a corner and through one of the myriad doorways that led to the corridor that led to the library.

It was locked. She should have guessed that Aidan would want to ensure that no one wandered where they weren't wanted. It left her standing in an old, damp, cold corridor wishing she could escape to her room or, even better, back to Dublin. But she wouldn't give Nessa the satisfaction. She would allow herself five minutes to stand here and breathe, then return for the supper and make sure she was widely seen to be nowhere near Philip.

As she habitually closed her eyes when she was breathing for calmness—and because of his damn ability to move like a cat—she only knew Aidan was in front of her when he said, "Trying to wish your way through the lock?"

Her eyes flew open, and some of her anger at Philip—and herself—poured out. "Doesn't anyone in this bloody family announce themselves before walking into what is clearly meant to be a private moment? Do I need to wear a do not disturb sign everywhere I go? If it's Nessa who sent you in search of me, you can tell her to mind her own damn business and that I'll come back if and when I want to."

"It wasn't Nessa. When I couldn't find you, I thought you might be here. It's where I would have come if I could. If you like, I'll let you in and lock it behind you so no one can bother you."

"And what happens when you get so distracted with your other guests that you forget to let me out?" Why did she have to picture the sort of distractions the gorgeous brunette might provide?

He said, with the gravest amusement, "You could sleep on the table. And I don't think you'd starve in one night."

"Who's the woman?" The question tumbled out, and she winced. But backtracking would make it even more awkward.

"What woman?" But she could see from his expression that he knew who she meant. "Ah. Her name is Penelope Costa. A friend from London."

"You looked very friendly." Why did these words keep spilling out of her mouth?

"We used to date. Not any longer. But Pen is someone who knows my past without ever trying to make me relive it. It makes things easier."

That stopped her irritation in its tracks. "I get that. Sorry."

"For what? That I have problems making friends?" Had he moved closer, or was it her imagination. "Or that you were jealous?"

"You rate yourself very high, Aidan Gallagher."

"The arrogance is for public view. I think you understand that as well."

"You're trying to tell me you're really shy and unassuming."

The sound he made was part laugh, part pure exasperation. "Only with you. Probably because I never know what you're think-ing." He raised a hand and lifted a strand of hair off her neck, his fingers brushing her skin. "What *are* you thinking, Carragh Ryan?"

That you've lost your mind—that I've lost my mind—that Nessa would not like this at all—oh dear, I really am a gothic heroine . . . Her Boston-bred attitude came to her rescue. "I'm thinking that you've had too much to drink."

"Is that true?" he whispered. His hand stayed cupped between her neck and her cheek, not quite a caress but not quite anything else. "Or are you thinking what I am?"

"And what is that?"

"How much I want to do this."

His lips touched hers at the same moment his hand tightened and his fingers caught in her hair. His other hand came up to match it, and Carragh found herself being thoroughly kissed in a way she never had been before. She had experienced seductive and aggressive and playful . . . but no one had ever kissed her as sweetly as did Aidan Gallagher.

When he pulled away, they both had to steady their breathing. "Was that what you were thinking?" he asked softly.

A gothic heroine would have said a silent yes with her eyes and a socially acceptable no with her mouth. To hell with that. "Yes."

"I'm glad." He stepped back and offered her his arm. "Then if you're not going to let me lock you up in the library, at least let me escort you back. Mrs. Bell makes an amazing apple cake. It will disappear fast."

There were glances when they returned—mostly discreet, the exception being Nessa, whose scrutiny was unmistakable. Philip looked none too pleased, either. Carragh deliberately turned away from them and concentrated on Aidan at her side. He introduced her to a few people—including the beautiful Penelope, who engaged her in vivid conversation about Boston and Harvard, where it turned out her older sister had gone to school. All in all, she could hardly believe how fast time went. People began departing before she could realize she was tired.

Aidan, with the exquisite judgment of someone who knew his family well, sent her off to her room before she could be trapped by anyone. "I'll see you in the morning," he said, his hand on her elbow at the bottom of the staircase. "I thought we'd leave for Glendalough by eight?"

She agreed and floated upstairs like the gauzy princesses she professed to despise. The weariness she felt was the pleasant sort that promised deep sleep and good dreams.

When she opened her door, it took a few seconds to understand what she was seeing, and then she caught her breath in dismay.

Her bed was a heap of various fabrics—velvet, satin, silk, lace—cut and ripped and tossed on top of each other in what looked like fury. Every single item of clothing borrowed from both Kyla and Nessa had been deliberately destroyed.

With malice aforethought.

That phrase swam dizzy laps through Carragh's mind ten minutes later while the Gallagher family stood in her bedroom and argued about what had happened and what to do about it.

Philip wondered aloud why no one was calling the police. Nessa, looking pale and fragile, picked through fabric as though trying to reconstruct what had been destroyed. The vintage items, she pointed out to no one in particular, could never be replaced. Carragh stared at Aidan, leaning against the closed door with arms crossed. He was staring at Kyla, standing just inside the doorway.

"What do you think?" he asked his sister.

"Me? I suppose the logical response is to call the police."

Nessa stopped fussing with the fabric. "There's no need for that."

"I said it was a logical response, not a proper one," Kyla offered. "I agree with Nessa, there's no need to involve outsiders in a minor case of vandalism."

Aidan's face was stony. "Vandalism that involved a measure of violence."

His sister remained calm. "If it's Miss Ryan you're concerned about, Aidan, I might point out that the destruction was directed at Gallagher possessions, not hers."

"Someone was in this room with shears strong enough to cut and

an anger that overrode common sense. If they wanted to merely attack Gallagher possessions, there are many more public spaces in
which to do it. Whoever did this had a personal motive."

"Or wished to make us think so."

It was as though Kyla and Aidan were the only two in the room.
There was intensity in the way they stared at each other, trying to
divine what might lay behind the other's words. The tension was so
thick that it took Carragh a minute to understand what Kyla had
implied.

"She means me," Carragh said flatly.

Everyone swung their gazes to her then, even Nessa looking
faintly surprised.

"She means I might have done all this myself."

"Why?" Aidan asked. The sharpness of the word was a reminder
that he wasn't just a Gallagher—he was a police officer who presumably knew how to interrogate suspects.

Swinging between defensiveness and real fear—Carragh didn't
think violent destruction of haute couture the sort of thing friendly
ghosts did—she answered, "As I didn't actually do it myself, I can't
give you the reason. To get attention, maybe?"

"That's absurd," Aidan said. "Anyway, you were never out of sight
long enough to do something like this."

Philip spoke up. "She was gone for a good fifteen minutes right
before supper."

Carragh wondered what she could say in her defense without
exposing that private moment outside the library. She didn't want
the precious memory turned over and over by others. Aidan took the
decision out of her hands. "She was with me," he said coldly, his expression daring Philip to press the issue.

"She wouldn't have had to disappear," Kyla pointed out. "It's her
room, no one's been in it since she left."

"You think I did this before the party even started?" Carragh was
astonished, then furious.

"I think it would be folly to overlook the obvious."

For the first time, Carragh realized that Kyla truly and heartily disliked her. Maybe even hated her. Was it possible she'd found out about her affair with Philip? If so, then cutting up gowns and throwing the blame on Carragh seemed quite likely.

Aidan said, "It's late and we're all tired. We'll talk about it tomorrow. Everyone go to bed."

Carragh hadn't heard his lord of the manor voice before—despite her egalitarian views, it was impressive. He stood at the door, waiting for the others to file out. Nessa was the last, pausing to lay her hand on Carragh's arm. Her palm had the same powdery texture as the onionskin pages of the library catalog.

"I'm sorry to have exposed you to such unpleasantness, Miss Ryan. I assure you, my only intent in bringing you here was to help with the library. But it seems the castle has other plans for you. You should be careful."

When Nessa had exited, Aidan said, "Lock your door behind me."

As if that would help her sleep easily after everything that had happened.

She stared at the painted Jenny Gallagher in challenge. "Now would be a good time for you to start talking," she said to the woman in the painting. "Perhaps the name of whoever did this?"

But Jenny merely looked back at her with that serene, timeless gaze.

CHAPTER THIRTY-TWO

Carragh and Aidan slipped out of Deeprath Castle as the sun was rising. He'd knocked on her door at six, asking if she could set off earlier than planned to avoid being caught by any of his family. After her princess outfit of last night, the jeans, hoodie, and trainers she wore were a reminder that this wasn't actually a fairy tale. Even if the two of them were hunting treasure, of a sort. In her backpack she had protein bars, a notebook and pen, and a copy of the Bride poem she'd been studying. She assumed Aidan had much the same in his. They were half a mile from Deeprath before either of them spoke.

"I didn't do it." Carragh had been practicing ways to say it to convince Aidan to believe her. Not too belligerent, not too needy, no craven appeal to whatever personal feelings had been expressed in the corridor . . .

Aidan's surprise was evident. "I know that. You're not that stupid."

"Thank you for trusting to my intelligence and not my morality," she said drily.

"Please. If you were going to break any moral codes, it would be to steal half my library."

The clever—and accurate—remark made her laugh despite herself. "That is true."

He showed no desire to speculate about who might have destroyed the clothing, but Carragh had her own ideas. She had carefully retrieved each piece of fabric last night and laid them in a neat pile on the desk, assuming that Mrs. Bell would be tasked with removing them. And while she'd worked, Carragh had turned over the possible identities of the vandal. If not Kyla, then she'd bet money on Philip. He knew she'd been out of sight of Nessa and the others last night, no doubt watched Aidan slip away after her, and was certainly malicious enough. Carragh didn't fool herself that it was because she was such a fascinating creature—Philip merely believed in controlling his women and not the other way around. Her rejection must have seriously wounded his ego.

Once again the Round Tower was the first thing she saw, its conical cap drawing the eye up and pointing it toward heaven. Or the sky, if one was less religiously inclined. Approaching as they did from the southeast, they had to traverse the length of Glendalough. With no one else in sight at this early hour, Carragh could almost imagine the distant figures of monks and clerics and students—and Darkling Brides—pacing slowly along the green paths to their various duties. Or hear the bells ringing from the seven churches that Glendalough had been known for.

Aidan pointed out Trinity Church in the distance to their right, much closer to the road than the rest of the ruins, with local Laragh houses looking down on it. They crossed the river and came up the path that bordered St. Kevin's Kitchen—with its own round tower, which looked like a chimney—and St. Kevin's Cathedral. Next to the church an enormous stone cross loomed over the surrounding graves. Unlike most Celtic crosses, this one had no carving on its face.

"Stop a minute," Aidan said. He stepped next to the eight-foot cross. "Legend says that if one can stand with one's back against St.

Kevin's Cross and reach around to touch one's fingers together, one's wish will be granted."

Carragh studied it skeptically. "That certainly seems to favor someone with longer arms. Have you ever done it?"

"Tried, but you're right, a seven- or eight-year-old's arms aren't long enough. You should try it."

She laughed, but dropped her backpack in the grass and pressed her back firmly against the stone cross. "Now I just . . . reach?"

No matter how hard she tried, she couldn't quite make her fingers touch. Aidan encouraged her. "Just another inch, even half an inch—"

Carragh stepped away. "I could only get another half inch if I dislocated one or both of my shoulders. And then I should merely have to wish them whole again. You do it."

From the moment Aidan put his back to the cross, his mind seemed to be elsewhere. Or, more accurately perhaps, else *when*. Had his mother stood here and cheered him on as a child?

When his fingers met, she crowed, "And there's a wish the saint shall have to grant you. What will it be?"

"I can't tell you that," he said with mock sternness. "But don't worry, I won't waste my wish on something . . ." He paused, the look in his eyes similar to the one he'd turned on her last night. Just before they'd kissed.

She swallowed. "On something trivial?"

"On something I figure I can accomplish on my own."

"What have I told you about arrogance?" But Carragh couldn't help smiling. "Keep your wish, then. And lead on."

To get to the Lady Chapel—St. Mary's Church, as it was known today—they had to veer southwest from the Round Tower, past the Priest's House and through the main part of the monastic grave-yard. The remains of the nave and chancel church were soft-edged against the iffy light of the morning, the stones looking less jagged and more inviting. The nave dated from the tenth century, and Aidan took her around to the west side, where the original doorway remained, with its granite jambs. When they passed beneath it, he directed the flashlight he'd brought above their heads.

"Look up."

Carragh stretched onto her toes, straining to see.

"Look just there." Aidan guided her eyes with the light. "It helps if you know what you're looking for. It's the center of—"

"A saltire cross!" Carragh cried.

"Yes."

The saltire was a diagonal cross, most commonly seen on the flag of Scotland. The four arms of this one reached out from a central circle, each arm also ending in a circle.

"Why is it here?" she asked.

"Probably another form of sanctuary cross, like the one at the gatehouse. Since the chapel was outside the inner circle walls—and likely was a dedicated church for women—perhaps this was a safe space for women who needed sanctuary? No one knows for certain."

They passed into the remains of the nave, elegant in its proportions despite the lack of roof and the jagged walls that ended at various heights. Through another doorway they could see the chancel, which had been added at a later date, but Carragh wanted to linger in the nave.

"Do you know," she mused aloud, "I used to say that I wished I could live in the past. But my mother is a terribly practical woman—judges mostly are—and she used to point out all the difficulties. Lack of sanitation and hygiene and bad diet, not to mention the fact that the odds that I would have been living in a castle as a noble were dreadfully low. Much more likely, she used to tell me, that I'd be born a peasant, either die in childhood or live long enough to bear ten children and count myself lucky if three or four of them lived to grow up."

"So you gave up your fantasies."

"No, I simply decided that if I actually did wind up in the Middle Ages or the Renaissance, I'd have taken the veil."

He laughed. "Become a nun?"

"Why not?" she challenged. "If you were of sufficient birth, you could get an education that most women weren't offered. And even if you were a peasant, at least you had somewhere stable to live and eat. And it removed at one stroke a woman's highest risk of death—childbirth."

"I suppose that's true." He regarded her closely. "I suppose I can see the studying part, but—"

"But how would I manage to live without a man like Aidan Gallagher offering to kiss me?" She couldn't help teasing; it had been so long since she'd met anyone she wanted to talk and laugh with, and not just touch.

That didn't mean she needed to throw herself at him. "Didn't we come here to see the graveyard?" she reminded him.

There wasn't much to see—a few stone slabs in the grass, broken reminders of the lives buried beneath them. "Not many markers," Aidan pointed out. "But then, there wouldn't be, would there? Not as it was meant for unbaptized children."

Hard to get more depressing than that. Carragh steeled herself against sentiment and said, "We're here to find a clue. I hope you can figure out what your mother intended."

As Aidan walked slowly through the overgrown grass, Carragh watched him and held her tongue. *Figure out what your mother intended. Your* dead *mother.* She considered how she might feel if their positions were reversed, and her instant shudder told her everything she needed to know about the strain he must be under. Hadn't she flatly refused to open the door to her own past?

Impulsively, she stepped to his side and touched his arm. "We don't have to do this, Aidan. Wherever your mother's hunt wandered, surely it ended at the castle. And who's to say this has anything to do with their deaths? We're probably just wasting our time."

Something flicked her ear. Carragh's hand went up automatically, but she already knew there wouldn't be any convenient bug or errant leaf blown there. Not when the flick had been accompanied by a sigh of pure exasperation.

"You're right," Aidan announced, oblivious to the invisible. "Not about it being a waste of time—we both know it isn't. But let's forget the clues, forget the hunt, for a few hours. Let me take you out on the Upper Lake. I know someone with a boat nearby—I want to show you Temple na Skellig."

Carragh half expected another sign or sound of displeasure, but Aidan's plan seemed acceptable to whatever force of heaven or imagination walked with her. "As long as you promise you know what you're doing," she said. "I don't swim."

You could tell the temperature of a family by appearing when they did not expect it. The temperature at Deeprath Castle was distinctly frosty this Saturday afternoon. Sibéal could feel it the moment she pulled her complaining car into a makeshift parking spot. Afraid her car would not be able to tackle the long rocky drive again, she left it just before the open iron gate and walked the mile to the castle with a distinct sense of moving back in time.

What was it Philip Grant had said about Deeprath? "Nothing happens there that the castle doesn't know about." Now to just figure out how to get the castle to talk to her.

She had learned to recognize the clues her body gave her as a case moved to a close. A muddled case that didn't reach a clear conclusion was accompanied by muddled physical symptoms like congestion and inflammation. But when a case was on the verge of breaking, her senses sharpened and clarified, often leaving her with tension headaches and muscles that hurt at each day's end from being held tight all day. She had that feeling now, and knew if she could keep her head and not be lost in the minutiae of details and possibilities, she would have the answer Superintendent O'Neill had demanded by Monday.

Whether she could prove it would be another matter.

Philip answered the door, to her surprise. He looked a bit worse for wear, with the bloodshot eyes and tight expression of someone with a vicious hangover.

"You didn't tell me you were returning to Deeprath when we spoke yesterday," Sibéal said accusingly.

"You didn't ask. What do you want?"

To talk to the castle . . . "I want to visit the library and the tower."

"To look for clues? After all this time?"

She smiled politely and did not elaborate. Before Philip could make more snide comments, Nessa Gallagher appeared at the door. In the week since their first meeting, Nessa seemed to have aged several years, her iron will increasingly less visible beneath the paper-thin skin and cautious balance.

But her voice, at least, remained the same. "Inspector. I'm afraid you find us somewhat disarranged. You know how it is after hosting an event."

As Sibéal had never been able to cram more than a dozen people into her little flat, she doubted it was quite the same. But at least it gave her a clue to Philip's morning-after state. No doubt there had been plenty of alcohol involved.

"I won't get in your way," she promised. "I think I can even find the library on my own. And the tower opens up from there as well, doesn't it?"

"It does," Nessa replied. "I believe it's still locked. I'll come with you and show you where the key is kept. Something happened here last night that I think you should know about."

Intriguing. But Nessa said no more until Philip had been dismissed and the two of them reached the library itself. Nessa retrieved the key from a glass-fronted cabinet and showed Sibéal the inner doorway that opened into the base of the tower. "You will be careful, won't you? The steps are centuries old and extremely worn and uneven. At least you're not wearing heels," she said, though she looked doubtful about Sibéal's loafers.

"I'll be careful. What did you want to tell me?"

"A serious act of vandalism occurred here yesterday. Some very valuable items were destroyed beyond repair."

"Items connected to the past murders?"

"No."

"Have you notified the local police?"

"My great-nephew does not wish the matter to be handled officially."

Sibéal cocked her head. "Then what do you want from me?"

Nessa, she decided, only ever hesitated for effect. "I would like you to finish up this investigation as soon as possible so that our lives can return to normal and we can dispense with the services of outsiders. We should never have brought a stranger into our home."

Even more intriguing—it seemed Nessa was not a fan of Carragh Ryan, either. Sibéal couldn't think whom else she might mean. Though she knew she shouldn't involve herself in this, Sibéal said, "Why don't you write me a brief statement of what happened, and I'll take a look at it and the property damage after I'm finished here."

Nessa departed, leaving her alone in the library. There were stacks of books on the table, and several open registers, one of them very old-fashioned. She supposed the other notes, all in the same neat hand, had been compiled by Carragh. As she wandered through the bays she noted that some of them were clearly a work in progress, with gaps on shelves and some books stacked on the floor in a method she could not divine.

Sibéal stood with her back to the main door, soaking in the space of the former chapel. She was religious enough to feel a shiver of unease at the desecration of the space—if not by books, then by the violence committed here. Was that why the library atmosphere was so charged?

Stop it, she commanded herself. *Don't daydream. Don't anticipate. Start with the facts and walk the crime.* A concept her first partner had drilled into her.

Fact: Cillian Gallagher died from a blow to the head while standing near the library table.

Fact: whatever caused that blow had not been found in the library at the time.

Fact: the marble cross discovered with the "stolen" antiquities two miles away was stained with human blood and hair, and the pathologist had confirmed that it was in keeping with the description of the damage to Cillian Gallagher's skull.

Fact: during the first police search of the grounds, Lily Gallagher's body was found at the foot of the ancient Norman keep, with injuries consistent with a fall. Among those injuries, might there have been one inflicted by the same marble cross?

No, now she was moving out of the realm of facts.

Supposition, verging on fact: Lily Gallagher did not kill her husband, tramp two miles into the mountains to hide the marble cross and antiquities, and then return to Deeprath to commit suicide. The timeline alone would not support it, no matter how many people wanted her to reach that conclusion.

There were three ways to kill a person: accidentally, in a moment of temporary passion, or deliberately and "with malice aforethought." The careful disposal of the offending weapon and stolen antiquities almost surely ruled out accident. That same logic ruled out a crime of passion—at least, not solely of passion. Cillian Gallagher might very well have been hit in the head without previous intent, but the careful cover-up that followed was both rational and cold-blooded.

Despite Sibéal's normally pragmatic outlook, the walls of the library seemed to be pushing in at her, as though trying to help her see what they had seen on that tragic day.

Walk the crime. She stood at the table across from where Cillian Gallagher had fallen and imagined facing him. She knew from photographs that he had looked a good deal like Aidan, so she imagined a shockingly good-looking man about to turn fifty, tall and intimidating in presence, confronting someone with hostile intent. He would not have expected violence, surely, for he was a man of control and would expect to be able to handle whatever situation arose.

Especially if it was someone he knew. And it was surely someone Cillian knew.

So . . . Cillian died without expecting it. And then? What had the killer done then?

The answer depended on whether Lily Gallagher had died *before* or *after* her husband. The timetables of people's movements through the castle that day were unsatisfyingly vague and incomplete—not necessarily suspicious in itself, because most people don't walk through their lives constructing alibis as they went just in case one was needed. In a place the size of Deeprath, it was no wonder that individuals dropped out of sight for long stretches of time.

But the timetable firmed up considerably from the moment Aidan had found his father's corpse. Mrs. Bell's call to the police was made at 4:15 P.M., the first officers on scene arrived at 4:37 and the coroner at five-ten.

Taking advantage of the enormous library table, Sibéal sat down and reviewed the timetable she'd constructed from the records.

> *3:00—Mr. Winthrop, the Rathdrum solicitor, leaves Deeprath Castle after a meeting with Cillian Gallagher and the steward, Robert Bell.*
> *3:20—Mrs. Bell takes a tea tray to Nessa Gallagher in her bedroom.*
> *3:25—Mrs. Bell takes tea to the library for Cillian Gallagher, who is expecting his wife to join him.*
> *3:40—Mr. Bell and the gardener head into the woods to examine some trees that need cutting down.*
> *4:00—Mrs. Bell sees Aidan Gallagher return from Glendalough; he asks her where he can find his father and heads in the direction of the library.*

Fifteen minutes had elapsed before the boy's screams brought the housekeeper running. What had Aidan been doing for that quarter hour? Sibéal wondered. Why had no one bothered to ask him that at the time?

By the time the police and emergency services arrived at Deeprath, every member cf the household was present and accounted for—save only Lily. It had been then-constable O'Neill who had discovered her body at the bottom of the tower, fallen into a tussock of tall grass against the weathered stones.

So . . . between three-thirty and four-fifteen someone entered the library, hit Cillian Gallagher in the head, and removed the cross and antiquities. All of that was straightforward enough. The oddity was Lily. Why hadn't she died in the library? Why had she gone to the top of the tower? And when?

As Sibéal stood there, the library seemed to shiver in her sight, and she had the sudden certainty that she was seeing it as Lily had. Facing her husband, the antiquities scattered across the library table, Cillian's expression changing from surprised to furious. She could see it all through Lily's eyes . . . except for one thing. Just out of reach beside her, just beyond her sight, stood someone else. The killer.

She breathed deeply, knowing she was on shaky evidentiary ground, but certain all the same that Lily had been in this room when her husband died. And in trying to get away from his killer, she'd bolted up the stairs of the tower.

Sibéal now walked the crime with her feet as well as her thoughts. The door between the library and tower opened fairly easily with the key. It must have already been open that day, for someone running for her life could not have paused to unlock it.

She took care as she went up, for Nessa had not exaggerated the condition of the stairs. Sibéal hadn't made a habit of visiting medieval ruins, and she found the boxed-in spiral staircase claustrophobic. The arrow slits let in pitifully little light—even less considering that clouds were boiling up, from what she could see through the narrow openings. Better hurry.

The Victorian sitting room floor was something of a shock, completely inconsistent with the empty floors below. There was something nightmarish about the space, from the damaged books to the rotting sofa. It took first place for weirdest room she'd ever seen.

And then she went up the last flight of stairs.

If the sitting room was macabre, the bedroom she emerged into was terrifying in a "mad wife in the attic," Jane Eyre kind of way. It was like an old-fashioned asylum: plain iron bedstead, a small table, and straight-backed chair . . . and then there were the walls.

"Now that's disturbing," she said aloud, staring at the white walls covered in black writing. Who had been kept up here? And what had they written?

Not Lily, she reminded herself. *Which means it's not the crime I'm investigating.* Wrenching her gaze away from the hypnotically horrifying walls, she went to the only door in the outer wall, a short, narrow door that even a medium-sized man would have to turn sideways to get through.

There had been a lock installed on this door, but it had been disabled at some point. Sibéal stepped gingerly through the doorway onto the open battlements. She made herself look down, and for a second she could swear she saw something at the tower's base—an illusion of broken limbs and white fabric.

Shuddering, she stepped back as a streak of lightning and crash of thunder occurred almost simultaneously. Within seconds rain sheeted down so heavily that she might as well have been standing in a crow's nest at sea.

"You're not very subtle," she complained to the skies above and the stone beneath. "I get it, you want me to stay. Fine. Now make it worth my while."

CHAPTER THIRTY-THREE

May 1881

Evan spent the last four weeks of Jenny's pregnancy watching her every move. She seemed to find his attention endearing—but when her father tried to do the same, she shied away sharply.

"This is not his baby," she complained to Evan a week before her due date. "I wish we could go away for the birth."

Jenny was wise enough to know why she could not, which Evan took as a sign that her illness was not really madness. If she were insane, she could not be this reasonable. He had toured lunatic asylums as research for his third novel. Of course, Bedlam was the most famous and by far the most disturbing. But he was a rigorous researcher and so had also visited several progressive asylums in Europe, as well as two privately run institutions in England. In every place, he'd seen men and women who were kept securely for their own good and safety as much as—if not more so—that of others.

And in none of those places had he found anyone half so reasonable and intelligent as Jenny.

She went into labor on a Tuesday evening when the Wicklow light had just begun to take on the glow of spring. All through the night she labored in their bedroom, with the ever faithful Dora Bell and a midwife to attend her and a medical man to oversee. Jenny did not like the doctor, but that mattered little to Michael Gallagher. The healthy birth of the next Gallagher generation must be assured by every means wealth and position could arrange.

Evan could have escaped overhearing any of her cries; his father-in-law shut himself up in the library at the opposite end of the castle. But he haunted the staircase and corridors near their room.

For that, he was rewarded by hearing his child's first cry. It brought him to the threshold of the room, where he hovered until Dora came out a few minutes later with a bundle of sheets and towels. There was no small amount of blood.

"Is she all right?" he asked, panicky.

Jenny heard him, and called. "Evan."

He ignored the doctor's and midwife's objections and went straight to where she rested against a pillow, face sheened with sweat. He pushed her hair back from her forehead. "Are you all right?"

But Jenny wasn't interested in her own condition. "Did you hear him?"

"I did . . . wait. It's a boy?"

The midwife answered, bringing with her a tightly wrapped bundle. "It's a boy, right enough. And mad as sin at all the fuss."

The woman didn't trust either of them to hold the precious bundle, but allowed them time to marvel at his screwed-up face, his eyes and nose and mouth, every familiar human feature turned to brilliance by the fact that he was theirs.

Finally, as Jenny grew sleepy, Evan allowed himself to be pushed out. But not before his wife murmured, "My father will finally be happy."

DIARY OF JENNY GALLAGHER

11 May 1881

Dora would not bring me my diary, so I begged the night maid in-
stead. What can possibly be too strenuous about leaning against bed
pillows and writing this on a lap desk? After being turned more or
less inside out, this is positively restful.

We have named him James for Evan's grandfather and Michael
to please my father. I know all mothers are biased, but he is truly
beautiful. He has my black hair and Evan's strong nose so that he
looks like he has been formed from the very landscape of our Wick-
low Mountains. Dora says the hair will not last—that I myself was
born blonde and then, after losing it all by the age of three months,
it grew in black—but I'm sure my James will be beautiful whatever
God has in store for him.

It is not often that I dwell on my mother, for she was ill for so
long, and my life since her death has been so dominated by my spells
and the tower room that she seems to belong to a part of life I
hardly believe was once mine. But I feel that she has been with me
all day, that it was she who held my James in her arms until the
last moment when he was placed in mine. I pray that her love and
care will keep my baby safe.

I told Evan that my father would be happy, but even I did not
expect the tears in his eyes and the wonder in his expression when
he first laid eyes on his grandson. For a moment I was shamed to
think I have ever thought him overbearing. I know that what he
does, he does for love of me.

Then he said, "The Gallagher line seems assured with this
one—but another two or three will be even better."

CHAPTER THIRTY-FOUR

Of course, Aidan knew someone nearby with a boat. He probably knew someone with a cannon and battering ram. John Quinn, it turned out, knew not only Aidan but his father and even his grandfather. The wiry old man lent them his truck and trailer to pull the boat with, keeping a wary eye on the sky and issuing a gruff warning.

"Storm coming in."

"Not till after dark, they say," was Aidan's answer.

"Just don't let yourself be distracted." Quinn gave Carragh a suspicious look, as though she was a siren in disguise. "Going to be a bad one. You won't want to be on the lake when it hits."

"We'll be well back before dark," Aidan promised.

As it was only ten o'clock in the morning, Carragh certainly hoped so. She didn't mind being outdoors—her brothers had often dragged her hiking—but she was dubious about small boats on open expanses of water.

She watched Aidan maneuver the boat off the trailer. "You know what you're doing, right?"

"Do you think Quinn would let me near his precious boat if I didn't? He's the one who taught me, no worries."

Once Carragh let herself relax—and put on a life jacket—she quite enjoyed the beauty of the Upper Lake. No wonder St. Kevin and his followers had wanted to live here. Aside from the occasional car passing on the road above, they might have been in any century from the eighth to the eighteenth.

Aidan seemed to have the same thought. "When I was little, we would have had a lot more company on the lake. They closed it to tourist traffic some years ago."

"So what happens if someone sees the boat?"

"I might get yelled at. Nothing I can't handle."

"You're telling me that being a Gallagher gets you special treatment?"

"I'll take what I can get."

They tied up at the bottom of a projecting shelf of rock and Aidan helped her up the steps cut into it. This brought them to a shallow section of level land that looked as wild to her eyes as it must have fifteen hundred years ago. All that time, all those pilgrims, all those monks passing in their silent ranks of the dead . . .

I don't have time for monks, she scolded them silently, feeling only a little ridiculous. *Just keep on doing your ghostly things and leave me be.*

"Temple na Skellig," Aidan said, "means Church of the Rock. It was built long after Kevin, but excavations in the 1950s confirmed that he and his earliest followers had lived here. At least long enough to build wattle huts connected by paved paths."

"Is there anything you don't know?"

"About Wicklow? Not much. My mother loved Glendalough, and Nessa made sure we knew our place in these mountains."

She examined what man-made things she could, which weren't many. The foundation of the church, one wall partially standing, the uncovered remains of the wattle huts, and the view itself, which was not man-made but surely one of the reasons people had been coming here for generations.

"For a man who prized isolation as much as St. Kevin, he couldn't get away from his own reputation," Aidan told her. "All he wanted was the quiet life of a hermit, to pray in solitude. But he was too good to send away those who came to him to learn. So they came out here and built their huts and learned whatever Kevin taught them."

"Good deeds never go unpunished," she murmured, studying the sloped cliff face behind them with the faintest suggestion of carved steps. They were practically vertical. "What's up there?" She pointed to a low rounded opening in the rock above them.

"That is our destination—St. Kevin's Bed."

"St. Kevin's Kitchen, St. Kevin's Bed . . . will we be seeing St. Kevin's washroom soon? That would be convenient. How are we supposed to get up there?"

"The safest way is to climb up the face farther down, then come at the opening from above."

"You can't be serious."

He laughed. "I'm not. I've been up there once, but it was with my father and Quinn and we had proper climbing gear to make sure of our safety. My mother hated heights. She wouldn't have put a clue of any sort up there."

"Then why are we here?"

"It's beautiful. I wanted to show it to you."

Carragh couldn't help but laugh. "With everything that's happening, you wanted to take time for this?"

"More for *this*."

It was possible, she discovered, to manage a comfortable position on the bracken between the stones. When they separated enough for her to speak, she teased, "If I didn't know that you left the mountains at age ten, I'd say I'm not the first woman you've brought here."

"I've never brought any woman anywhere near Ireland. I've hardly come here myself. When I was eleven, I went to a Benedictine school in England, then university. I lived with Nessa in Kilkenny during school holidays and I've visited Kyla there about once or twice a year since her marriage. But I never came any closer to home."

"Why not?"

He leaned over her with those amazingly gorgeous eyes and asked, "Is it really talking you want to be doing just now?"

A burst of light, a crackle of power in the air, and a split second of every nerve ending alive with energy . . . then the rain came like hundreds of needles driving into every bit of exposed skin.

"Quinn's going to kill me!" Aidan shouted.

Her laughter turned to choking when rain got in her mouth. Aidan lifted his head, then ducked it back down close to hers. "We can't go on the lake like this. We've got to find shelter of some kind. Farther downshore, where we aren't kept on such a narrow spit of land."

"Okay."

"Hold my hand. Don't let go."

She thought he was overreacting until she tried to get up and fell straight back again. Aidan hauled her up by the arm, keeping his body angled between her and the wind as much as possible. That mostly ensured that they remained pressed up together, and it made for awkward movement. She clung grimly to his arm, determined not to let go whatever happened.

It quickly became apparent to Carragh that there was no sufficient shelter to be found, a fact Aidan must have known before they even started. They would simply have to back themselves up against the cliff face and hope for the best. Hope the waves wouldn't be whipped up too furiously on the lake and dash against them. Hope the lightning wouldn't strike or the winds bring down trees upon their heads. She could hear the creaking of wood all around them.

Beneath the instinctive fear, Carragh told herself they would be fine. If only because she couldn't imagine a more foolish time and place to die.

She didn't realize Aidan had stopped until he dragged her back a few steps. He put her back against the rocks and faced her, arms spread on either side of her shoulders so he took the brunt of the rain for a moment. He leaned down to speak against her ear, so close she could feel his breath.

But what he said was not in the least romantic. "We're going to have to go up."

"What do you mean 'up'?" Just after the words left her mouth she answered her own question. "To the cave? Are you insane? You said it wasn't safe."

"Neither is this."

"If we fall, we die!"

"It's not that far. And you won't fall." His lips pressed against her earlobe for a moment. "I promise."

It was hellish work. Aidan sent her up first, to provide stability behind her. He kept up a running commentary of guidance and reassurance, most of his words snatched away by the wind.

In the end, Carragh was fairly certain that the only way she made it up the cliff was through sheer irritation and fury at the entire situation. She turned it all on Aidan the minute they had both crawled into the cave—on hands and knees—after managing to bang her head three times in the process.

"What the hell were you thinking?" The enclosing rock echoed her words, so that her voice reverberated against and inside her skull. She modulated her volume down. "This is why I hate camping."

"If I'd taken you camping I'd have been better prepared."

"So we just stay up here . . . how long?"

"At the very worst, overnight. But the worse the storm, the faster it passes."

"So now you're a meteorologist. Aren't you the one who said the storm wasn't coming until after midnight?"

"It will be fine. We've got some food and water. And lightning can't reach us here."

"At least lightning would be warm."

He switched on his flashlight then, and she saw the very real worry in his eyes. It made her pause and say grudgingly, "It's okay. I'm not that cold."

But she was, and he could see it. "This cave was built for one—

St. Kevin wasn't much for company in his bed—and that means we're forced into close proximity. That will keep our body heat conserved."

She felt the corners of her lips twitching up. "And you mean me to believe you didn't plan this."

"If I were going to maneuver you into a compromising position, Carragh, it wouldn't be in a cave that I can't even stand up in."

"Who needs to stand?"

Body heat made a significant difference, she found. And the creating of it also managed to pass the time pleasantly. At least until both of them had accumulated a number of minor bumps and scrapes. As Aidan had pointed out, the saint had slept here alone.

Finally they set about making themselves as comfortable as possible in a space of only a few meters. In the process, Carragh hit herself so many times on various outcroppings that Aidan finally remarked, "I've never known anyone likelier to injure herself by simply breathing."

"Fine, I'll stop breathing. Can I eat something instead?"

She could get used to homemade bread. And country ham. And Mrs. Bell's shortbread. Maybe she would learn how to cook. Once she had a kitchen that wouldn't explode the first time she switched on the stove, that is.

"Now," Aidan said with an annoying air of command, "it's your turn to talk. I feel like all we've done in the last ten days is wade through my family's issues—past and present. I'd like to hear about your family."

"You know what you need to. Irish-born father, Irish American mother, three older brothers who love public service and football in equal measure, and an upbringing in which education rivaled the Church for importance."

"That's the family who raised you. What about your real parents?"

"As opposed to my imaginary parents?" Her voice rose. "I hate that word. *Real*. It elevates the most basic transfer of genetic material into an obsession. Just look at you Gallaghers. I've never met people more obsessed with blood, but what makes your family more real than mine? Your money? Your castle and houses? Or is it the fact that you can hardly stand to be in the same room with each other?"

"I'm sorry. I know intention doesn't matter, but truly I didn't mean to insult your family. Truth be told, I envy you."

"Right."

"It's not a competition, but if it were, I guarantee I would win. What could be worse than two dead parents, your mother rumored to have killed your father?"

"How about a dead mother and a father who most definitely killed her?"

She had never said it so plainly. Of course she'd talked about it—her family was Irish, not the usual reserved and repressed New Englanders—and she had refused to hide from the facts.

But hiding from emotions was entirely different, and that was a skill she was extremely good at. Maybe, she reflected, not so different from the Gallaghers after all.

She had no idea she was crying until Aidan touched her cheek and brushed away a tear. He said nothing else, asked no further questions, made no further pleas. It was his very reticence that served to break her. She knew how to withstand questions and opinions, knew how to hold her own against her mother's determined efforts to get inside her heart. But gentleness and silence, it seemed, was a weapon against which she had no defenses. Within moments she was full-blown sobbing, in a way she hadn't since she was four years old.

By the time she had subsided into undignified hiccups, Aidan was holding her lightly. The moment she moved, he dropped his hands and allowed her to straighten up without comment. Until she banged the side of her head against the wall, when he murmured, "Always bumping into things."

She began to talk. "In August 1991, residents of a Boston apartment building began to complain about a foul smell. Around the same time, one or two of the more neighborly types realized they hadn't seen a particular tenant in a while. The building superintendent called the police and unlocked the door for them.

"They found the tenant—a twenty-five-year-old woman from Hong Kong—decomposing on the kitchen floor. She'd been strangled. The same attentive neighbor also told the police that the dead woman had a daughter.

"The child was in a closet, locked from the outside. She had been there two days, with a pack of juice boxes and a carton of animal crackers. The first thing she said when they opened the door was, 'If you're loud, he'll find you.'"

She chanced a look at Aidan and saw the same terrible sympathy she'd seen on too many faces. And yet . . . there was something else in his eyes. A faint spark that kindled in recognition. *I, too, have suffered death up close.*

With a decisive clearing of her throat, Carragh took control of her runaway emotions and memories. "If you really want the details, you can find them online. The dead woman's former boyfriend hanged himself afterward. And the police sergeant who had found the little girl in the closet used every connection he could to ensure that a good family would adopt her. And that's how the child of a dead Chinese student and a privileged California sociopath came to be Carragh Ryan."

She waited for Aidan to say the obvious. *I'm sorry. How horrible. How lucky you were.*

He said only two words. "You win."

It surprised a laugh out of her. Anyone else would have found it highly offensive, or at least insensitive. But Ryans were tough, and Carragh had learned only to shun the trap of self-pity. She might fail now and again, but Aidan's words reminded her of who she was.

"Can I ask you something?"

What secrets did she have left to reveal? "Yes."

"What was your name, before you were Carragh Ryan?"

To Mei-Lien, daughter of my daughter, Mei-Li . . . "Mei-Lien Lu," Carragh replied. "Mei-Lien remains my middle name. My parents called me that for a few months when they took me in, until I asked them to call me something else."

Not my name, she'd told them. And though she couldn't articulate it at the time, she knew later that it was her way of shutting up the first four years of her life and locking them away in the same closet where she'd hidden while her father murdered her mother. She'd thought it necessary. Healthy, even. But working at Deeprath had begun to teach her that things covered up don't disappear. They lurk, waiting to seize their moment.

Perhaps that was why the castle—or Lily—or Jenny—seemed to be calling to her. She could see so clearly the necessity of the truth, the whole truth, for the Gallagher family to move on, and could not understand why they were so determined to ignore the past.

She just hadn't wanted to believe that the same answer applied to her.

CHAPTER THIRTY-FIVE

It's an adventure, Sibéal told herself. How many people get to spend the night in a medieval castle during a furious storm with only candles and oil lamps for light? It should be positively romantic. Unfortunately, she was shut up with the most difficult and uncongenial family one could imagine. And one of them, she was convinced, was a murderer.

Not that she thought herself in imminent danger. It just made for a highly unpleasant dinner. Nessa Gallagher insisted on eating in the dining room, and at least the food was surprisingly hot. Sibéal supposed that was one of the benefits of living in a place so ancient—you still had enormous fireplaces and coal or wood stoves hanging about. She had borrowed leggings and a tunic dress from Carragh's belongings, the only things that would fit her to some degree, and reminded herself sternly that this was a golden opportunity to observe the Gallaghers at ease.

No one was at ease, though, for Carragh and Aidan had not returned from wherever they'd gone early that morning and no one had heard from them. With no mobile service here on the best days, and the telephone lines knocked out along with the power, the two of them had no way of contacting Deeprath, which left Nessa, at least, fretting.

"I do hope he hasn't done something reckless."

"Aidan?" snorted Philip. "He's the least reckless man I've ever known. Whatever he does, he makes sure he's the one in control. No doubt they're comfortably ensconced somewhere with electricity."

"Lucky them." Kyla was jittery tonight, her good manners slipping more and more with every drink she took.

Police instincts warring with the desire to ease the tension, Sibéal asked her, "How are your girls? Are they not still here?"

"I sent them back home with Louise. They can't stay out of school any longer."

Sibéal could not envision sending May away from her with only a hired au pair, and had to quash the instant thought that her daughter had spent more time this month in Josh's home than with her. Perhaps she shouldn't be so quick to condemn.

"Aren't you going to ask my wife what she does with herself now that the girls are in school all day and Louise does everything domestic?" Philip said, smooth and nasty. "I, for one, would like to know."

Sibéal would have expected Nessa to intervene by now, but the woman looked drawn and more delicate than she had two days before, with no energy to spare for the sniping of her younger relatives.

Kyla raised her glass to her husband, her smile dripping acid. "Perhaps I'll spend my weekdays in Dublin with you, Philip."

This was getting more than awkward. Sibéal reached into what she knew of Kyla's history postmurder. "You did a business degree at Trinity, didn't you? That's impressive."

"Is it? I was told I was simply filling in time before having children, when I was expected to restrict myself to charitable boards and local galas."

"Is that how your mother filled her days?"

Kyla's cheek twitched and for a moment she looked like a little lost girl. Like May when she fell off her bicycle or popped her balloon. "My mother had the gift of loving everything she did, no matter how boring."

Sibéal swallowed a spoonful of soup, considering. "Maybe it was just that she chose the things she loved, however boring you may have thought them."

"But what if I have no idea what I love?" Kyla eyed Philip. "Or who?"

"Don't be silly, darling," he retorted. "You know I love you enough for both of us."

"I know you love my money."

Mercifully, Nessa finally intervened. "That is enough. Marital disagreements should be handled privately, not at the dinner table." Not that there was a lot of actual dining going on. Just pushing food around. And drinking.

"That only works so long as he takes care not to make his infidelities public," Kyla retorted. "Who is it this time, Philip? Clearly someone who walked away before you could. I haven't seen you this bothered since—what was her name? The French girl who 'interned' for you three years ago?"

As though in answer to Sibéal's prayers, an enormous crash sounded. Like someone had driven a car into one of the castle walls. With the sound came a shockwave of vibration rolling through her body as though she was one with the structure around her.

They had all frozen reflexively, and all four of them now moved in concert. Nessa calling for Bell, Philip taking Kyla's arm (she shook his hand off immediately), Sibéal reaching for her phone even though she knew she couldn't get a signal and had no idea who she would call if she could.

"What was that?" she asked.

"The roof falling in?" suggested Philip.

"Lightning, I think." Nessa conferred briefly with Robert Bell, in voices low enough not to be heard.

"Can I help?" Sibéal asked Nessa, since she was so clearly in charge.

"Nothing can be done in the dark or during the storm. Both will pass and then we will see precisely what needs doing."

"What was hit?"

"At a guess, the Bride Tower. It wouldn't be the first time. The great advantage of the tower's age is that it has never been electrified or greatly modernized, which reduces the damage a lightning strike can do. Still, Bell will make a careful search of the castle to ensure no fires result."

"I'll help," Sibéal offered.

"As you wish."

With a cultivated drawl, Philip said, "We've had quite a run of bad luck since you showed up, Inspector. No doubt we'll be much happier when you are out of our lives."

"Your bad luck didn't start with me. But I will gladly leave—with an arrest made. Surely that's what you all want?"

They locked eyes. "Of course." It was Philip who answered, but she knew he spoke equally for the Gallagher women. The right answer . . . and a lie. The only Gallagher who was truly interested in justice was Aidan.

Who knew that Aidan Gallagher had so many stories in him? Or could sing? All through that long, dark, cold, and physically awful night in St. Kevin's Bed, he took up the burden of distraction and entertainment. They ate sparingly of what they had brought and drank even more sparingly. They managed to situate the backpacks into supportive positions and half sat, half lay against the back of the cave. Carragh dozed at some point, then woke herself with a crack to the head when she abruptly shifted position.

Aidan laughed, then stopped when she swore at him, and perhaps feeling penitent, he began to tell her stories. About Glendalough and the Wicklow Mountains. About the United Irish Rising and how Michael Dwyer had hidden from the British not far from here.

Stories of Gallagher ancestors, their far-flung adventures in the world, and how they had always come back to Deeprath. Stories about arts and antiquities crimes, including famous unsolved thefts like the one at the Gardner Museum in Boston. Carragh could add to that one, with her personal knowledge of the museum.

"It's very sobering," she told him, "standing in front of the blank spaces where the canvases had hung. Do you really think they ended up in Ireland?"

They discussed the intricacies of drug crime, gun running, the IRA, and art theft. He wanted to know about her Irish studies at Trinity, and it turned out he not only knew the words of many ballads, but their melodies. Carragh had a rather shaky alto that he helped her tune to his tenor and they sang "Erin go Bragh" and "The Isle of Inisfree" and "The Battle of Benburg."

That was the last thing she remembered before she woke—less violently this time—curled against Aidan. He was still asleep, and she thought it was ridiculously unfair that he should look even sexier after a night in a cave. Then she realized that she could see his face because there was light coming from the entrance. Not a huge amount, for it was still pouring, but at least it was only rain that she heard now instead of the ferocious roar of the storm.

"Aidan." She leaned in, touching his shoulder. "Aidan, the storm is passing."

They heard the shouting after they left the cave, before they were all the way down. Aidan had gone first, and Carragh half climbed, half slipped into his arms. "I think you're being called," she said breathlessly.

He was, indeed, by a Search and Rescue team alerted by Quinn late the night before. The boat, Carragh saw mournfully, had been smashed by the wind into the rocks. "He's definitely going to kill me," Aidan muttered grimly.

The search team took them across the lake in their own boat, and soon enough they were damp and shivering in the lobby of the Glendalough Hotel as the receptionist rang Penelope's room. She was downstairs in two minutes, robe thrown over silk pajamas, and shook her head at them as if they were children who had disappointed her.

"Were you trying to get yourselves drowned?" she asked caustically.

Aidan simply said, "Could we possibly use your shower to warm up?"

The shower did warm Carragh up, but it did nothing for her nerves. It was not at all awkward, she told herself afterward, being locked up with Aidan's former lover while he showered in her bathroom. Not at all. At least Penelope didn't seem interested in flaunting her former status or in emphasizing the fact that she was gorgeous. And smart. Probably rich as well.

"How's he doing?" Penelope asked her without preamble.

"In the shower? You would know better than me." Why did she say these things?

Penelope smiled but refused to be diverted. "Being back at home."

"I just work in the library."

"You're an awful liar. Almost as bad as Aidan. Look, I came to Ireland because he asked me, and because I thought he needed help coping. I may have been wrong about that—he appears to be coping just fine. And I don't need a psychology degree to know you're part of the reason why."

"When you both come from trauma, you can understand one another," Carragh replied, and stopped herself there. Damned if she was going to spell out her past for this elegant creature.

"Fair enough," Penelope said. "Did you know he's interested in being hypnotized?"

The non sequitur made Carragh's already light head spin. "Hypnotized? Why?"

"It's a tool I've used in my psychology practice from time to time.

It's not what you think, if your horrified expression is anything to go by. It's a relaxation technique, more than anything. When both the body and the mind are relaxed, it's possible to recall things one has long suppressed."

Pounding on the door . . . *"Let me in, bitch"* . . . *Blinking up at her mother from the closet floor* . . . *"Be quiet, Mei-Lien. If you're loud, he'll find you"* . . .

Then nothing. A black blankness that doesn't lift until a police officer breaks open the door of the closet. *"Oh sweetheart,"* the young man had said to her. *"You're safe now."*

"Does it really work?" Carragh asked Penelope, endeavoring to sound skeptical.

"Depends on the person. Sometimes, no matter how much they think they want to remember, they really don't. I can't make someone remember something part of them is determined to hide."

"What does Aidan want to remember?"

"You would have to ask him," Penelope said with a kind finality.

Would Aidan talk about her to his . . . friend? Carragh wondered. Counselor? Woman he'd be happy to go back to bed with?

Penelope gave them a lift to the castle, but Aidan had her drop them at the top of the drive, next to a blue Volkswagen. "No use trying to get down the drive in that," he said, dismissing her little rental car. "Thank you. I'll be in touch."

"I guess the police are here," Carragh said, looking at Sibéal's car after they got out. Aidan didn't reply.

They had to pick their way carefully through the storm debris, including several downed trees that would have to be moved before any vehicle could get in or out. "I wonder why Bell isn't up here yet with the chain saw," he said uneasily.

He was right to sound uneasy; when the castle and its ring of cultivated grounds came into view, the reason for Bell's failure to deal with the trees was immediately evident.

"Damn."

A jagged black line streaked down the proud, ancient face of the Bride Tower as though painted on. But the gap in the crenellated battlements was no artistic statement. Nor was the tumble of damaged stone at the tower's base. The household stood there as they approached, surveying the damage. Nessa, Philip, Kyla, both the Bells, as well as Sibéal McKenna.

"Everyone all right?" Aidan called as they drew closer.

Nessa actually gasped, and then hugged a bemused Aidan. By the time he broke the embrace, the old woman had recovered herself. "We're perfectly fine. No power yet, but no significant damage except here. It's a pity, but I suppose even stone can only be struck by lightning so many times over the centuries before giving way."

"Is the interior stable?"

"Stable enough for now, but we'll need an engineer to check things over," answered Bell. He straightened from his examination of the rubble, and his expression alerted Carragh. Something was not right here.

Aidan had seen it, too. "What's wrong?" he asked the estate manager.

"Not altogether sure."

Carragh moved toward the tower, her curiosity stronger than her manners, and Philip pulled on her arm none too gently. "Careful. Wouldn't want you tripping over anything."

She shook him off, aware that Kyla was watching, and stepped out of reach, unwilling to be reprimanded. From where she stood, she could see only the tumble of lightning-blasted stones.

Aidan crouched down. "Is that . . ."

"I think so," Bell confirmed.

"Is that what?" Carragh heard one of the women demand. It could have been Kyla or Nessa, or even Sibéal, the voice roughened by weariness and surprise.

Aidan continued to stare. It was Bell who answered. "Bones."

→ ←

Sibéal watched the faces of everyone gathered outside the tower with extraordinary care. Carragh, she could dismiss. Not Aidan, though. A ten-year-old would not have been able to dispose of a baby's body so cunningly—and those bones could only have come from a very small child. But just because she didn't think Aidan had committed this crime didn't mean he didn't know something about it.

She knew she was making assumptions. There were probably any number of missing skeletons in the Gallagher family tree that she didn't know about. After all, the family had lived here for centuries. And these tiny, fragile bones and miniature skull, its hollowed eyes flaking around the sockets, looked too ancient to be relevant to her case. But hell if she was going to take the risk.

"I need to secure the site," she announced. "And I need to get somewhere I can get a mobile signal."

Aidan looked up from where he knelt, his face white. "Why?"

"Mysterious bones tumbling out of the same tower where your mother died? You know why, Detective Inspector Gallagher." Using his professional title was the quickest way she could think of to knock the stunned expression off his face and get his mind working.

After quick consideration, Sibéal left Bell to watch the site—of them all, he was the most likely not to interfere in anything. Then she hiked to the top of the drive to get a faint cell signal, and when she did, ordered Sergeant Cullen to bring down everything necessary from Dublin. She also instructed him to notify the Wicklow coroner. It didn't matter where or how human remains were found; they required investigation. All the while, she marveled at what a very strange family the Gallaghers were.

If it had been McKennas finding bones apparently hidden in their house, no shortage of loud speculation and/or accusation would have ensued. Unless it was political, no one in her family had ever been able to keep their mouth shut about anything at all, least of all something as enormous as murder.

One could almost believe the Gallaghers were English, with their stiff upper lips and cool control. But beneath the surface, she knew a tempest had to be brewing. She could only try to direct it and hope to bring down their defenses as surely as the storm had brought down the battlements.

CHAPTER THIRTY-SIX

August 1992

"Now think hard, Aidan. Where do we need to go next?"

Lily smiled encouragingly at her ten-year-old son as he screwed up his eyes and concentrated. She knew how much her Aidan wanted to get this right, without any help from his mother. He wanted to prove that he was more fun than Kyla, who at fifteen just rolled her eyes at the games and puzzles she'd once loved playing as much as he had. Like their mother's scavenger hunts.

He bit his lip and chanced an answer. "The globe in the library." His voice wavered on the end, not quite allowing it to be a question.

"Bravo!" She clapped her hands. "Lead the way, my brilliant explorer."

They trooped through the castle, passing Art Deco clocks and fragments of Roman mosaics and Louis XV sideboards and Gainsborough paintings—things that still sometimes made Lily blink twice and wonder if she really lived here. For a girl raised in a minimalist steel-and-chrome New York penthouse, Deeprath Castle had been a revelation. Cillian still teased her that she'd said yes to the house rather than to the man. Which he could tease about, because he knew how wildly she loved him.

She allowed Aidan to lead the way into the library, shoving rather hard at the carved oak door while trying not to let the effort show. He was so anxious to grow up, and she was so anxious for him not to . . . Look, she'd been a terror herself as a teenager. She had complete faith that all of them would survive Kyla's hormonal moods and surges of independence, but when Lily thought of her sweet boy descending into the silent indifference of typical teen males she wanted to hold back time by force of will.

Aidan went directly to the standing globe hand painted by one of his ancestors and hesitated only briefly before triumphantly snatching up the square of paper she'd tucked beneath the stand. He'd successfully reached the end of the scavenger hunt, and his reward, the paper told him, was a mother-and-son picnic at Glendalough.

"Really, truly?" he asked. "Just us?"

"Just us. Mrs. Bell has everything ready in the kitchen. You go put on your best walking shoes and bring a jacket. I'll meet you in the hall in twenty minutes."

Aidan shot off, all eagerness and light. What a contrast to his sister. Lily was shaking her head over it when someone spoke from one of the darkened bays.

"Lucky boy, getting you all to himself."

If it had been her husband, it would have been a compliment. But coming, as it did, from the arrogant—and young—mouth of Philip Grant, Lily put on her "lady of the manor" air. "Shouldn't you be working?"

What, exactly, the boy did, she wasn't sure. Cillian had agreed to have him as an intern this summer because Philip's father was a banker and MP with whom he'd done business in the past and hoped to do again in the future. It seemed to Lily that mostly Philip had spent these weeks idling in the gardens, turning Kyla's head with entirely inappropriate flirtations, and seeing just how close he could come to crossing the line of propriety with his boss's wife.

"Lord Gallagher sent me here in search of this." He held up what looked to be some sort of old ledger, though it may have just been the most convenient thing at hand for him to grab in excuse. And yet . . . he always seemed to know when to rein it in. Proving, perhaps, that he was a politician's son.

In a less familiar tone, he continued, "Your son is very lucky. I would have liked to have my mother's full attention at his age. Well, at any age, really. She's always been rather more concerned with her charities."

Which was common gossip in society, and made Lily forgive him more easily than she otherwise might have. "I consider myself the lucky one. Best go off with that . . . my husband has many virtues, but patience is not one of them."

It was as well, she thought, that Kyla was not there to see the utterly charming smile Philip gave her as he left. Except no, there she was, coming into the library as Philip exited. It was like Kyla had a magnet attached to the boy that drew her everywhere he was, and at the most inconvenient moments.

She heard her daughter's laugh against Philip's low murmur and wished she could just ignore all of this and go on her picnic with Aidan without anything to trouble her mind. But if she wanted that, she was fifteen years too late, she thought mordantly. And erased the treacherous thought as she looked at Kyla. At fifteen, her daughter had lengthened into a Gallagher height that passed Lily by three inches, making her long and leggy in the shorts and miniskirts she insisted on wearing even when she had to top them off with a wool sweater in the Irish summer. Beneath the sulky roundness of her cheeks, she had the good bone structure of her great-aunt Nessa and the same abundant russet hair that appeared in photos of her late grandmother.

The only thing of Lily's she shared were the brown eyes, something Kyla had been known to lament, complaining that striking blue eyes and sooty black lashes were wasted on her little brother.

"Aren't you too old to be flirting with someone half your age?" Kyla asked her mother, attempting the bored expression of a society lady. But beneath the hostility, Lily could always see the frantic little girl who was afraid of being overlooked. Most of the time, that allowed her to keep her temper.

And she absolutely refused to be drawn into Kyla's games about Philip. "I'm off to Glendalough with Aidan. Have you finished your summer essay assignment on Montaigne?"

"You just want to keep me shut up in my room so he can't get near me!" she cried with all the melodrama of youth.

"You're not Rapunzel, darling." *And for certain Philip is no Prince Charming,* Lily added silently. "But Philip is expected to work during working hours, so you might as well do the same."

Her husband's first instinct upon realizing Kyla's crush had been to forbid personal contact between her and Philip, but Lily could see that their daughter half wanted him to give that order just so she could flout it and have another excuse to play the persecuted heroine. Cillian had been persuaded to the compromise of keeping Philip on a very tight leash while he worked, insisting that he attend family dinners with all of them, and sending him back to Dublin or his family on the weekends.

Just ten days to go until Philip left Deeprath for good. And two days later Kyla would return to boarding school. They had almost made it. And maybe, in this next year, Kyla would grow into her own confidence. Maybe then she'd be less likely to treat her mother as the enemy.

"Be a good girl, darling," Lily said as she passed. "Write your essay. You can work in here or the dining room or the music room, if you like. It was never me who said it had to be written in your room. The house is yours."

"But it's not, is it? It's Daddy's, and then it's Aidan's. I will never be any better than Aunt Nessa, allowed here on sufferance so long as I behave. I can't wait until I'm eighteen and never have to come back here again!"

Oh my girl, my girl, Lily mourned to herself as Kyla whirled and ran out in angry tears.

Sometimes she hated being a mother.

CHAPTER THIRTY-SEVEN

Carragh gladly escaped the outdoor scene, desperate to take a hot bath—a shower borrowed from Aidan's former lover was not that relaxing—and put on the warmest jumper she owned. She should have known better than to expect peace at Deeprath.

But nothing could have prepared her for the disaster that met her eyes when she opened the bedroom door.

If the window and walls weren't intact, she would have assumed the storm itself had blown through here. But this was fury of a different—human—kind. The books she'd brought with her now littered the room like drifts of paper ghosts, Evan Chase's words flung far and wide. Her notebooks had suffered the same fate. Worst of all was her computer. The laptop looked as though someone had taken a hammer to it. Luckily for her, she saved everything she did to the cloud.

Only one item belonging to Deeprath had been touched. Laid flat in the center of the bed was the Bride portrait. Someone had taken a knife to it—or the shears that had cut up the valuable borrowed clothing night before last?—slitting both Jenny Gallagher and the mirrored bride to shreds.

Why?

Carragh was still contemplating that question, horrified and sick, when someone spoke from the open doorway. "How long have you been sleeping with my husband?"

She whirled to find Kyla, her elegant voice rough with anger. She did not even appear to notice the vandalism, so intently focused was she on Carragh.

There was no point lying—the guilt must be written all over her face. "It was months ago. I'm so sorry. I had no idea he was married, I swear. And the minute I found out I walked away."

"Of course you walked away, clever, independent girl that you are. Much too smart to stay with a man who lies to you, not like his stupid wife—isn't that what you tell yourself in your smug working-class way?"

Oh dear. While she was still desperately seeking any other apology she could think of, Kyla continued to shoot questions at her. "How did it start? Did you do temp work for him? You're registered with a temp agency."

"How do you know that?"

"Money buys you a lot of information. I knew he was sleeping with an Asian girl. I've got someone on staff at his flat who lets me know when he brings them home. Where was he bringing you from?"

"Kyla—"

"Where?" she shouted.

"A club. I was drunk and very, very stupid. I swear there has been nothing between us for two months. And when I took this job, I had no idea he had any connection to the Gallaghers."

"You expect me to believe that?"

"I came here for the library. That's all."

"Is that what you told Aidan? My brother is remarkably naïve where a pretty face is concerned."

And right on cue, as though summoned by his sister's rage, Aidan appeared. "What's going on?"

Carragh had thought she wanted to die when Philip showed up without warning at Deeprath. This was worse. Where were her helpful ghosts now? Couldn't they drop a convenient painting on her head or set something on fire?

To her enormous surprise, Kyla didn't jump at the chance to reveal her sins. Instead, she waved at the disordered room and said, "Seems our vandal has struck again."

Aidan stepped past Carragh, assessing the damage. "Is this all yours?"

"Yes."

"Including your laptop."

"Yes."

"So either someone doesn't like you or someone doesn't like what you're—we're—doing."

Aidan stared at the mess all around them, then at the Bride portrait in tatters on the bed, a sight that made him draw his breath in with a hiss. "That does not belong to you. So why was it destroyed?"

Kyla seemed to see the damage for the first time. Studying the wrecked portrait, she shrugged. "Miss Ryan must have done it herself."

"When? You can see the bed is made up. That means Mrs. Bell was in here yesterday morning, after she and I left Deeprath. She surely would have brought it to someone's attention if the room had been in this condition. And as Carragh and I have been within ten feet of each other ever since, she hasn't had time."

"Really, Aidan, do you think I'm fooled by your show of logic? You don't think Miss Ryan did it, because you're hoping to get her into bed."

Aidan kept his temper, though his voice was distinctly frosty. "Whatever has upset you, Kyla, there's no need to take it out on the innocent. If Philip is behaving badly, then send him away and be done with it."

Kyla gave a hysterical laugh. "That would be rich, and exactly what Philip wants. Send him away at the same time as his slut. Or didn't you know your precious librarian was sleeping with my husband?"

All the air in the room vanished, and Carragh thought she heard a soft sigh of sympathy in her ear. She instinctively closed her eyes, then forced herself to open them. Not surprisingly, Aidan was staring at her.

He had gone dead white. But years of control came to his aid, though it took an almost visible effort. "Kyla, none of this is helpful. Please, come away. I can take you home, if you like. It was a mistake coming back to Deeprath. I knew it."

"It's too late, Viscount. There will be no peace for any of us now until our dead are laid to rest."

She stalked away and, with only a slight hesitation, Aidan followed her. Carragh called after him, "I'm so sorry, Aidan. It was a mistake, before I came here, I didn't know—"

All he did was hold up his hand, but the tension in his body made his meaning clear. *Not now.*

Maybe not ever.

Aidan drove Kyla home to Kilkenny himself, once he and Bell had managed to clear the drive of fallen trees sufficiently to get the Land Rover out. He also told Bell to do his best to get Philip out of Deeprath and on a train that night. Kyla hadn't even bothered to pack, bringing only her purse with her.

Neither of them said anything until the outline of Strongbow's castle came into sight on the horizon. Finally, Kyla spoke. "I suppose you think I'm the one who vandalized Miss Ryan's room. I didn't, for what it's worth. If I went around wreaking vengeance on every woman Philip seduced, I'd never have time for anything else. Besides, it's not his women I hate."

When he didn't say anything, she asked, urgently, "You believe me, don't you? That I didn't do that to Carragh's room, or the Bride portrait?"

"I believe you." Did he, though?

"I've got nothing against her personally," his sister said. "It's just her bad fortune to be the straw that finally broke my back."

"Are you saying your marriage is over?" He asked it cautiously, afraid to frighten her off the subject.

"My marriage was over years ago."

"Do you want me to call Winthrop?"

"For a divorce? I'll do it. I don't need you doing all my dirty work for me."

He eyed her sideways. "You're really going to file?"

A wry smile tugged at the corner of her mouth. "Do you want to know a secret? I've had the papers drawn up for three years. Ever since the French girl that he slept with for a year. He even took her to Tahiti over Ellie's birthday. Told me it was a work thing."

"Philip was never good enough for you, Kyla."

She shrugged listlessly. "What options did I have? At least Philip understood me, knew where I'd come from. Don't tell me you haven't done the same. The reason you've never found someone good enough for you, Aidan, is because you've never wanted to explain that your parents' murders destroyed your family beyond repair. Better to remain aloof, and pretend that you are not afraid."

He pulled to a stop before the carriage house and faced his sister. Her eyes were enormous in her face, and he realized suddenly that she had lost weight; her collarbones were jutting out.

"What am I afraid of, Kyla?"

"That I'm the one who killed them both. Do you think I can't piece things together? I know murders like these are mostly domestic. I know I'm the most likely suspect, with or without Philip's involvement. I don't blame you for wondering."

"Kyla—"

"Good luck with the bones." Kyla left him, entering the house she had prudently bought in her own name.

Before Aidan left his sister's driveway, he pulled out his phone.

Where are you, Pen?

Walking around Glendalough. And remembering why I like in-
door activities.

Can I come see you?

You just saw me.

Alone. I need you to help me remember. Nothing will ever be right
until I can remember.

A long wait, then:

Come to my room. We'll see what we can do.

No more fear. The truth had to be better than this endless twilight
fog. Kyla was right—he had lived the last twenty years half afraid that
she'd been involved in brutally ending their parents' lives. Ironically,
only just now when she'd dragged it into the open had he become
certain that she was innocent. He didn't know why, but he felt it must
be connected to that nagging memory of Kyla on the day of the murders, the memory locked behind the defensive walls of his brain.
Something, he could only hope, that would prove her innocence.

Time to explode those walls and follow this to the end.

By late afternoon Carragh had cleaned up the chaos in her room and
gently placed the damaged Bride portrait prone on her desktop. She
hoped it could be restored. Aidan would probably know someone . . .

How he must hate her. She hated herself for the hurt she'd caused
an innocent woman. She'd felt guilty before knowing it was Kyla—
now the weight of it was crushing. No, she hadn't known Philip was
married. But she hadn't even tried to find out. And if she had known?
She might just have been angry and reckless enough at the time to
have gone ahead and slept with him in spite of it all. What a coward
that made her.

If she'd had the Hong Kong letter with her, she would have

opened it then and there as punishment for her cowardice. All she could do was vow that at the first opportune moment she would read it and face whatever it contained. She was not that frightened child anymore. And what had she to fear in not being wanted by people she'd never met? She had all the love and belonging and closeness anyone could ever want—even more. As she'd told Aidan last night, she was a Ryan.

She'd have left Deeprath if she could, but Aidan had taken the Land Rover. Nessa was in seclusion in her rooms, and Philip had prudently disappeared. Finally, Carragh wandered outside to see what was happening by the tower.

Inspector McKenna had managed to get a team out there—if one used that word in the loosest sense. In this case, it meant two garda from Dublin and a forensic archaeologist. Carragh was introduced to McKenna's partner, Sergeant Cullen, who looked refreshingly open and good-natured after the cloistered atmosphere of Deeprath Castle. He narrated it all for her.

"No spotlights—not likely to get any in here now, what with storm cleanup—so they want to work as quick as they can. Closest we can figure is someone hid those bones inside the tower wall all the way up there. Must have taken some work." He eyed the tower speculatively, hands shoved into a city raincoat that looked at odds with the muddy surroundings.

"Not as much work as you think," Carragh told him. "Medieval castles might have walls fifteen feet thick, but most aren't solid stone. The stones form the outer and inner side of the wall, with rubble filling the hollow space between. Find a weak spot to chisel out a stone, and a determined person wouldn't have much trouble creating a hiding space." She watched the garda, slipping in the overgrown, rainsoaked grass as they followed the directions of the forensic specialist. Then she looked back at the sergeant. "The question is why bother to hide a body like that at all?"

Cullen had listened to her intently. "Maybe the document case will tell us why."

"What document case?"

"Once we got everything photographed and could start carefully moving things, we found a leather case that came down with the stones. One of those old ones, that writers could roll up and buckle."

"What's in it?"

Cullen shrugged. "We're waiting on the coroner for the bones, but the inspector has called the National Library just in case it's something valuable. They can't send someone until morning, so that's me with a long night's job ahead of keeping an eye on the site."

"It will be good for you." Sibéal McKenna had come up behind them, her footsteps lost in the high grass. "Go help them secure things before it gets dark."

When Cullen had gone off, McKenna turned to Carragh with a casual air that spoke of deliberation. "What happened in the castle earlier?"

"What do you mean?"

"First you went off inside, followed by Kyla Gallagher, then her brother, while Philip Grant stood around out here looking like he'd cheerfully set the house on fire. Then Lord Gallagher comes outside again and sends Philip about his business—without raising his voice, more's the pity for the eavesdropper—and proceeds to tear apart those downed trees like they have personally insulted him. Then he roars out of here with his sister in tow, leaving Philip looking as though he just lost a fortune. So tell me . . . what the hell happened?"

Where to begin? Carragh didn't feel the need to lie, but she was too emotionally battered to get into the many details of her sins. So she put it as baldly as she could, for what did she care what this police officer thought of her? At least she wasn't a murderer.

"Three months ago I had a brief affair with Philip. I didn't know he was married, and I certainly didn't know who he was. It was over weeks ago and I got the shock of my life when he turned up here as Kyla's husband."

Sibéal nodded. "I know."

"Is there anything you don't already know?"

"The nature of my job, I'm afraid. You can't tease out just the secrets you want—there's always a tumbled skein of them pulling and twisting on one another. Mr. Grant was far too eager to point me in your direction, considering you could have no connection to the past crimes. I'd say you bruised his pride severely. Probably doesn't happen that often."

"Good. He's a pig." But honesty compelled her to add, "Not that I'm winning any prizes for my conduct. I behaved very badly."

"So what exactly happened earlier?"

"Kyla had found out. She yelled at me—no more than I deserved—and Aidan got caught up in it and everything was in such a mess in my room and the portrait slashed and Kyla accused me of doing it myself . . ."

She was aware of how overwrought she sounded. Logically, she knew it was because she hadn't slept properly in two days, save for a few brief, uncomfortable stretches in the cave last night. And Aidan had looked so grim when he'd walked away with Kyla. Should she make sure to be gone before he returned? Or would he want to see her again—to yell at, if nothing else?

"What else did Kyla accuse you of doing?" The inspector had the skill needed to calm any situation and refocus on one point at a time.

Carragh drew a deep breath and let it out slowly. It helped slow her mind down as well. "My room was vandalized. Nothing taken, just messed about. Destroyed books and notes and my laptop is in pieces."

"Show me."

"I've already cleaned it up."

"Show me anyway."

The light was going and the power was still out. Carragh lit an available lamp and, as requested, described as best she could where everything had been. The position of things on the floor. Were the clothes beneath the book pages? What had been touched first? Meanwhile, McKenna, using a flashlight, moved methodically, viewing the room from different angles.

She whistled at the damage done to the laptop, her fingers touching the indents made by whatever had been brought down on it. "Fury," she said under her breath.

Last of all was the painting. "This was the only thing not belonging to me that was damaged," Carragh said.

McKenna studied the tattered images. "A Gallagher, I presume?"

"Jenny Gallagher. She died in 1882."

"Unnerving," was the officer's judgment. She looked at Carragh, the flashlight beam carving odd shadows on her face. "Is there anything else you'd like to tell me?"

About what? About the fact that the damn painting had been haunting her since she arrived? About the sympathetic sighs she heard, and the laughter in the dark? About the trail of Lily Gallagher's treasure hunt, her distinctive voice echoing from the grave to lead her son to . . . what?

If she'd had anything concrete to offer, she would have spoken up. Or so she told herself. But she and Aidan had nothing more than cryptic clues in poetry and graveyards to go on, nothing to prove a connection to his parents' murders except a feeling. Anyway, it was Aidan's story to tell, if he chose, not hers.

"There's nothing else," she replied.

McKenna gave her the look of a mother who knows better but is holding her peace for strategic reasons. "I recommend that you sleep elsewhere in the castle tonight."

"Don't you think I should leave altogether? Surely the Gallaghers will want me gone."

"Honestly? I think you're a convenient lightning rod for the tension running through this family. That tells me you're an important piece of this case now, and I like to keep an eye on all the pieces. Also, you were hired to do a job. Unless you're keeping something from me, neither Aidan nor Nessa Gallagher has released you from that contract. And surely there is plenty more to do in that library."

"You want me to catalog books in the middle of all of this?"

"What do you have to lose?"

Very little, Carragh decided. Only her pride, which was pretty much shot to hell anyway. She would go to the library and lock herself in and work until she dropped. And then she would take the officer's advice and sleep elsewhere. It's not as though there weren't dozens of empty rooms. She could even go into the tower . . .

A reflexive shudder passed through her. Not a chance, not without electric lights. She'd rather sleep on the library floor.

As though she could read Carragh's mind, McKenna warned, "Keep out of everyone's way. I'll be around to keep an eye on things. I'm not going anywhere until those bones are safely removed tomorrow. You might want to slip into one of the empty bedrooms near me."

"May I make a suggestion, Inspector?"

"Only if you'll call me Sibéal."

"All right. Sibéal."

"What's your suggestion?"

"Once you get that document case out of the stones tomorrow, is there some way you can keep from opening it here? I don't think the Gallaghers should be part of it."

"You don't trust them?"

"Do you?"

McKenna—Sibéal—studied her for a moment. "I'll make sure it's not opened here. Can I ask what you think is inside?"

"I don't really know," Carragh said.

Strictly speaking, that was true. But she suspected it was a motive for murder.

CHAPTER THIRTY-EIGHT

Aidan never did anything without extensive research and preparation. But he had deliberately stayed away from learning about hypnosis for memory recall. Now here he was, in a hotel room with Penelope, Glendalough's Round Tower outside the closed drapes, trying to get comfortable in the armchair while she sat cross-legged on the bed.

She had been bracingly clear on the limitations of what she could do.

"I'm not a magician," she said. "Or an illusionist. This isn't America in the eighties, when therapists convinced entire courtrooms that hypnosis could recover lost memories. All I can do is help you relax enough to lower your guard. Which, granted, would be no small accomplishment."

Not really, he thought. I lowered my guard for Carragh.

Who'd slept with Philip.

He said tightly, "Just do what you have to."

"I'm not putting you in a trance. I'm not going to control you or command you or draw out anything that you don't want known. All hypnosis is self-hypnosis in the end. I'm here only to guide the process. It helps if you have a specific goal in mind.'

"I do."

"You should say it aloud."

"I want to remember where I saw Kyla the day of the murders."

"Good. Then let's begin."

Penelope had a musical voice even in everyday speech—now she used that talent to weave a cocoon of safety around him.

"Breathe in slowly," she began, setting him an example. "And out. Pick something small to focus your eyes on and keep breathing in that rhythm."

Aidan focused on the inoffensive landscape painting hung above the bed and concentrated on his breathing. He knew he was too alert, he was trying too hard, which meant he was thinking about all of it, and that would never be useful . . .

"Aidan, listen to my voice. There is nothing in the moment but my voice."

Slowly, delicately, Penelope led him through the process: tightening and relaxing every muscle group from the toes upward, letting his eyes close as they grew heavy, keeping his breath deep and even. She walked him down the steps she'd asked him to visualize—he meant it to be the main staircase of the castle but his mind kept drifting until he gave in and visualized himself descending the stone steps of the Bride Tower.

"You're at the bottom." Penelope sounded distant now. "There is a door before you."

There was—the narrow, pointed-arch door leading to the library. Of course these were the steps he'd needed to come down.

"Open the door and tell me what you see."

"The library."

"Describe it exactly as you see it."

"I see the shelves on either side of me like a tunnel. I see the spines of the books to my right—I drag my hand on them as I walk past. Aunt Nessa always scolds me for not respecting them."

He described it as he went—the books, the shelves, the lighting that never quite banished shadows—until he got to the long library table.

"What do you see on the table?"

"Books. Papers. My father's fountain pen."

"What else?"

"There's a chair shoved back from the table. Like someone just got up."

"What do you do?"

"I call for my father. There's no answer." His breath hitched. "Something's wrong."

He doesn't need her measured voice now, for he has always remembered this part, despite his best efforts to forget. "I call again, but I know he won't answer. I walk around the table to push the chair back in but I can't because there's something on the floor. Why is my father on the floor? I bend down and his head is all wrong, the shape is wrong, it's caved in over his ear, and I scream for him to get up, I keep screaming and screaming—"

"Aidan, stay with me. One breath at a time. What happens after you scream?"

"Aunt Nessa's there, and Mrs. Bell. She screams, too, until Aunt Nessa slaps her and tells her to call the police. She's taking me out of the library and I want my mother, I keep asking for my mother, and Aunt Nessa grabs the cook and tells her to find Lady Gallagher and bring her to the music room."

"Very good. Let's go back now. Before you opened the library door. Where were you?"

"The tower. I'd just come down the spiral stairs."

"Go backward in your memory, up the levels of the tower. How high were you?"

He could see it now, grainy and jumpy like an old filmstrip damaged by time. "All the way up top. To leave flowers for the Bride.

Whenever I went to Glendalough, I brought her something back. It was hedge roses, they kept pricking my fingers. I had to suck the blood off."

He could taste the blood, hear his steps echoing in the enclosed spiral staircase . . .

He was lucky not to have been seen. He wasn't allowed up here alone. But he knew the secret of the tower keys: one set in the library, one set in the Bells' sitting room off the kitchen. He'd swiped that set after asking Mrs. Bell where his father was. No one had ever caught him before he could return them, though sometimes he thought Mrs. Bell knew. Mother said he would have nightmares. Father said he could fall through the floor. But he wasn't afraid. He liked it in the tower, even when a mouse ran across the floor.

He climbed all the way up, past the creepy sitting room, to the almost bare top floor where he laid his flowers on the table. Then he pulled open the door to the outside just a crack, and slipped carefully onto the battlements that surrounded the tower.

He liked to imagine he was a knight defending Deeprath from the English—or other Irish, he wasn't picky—and played at spotting an enemy approach and preparing his bow to shoot them down. Sometimes he used boiling oil or pitch to chuck over the side, sometimes he allowed the enemy to make it inside so that he had to fight with his sword high in the air.

He always won.

When he caught movement below from the corner of his eye, he dropped his sword hand and pressed himself up against the taller buttress so he wouldn't be seen. The crenellations meant he could peer down at an angle and see the ruined oratory and half the stable blocks. He could see . . .

With a gasp like one surfacing from underwater, Aidan opened his eyes. Penelope regarded him with unaccustomed gravity. "You remembered."

"Yes."

"Do you want to tell me?"

His heart beating swiftly, Aidan fixed her with a level, professional gaze. "No."

She must have known from his expression that he meant to be reckless. "Aidan—be careful."

Aidan thanked Penelope and then sat in the Land Rover for twenty minutes, allowing his pulse and breathing to normalize while considering what to do next. What he wanted to do was go after Philip and knock the fear of God into him, and then go to Carragh and shake her until he could understand why she'd slept with the man. Neither were very practical. And if he had learned anything in twenty years, it was practicality.

So he pulled out his phone and made a list for himself, noting as he did so how similar it was to the one Carragh had found in his mother's handwriting. They even had a couple of the same reminders.

1. Father Hennessy
2. Parish-held family records
3. General Register's Office
4. Kilkenny

He looked at his watch—almost 7:00 P.M., on a Sunday. Father Hennessy lived just up the road, so he might as well deal with the first two items while he was here.

Father Hennessy had been the priest at St. Kevin's parish since Aidan's own baptism. He was of that priestly school that had little interest in ambition or promotion, who genuinely sought to do good in their parish and were happy to live decades alongside the same families. Aidan had always thought him old, but he couldn't be more than sixty now. Which meant he'd not been much older at the time of the deaths than Aidan was now.

Tall, lean, ascetically spare, Father Hennessy welcomed Aidan inside without unnecessary fuss and, without asking, poured him some brandy. Once settled before the electric fire, the priest said, "I expected to be visited by your guest, the young woman working in the library. We had an appointment yesterday afternoon."

"Did you?" Carragh hadn't mentioned it to Aidan. "I'm afraid we were caught across the Upper Lake when the storm blew in. But I imagine our questions might be similar. Though I admit I feel badly coming to you only because I need something."

"The nature of the job," the priest answered cheerfully. "So what can I do?"

"I have two questions, Father. First, can I see the parish records beginning with the famine years? And second, by any chance did my mother make the same request to you before she died?"

His gentle smile was answer enough. "Yes, you may, and yes, she did."

"What did she want to know?"

"She told me she needed to see original documentation of births and marriages, those sorts of things, because the family library was missing a large section of those records."

So the absence Carragh had noted in the family records predated his mother's interest. "Father, I know it's late and I'm imposing. I need to be in Dublin tomorrow morning and I was hoping to have finished here first. If you'll point me in the direction of the parish registers, I'll gladly lift and carry and sort through everything myself."

"You could look online, you know. It's all been digitized these days. But I suppose you want to see the original notations, just like your mother."

"I do."

Unlike some priests, Father Hennessy kept the parish records in good order, including the wrapping and safe storing of centuries old registers. The trunks in which they were kept were dated on the outside, so it was a relatively simple matter to locate the right ones. Soon enough Aidan was tracing the spidery handwriting of the long-dead priests who had presided over the Gallagher family in their religious rites. He noted only one anomaly, which he brought to Father Hennessy's attention.

"This lists the reading of the banns for the marriage of Jenny Gallagher and Evan Chase, but not the marriage itself."

"They were married in Dublin, at St. Patrick's," the priest explained, "by special license, so they could have skipped the banns. But the Gallaghers always liked to keep the parish part of their lives."

The next Gallagher event was the baptism of James Michael in May of 1881. A safe twelve months after the wedding; no scandal there. In early January 1882 came Jenny Gallagher's death and burial in the family plot at Glendalough cemetery. The priest must have bent his professional conscience there a bit, for even then no one seemed in real doubt that she had deliberately jumped to her death. Suicides were meant for unconsecrated ground. The inquest, Aidan knew from his mother's notes, had officially found for "accident," sparing the grieving family the additional indignity of being refused a church service.

No Gallaghers to be found again until the burial of Jenny's father, the fourteenth Viscount Gallagher, in August 1889. Then the long break until the new viscount grew up and, in his turn, married and had children. His first marriage in 1911, and a son the next year, who became Aidan's grandfather. Then, after a long time as a widower, remarriage and the birth of a daughter, Nessa, in 1931.

Aidan stared at the various relevant entries until his eyes began to cross and wondered if his mother had found more in them than he could see. Why the missing fifty years of family documents? And who had removed them, if not his mother in her research?

After he put everything back the way he'd found it, he went to thank Father Hennessy.

"I have something else for you," the priest told him. He had another old parish register open, and it looked as though he'd been taking notes.

"What is it?"

"When your mother came asking these questions, she had an additional one you have not asked. I don't know if it's at all relevant, but it can't hurt. She wanted a list of the families who came to the mountains during the Famine and were aided by our parish, and especially the Gallaghers. At one point the family had nearly eighty people living on the estate. Some of them, like the ancestors of the Bells, remained at Deeprath even afterward, with the rest resettled by the thirteenth viscount in one of his factories or shipyards in Wicklow or Wexford. In any case, I thought I'd look them up for you and pass them on."

There were five names on the list: Byrne, Farrell, Lynch, O'Brien, and Ryan. "Thank you," he told the priest warmly. "I wish I could repay you adequately."

Father Hennessy studied him without his usual humor. "The Gallaghers and the mountains go hand in hand. It's a pity for that chain to be broken."

Was there anyone in the mountains who thought it a good idea for Deeprath to be sold?

Carragh stayed up as long as she could physically manage, using oil lamps to work in the library. Not only did it pass the time, but she was feeling a sense of urgency. Even though Aidan had delayed the donation of the castle, the thought of all these books being sent away from their home . . . Okay, it was sentimental and silly. But no more silly than anything else that had happened here.

Aidan never returned. She finally admitted defeat at two in the morning when her eyes would not stay open. Taking both oil lamps with her, she followed Sibéal's advice and crept quietly through the Regency wing and into the room next to the police officer. Someone— presumably McKenna—had left a blanket and pillow on the bare, empty mattress. Carragh just managed to take off her shoes before falling asleep.

An hour later—or three—or maybe just twenty minutes—she woke with a jolt, sitting straight upright in the pitch black straining to identify whatever noise had jerked into her dreams and pulled her out. Simultaneously, she fumbled for the flashlight she'd left next to her pillow and switched it on. The light wavered and jerked and the only thing she could hear was her own harsh breathing.

"This is ridiculous." Was she speaking to herself or unseen listeners? She had about as little patience with both just now.

But damn if she was going to let this go on without figuring out what the hell "this" was. Climbing off the bed, she opened the door to the corridor cautiously. All remained quiet. She padded down the corridor, bare feet flinching from the cold, trying to assemble a map in her head of the castle, to anticipate where she was headed. The Regency wing contained the music room and breakfast parlor on the ground floor before joining up with the Tudor hall that stood in the center of the castle.

Now she could hear something, a hush and rustle of whispers just beyond her comprehension. *Really? Can't you just tell me what I need to know?* But there was that curiosity kicking in, beckoning to her with the seductive promise of a mystery just on the verge of being solved . . . She definitely hadn't had enough sleep.

Long before she reached the appropriate corridor, she knew she was being led back to the library. At least, she hoped it was only the library. If the whispers tried to lure her into the tower, she'd tell them to go to hell.

But the whispers died away before she reached the library door. In case they started up again, she decided to go ahead and check things out. After which she'd curse them all and go back to bed.

The smell hit her first. She didn't want to recognize it, but she did . . .

Smoke. She knew better than to fling the door wide, but it was surprisingly difficult to control her adrenaline and merely crack it open. That was enough for her to hear the crackle of flames.

The library was on fire.

Fight it, or run for help? Her body made the first decision, heading straight for the fire extinguisher Aidan had pointed out to her the first day.

It wasn't there.

She ran back to the Regency wing, shouting "Fire!" as she went, and found Sibéal already up when she reached her room. "The library's on fire."

The police officer was only a few steps behind Carragh as she ran back the way she'd come. She knew the Bells were sleeping somewhere beyond the kitchens . . .

Sibéal ran out the front door, heading up the drive until she could get a mobile signal to phone for help. How long would it take for a fire truck? Carragh wondered. And not just any fire truck, but one that could pump its own water, or access the castle's water sources and— She had no idea how it worked. But she was pretty sure it would all take time.

She ran straight into Mrs. Bell coming into the kitchen. "The library—"

"Aye. We heard you. Rob's got equipment in the storeroom. Go help him, I'll wake Lady Nessa."

God bless the Bells and their practical years of stewardship— Bell thrust a commercial-sized fire extinguisher into her hands when she reached the storeroom behind the kitchen and carried another two himself.

"Tie something over your mouth and nose," he shouted to her just outside the library door. The corridor was already beginning to feel warm. Carragh pulled off the cardigan she'd fallen asleep in and wrapped it snugly just beneath her eyes. Bell looked at her, nodded once, and opened the door.

Smoke—thick, black, choking—rolled into them like ocean waves seeking to pull them under. She coughed and plowed on, looking for a source.

There were two—the family cabinets at the former altar end of the space, and the doorway leading to the Bride Tower. Bell headed for the cabinets. Carragh tackled the flames that were now up the shelves on either side of the tower door.

She had barely finished emptying the canister when another one was thrust into her hands by Maire Bell. It was enough, thankfully, to extinguish the last of the active burning. And it seemed her husband had managed to put out most of his fire, using a heavy blanket his wife had dragged in to smother the last bits.

The family cabinets were little more than ruins of wood and paper and ash. The door to the tower keep still stood recognizable, though blackened and warped. Almost half the length of each bookcase flanking it—a good five or six feet on either side—was either burned or covered in chemicals. Not to mention the smoke, which must have permeated every precious volume in here . . . the damage to material goods was severe. The damage to history was worse. Carragh's eyes were tearing from the smoke, her lungs heavy and thick, and she felt like crying over the destruction.

Sibéal returned, with Sergeant Cullen in her wake, and regarded everything grimly. The two police officers began to help the Bells and Carragh move what they could of the relatively undamaged books. Silently, they stacked them in the corridor and the ground floor of the tower keep. Nessa came down at some point, wrapped in a dressing gown, her face carved in deep lines and dark with shadows. She said nothing at all.

The fire truck arrived, bringing official order to the scene. Not far behind was a sour-looking man who eyed Inspector McKenna with distaste.

"What are you doing here?" she snapped in a manner that made Carragh's head swing around in curiosity. Clearly Sibéal did not like this man.

"This is my district," he answered sharply. "You can investigate a twenty-year-old crime to your heart's content. But a possible crime committed today? That's my business. The fire chief thought I should know."

"Inspector Burke." Nessa rose from the chair Mrs. Bell had set for her in the corridor. "It's quite clear to me, as no doubt the firemen will confirm, that this blaze was deliberately set. For one thing, the castle has not had power for more than two days, so it could hardly be an electrical accident."

She turned on Carragh, her upper-class face and voice both devoid of emotion. "I would appreciate it greatly, Inspector, if you would arrest Miss Ryan on charges of arson."

CHAPTER THIRTY-NINE

July 1881

Everything at Deeprath changed in the weeks after James's birth. He wasn't a particularly quiet baby—he seemed often to be complaining about something, usually at the top of his lungs—but with his mother he mellowed. Jenny insisted on nursing him herself, despite her father's objections, and nothing could have shown more clearly what her delivery of a grandson had bought her than his easy acquiescence to her wishes. When she sat with James for a photograph, her father beamed with pride.

As for Evan, he was writing at a furious pace. Finally. Charles had been hounding him for months, as Evan's promise of a finished manuscript continued to be just that—a promise. A chapter here, a telling scene or two there . . . it gave him the comforting illusion of working on it. The illusion burst one month after James's birth, when Evan sat himself down in the library and looked over what he had. The pages were depressing in both amount and quality. He'd always been a fast and careful writer, and at first he feared Ireland had swallowed that. But once he began forcing words onto the page, he realized that he could still do it despite the "entanglements of a wife and child," as Charles put it despairingly.

His Bride was not, whatever others might think, a thinly veiled portrait of Jenny. That's not how he wrote. Sure, aspects of her colored the story, but no more than aspects of himself always did. So the wicked Bride of legend carried with her a touch of melancholy, a fear within herself that she could not banish. And the resilient heroine, Anna, faced her own terrors with kindness and a little humor.

Then Jenny fell ill. At first no one thought it more serious than a cold, until she fainted while nursing James. Within twenty-four hours she had a serious rash that the doctor proclaimed as measles.

Her immediate concern was for her son. "He must go away. Promise, Evan, to take him somewhere safe. Measles would be dangerous for him, he's so small. Promise me."

He didn't have to promise—his father-in-law had already taken James away. "He's safe, love," Evan assured her. "Your father has found a wet nurse for him in Wicklow. The nanny is with him as well. He's only a day's ride away, and we'll bring him home as soon as you're well."

For almost a week Jenny was very ill indeed. She could not bear the light because of the pain it caused her, so Evan stayed with her in a darkened room. Her fever spiked, causing a delirium that he feared meant she was tipping into a dangerous mania, but when her temperature came down those symptoms eased. Even after the doctor pronounced her out of danger, her lingering cough turned into bronchitis. Though she would not hear of James's return until she was in perfect health, the separation weighed on her spirits. To pass the time, she took to writing in a floral cloth-covered notebook, different from her usual diary.

"My mother gave it to me when I was a child," she told Evan. "I never used it for more than copying out verses I liked."

She would not show him what she wrote, or talk about it, which he conceded wryly was fair enough considering his own writerly reticence. But she began to lose herself for hours at a time in writing, and though this was something with which Evan was intimately acquainted, there was something . . . eerie about it. As though, each time she emerged from the fog, she left a piece behind her. Or maybe brought back a new one.

Once, he heard her talking to someone as he entered the room—the otherwise empty room—and when he asked about it, she said, "The Bride likes it when I talk to her aloud. She's been lonely for so long."

Uneasily, he let it pass. And determined to bring James home as soon as possible.

It had been a full twelve weeks of absence before Lord Gallagher made the trip to Wexford to bring his grandson home. Evan was hard put to keep Jenny calm until their return. She could not settle to anything, not even listening to him read from the new manuscript. Every time the story mentioned the original Darkling Bride, Jenny would interrupt with, "That's not what she said," or, "She would never be so silly."

So he put the manuscript away and prayed that James Michael would be the medicine to put her right.

Jenny dashed outside the moment she heard carriage wheels, barely waiting for the nurse to emerge before snatching James out of her arms. "My child, my heart," she cried, and whirled him around while both the nurse and Lord Gallagher tried to stop her. But James loved it, gurgling in delight at his mother's enraptured face.

Because Evan was watching so closely, he was the first to see the light in Jenny's eyes flicker and dim. She shook her head hard, as though dislodging a bee, and stared and stared at James. Then, with a violent suddenness, she thrust him back at the nurse.

"What have you done? Take him away, I don't want him, what were you thinking bringing him here . . ."

It was like the theater night in Dublin on their honeymoon, all panic and mania and a torrent of words that made no sense.

"Jenny," Evan intervened desperately, keeping hold of her shoulders. "Jenny, my love, come inside, please. Come in and take a breath. You need to calm down."

Latching onto him with a grip that hurt, she implored, "Promise me you'll take him away. Promise me, Evan. Take him away!"

"Love, you're frightening James. Come away and calm down and all will be well."

She dropped her hands, and all her violence and fury stilled into a moment of utter calm, so that no one would guess she was anything but perfectly lucid. "That is not my son. Take the changeling away and bring me my son."

CHAPTER FORTY

After a considerable amount of arguing (between Sibéal and the Rathdrum inspector, Burke) and icy orders (from Nessa), Carragh was taken to the Rathdrum police station. She was not under arrest, merely "helping police in their inquiries." She knew what that meant: Inspector Burke wanted to oblige the family by removing her, but was covering himself since there was no evidence, only Nessa's assertion that Carragh disliked the family.

She fell asleep in the interview room where they stashed her, probably intending to leave her long enough to grow increasingly nervous as time passed. Inspector Burke regarded her with dislike when she jerked awake upon his entrance. Her neck and shoulders were sore from laying her head on the table, but her mind was working better now than it had since leaving St. Kevin's Bed after the storm.

Though his expression was unpleasant, he spoke neutrally enough—and with perception. "Why is Nessa Gallagher so eager to get you out of Deeprath Castle?"

"Is this an official interview?"

"If this were an official interview, I would have someone with me and we would record it. This is simply a conversation."

"Which means I am not required to answer."

"No, Miss Ryan, you are not."

She studied the man, thinking hard. Despite his abrasive personality, he seemed intelligent enough, and he wasn't falling over himself to fulfill Nessa's outrageous demands. But Carragh knew something about jurisdictions, however hazy, and certainly he and Inspector McKenna were at odds if their shouting match earlier were any indication. And whatever the library fire had been meant to accomplish, it surely had everything to do with the murders of the past. That made it Sibéal's case.

"Lady Gallagher," she said, navigating her answer with care, "will always look to an outsider when blame must be laid. No doubt she is correct that the library fire was arson—it could not have simultaneously started in two separate areas otherwise. And also, the fire extinguisher kept in the library itself was missing."

"I know," the inspector said. "It was found in your bedroom."

A bit obvious, that. But then, Carragh was coming to understand that her opponent—Surely *enemy* was too strong?—had no objections to big red flags waving in her direction. Through personal dislike, or a desire to confuse, or both. Because Carragh knew that as long as she was being examined, the past was not.

"I suppose you've considered that Philip Grant was more or less forced to leave Deeprath Castle yesterday after a ... family argument. He might have cause to want revenge."

What she wanted was the inspector to not only agree that Philip had cause, but to somehow let her know if he also had opportunity. She didn't know where he'd gone after Kyla and Aidan left. He appeared to have left Deeprath, but he could have made his way back in the dead of night.

Beneath what seemed to be Inspector Burke's perpetual scowl lurked thoughtfulness. "I am not entirely unaware of that situation,

Miss Ryan. For now, you are free to go. I would advise you to stay nearby for the next few days. Leaving the area might be seen as prejudicial. There's a solicitor outside waiting to tell you the same, no doubt."

A solicitor? Carragh followed the inspector to the reception area wondering who on earth was waiting for her. It took her a moment to recognize the older man with stooped shoulders dressed in an inoffensive gray suit. Behind his wire-rimmed glasses, however, his eyes were sharp. It was the Gallagher family solicitor.

"Mr. Winthrop," he confirmed, shaking her hand. "I was asked to come down and ensure you were not being unduly harassed in any manner."

He handed over her purse, which they had taken from her. "I believe you will find on your mobile telephone a message from Inspector McKenna."

Bemused, Carragh turned on her phone.

"Carragh, it's Sibéal. I've gone back to Dublin, but you'll be fine. They'll probably ask you to stay in Rathdrum and I'll be in touch as soon as I've got things sorted with my superintendent. An archivist at the National Library has opened the document case found with the bones. I don't entirely understand what he found, but I think you might and I think it matters. I'll tell you about it when I get back to Rathdrum. Let me know where you are."

Really? That's all she was going to leave her with? Mr. Winthrop regarded her with an air of endless patience. "Sorry," she said. "It's very good of you to go to all this trouble."

"It's my job to do as my clients wish."

"Your client?" But there could be only one answer.

"Lord Gallagher was notified by Inspector McKenna, I believe. Concerning both the fire and the unfortunate accusation against you. He wished me to ensure your good treatment. And he asked me to take you back to Deeprath Castle when you were released."

The castle? Had Aidan lost his mind?

With a smile that hinted understanding, Winthrop said, "He told me to tell you that he trusts you. And that you should trust him in turn. Lord Gallagher also said that he will meet you at Deeprath as soon as he is able."

She wondered what the mild-mannered solicitor would do if she flat-out refused. Not that she would. Even without Aidan's request, curiosity would have driven her back to Deeprath. Curiosity—and sheer bloody-mindedness. Whatever was inside that document case Sibéal had taken away, it was the castle that surely held the final answers. And Carragh was determined to be there when they were revealed.

After Inspector Burke had taken Carragh away, Sibéal, still fuming, gathered up her few belongings and hiked back up the drive to where her car had managed to sit out the storm without damage. Stowing her belongings, she phoned Aidan Gallagher and, just as everyone else had when trying to reach him for the last twenty-four hours, reached only his voicemail. Her message was terse: "Your great-aunt is accusing Carragh Ryan of trying to burn down your library. She's been taken to Rathdrum Garda station for questioning. You might want to consider coming out of hiding."

As she started back down the drive, the coroner arrived. Sibéal delivered her to the site to begin the delicate task of finding and removing as much of the skeleton as could be identified after its un-dignified fall to earth. Not far behind the coroner came the National Library employee, eager and talkative.

The conservator finished quickly, for Sibéal asked him not to open the case until back in Dublin. "I wouldn't have, anyway," he answered. "This isn't the best environment for old documents."

He cast a wistful, covetous eye at the library's exterior. From where they stood, the only visible damage was the priest's door, which had been wrenched wide for the fire hoses. "I hope we can get in there soon," the young man said. "There's been too much damage done already."

Sibéal had expected to deal with at least a few questions from the castle—no matter how reduced the current household—but the experts were left strictly alone. Once she'd seen the librarian off with the case, she headed back to Dublin.

Her instinct was to go straight to Phoenix Park, but she had enough of a sense of self-preservation to go home first. A shower, clean clothes, and a mix of sugar and caffeine got her ready to face whatever was coming at her from O'Neill.

"What the hell is going on down in Wicklow?" the superintendent demanded the moment she walked into his office. "I've had zealous officers and I've had cold cases solved because of that zeal, but I swear by the sweet Virgin Mother I've never had anything like the maelstrom you've stirred up in those mountains. Fires, holy wells, lightning-struck towers, bones tumbling out—"

"It's not like I knocked over the tower battlements myself," she protested. "And if the Gallaghers had taken care over the years to bury all of their dead properly, there would be fewer bones."

"Tell me what you have," he commanded. Beneath his furious air, Sibéal could see the intelligence and genuine interest that made him a superb officer.

She led him through the last few days—Philip Grant's history of alleged statutory rape and her subsequent interviews with him, Lily Gallagher's fascination with the family history immediately before the murders, Nessa's eagerness to bring the investigation to a hasty conclusion—and ended with the early morning library blaze and Carragh Ryan being escorted to the Rathdrum police station for questioning.

"I believe more than ever, sir, that the Gallagher murders were a domestic affair. And that the family's return to Deeprath Castle has begun to crack the killer's composure. Why else would Miss Ryan be a target of vandalism and accusations? It's a literal smoke screen."

"Belief and instinct are all well and good, McKenna, but there can be no charges laid without evidence. So I must ask—is there any reasonable prospect of getting the necessary evidence to make an arrest? Most cold cases are resolved because of DNA evidence or confessions. And the Gallagher case has no DNA to test, beyond confirming that the marble cross was the weapon used on Lord Gallagher."

"So I need a confession."

He shrugged. "That's about the way of it."

"Yes, sir."

Sibéal retreated to her office and summoned Sergeant Cullen to help devise an interview strategy that would make one of her three prime suspects crack and confess. Philip Grant and Kyla Gallagher, either alone or together, and then the long shot . . . Nessa Gallagher. The first two had plenty of motive between them to encompass a crime of passion or greed. What the old lady's motive could have been, Sibéal had little idea. But Nessa'd had the opportunity. And she'd gained by the crime in the sense that she became guardian of Aidan and Kyla and had access to their trust funds.

She set Cullen the task of trying to get the cryptic Winthrop to release any information about the Gallaghers' financial affairs, specifically during the children's minorities, and mulled over which member of the unhappy marriage to tackle first. It would have to be Kyla, she decided. The woman seemed much nearer to collapse than her husband.

Then her direct line rang. "Inspector McKenna?"

It was the young man from the National Library. "Do you have something for me?" Sibéal asked.

"I don't know if it will be of any use to you," he answered, "but it's certainly interesting. There's a manuscript of some sort—the date on the first page is 1882."

Sibéal remembered Carragh Ryan's story about a Victorian writer: he came to write a book, and ended up marrying the daughter and heiress of the house. She felt as though she were on a precipice, that last, breathless moment before tumbling down the slope into understanding. "What does it say?"

"There's a dedication, like you find in most books. It reads: 'For Jenny. And in memory of James Michael Gallagher, gone too soon and left unmourned.'" The man paused. "Then there's a signature: Evan Chase."

Aidan spent the night in a Dublin hotel and in the morning walked to the General Register Office. His route took him through St. Stephen's Green, up the pedestrian and tourist-friendly Grafton Street to Trinity College, then west to Dublin Castle. He remembered his father bringing him here, touring the remains of the stronghold built by King John of England in 1204. "Almost as old as Deeprath," Aidan had said, somewhat disappointed to realize his home wasn't absolutely unique.

"Yes," his father had laughed, "but King John's descendants aren't still living in Dublin Castle today, are they?"

The castle, for so long the center of English political and military power in Ireland, was today a combination of tourist site, police offices, and government buildings. Including the General Register Office and its public research facility, which held the records of Irish births, marriages, and deaths back to 1864. Just far enough back to be useful to Aidan.

God bless Father Hennessy, for the priest had given him several pieces of information to help solidify his vague instincts. Five surnames—Byrne, Farrell, Lynch, O'Brien, Ryan—and two places— Wicklow town and Wexford. He began calling up records to examine and threw himself into research.

Aidan knew he had forgotten himself too much since returning to Ireland. Not everything that had happened since he was ten years old was a mistaken attempt to wall off his past. He was thirty-two and old enough to know at least some of his talents, and he knew that he'd been a bloody good Arts and Antiquities officer because he was tenacious when on the scent. Willing to plow through financial records and auction catalogs and witness statements from long-ago cases that might hold a hint to a missing artwork or a current crime organization using art as capital. He had an almost sixth sense for relevant information that he used today by pretending this case had nothing to do with him, but was simply a random crime to be unraveled.

With the records not quite reaching the Famine years, Aidan had to make some educated guesses about which families in the two towns might have had ties to Deeprath Castle. Just because they bore one of the surnames Father Hennessy had listed didn't mean they were relevant. He could hardly research every O'Brien in southern Ireland, for example. But census records helped narrow things down, with occupations listed, and slowly his mass of indecipherable notes began to narrow into a single line of inquiry.

In 1865, Elinor O'Brien married Robert Lynch in Wexford. The bride was twenty-four, making her just old enough to remember the Famine and, quite possibly, the Gallagher family who had sheltered them. It was certainly true that both Elinor's father and her new husband worked at a Gallagher-owned import company in Wexford. In 1866 came the birth of their first child, a daughter named Mary. They had five more children over a period of eleven years, before Robert Lynch's death in 1877 at the age of forty.

Though focused on dates and facts, Aidan felt the tendrils of grief and hard work and poverty woven into this story. Even if he hadn't felt that he was on the right track, he might have kept researching just to find out what happened to Elinor and her children.

In May 1881 the birth of Rory Lynch, "bastard son of Mary Lynch," was recorded. The girl, still living with her widowed mother and siblings, had been only fifteen. Perhaps it was for the best, then, that the baby died just four months later. Easier for Elinor's daughter to make a new start, one would suppose. But if she had, it had not been in Wexford. In fact, not just Mary Lynch, but Elinor O'Brien Lynch and every one of her children vanished from the county records after September 1881.

They must have moved elsewhere. But where, and how? Widowed mothers with large families to care for rarely had the resources to relocate, even if they were able to find work. What had happened to Elinor Lynch, her daughter Mary, and the rest of them after 1881?

When he came to himself and checked his watch, Aidan was startled to find he'd been researching for six hours. No time now to try and trace the Lynches. They might have gone to any county in Ireland. Possibly even to America. He might be intellectually curious about them, but at the moment he had what he needed. If it wasn't exactly what he'd been looking for . . . But then, he'd come here today not knowing what he was looking for. Just following his mother's trail and his own instincts.

He turned on his phone upon leaving and found eight missed calls from Inspector McKenna and one from Winthrop. He listened to the messages both had left, swearing aloud in surprise several times. The library was set on fire? Carragh was accused? The Rathdrum police took her to the station for questioning?

His first call was to the solicitor, telling him to get over to the station at once, ensure that Miss Ryan's legal rights were being respected, and to get her released if he could. Then he called Sibéal McKenna.

"Where the hell have you been?" she yelled at him as though she were his sister. "Never mind. Miss Ryan has been taken to Rathdrum—"

"I know. I listened to your message. I've sent my solicitor over to take care of it. Look, Inspector, would you meet with me tomorrow? I think I'll have some information for you by then—information you will want."

"Is that so? Well I have information *today*. There was a document case found amongst the bones and fallen stone from the tower."

"Yes," he answered warily, his pulse quickening.

"It contained a manuscript that a National Library specialist is examining. The cover page appears to have been written by Evan Chase and contained a dedication to James Michael: 'gone too soon and left unmourned,'" she quoted. "Tell me, Lord Gallagher, why would Chase write that about his son, who lived to be ninety-two, and whose funeral in 1972 was attended by hundreds of mourners?"

Aidan thought rapidly—almost as rapidly as his heart was beating. "I appreciate the call, Inspector. I have things to do now. I'll call you tomorrow."

He could almost hear her shouting at him even after he'd turned off his phone.

CHAPTER FORTY-ONE

Carragh had Winthrop drop her off at the top of the castle drive, and felt serious qualms as his car disappeared. Had it really been less than two weeks since she first came here? Impossible to remember any time before Deeprath Castle. Or envision any time after.

Each step down the drive increased her sense of unreality. There was a shivery quality to the air and a gossamer look to the trees—as though reality itself was fading in and out. Or, perhaps, fading from one time and sharpening into another?

The castle frontage reared up before her, and there was nothing in that sight to indicate whether she still stood firmly in 2015 or had slipped into another time stream. *Get a grip!* she scolded herself, and wondered about the best way to get inside without being seen.

The answer was obvious—the library. The outer priest's door had been pulled open by the firefighters, and it seemed no one had bothered to close it since. Stepping gingerly past the scorched rood screen, she stared mournfully at the wreckage of the main library. She couldn't work in here even if she'd wanted to. But right now her object lay beyond.

She pulled out her sturdy flashlight (*best gift ever,* she silently thanked her father) and switched it on. Even if the electricity at the castle was working—and she hadn't seen any lights in the windows—those lines did not extend to her destination.

Slipping on the mess of chemical foam and fire debris, Carragh edged her way to the keep door. Here, the damage was the worst. The family cabinets and the Bride's Tower entrance had clearly been the targets of the arsonist's anger. She could only be glad that the keep itself hadn't been set on fire. The shell and stairs might be stone, but the levels could have collapsed on one another if that had been the intention. But she didn't think so, having a fee for her opponent now—a person anxious to mislead and misdirect, not destroy the very fabric of the castle.

She shone the flashlight up the spiraling steps and took a deep breath. A series of deep breaths. It didn't make stepping into that claustrophobically dark space any easier.

The late afternoon sunlight pierced through the arrow loops and the lancet windows on each level. The frozen-in-time sitting room had the best light, for it had been set up in what was undoubtedly the original solar, the level on which the lord and his family and most important retainers had lived in relative comfort. There were more windows here, a little wider than the ones below and fitted with glass sometime in the nineteenth century. Carragh opened all the interior wooden shutters. She had not spent any time here in daylight since her first brief exploration, so she turned off the flashlight and made a more detailed examination.

This time she wasn't exploring for curiosity's sake, she was looking for a few specifics. She took down every remaining book on the fitted shelves and examined each from front to back. Nothing loose fell out, and no notes or marks had been made in the text. She had to discipline herself from imagining Jenny turning these pages and wondering if she had found pleasure in reading or just a tedious method of passing the time. This wasn't about identifying with Jenny Gallagher. It was about teasing the truth from the myth. Or if not truth, then at least the facts.

She found nothing in the books. Nothing in the cupboards and linen chest but fragile remnants of cloth and dust. She even turned the carpet over to ensure there were only floorboards beneath. She left the Louis XV walnut desk for last.

The outer drawers held blank writing paper embossed with the Gallagher griffin at the top, some dried inkwells, and a beautiful fountain pen with gold nib, etched with geometric designs in red and black. Carragh couldn't help but hold it, running her fingertips across the surface and appreciating the weight of it in her hand. Then she replaced it where she'd found it and continued her hunt.

She pulled down the sloping cover to its desk position and began on the inner drawers. Expecting only more emptiness, she searched quickly. In the fourth drawer, to her surprise, she found a single cabinet photograph.

The four-by-six-inch photos had been a popular item in the late nineteenth century: the images, usually sepia-toned, were pasted to a cardboard backing, then displayed on cabinets. Carragh had seen some in her grandmother's attic. The photo she was studying now showed a young woman with abundant dark hair plaited in the semblance of a band framing a rounded face. She wore a loose-fitting robe of some dark material, probably because she had recently delivered the baby she held in her arms. The infant was little more than big eyes, a rosebud mouth, and a drift of dark hair all drowning in the traditional long white ceremonial gown of the Victorian infant.

It was one thing looking upon the oil painted version of Jenny Gallagher's face. To see the purity of her profile, the curve of her cheek, and the not-quite visible smile with which she looked on her son gave Carragh an uncomfortable sense of spying on an intimate moment.

The desk held nothing else.

There was nothing left to examine but the upper floor and its haunting walls. Someone in the past had put a more modern oil lamp in the sitting room and a convenient box of matches. Oh, who was she kidding? "Thank you, Lily," she murmured, and was only a little startled at the soft laugh that echoed in her ears.

Lamp in one hand, flashlight in the bag slung over her shoulder, Carragh moved cautiously up, her irregular breathing fluttering her lightweight jumper. I'm coming, she thought. Help me find what you need, Jenny.

There was no way she could read large swaths of the writing directly on the walls, but she needed to try. If she was right, then just two or three sentences was all she needed to confirm her suspicions. Someone had made sure to destroy the enlarged photographs and her laptop. She didn't necessarily need either one.

With her memory of the section she had transcribed, Carragh scanned the walls a few inches at a time, starting to the immediate right of the staircase. Soundlessly, she repeated the distinctive phrases she could remember: *disdaining those spirits . . . darkening days and endless nights . . . first sin of the fae . . . the darkling shadows . . .*

And at last she found it.

The Bride had forgotten them. She had fled her bright world for the darkling shadows of the mortal one and counted her people well lost for her pride. But sin casts a long shadow. Where one child is lost, another may be found. If the girl would not return of herself, then let her pay the price.

Where one child is lost, another may be found.

Carragh thought of the photograph below, of a mother's love, of a woman judged mad and locked up to . . . what? Keep her from harming herself? Keep her from harming others with her ravings?

Or to keep others from the truth?

She continued to scan the walls, looking for more than just vague hints. But when it came, it was in a form she could never have guessed. *My child, my heart, my baby lost . . .* At first she couldn't think where she'd heard that phrasing before. And then, as clearly as though he were standing next to her, she heard Aidan reading aloud in the library:

"My child, my heart, my baby lost
I will find though balked and crossed."
They locked her in a tower bossed
With iron locks, and grief did frost
The Dark Bride of Deeprath.

The words on the wall were not arranged in the same visual form—but they were undoubtedly from the Poem of the Bride. The poem dating from the era of Evan Chase, captured only in a privately printed family book. A poem—it now seemed—written by Jenny Gallagher.

And painstakingly copied out by hand by the boy called James Michael Gallagher.

Something sounded in the staircase and Carragh's head jerked up. That hadn't been any sort of ghostly noise. She heard it again: a series of rhythmic knocks coming from the direction of the enclosed stairs. With a firm grip on her flashlight, she called out, "Who's there?"

"It's just me." Aidan appeared, hands spread out as though ensuring her that he wasn't going to attack. "I wanted to make sure you heard me coming."

She blinked and realized it had grown dark outside. "What time is it?"

"Just after nine. How long have you been here?"

"Didn't Winthrop call and report on my movements to the lord of the manor?" He raised one insolent, interrogative eyebrow, and she nearly flung the flashlight at him in an excess of nerves. "Where the hell have you been?"

"Dealing with my sister," Aidan answered evenly.

Only then did Carragh remember that awful moment when he'd learned of her affair with Philip. She braced herself for whatever came next, but he merely said, "Then I spent time with Penelope and after that I had some things to set straight."

What kind of time did you spend with Penelope? Not that it was any of her business. Not at all. Certainly not after . . . was it really just yesterday?

"What are you doing up here?" Aidan asked her.

"Presumably what you meant me to do when you told Winthrop to bring me back here. Unraveling this puzzle to its end. I assume that's what you've been doing as well?"

He simply smiled. "Come down and we can share."

The lights were still out, but he led her to the kitchen and the marble-topped island used by generations of cooks to knead dough and press out cookies and chop vegetables. Mrs. Bell kept multiple oil lamps for her use there, and soon they had plenty of light.

"She doesn't mind us in her kitchen?"

"I sent them home for the night."

"Why?"

"Why do you think?" He held her gaze steadily. So, he'd reached some of the same conclusions she had. "Whatever happens next, it's a Gallagher problem."

"All right," Carragh agreed. "Tell me what you found."

"After I took Kyla home, I went to see Penelope and had her hypnotize me. It worked. I remembered what happened in the half hour or so before I found my father. Then I went to see the family priest, then to Dublin for some research, and back again to Kilkenny earlier this evening."

"Why Kilkenny again?"

"To prove a point. I proved it." He pulled a notebook bound in peacock blue leather from his backpack. "I found my mother's missing journal."

CHAPTER FORTY-TWO

September 1992

CLUE #5

This is it, my love. One to go. The hunt ends at the
spot where you asked me to marry you. Not the Official
Proposal—in the castle drawing room with all your family
present—but the one just for us. Remember?

Go there, look two feet to the right of the door at floor
level, and you will find my gift concealed behind stone: one
untold story, hidden long ago by a man in his grief. A
story . . . and a life.

Love always and forever!
Your Lily

Lily sat at her dressing table and sealed the last clue. She set it
down next to the rolled leather document case, stiff with age but
keeping its contents secure enough. She would replace the case
where she'd found it, then place her last clue. This time tomorrow
the hunt would be over.

Nessa knocked once and entered without waiting to be invited, trailing that air of possession that went beyond security in herself to encompass all of Deeprath Castle. Lily could only hope her aunt-by-marriage wouldn't haunt the place when she was dead. Nessa would be a much less congenial ghost than the musical Martha or Thomas Gallagher striding the battlements.

"So you are seeing this game through to the end?" Nessa frowned.

Lily looked at her without enthusiasm, wishing the woman hadn't insisted on being at Deeprath for Cillian's birthday. She had resisted Nessa's attempts to keep her apprised of what she was doing, though Nessa had held it to be her right when she'd learned that Lily was sifting through the Gallagher family history.

"Cillian loves my games," she replied brightly, unwilling to spark a confrontation today. "I am going out just now. Perhaps you'll join Cillian and me for tea at three-thirty in the library? He's going to show me the antiquities up close."

Nessa studied her with that sculpted, unreadable face that would no doubt look the same when she was ninety. "I suppose."

Lily took care that no one saw her enter the tower, and locked the corridor entrance behind her. The door to the library was ajar, but she avoided it so Cillian would not hear her. Going up, as she had so many times in the past, she walked softly, as though wary of disturbing Jenny Gallagher. She had felt the woman's presence for weeks now, and hoped she was doing what Jenny wanted.

On the top floor, Lily exited to the battlements, then knelt. On the exterior wall, she eased out the loose stone that she'd discovered two weeks ago and gently replaced the document case. When she'd settled the stone, she crossed herself, still kneeling, and sent up a prayer for the tiny bones that also lay within. This had started as a game, a pastime, an intellectual exploration of a family's history. And God—or fate—or the dead—had taken that game and used her for something much more important. Soon, those bones would truly rest.

Lily returned to her bedroom to change out of her jeans for tea. Moving to her dressing table, she stopped suddenly and stared at the empty space where, when she moved into this room twenty years ago, she'd always kept her current journal. It was gone, along with the final clue for Cillian.

And no prizes for guessing who had taken it. Nessa, who had pressed and prodded her this last year. Who had tried to talk her out of pursuing Jenny Gallagher's life and death. Lily knew that the old lady didn't like the taint of even an unacknowledged suicide in the family's past. But if Nessa had now read her journal . . . she would know far more than she should, at least without having been adequately prepared.

Lily went directly to Nessa's room. A tea tray stood on the rosewood desk, but the room was unoccupied. With sinking heart, she headed for the library. She could easily imagine Nessa's outrage—of course she would go straight to Cillian and complain.

Well, Nessa wasn't going to complain without her there to defend herself—and the truth. Furious as she might be, what could Nessa do about it? The past cannot be changed. It's not as though Lily proposed taking out a banner ad in the *London Times* to announce what she'd found. But nor would she let an old woman's misguided pride keep the rest of the Gallaghers—especially Kyla and Aidan—from knowing their own history.

Prepared for battle, Lily opened the library door.

Nessa was shouting at Cillian. "Your wife has gone mad! You must stop her. She's making up all sorts of lies about us, will make us laughingstocks—"

"Nessa!" Cillian had what Lily and the children called "his work voice," and he used it now to good effect. He caught sight of his wife and motioned her in. "Let's talk about whatever is going on like adults."

Lily knew at once that would be impossible, for Nessa looked on the verge of a collapse. Red-faced, furious, she whirled on Lily. "Where have you put it?" she demanded. "Where is all this 'evidence' you claim to have?" In her hand, she held Lily's journal, shaking it at her.

"Give me back my journal."

Nessa threw it on the library table, where it landed against the marble Celtic cross that Winthrop had brought as a gift for Cillian's birthday. "You're not doing this," she announced. "I will not let you ruin our family."

Beneath Cillian's exasperation, he was beginning to look alarmed. "Nessa, sit down and speak calmly."

But Nessa seemed to have forgotten everything except Lily. "Take it back," she hissed, like a child insulted on a playground. "Take it all back."

"I can't. It's true."

"What's true?" Cillian asked, bewildered.

Nessa was through talking. She flung herself at Lily, scratching like a wildcat. Lily stumbled back and Cillian pulled his aunt away. But despite her age, Nessa was a woman in excellent condition, thanks to decades of riding and hunting. She twisted out of his grasp, snatched up the marble cross, and swung it wildly at Lily.

But Cillian had stepped between them. With a horrible *crunch*, the cross connected with his skull just behind his right ear. He fell.

Lily cried, "What did you do?"

Nessa, a blankness in her eyes, as though she saw nothing except her target, continued swinging at Lily. With Nessa between her and the door, Lily bolted for the only escape.

The Bride Tower.

CHAPTER FORTY-THREE

Aidan watched Carragh's face, her surprise and satisfaction lit by the changing lamplight. Her eyes were so dark he could swim in them . . .

She blinked, and he realized he'd been staring. "Did you say something?" he asked.

"I'm sorry about Philip," she replied. "And I'm so sorry to have hurt your sister. I feel sick about the whole damn thing, I knew he was trouble, but I was so unhappy and tired and mixed-up, and I swear, it was only a few weeks and I've despised him ever since. Almost as much as I've despised myself." The words seemed to tumble out of her like a flood.

It was his turn to blink. "Is this really the time?"

"Please, Aidan, say you understand. I mean, I know you kissed me but maybe it's different seeing how much I hurt Kyla. I won't ask you to forgive me, but tell me you don't hate me—"

"Carragh, there's nothing for me to forgive." If she wanted to do this now, then best do it thoroughly. "You can take that up with Kyla. And I don't hate you. I hate Philip, but I hated him long before you came along. I hate him for what he's done to Kyla all these years, and because, God yes, I'm jealous. I'm jealous of every man before me who has ever touched you and made you smile and made you hit your head on walls . . . but when I think of you and Philip, I really think I might kill him if I could. It's pathetic, I know. I don't like that about myself. And God knows I'd never use my feelings to make a judgment of your past. I'm not that much of a bastard. But I'm looking at you now and I'm not thinking about anyone or anything except how much I'd like to take you to bed this very minute."

One of the pots on the hanging racks above crashed onto the table between them. Even Aidan jumped, and Carragh swore, then laughed. "And there is our reminder that—as you said—now is not the time."

"A reminder from the castle?" But Aidan didn't say it as skeptically as he would have before.

There was a definite tang to the air, in addition to the lingering ashy scent from the fire, as though more than just the two of them were in this kitchen, waiting for the final truth to be unveiled.

"So," Carragh said briskly. "Your mother's journal. Where did you find it?"

"Take a guess."

"Well, considering that you said you've just come from Kilkenny, I'd guess either at Kyla's house . . . or Nessa's."

"Nessa's," he confirmed. "Took ages to find it, and I may have made a bit of a mess in her beautiful home."

"How did you know to look there?"

"Because," he answered slowly, "of what I remembered with Pen's help."

He liked to imagine he was a knight defending Deeprath from the English—or other Irish, he wasn't picky—and played at spotting an enemy approach and preparing his bow to shoot them down. Sometimes he used boiling oil or pitch to chuck over the side, sometimes he allowed the enemy to make it inside so that he had to fight with his sword high in the air.

He always won.

When he caught movement below from the corner of his eye, he dropped his sword hand and pressed himself up against the taller buttress so he wouldn't be seen. The crenellations meant he could peer down at an angle and see the ruined oratory and half the stable blocks.

He saw Kyla coming out of the woods behind the oratory, looking around rather like he did himself when he didn't want to be seen. As he watched her, Kyla's head came up toward the tower, and he froze, knowing she'd be more likely to see him if he moved. But she seemed satisfied that she was alone, and headed into the castle. He remained motionless on the battlements, pretending he was spying on an enemy camp. He was rewarded a few minutes later by Philip leaving the woods at the same spot Kyla had.

"Lady Nessa." Philip's voice floated up from the ground, airy and insubstantial.

He risked craning his neck, and saw his great-aunt nod once to Philip, whom she did not like.

While Philip entered the castle, Aunt Nessa, her red leather carryall on her shoulder, continued into the stables where the cars were kept. He decided that she must be leaving already, which cheered him a great deal. Supper would be much more fun without her going on about his table manners all night.

But when Aunt Nessa left the stable, it was on foot, as she had gone in, and she seemed to be coming back into the castle.

He sighed. Might as well give up the game for now. He'd go and ask his father how much longer Aunt Nessa planned on staying.

Carragh listened closely as Aidan described what he'd seen. He had noticed that, when deep in thought, the tip of her tongue showed. "As a boy," she said, "you'd hardly have thought any of that important in the aftermath. Not unless someone had thoroughly and skillfully questioned you. But as an adult . . ."

"As an adult, it was certainly suggestive. As a police officer?" Aidan shrugged. "I know how to construct a basic timeline. Both my parents were dead before I went up the tower. I can't have missed the killer coming back down the tower steps by more than a few minutes. Kyla had been in the woods—with Philip, something I confirmed with her tonight. She'd never said because no one had ever asked her directly. Why borrow trouble? she told me. Because yes, of course, they'd been having sex. That left Nessa."

Nessa, who had left the castle with her bag and then returned without it a minute later. Nessa, whose big red bag was unmistakable and could have held a supply of army munitions, let alone a smallish coffret filled with antiquities, a bloodstained marble cross, and one blue leather journal.

"Why didn't she bury the journal in the holy well with the antiquities? Or no," Carragh corrected herself. "Why did she hide the journal all these years and not simply destroy it?"

He shook his head. "That, I don't know. But I wonder . . . is it possible she kept it so she had a convenient piece of evidence to plant on someone else? Just in case the police were suspicious and considered her."

The thought made him shiver. Would Nessa really have sacrificed someone else? But the moment he asked himself, the answer was clear: Nessa would sacrifice anything—or anyone—for what she considered to be the greater good of the family.

Carragh nodded thoughtfully. "A week ago—even yesterday—I'd have laughed in your face. What possible reason could she have for killing the Viscount Gallagher, when it seems the only thing she worships in this world is her family and its name?"

"And now?" Aidan asked.

"There's something you should see in the tower. All the way at the top. You know the writing on the wall up there? I know what it says."

Aidan had the General Register Office records, as well as the tantalizing fragment read to him by Sibéal McKenna over the phone. He didn't know why he hadn't led with that, except for the desire to lay out this puzzle the two of them had started on one piece at a time.

Be honest, he chided himself. *You wanted to impress Carragh.*

He stood and claimed a lamp. "I left some things in the Land Rover that I think you'll want to see. I'll meet you in the tower."

Carragh took a lamp in one hand, her enormous flashlight in the other, and Aidan could not resist. He leaned in—carefully, for the flames they both held—and kissed her.

As he went in one direction and Carragh in the other, he could swear he heard a hint of approving laughter in his ear.

When all this is over, Carragh promised herself, *the first thing I'll do is have an electrician put twenty light fixtures in every room of my house.* She had to tuck her flashlight away when she got to the tower stairs—no way was she going to tackle those steps without at least one hand free. So with her right hand on the railing and the oil lamp held in her left, she started upward. Again.

Almost there.

"And the second thing I'm going to do," she said fiercely to the shadows, "is spend a week somewhere without ghosts bugging me all the time."

With Aidan? Carragh had no idea if the question was her own . . .

With the last circular turn of the stairs, a flickering light played from above. She stopped, a surge of adrenaline making her heart skip. One thing she knew for sure—ghosts did not require light.

She had begun to back cautiously downward when an icily elegant voice floated down. "Do come up, Miss Ryan. Unless you feel all your questions have been adequately answered?"

Curiosity warred with prudence. Briefly. Aidan would be here any minute, and what had she to fear from an eighty-eight-year-old woman? She could knock Lady Nessa down without even resorting to her heavy flashlight. But just to be on the safe side, she pulled it out, and the moment she had edged up the steps and far enough into Jenny's tower bedroom, set down the oil lamp on the floor.

Nessa Gallagher, wearing tweed trousers and a heavy, fawn-colored jumper, sat bolt upright in the desk chair. Everything about her bearing was as Carragh remembered it from their first meeting. Even the repurposed Victorian cane laid lightly against her lap. All of it the same save one, critical, detail—Nessa Gallagher was pointing a rifle at her.

Eyeing it with disbelief, Carragh blurted out, "Where did you get a gun?"

"I've been hunting waterfowl since I was thirteen years old. And yes, if you're wondering, I am an excellent shot."

Chekhov's gun on the mantelpiece, Carragh thought, *except I didn't see it at the beginning so it's not fair for it to appear now* . . .

Nessa motioned with the rifle. "Come away from the stairs," she said, as calmly as though they were taking tea in the music room. "But don't bother to make yourself comfortable. This won't take long."

Unlike some of her friends, Carragh did not loathe guns. With seven police officers on her mother's side of the family, she had been taught how to handle and fire them safely, but she'd never wanted to carry one herself. She almost regretted that, as Lady Nessa kept the rifle firmly sighted on her while Carragh drew level with the iron bed frame. All around them swirled Jenny's writing, like a curse. *The Dark Bride of Deeprath* . . .

"What a mistake I made," Nessa remarked. "I thought I was hiring an inexperienced, easily influenced girl. Instead, I brought a dangerously independent agent right into the heart of my home."

"It is Aidan's home," Carragh pointed out. Forget gothic—now she was in a mystery novel, trying to keep the villain talking until help could arrive.

Nessa's face tightened. "If Aidan believed that, he would not be giving Deeprath away like an unwanted overcoat. He has been allowed for too long to forget his responsibilities. I thought I would be able to remind him, once he was here. But you meddled even with him, so that now he does not know what he wants or who he is."

"He knows who he is," Carragh said firmly. "I think it is you who do not know yourself."

It was—almost—a shot in the dark, for they had no way of knowing what Nessa had guessed about the past. But from the immediate darkening of the old woman's eyes, Carragh knew she was right.

"I am a Gallagher," Nessa said fiercely. "From the day I was born until the day I am laid in the earth. Nothing you say or do can change that."

"Is that what you told Lily before you killed her?"

But the old woman was not so easily led, or broken. "I am afraid the time for talk is at an end, Miss Ryan. No doubt my great-nephew will be with us shortly."

Where was Aidan? Why did this castle have to be so ridiculously enormous? And why had her supposedly helpful ghosts decided to vanish now? Not that she had any useful ideas about what they might do. She didn't think Nessa likely to be frightened by falling pots or trailing laughter.

Nessa stood, and any hope Carragh'd had that she would be unsteady and unbalanced without her cane vanished. The old lady smiled. "You see, I am not quite as infirm as everyone thinks. No doubt you could outrun me, or fight me by hand—but you cannot beat a shotgun shell. So if you would be so kind, my dear, as to go onto the battlements and jump."

Carragh stared. "I don't think so."

"You will jump, or you will be shot. I would prefer the first."

"Did you give Lily that choice?"

"There was no need. She panicked, poor girl, and chose the wrong direction to run. It was not terribly difficult to corner her. And the battlements were dangerously low even before the lightning brought down a good third of them."

"How do you plan to explain my death?"

"The poor, sad girl who could never belong to Ireland and became obsessed with Deeprath and the Darkling Bride and the present Lord Gallagher . . . it explains itself. You've helped me along very nicely by sleeping with Philip as well. So when Aidan scorned your unhealthy obsession, you killed him. Then flung yourself to your death just like Jenny Gallagher."

"You're going to shoot the seventeenth Viscount Gallagher," Carragh said flatly. "I thought the title was sacrosanct."

"Only to those who honor it. If Aidan cannot be brought to himself, then we will wait for another. Kyla is young enough to still have a son. And if she fails, there are her two daughters."

"You're mad. Really, truly, clinically disturbed. No one's going to believe in a second murder-suicide, or murder-anything. Sibéal McKenna is much too smart, and she doesn't give a damn about your name or position. She's coming for you already."

"Then what do I have to lose?" The sculpted face, still so beautiful in old age, did not change.

"All this because of something that happened a hundred and forty years ago? No one will care. You are still yourself, whatever is in your blood."

And now, for the first time, Nessa's cool poise broke. She practically snarled, "I am a Gallagher. My father was a Gallagher, no matter what his poor, lunatic mother may have claimed. No American with a dubious bloodline can come in here and tell me differently!"

Nessa recovered almost as quickly, the shotgun unerringly pointed at Carragh's chest. "Outside now, move slowly."

Carragh hesitated, then took a careful step toward the outer door. The longer she could play for time, the better chance that Aidan would arrive. And she didn't want that shotgun anywhere near the spiral stairs when he emerged. She didn't want either of them to be shot tonight.

As she stepped into the open air, she could swear she felt a hand take hers in a gesture of support. *Thanks*, she thought. *Now do something.*

She swung around to face Nessa, who showed no signs of weakening or dropping the hand holding the gun.

"Just think," Nessa said in a terrifyingly calm voice, "you will be linked forever with Jenny Gallagher. That should please you."

"I won't jump."

"Jump, or I shoot."

"You'll have to shoot me, because I am Not. Going. To. Jump."

Carragh stood with her back to the battlements, the lightning-scarred section dropping into nothingness just a foot or two away. Nessa faced her directly. She could hardly miss. They stared at one another, each waiting to divine the first movement of the other.

She saw the slight tightening of Nessa's jaw and just had time to think, You've got to be kidding me, when a burst of light exploded around them. Like a lightning bolt, or a dozen flare guns going off at once. The brilliant light made Nessa instinctively raise her arm to shield her eyes.

In two steps Carragh was within reach, swinging her heavy flashlight against Nessa's shoulder and arm. She heard something crack, and the gun dropped to the ancient stones.

Instantly, she was on her knees, scrabbling for the weapon. Nessa threw herself against Carragh, as though intending to bodily throw her off the tower. She wouldn't even have to throw her—just pull her close enough to the crumbling edge. But the best of intentions cannot resist the weakness of old age—or a second flare of light, an echo of the first. Nessa Gallagher was still blinking, right arm hanging crookedly, when Carragh turned the rifle on her.

She would take no risks, so the two of them simply held like that, facing each other, for what could have been minutes or hours, for all the sense of time Carragh had. Finally, she heard footsteps and then saw Aidan, his stupefied gaze swinging from her to his great-aunt and back again.

But as a police officer, Aidan had the training and instincts to act quickly in a crisis. Taking Nessa's arm securely in his, he said to his great-aunt, "Come down. I'm not letting you take the easy way off this tower."

With withering scorn, Nessa replied, "As if I would. I am a Gallagher. I do not run away."

Aidan looked warily at Carragh, still pointing the rifle in their direction. Slowly, she laid it on the stone floor of the battlements.

Reaction had hit her now, teeth chattering from delayed shock. "I'm fine," she assured Aidan. "Take her down. I'm coming."

Carragh waited until she could no longer hear their footsteps. Until the dark and timeless quiet of Deeprath had settled once more on the tower. She stood in the open doorway, firmly and safely away from the drop, waiting. And watching.

She and Nessa had not been alone on the battlements. In that first burst of light, Carragh had seen two figures. Even now, she felt that if she could just turn her head quickly enough, she could glimpse them again.

Two women, both with long black hair and soulful eyes. Two women who had brushed words against her mind even as the light vanished. *Thank you.*

Jenny Gallagher. And the other? Not Lily, as Carragh might have expected, for she knew Aidan's mother had been blonde and sleek. No, Jenny's companion had been quite *other*, in every sense of the word: a woman who had outlived even her name until she had become no more than the whisper of a memory.

The Darkling Bride.

CHAPTER FORTY-FOUR

DIARY OF JENNY GALLAGHER

1 January 1882

I do not know what day it is. I know it is cold. They would not bring me my diary for a long time, until I gouged my skin enough to bleed and try to write with that on the walls. Only then was I allowed both ink and paper . . . but paper will not do. Paper can be destroyed. I will not let the truth be buried.

My son is out there. They have stolen him, those jealous fae who never forgave the Bride for choosing a human love over her birthright. The changeling in my house must go back—I will bargain—I will plead—I will sacrifice all to break the curse of the Darkling Bride.

The first day of 1882 passed in the same deep melancholy that had pervaded Deeprath since Jenny's September collapse into complete insanity. Evan had learned a great many things in the last three months, one of them being how exhausting fear and sorrow could be. When he was awake all he craved was sleep, and when he went to bed all he could do was stare into the blackness

Some days Jenny thought she was the Darkling Bride. Some days she called him Niall. Some days she would not speak to him at all. But on no day at all would she accept her son. Twice, when her behavior had appeared docile and even clear-headed for some time, they let her leave the tower. Both times she ran away. The second time it was the dead of night and she was clad in only her night robe and slippers. "I have to find him," she kept insisting. "Let me find him!"

Lord Gallagher had had enough. The day after Christmas, he'd summoned a leading doctor who ran a private, forward-thinking asylum in northern England.

"I promise you," Evan had once told his wife, "that for the rest of my life your care and happiness will be my only concern." But what did one do when "care" and "happiness" were mutually exclusive?

James continued to thrive physically—and he had no shortage of love from his nurse and Dora Bell—but how would he grow up, Evan wondered, without his mother? The only thing he could think of was to pray for a miracle: Jenny, fully restored. Jenny, once more in his arms and smiling into their son's face.

When he went to see her that evening, as he did every evening, a miracle of at least a smaller order had occurred. Jenny was neatly dressed in a pale blue frock and reading in the sitting room under a nurse's eye, rather than painting the walls of the upper bedroom with scrawls of ink. The doctor had told them not to forbid her this outlet, but to encourage her away from it gently by showing no interest.

Evan dismissed the nurse, as always, and cautiously sat next to his wife on the sofa. "What are you reading?"

She showed him the book—one of his. He refused to ask her if she was enjoying it, for that was taking writerly pride too far, so he asked the most useless and vague of questions: "How are you feeling?"

"Quieter." She laid the volume down and turned to him. "As though I have been in the midst of a great storm without knowing it. But now . . . I begin to believe in calmer waters. I know that I must leave. I do not want to go. But I understand now. I see it all, and I am sorry."

He was afraid to hope, but too young not to. They stayed in that quietness until the nurse returned two hours later, Evan stretched on the sofa, with Jenny curled against him. And when he said good night, she pulled him down for a kiss. The first since James had returned.

As a frosty, bitter dawn rose in the mountains, they found Jenny's body at the bottom of the Bride Tower. It seemed she had squirreled away hairpins over the weeks, and finally managed to pick the iron lock of the outer door. There, she must have stood on the battlements and jumped.

Numb as a leaf tossed on the violent winds of the household's grief, Evan picked up the book Jenny had been reading that last night. He turned the pages, wanting only to linger over the last object she had held, and found the note she'd left him.

I did not lie, my love. I do understand now. I had thought my son stolen and replaced by a changeling child. But that was only my mind trying to protect me. The poor baby boy in this castle is no changeling . . . he is a human child. A stolen human child. And our son is dead.

If you cannot believe me, ask my father one question from me: what have you done?

We will wait for you, Evan, our son and I. All my love forever,

Jenny

CHAPTER FORTY-FIVE

Three weeks after leaving Deeprath Castle, Carragh returned to the Wicklow Mountains. The gentle May afternoon in the cemetery at Glendalough bore little outward resemblance to the freezing January rain at Glasnevin Cemetery when her grandmother had been buried. But the words of the committal rite were fresh and expressive in her mind.

We commend to Almighty God our brother . . . and we commit his body to the ground, earth to earth, ashes to ashes, dust to dust.

They had foregone a vigil and mass, preferring this quiet burial with only Father Hennessy, Aidan, Kyla, the Bells, Sibéal McKenna, and Carragh to witness. Nessa Gallagher remained in the women's center of Mountjoy Prison, awaiting trial. She had made one statement—in which she admitted destroying her own and Kyla's clothes the night of the reception, ripping up Carragh's books and damaging her laptop, and setting fire to the library. And yet somehow she'd still managed to blame Carragh—Sibéal had discreetly leaked her the details. *Miss Ryan was a troublemaker who couldn't keep to her place. If not for her meddling, none of this need ever have come to light.*

Since that statement, Nessa Gallagher had refused to speak to anyone. And though she had admitted to slashing the portrait of Jenny Gallagher and the Darkling Bride, Nessa had not claimed responsibility for its earlier, eerie wanderings.

Carragh did not believe that had been done by human hands.

Lord God, whose days are without end and whose mercies beyond counting, keep us mindful that life is short and the hour of death unknown.

The grave of Jenny Gallagher had been quietly opened two weeks earlier. Forensic specialists had sampled her humerus bone for DNA testing against the infant's skeleton found in the tower walls. The report had concluded—with all the standard caveats about testing methods and the degeneration of material over long periods of time—that it was more likely than not that the two bodies were closely related. Today, the remains of Jenny's son were being laid to rest with his mother.

"Eternal rest grant unto him, O Lord," Father Hennessy said.

"And let perpetual light shine upon him," those at the graveside replied.

After the last prayer, Aidan asked Carragh to walk with him along the river. She felt almost shy, for they'd had little contact since that night on the Bride Tower.

If he felt shy, he didn't show it. "I'm moving back to Ireland."

Carragh suppressed the instant leap of happiness and asked, "Why?"

"Because Nessa was right about one thing—Deeprath is not mine to sell or give away. It is a heritage that is in my care, and Kyla's. You know, when I first decided to donate it, Kyla wanted me to create a foundation instead. One that could administer Deeprath as a trust, allowing us to choose how it is used in future. Turns out she'd done her homework. Business models, a plan for a board of trustees, pages and pages of research on places like Malahide Castle that manage to make money. The problem was always going to be freeing up the ready cash to start it."

"And you've found it?" she asked.

"I'm selling the London house. Once that decision was reached, it was easy to decide to leave England altogether."

"So, you're coming to Ireland to run this foundation with Kyla."

"I think she'll be rather better at that than I would. I'm not quite sure what I'll do. Inspector McKenna seems to think the Siochana Garda would be glad of my services. But I don't know that I'm entirely committed to the police. It was always the art and antiquities part that excited me."

They crossed the river in silence and onto the path leading to the castle. Carragh kept sneaking glances at Aidan. He looked, not younger, exactly, but freer. The tightness of his expressions had eased and the blue of his eyes was even more brilliant than before.

"How are you?" Aidan finally asked. "And your family?"

"Am I speaking to them, do you mean? Yes. My parents not only told me in no uncertain terms that I am not permitted to sell my grandmother's house, but they sent my brother over to help renovate. In all his various starts and stops and adventures around the globe, Francis has become rather handy. We're turning it into two flats, so there will be rent money to keep things up Sibéal McKenna and her daughter are moving in next month."

Carragh had also, at last, read the Hong Kong letter. It contained a restrained message from her birth grandmother—who wrote that her husband had preferred to cut all ties, but with his recent death, she herself wished to tell her granddaughter that she had always thought of her—and a dozen photographs of Mei-Li in Boston with her little girl.

We wrote infrequently and in secret, Mei-Li and I, her grandmother wrote, *out of respect for my husband. But she managed to send me these and wrote of her great love for you. If you would like, I could have those letters translated.*

Not quite ready to discuss all of that openly, Carragh changed the subject as deftly as Aidan might have. "Have you been able to discover how your mother found out about Jenny and her baby?"

"It was all in her journal. The turning point was a letter that

Evan Chase wrote to his publisher after Jenny's death—a letter that your grandmother helped my mother find. In it, he announced that there would be no book forthcoming. I don't know where that letter is now—maybe Nessa found and destroyed it, maybe it's still hidden somewhere as part of my father's intended treasure hunt. But my mother wrote in her journal that Evan had inserted some kind of puzzle or riddle in the letter that allowed her to find the stone in the tower behind which he'd interred his son and his manuscript."

"I know you said the document case didn't include Evan Chase's lost book. So what, exactly, was in it?"

"Ah," Aidan said, with that smile that was just so unfairly attractive. "The manuscript in question was not, as I said, the novel Evan Chase came here to write. But it is a book, and it is entitled 'The Darkling Bride.'"

Somehow—perhaps because she could feel the faintest shiver of a presence she had last felt at Deeprath—Carragh knew what he was going to say. "Are you telling me—"

"He wrote about Jenny," Aidan confirmed. "He wrote about Ireland and their first meeting and how they came to love each other. He wrote of their marriage and their son . . . and he wrote of her father's betrayal. James Michael Gallagher died at seven weeks old in June 1881, after having been removed from Deeprath to protect him from measles. When Jenny's father learned of it, he decided to substitute a newborn child from one of the families who had been rescued by the Gallaghers during the Famine. A poor family, it goes without saying, who could not easily refuse."

"You've read it?" Carragh tried, not very successfully, not to yelp.

His smile became a boyish grin, and if she'd had any heart left to lose, it would have gone now. "I've read it," he answered. "But *you* are going to edit it. I want you to prepare it for publication."

She couldn't decide whether to scream or weep. "Are you sure you want all this information out there?"

They had reached the end of the path. Deeprath Castle rose before them, much as Carragh had seen it on her first day.

"What are they going to do?" Aidan asked. "If they—and I have no idea who 'they' would be, since the Gallaghers were never an extensive family—really want the castle and the title, then we can fight over them. But no one can take my name, or my family." Tilting his head down, he said softly, "I believe it was you who taught me that truth."

He kissed her then, and Carragh didn't know which was making her pulse race more—Aidan's touch, or the thought of getting her hands on Evan Chase's last work.

Deeprath Castle watched them as though called to bear witness to this particular moment of its history. Because the story of Deeprath was always and forever the story of the Gallaghers.

The castle knew her own, and jealously kept their secrets.

She alone knew what was lost
And would not lie, whate'er the cost
To love and life and tears that glossed
O'er hearts of two that were star-crossed,
The Dark Bride of Deeprath.

ACKNOWLEDGMENTS

We have a collection of three-word mottoes in our family. But it was five words I lived by while writing this book: *I can do hard things.* That is true. It's also true that I can do nothing—hard or otherwise—without help.

Tamar Rydzinski: for your kindness, your steadiness, your patience, and for being simply one of the best humans I know, thank you. I would not have written this book—or any book in the last two years—without you.

Kate Miciak: your faith in me and my writing has sustained me through both professional and personal droughts. Any success this book enjoys belongs to you.

At Random House, I have been supported by the finest and most enthusiastic people in the business: Alyssa Matesic, who deals with my every deadline and delay and query quickly and with good humor; Shona McCarthy and Nancy Delia, who magically produced an actual book from the jumble of words I provided; Peter Weissman, who must think I never speak in complete sentences if the amount of ellipses he has to copyedit is any indication; Victoria Allen and Caroline Cunningham, who have designed the atmospheric and beautifully Gothic cover and interior of my dreams; and Catherine Mikula and Maggie Oberrender who present my books to the public in the most flattering light. I owe each of you dinner and flowers and chocolates and whatever else your heart desires for working so hard on my own heart's desire.

And my family: we're still here. Every one of us. That is a gift I never take lightly. Each word I write is made possible by your love.

ABOUT THE AUTHOR

LAURA ANDERSEN is married with four children, and possesses a constant sense of having forgotten something important. She has a B.A. in English (with an emphasis in British history), which she puts to use by reading everything she can lay her hands on.

lauraandersenbooks.com
Facebook.com/laurasandersenbooks
Twitter: @LauraSAndersen

ABOUT THE TYPE

This book was set in a Monotype face called Bell. The Englishman John Bell (1745–1831) was responsible for the original cutting of this design. The vocations of Bell were many—bookseller, printer, publisher, typefounder, and journalist, among others. His types were considerably influenced by the delicacy and beauty of the French copperplate engravers. Monotype Bell might also be classified as a delicate and refined rendering of Scotch Roman.